BREAKDOWN ON THE BRINK . . .

Neston looked over the instruments of the communications console, while Bill Stanton frantically checked the circuitry. When he turned, his anxious look matched his words.

'The NASCOM circuit from Madrid has gone dead,' he told them. 'We're getting no signals to or from the d...
to patch in
'How long
'Ten minute
security pro
our facilities
'Work on it – .... iviatthews
then faced Harper with a question. 'What about the dog? While our communications are out, will he stop?'

The Lieutenant's tone was grim. 'No, General. He's received his commands . . . they're part of his memory now, and he won't forget them. Without further orders, he'll keep heading towards the target . . . *but with no idea what to do once he gets there!*'

Also by Gary Alan Ruse in Sphere Books:

A GAME OF TITANS

Houndstooth

GARY ALAN RUSE

SPHERE BOOKS LIMITED
30/32 Gray's Inn Road, London WC1X 8JL

First published in Great Britain
by Sphere Books Ltd 1979
Original American edition published in 1975 by
Prentice-Hall, Inc., Englewood Cliffs,
New Jersey, USA
Copyright © Gary Alan Ruse 1975

TRADE MARK

Filmset in Photon Times

Printed in Great Britain by
C. Nicholls & Company Ltd
The Philips Park Press, Manchester

For my family,
for just about everything . . .

ACKNOWLEDGMENTS

In gathering the necessary information for a book of this nature, it is impossible to do so without the assistance of others. The author wishes to take this opportunity to recognise those individuals and organisations, and to express his grateful appreciation to all of them.

For supplying invaluable official reports and other materials concerning the Soviet space programme, I must thank Lester S. Jayson, Director of the Congressional Research Service, Library of Congress, and Senator Frank E. Moss (Dem., Utah) of the Committee on Aeronautical and Space Sciences.

For their aid in obtaining pertinent information concerning systems and facilities at the Lyndon B. Johnson Space Center, I wish to thank John E. McLeaish and John E. Riley of the NASA Public Affairs Office in Houston, Texas. Also, Webster W. Sharp, manager of the Clear Lake Chamber of Commerce and the staff of the Houston Chamber of Commerce.

In the areas of brain implants and visual processing, I must thank Jacob Kline, Ph.D., Director of the Biomedical Engineering Department, University of Miami, Fla., for his courteous assitance in answering my questions and for pointing some of my later research in the right direction.

I also wish to thank Alvin Samet, Supervisor of Radar and Weather Services, National Hurricane Center, Coral Gables, Fla., for special help rendered in the area of international meteorological information.

The Public Information Office of the Homestead Air Force Base supplied data on aircraft and recommended other sources for checking certain important details, and the U.S. Coast Guard Search and Rescue Station of Miami, Fla., the Miami Office of the Federal Aviation Authority, and Dean Fay of the Miami Main Army Recruiting Station courteously answered my questions. For their help, I thank them.

Some of the information required in the development of this book was difficult to track down, and there are many people who simplified the task; among them – the Reference departments of the Miami Public Library's Main Branch and Coral Gables Branch, the University of Miami's Otto G. Richter Library, and the Information Bureau of *The New York Times*.

G.A.R.
Miami, Florida

Cape Kennedy, Florida, January 1 (AP) – On December 3 the Soviet satellite Cosmos 462 was launched from the Tyuratam rocket base. Within hours it zipped close to Cosmos 459, launched four days earlier, and exploded into 13 pieces. Both satellites were destroyed 150 miles above the Earth.

Western experts concluded that the Soviet Union had the capability of blasting from the skies American reconnaissance satellites, most of which operate 100–150 miles up.

The New York Times, January 2, 1972

USAF's Space and Missile Systems Organisation requested industry proposals two months ago for studies of an unmanned space system designed to intercept, inspect and, if necessary, destroy hostile space craft.

Aviation Week and Space Technology, June 19, 1972

CHAPTER ONE

Major tumbled down the chute, reached the end of it, and spun wildly for a second in midair. Twisting and turning in the utter darkness that surrounded him, he could only rely on his sense of balance to bring him into an upright position. Abruptly the cold, firm surface of the flooring was there beneath him. It had come with surprising swiftness, a sudden jolt after the agonising drop through emptiness that had seemed so much longer than it was. He landed on all fours, escaping injury, and managing it with a grace more fitting for a cat than a dog.

And Major was, after all, only a dog. Even if a very special one.

He waited, panting, muscles tensed. There had been games like this before. Always, in fact. His life thus far had been full of unending activities that were strange and perplexing. But there was a pattern to it all that could be learned, learned and accepted as routine. It was as simple as the rewards and punishments given for his performance. And Major had learned quickly. In the last year there had been only rewards.

As he waited, he became aware of light filtering in from some unknown source. It grew brighter, illuminating the flooring and delineating Major's muscular form. Purebred German Shepherd he was, with hard, lean lines and a healthy coat that was more black than cream in its pattern. And a marking, a blaze on his forehead, light in colour and shaped like a pudgy asterisk. It stood poised above two alert eyes that searched for some slight clue to this new puzzle . . . this new game.

In the brighter glow, he could see the four walls around him. They were more than four times his height or else he might have considered jumping them. No, there must be some other way. He would wait a second more.

With a slight humming of motors, a narrow section of the wall to his left moved slowly upwards, creating a doorway. Major hesitated briefly, then walked through it.

He was now in a narrow corridor that ran to the left and right of the spot where he was standing. Above him was darkness: no ceiling, only walls. Special walls whose placement could be altered. He had been in mazes before. Some had been hard, some easy.

The corridor seemed the same in both directions, each turning the corner a short distance away at a blind angle that prevented seeing farther along its route. Each was the same. Equal. Exact.

Which to choose . . . ?

Major knew the regular pattern for finding his way out of such a maze. Arbitrarily he would pick a direction, follow it as far as he could, and through trial and error, work his way out. And he would remember the path, so that when they tested him again he would be able to repeat it without hesitation. He did not know why it mattered to them, this game. But he did not care, as long as he won their favour . . . and the reward.

He turned to the left, started forward, and then suddenly froze. Something odd had happened, a feeling that was strange and alien to him.

He was going the wrong way. Major could not remember having been in this maze before – in fact, he was sure he had not. Yet he knew the way now. All of it, with a certainty that was perplexing and beyond his comprehension. He devoted no more thought to it, concentrating instead on the glowing bit of knowledge in his mind. So clear and easy was the awareness, so strong and crisply outlined. It was simple now. He knew.

Major turned around and headed off down the corridor to the right. His pace was regular and comfortably swift. He turned the next corner and continued, going partway down the next corridor before turning to the left. There was no difficulty to it. Left here, now right. Down one way, then backtrack along a different corridor. It would not be long now.

Other eyes watched the maze as well.

Above, in the carefully controlled darkness, an observation room was suspended from the supporting framework

12

of the ceiling. A complete view of the testing area was visible through the slanting, encircling windows. No sound could penetrate through to disturb the experiments, and the dim light of the room was of a colour invisible to animal eyes.

Inside the special booth, behind the layered glass, a tall man stood motionless and straight. At his temples the greying hair was cropped close, which seemed to increase the angular thinness of his face. The Army officer studied the movements of the dog, watching with an intense interest that marked the man as a participant in the proceedings, and not merely an observer.

He looked towards the computer terminal connected to the cables leading out of the booth, and smiled faintly at the man seated behind the keyboard.

'Perfect,' he said crisply. 'It's working better than I had hoped.'

The computer technician was younger, in his mid-thirties, with full, boyish features. He glanced up. 'Yes, Colonel Brunning. So far, the system is operating flawlessly.'

The third person in the room was a young man, also in Army uniform, whose collar bore silver lieutenant's bars. His dark hair was cut less severely than Brunning's, and he looked more a part of the midwestern area than either of the others. Brunning turned to him.

'You're quite sure the dog could not be operating on any innate sense of direction?'

'Yes, sir. In the maze, his sense of direction can't help him very much anyway — not the first time.' The lieutenant studied the chronometer attached to the clipboard he held. The second hand continued to sweep, showing the elapsed time of the experiment. 'Besides, at best he could only rely on dead reckoning, paying attention to the way he entered the testing area. The little spin we gave him down the chute prevented that. After that kind of disorientation, he's strictly on his own.'

'Yes . . .' The colonel's eyes went back to the maze below. 'Except for the system.'

Brunning watched the dog's dark form proceed swiftly through the maze. From his vantage point he could see each corridor, each obstacle, and anticipate each necessary turn. So far there had been no mistakes. The dog had followed exactly the correct path. If there was one area of fallibility in the system, it was that it did not totally control. It could only make information available . . . and relay instructions.

Lieutenant Halper also watched, but with an interest more personal than Brunning's. Halper's training of the dog represented only a part of the overall programme, but it was certainly one of the most important parts. Without the proper conditioning, the advanced technological systems involved were worthless. The dog's performance was as much a reflection of Halper's skill as of the dog's own capabilities. In a way, the lieutenant felt himself being tested in the maze.

'The next part should be interesting,' Brunning said softly. 'It's been easy so far. But will the system override instincts? Will it help overcome the dog's natural fears? That will be the telling factor, Halper – the telling factor.'

Watching the maze, Lieutenant Halper prepared to trigger the next set of controls. 'We shouldn't have long to find out. Even with the special training I've put him through, there's no guarantee he won't panic. Only the CAM system has a chance.' He turned to the computer technician. 'Stand by with the quelling signal.'

Major was nearing the outer section of the maze when the corridor he was now following turned sharply to the right and abruptly widened into a room of moderate dimensions. There was, at the moment, no other entrance or exit. Major paused, dimly aware that another stage, some new aspect of the game, was about to begin. And he was not wrong. Behind the transparent walls, an array of devices waited – waited only for the signal that would activate them. A signal that came . . . now.

Powerful arc-flashers suddenly erupted with glaring, near-blinding brightness. In rhythmic bursts of light, the flashers pulsed with an irritating frenzy that should have panicked the dog and sent him fleeing back the way he had entered the room.

That was the feeling that pulled at him, that tugged at his reflexes. It was a startling threat, creating a feeling of danger.

14

But Major did not panic. Despite the desire to flee, he stayed where he was. Although not sure why, he knew that the flashing of the walls would not harm him. Further, he knew that it was essential to ignore them, to avoid their disturbing influence. Something more would be expected of him, and he must succeed to win favour.

As the dog stood his ground, a panel at the opposite end of the room gave way to another corridor. Major headed gratefully towards it, and wondered why he only just now remembered it was there.

He padded along the flooring, his paws silently covering the distance between the room behind and that which was ahead. The goal was ever closer, almost within reach. His pace quickened.

Major was not aware of the control booth suspended above him in the darkness of the massive testing building, one of several on the grounds of the Animal Research and Development Command. In all the seemingly countless 'games' in which he had taken part, he had never suspected its presence. There were too many safeguards for that. Yet he was tied to it in a way he could never perceive.

From that booth now came another electronic command, and more of the maze equipment was brought into play. Though he could see the end of it now, the door that led to the outside 'world', there was one final obstacle. It sprang into life with a shooshing roar that filled the corridor with heat and light.

Gas-fed flames danced just above vents in the flooring and cut directly across the corridor. There was only the narrowest of gaps in the centre that would allow him to pass with absolutely minimum clearance. Between those two sheets of writhing fire, that gap seemed very, very small.

Again, it was something that should have stopped him. And again, he knew that there was no need to stop . . . and a greater need to continue. It would take effort, but it could be done. Major lowered his head, involuntarily shuddered once, then charged full speed at the wavering gap ahead.

'Excellent!' Colonel Brunning clenched a victorious fist as he saw the dog safely penetrate the flames and finally reach

15

the doorway that was just now opening for him. 'You've both done your work well. We can proceed at once.'

Halper breathed an inward sigh of relief and marked down the final time for the experiment. It had taken most of the day and early evening to set everything up, and Brunning's normal impatience had become nearly intolerable. Halper had never seen him quite so keyed-up before.

As Halper switched off the flame barrier control, the computer technician swivelled around towards Brunning. 'Will you want to run another test, sir . . . just to be sure?'

'No, I'm quite sure already, Carter.' He turned away from the glass. 'Besides, there isn't time for more experiments. There'll be no dry run for this, just the real thing.'

'As you wish, Colonel.'

Halper tucked his clipboard under one arm and deactivated the master controls. The maze and testing area were plunged into total darkness.

At the computer terminal, Carter flipped a switch from *transmit* to *reprogram*. The ready light appeared, and he typed out the coded instructions necessary to remove the layout of the maze from the memory banks. In another moment it was done.

'Will that be all for now?'

'Not quite. When you're through here, report to the main computer room. There'll be sealed instructions for you.' Brunning picked up his attaché case and headed towards the door that led by means of a catwalk and stairs to the ground floor facilities. Halper exchanged a curious glance with Carter, then followed silently.

At the door, Brunning hesitated, turning to face the technician once more. 'One other thing, Carter. The implant — how long will it be operative?'

'Barring damage, nearly indefinitely. But of course the energy cell that runs it is using power whether there's anything to receive or not . . . and that will only last a month or two at most.'

Brunning nodded, then opened the door. 'That should be quite long enough, I think. *Quite* long enough . . .'

Joyce Kandell was kneeling beside Major in the ground floor room, petting him as he ate the food tidbits that were a special treat for him, a reward for a job well done. But there was more to it than just the food. The young woman's soothing voice, her light and affectionate touch — these things made the testing worthwhile for him. In training of this nature, love was a more effective tool than even food or threats of punishment. At least that was Joyce Kandell's technique — and one that was sometimes at odds with the ARDCOM programme.

Colonel Brunning came through the door at that moment, quickly and quietly. Ryan Halper followed close behind him. Brunning stopped a few paces away from the dog, watching the young woman's actions with growing impatience.

'Let's not overdo it, Miss Kandell,' he said irritably. 'I wouldn't want to ruin a good animal.'

'Yes, Colonel ... I always try to keep a balance.' She meant, however, that she tried to provide a balance against Brunning's insufferable callousness with her animal charges. She knew better than to spoil the dog, but she also knew better than to ignore his need for attention.

Still kneeling, she manoeuvred her stethoscope beneath the dog's chest, checking his heartbeat and respiration. She wrote down the information, then began a physical inpection for signs of any injury, minor or otherwise, that might have occurred in the maze. Brunning's look of impatience increased, hurrying her on more effectively than words.

There were no problems, at least none revealed by her quick examination. Her fingers probed the slight lump just above the dog's left ear. The long scar there was hardly visible. She ruffled the hair back over it, then stood up.

'I take it the first test was successful.'

'Completely. And there'll be no more tests.'

Her dark eyes blinked. 'But — I understood that it might take a week or more to confirm the system's effectiveness . . .'

'That was optional from the beginning. My option. I hardly think it's necessary.'

Joyce's eyes shifted quickly to Halper, only to find her own confusion reflected on his features as well. She routinely

17

jotted down a few final notes on her data clipboard and hung it back on the wall. 'There are still so many unknown factors to consider . . . there could be psychological side effects as a result of the implant.'

'I doubt it. He's reacted perfectly so far, and doesn't seem in the least disturbed by the sudden presence of a second memory.' Brunning's tone had been hard and unyielding, but now it relented. His expression softened. 'Look, I . . . I know what's bothering you. You've grown attached to the dog. It's difficult to avoid, I know, and I'm not really surprised . . . but it only makes things more difficult. Whether we continue testing for another week or stop where we are, the dog still has a job to do for us — we can't change that.'

Joyce nodded but remained silent. Her face, a pleasant oval accented by strong cheekbones, was neatly framed with medium-length hair, raven-dark and shining.

'I suppose I have something of an advantage over you,' Brunning continued. 'Being a soldier and an officer, I've had to do things many times that I did not like or want to do. It's necessary if you put an important goal over personal interest.'

'I realise that, Colonel.'

He smiled faintly. 'All right. No more lecturing then. But try to remember that on a project like this, sentiment will ultimately make things harder for you.'

'I suppose so. . . .' She sounded unconvinced, but it seemed Brunning would let it go at that. She wondered. On previous occasions, she had seen that rigid façade change to one of apparent kindness and friendship. At times it appeared there was a vulnerable core beneath the surface, a core that could disappear in an instant behind the strict and orderly presence of the military man. But was the kindness real and the cold discipline only a self-protective shell? Or was it *all* a façade? Was it perhaps only an officer's training in psychology . . . a pep talk for the 'troops'?

Joyce leaned down and gave the dog a final pat, then opened the door to the small kennel facility that was now completely empty. Only a month before, there had been twenty dogs occupying the kennel. The rest were gone now, sent to different bases, some in far-flung corners of the world and a few in combat areas. One dog, the best, had been kept to receive additional training for an unknown purpose, and an implant.

Joyce snapped her fingers.

'Major!' She motioned towards the kennel and the dog immediately started through the door. She watched him trot down the centre aisle and into his section. He lay quietly down and gazed benignly back at her. After a brief hesitation, the young woman turned out the light and shut the door.

'As I recall,' Brunning said abruptly, 'the dog's original designation was not "Major". Who decided to make the change?'

Joyce's eyes met Halper's for a split second, then shifted away. 'Well actually, Colonel, it has something to do with the blaze on his forehead, the way it looks like an oak leaf . . .'

Brunning nodded. 'That much is obvious. But whose idea was it? Yours?'

Before Joyce could say anything further, Halper interrupted. 'It was my idea, sir.'

Brunning looked at him, slightly displeased. 'Your idea? I might have guessed.'

'I'm sorry if I acted without authority, sir. . . .'

Brunning ignored the apology. 'Will the dog still respond to command well enough . . . with his new name?'

'Yes, Colonel,' Halper replied, with more confidence. 'We made the substitution early enough in the training programme to avoid any problems.'

The colonel considered it for a moment, then sighed. 'All right, Lieutenant, we'll let it drop. Considering the blaze, it's an appropriate enough name; I don't see that it will do any harm. Training details are *your* jurisdiction – what I'm interested in are *results*.' He paused a moment. 'But if you find a pup with an eagle on its forehead, I trust you'll resist the temptation . . . ?'

Halper nodded, smiling. 'Understood, sir.'

'I hope so.'

The lieutenant checked his watch as another thought came

to mind. 'It's just now twenty-one hundred, sir. Have the others arrived yet for the staff meeting?'

'There'll be no others.'

Halper looked perplexed. And he could see that Joyce was as surprised as he. 'Not even Captain Stens ... or Major Samuelson?'

Brunning shook his head negatively. 'Major Samuelson is still tied up with the Oakland project. Besides, his function is primarily administrative and he has little experience that would be useful on this kind of special ... problem.'

Joyce slipped out of her laboratory smock and hung it on an OD metal coat rack that was many times duller than the bright green of her dress. She said, 'And Captain Stens?'

The corner of Brunning's mouth wrinkled slightly. 'The captain has been sent to Washington. He will be representing me before the Joint Chiefs of Staff, and will give a progress report on some of our current efforts.'

'But then ...' Joyce began slowly, 'if neither of them will be here, we can't very well have our staff meeting ...'

'On the contrary,' Brunning said gravely, turning for the door. 'It is absolutely essential that we have the meeting. I will expect you both in the conference room in five minutes.'

Halper and Joyce were silent after Brunning left the room. Joyce went about her remaining minor duties, checking the security locks on the filing system and inspecting her desk for loose paperwork. Finally she slammed a drawer and turned to Halper with a look of exasperation.

'Ryan, do you have any idea what this is all about — what they're planning to do with Major?'

Halper shook his head slowly. 'Wish I did. I've been told as little as you.'

'You wouldn't hold back ... under orders, I mean?'

Halper did not answer that one directly. 'I really don't know any more than you do on this.'

He went to his own desk and stored away the clipboard and timer. Rolling his chair under the knee well, Halper turned and sat on the edge of the desk, arms folded. His tall, lanky form was always more relaxed when Brunning was not present, and now it also showed the added weight of fatigue.

Joyce's gaze was still on him. 'You mean, Brunning hasn't hinted at anything . . . not even to you?'

Halper sighed. 'Honest. I'm strictly in the dark. The extra training I've had to put Major through is just added conditioning. I can't even guess what it's all for.'

Joyce turned away, suddenly looking very dissatisfied — with Halper, with herself, with the world in general. She shook her head glumly, looking nowhere in particular as she talked. 'When we started on the Computer Augmented Memory project, I understood that it was only intended as a new training experiment, a means of improving the dog's response and learning abilities.'

'Still is, so far as I know.'

'But this trial run today — a trial run for *what*?' Her eyes focused again on Halper. 'And why the sudden change from a temporary hookup to a permanent electronic implant?'

It was a question Halper had asked himself over the past weeks and he knew he had no convincing answer. 'I suppose it makes more sense for long-range testing. It's less awkward than that bulky collar receiving unit we've used with the other dogs.'

'Of course, but Ryan, can you imagine the *cost* of that micro-implant! They can't expect to keep using them. Our budget here was cut twice in the last six months. Without a special appropriation of some kind, we may not be able to complete half the projects scheduled. And now, all of a sudden, something that isn't even scheduled is obviously in the works. It just doesn't wash. I don't understand it.'

Halper shrugged. 'Look, let's not get worked up over it — there are people here who get paid to fret about the budget and which experiments we can or can't afford. Let them do the worrying.'

'It's not that simple and you know it.'

Halper hesitated. 'Because of Major . . . ?'

'Partly.'

'I *do* understand. When it comes time to ship him out, I'll miss him too. But in this kind of job, working with test animals all the time, you have to be realistic. There's a need for all this, and —'

21

'Don't, Ryan. Please don't. You're beginning to sound like Brunning and I don't think I can take that.' She turned away from him and headed for the other side of the small office. 'And as far as this job goes . . . there are times when I wonder if it's worth having.'

He watched her a moment, frowning. 'Don't forget that Uncle Sam will be picking up the tab for your advanced college work.'

'You don't have to throw that at me . . . that's not the only reason I took the job.'

'I know.' He almost regretted the remark now, but it was too late to retract it. Halper checked his watch from force of habit. 'We'd better get going. I'd rather be a minute early for the colonel's meeting than a second late.'

Joyce nodded and headed for the door. 'I'd just feel a lot better about this whole thing if we knew what was going on.'

Halper switched off the lights as they left the office, pulling the door closed behind him. 'Maybe we'll find out now. . . .'

Lieutenant Halper entered the conference room last, closed the soundproof door, and latched it. At the colonel's nod, he activated the electronic system of countersurveillance equipment. There were nearly a dozen devices in all, contracted by the government from a number of firms that guaranteed 99 percent efficiency. Halper had never bothered to ponder about how much that figure might be exaggerated, or whether or not the total security effect was cumulative or merely parallel. He simply pressed the lighted rectangular button and waited a second to see that the equipment was functioning.

The table that ran down the centre of the conference room was large enough to seat fourteen comfortably, but Colonel Brunning did not sit down, so neither did the others. He placed his attaché case carefully on the laminated top of the table, lining it up with the edge.

'Now we can begin,' he said smoothly. 'I don't doubt for a minute that both of you have been more than slightly curious about this project from the start.'

Joyce managed a self-conscious shrug. 'I have worked

22

under top-secret security before, but I must admit it seems I've been told a lot less about this project than most.'

Brunning nodded. 'So far this has been handled on a need-to-know basis. Up until six weeks ago, even I hadn't been informed. And even now there are no more than ten people who know the rough outline of the operation; only three who know the exact timetable and other details.'

'Sounds like something big,' Halper said.

'To give you a rough idea of the extent of it,' Brunning continued, 'let me mention that, for the time being, the usual chain of command has been bypassed and our installation is directly answerable to the Department of Defense.'

Halper considered it a moment, then as the information sank in, he frowned sceptically. 'Bypassing even the top Army command?'

'Yes, owing to the circumstances involved. And it's a joint effort, so Defense has to call the shots.'

'With all due respect,' Halper began carefully, 'what exactly do we have here that is so important?'

'The CAM project, Lieutenant. As it turns out, the system has an unexpected value . . . one which is urgently needed.'

If anything, Joyce seemed more puzzled than ever. 'And Major is a part of this?'

'Yes — a key element, in fact.' Brunning shifted slightly. If he was tired, neither his features nor his posture revealed the fact. 'I shall be acting as General Raskin's representative in this matter,' he continued. 'You, in turn, will be receiving your instructions directly from me, here on out. And I want you both to remember every minute — every second — of the way that this matter is being carried out under ultra-top-secret security. I can't caution you strongly enough on that fact. Your complete cooperation is vital.'

Joyce found her voice again. 'I . . . I'm afraid I don't understand, Colonel. If the testing of the dog is over, as you say . . .'

'The testing *is* over, but not your participation in . . . this matter,' he replied. 'I can't go into detail now, but rest assured that you will be completely filled in later, at the appropriate time. And there are others that we'll be working

23

with — civilians for the most part, from several government agencies that are directly involved. There will be a great many more people less directly involved, and they will be briefed only to the extent that is necessary for the performance of their duties.'

Halper frowned. 'But we *will* be in on the whole picture?'

'Yes. But only because it's necessary. There are more complicated aspects to this operation than yours — how complicated I can't tell you yet — but even so, the entire thing centres around the dog. He's the one absolutely essential element. And that makes both of *you* essential. I regret that I have to throw you into this all so unexpectedly, but it's quite necessary. I think you'll understand why later.'

'Sir,' Halper began cautiously, the question that had been bothering him at last forming itself into words, 'about Captain Stens. . . . Has he been sent away for some other reason? I mean, from all the information I had, the ARDCOM progress report was not required of us for at least another month.'

Brunning leaned back against the table and frowned, not at Halper, but at some point in space just above the floor. He was silent a long moment.

'All right,' he said at last. 'You may as well know. It might be important, it might not.' His hard gaze flashed at both of them. 'But what I say here tonight is not to go out of this room. Understand that.' He paused again, seemingly reluctant. 'You're quite right, Lieutenant. Captain Stens has been sent to Washington prematurely . . . and for an ulterior motive. It's a minor question of security.'

'*Security?*' Halper was himself surprised at the volume of his outburst. His tone immediately softened. 'But surely the Captain can't be suspect. Just to work here he would have to have a perfect security record.'

'He does . . .' Brunning responded, '. . . almost. Last year, during his previous command in Germany, there were three days during which his whereabouts were not accounted for — three days at the beginning of a leave that was supposed to be spent with his family, who were billeted there in the town outside the base. That's the way it's logged in our records,

24

but as it happened, in the course of a recent check we found out that his family did not see him for those first three days – they thought he was on official business outside the city. Where he really was, we've not been able to find out.'

'Why don't you just ask him?'

The colonel shook his head. 'Lieutenant . . . if only it were that simple. Captain Stens has had a perfect record so far. Since that disturbing little gap in Germany he hasn't made even the slightest wrong move. He's valuable to us, but . . .'

Halper was unconvinced, and his expression showed it. 'That seems like such a small point, sir. I mean, there were a few times while on leave that even *I* didn't know where I was.'

Brunning smiled vaguely. 'But *we* know. It might surprise you to learn how thoroughly we can account for your time. And that's the difference. Stens's missing days are probably perfectly innocent, at least as far as national security is involved. I myself am sure of it. However, in anything this important, the slightest doubt must be acted upon.'

'But you have no doubts about us?'

'Obviously not. As far as we're concerned, both your records are Polly-pure.'

Halper felt he should have been pleased, but the remark made him vaguely uncomfortable. He wondered if the colonel also knew of his growing relationship with Joyce Kandell, or about his moments of doubt about the ARDCOM programme. The kind of trust of which Brunning spoke was not simple blind faith.

Joyce spoke abruptly, her voice surprising both men. 'Colonel, you still haven't told us what it is we have to do. At least a rough idea . . .'

'I'm coming to that.'

Brunning snapped the latches on his attaché case and raised the lid. He extracted two folders with typewritten labels affixed to their corners, handed one to Lieutenant Halper and the other to Joyce.

'These contain your orders,' he explained. 'At least they are the orders that will officially cover your time and activities, and also your travel.'

25

'Travel?'

'Yes.' He checked his watch. 'At zero five hundred hours there will be an Air Force plane at the base airstrip. Although you will not be departing until zero five-thirty, I want you to be there ahead of time to supervise loading the dog and whatever supplies he may need for the next thirty-six hours. You'll also need to take whatever research information you have accumulated on the dog to this date, and Dr. Braydon's notes as well. That gives you ... roughly seven hours to return to your quarters, pack, sleep if you wish, and be back at the field.'

Halper raised the corner of his folder, enough to see the destination of the flight: Houston, Texas. *Texas?*

'That's it, then.' Brunning closed the case and locked it. 'The rest must wait. You may deactivate the security system, Lieutenant.'

'Yes sir,' Halper replied, after a moment's hesitation. He switched off the equipment and unlatched the door.

'Colonel —' Joyce inquired suddenly. 'You said to bring enough supplies to last Major for thirty-six hours. What about after that?'

'After that,' Brunning replied, 'he will be out of our direct control and care.'

As the door swung open, Brunning marched from the room. The others followed him into the hall. They were surprised to see two figures snap to attention in the dimly lighted corridor.

One of the men, the one who was not saluting, was Carter, the computer technician who had participated in the test just thirty minutes earlier. An apparently borrowed Army-issue topcoat now covered his civilian clothes, and he carried a bulky case used for transporting computer tapes and other programming materials. He seemed nervous.

The other man dropped his arm as Brunning returned the salute. A Special Forces master sergeant, the man wore a web belt with a .45 pistol neatly fastened around his dress greens. He waited in silence.

'Your jet's waiting, Carter,' the Colonel advised him. 'You know what you have to do?'

Carter's tone was one of resigned despair. 'Yes, sir.' He turned and headed down the hall with his escort.

Carter's hasty departure — to a waiting jet — only increased the tangible feeling of tension that was building. And the fact that a computer programmer was still needed was only a tiny piece of the puzzle whose limits were still beyond their knowledge.

One thing at least. Halper was grateful for having a little more time to get ready than they had given poor Carter. . . .

Two hours earlier and almost a thousand miles away, lights had still blazed in the fourteenth floor offices of *News-Scene* magazine on Lexington Avenue in New York City, but only a dozen or so employees still remained.

D. Thomas Lawrence, one of the news magazine's three associate editorial writers, stood momentarily still at the window. A heavy drizzle had begun to fall, and the street below was reflecting the myriad of moving and stationary lights that were a part of Manhattan at night. At least the view was better now than during the day, with the grimy and cluttered rooftops of shorter buildings invisible in the darkness.

Lawrence left the window and returned to his desk, but remained standing. He picked up a folded wire-service print-out sheet and began skimming it again. The boss was taking his sweet time in looking over the notes for the week's lead article, and Lawrence was growing impatient.

At that moment Harrison James, the executive editor and Lawrence's superior, walked into the small office. A portly man with puffy features and thinning hair, his eyes were on a handful of typewritten pages, paper-clipped together. He stopped a short distance from the desk, and, as Lawrence waited, continued to glance over several pages of Lawrence's notes.

Finally, Lawrence asked, 'What's the verdict — is the approach all right?'

'Yes, it should be . . .' James flipped back to the first page. 'But this heading you've indicated — "Will Mid-East Be Sacrificed At Summit?" — well, I think that's a little too . . . a little too alarmist, don't you?'

27

Lawrence shook his head. 'I'm sure you're aware of the rumours concerning increased Russian arms shipments to Arab states. It will be a strong factor at the summit. And from what I've been hearing, the President is going into the meeting with a weak bargaining position.'

James looked up at him, his eyes revealing a hardness not suggested by his outward appearance. 'You have something definite on that? Something beyond the hints you've mentioned here from "usually reliable sources"?'

Lawrence sighed. 'No, nothing really definite – you know what a news blanket they throw over everything before an event of this importance. But the general feeling in Washington right now is one of uneasiness, not one of confidence. I don't know why. I've heard that the weapons limitations talks are not going smoothly – the Russians are being very cagey, as if they have nothing to gain from cooperation. There might have to be a trade-off. And if our side has to make some concessions, the indications are that one of them would be a relaxed posture towards Russian involvement in the Arab states.'

'Maybe ...' James said softly, his eyes returning to the notes. 'But remember, only a few months ago just the opposite rumours were making the rounds – that the U.S. was in a stronger bargaining position. Tread easily, Larry. We don't go to press for three days yet, and the first day of talks is scheduled for day after tomorrow. Make use of the time – get the article ready to go, but leave yourself some openings in case there's an unexpected change. After all, we don't report on summit conferences every week.'

Lawrence gave a grudging look of agreement. 'What about the heading?'

The executive editor laid the notes quietly on Lawrence's desk. 'For now, let's just go with "Mid-East: A Key Issue at Summit." I think that will cover it just as well, and we can always pull a last-minute change if something out of the ordinary occurs.'

'All right ... you're the boss.'

James nodded, started to leave, then turned back. 'By the way – who did you assign to cover this for us in Moscow?'

'I decided Jeremy Meeker is the best man for it. He's followed the Secretary of State on some of his lesser trips and is well acquainted with Mid-East matters and the arms talks. He'll be leaving tomorrow with the Press Corps for Brussels, then after the NATO meeting he'll continue on with the presidential party to Moscow.'

'Good. It should be interesting. However the meeting turns out, it will affect the shape of international politics for years to come.' He headed for the door. 'Good night, Larry. See you in the morning.'

Lawrence watched him go, then picked up his notes for the article. He stared at them for a moment, then crossed out the heading and replaced it with James's suggestion. After that, he tossed the papers into his top desk drawer and locked it for the night, picking up his coat on his way out of the office.

Exactly seven and a half hours after their staff meeting, Lieutenant Ryan Halper returned to the ARDCOM testing centre. At five in the morning, he was in no mood for the bright office lights. He squinted into their glare as he made his way to his own office and the dog kennel beyond. When he opened the door, he was surprised to find Colonel Brunning waiting for him.

Brunning rose from a chair, eyes flashing to his watch. 'You're here a little later than I expected,' he said quickly. 'We'll use the section's van for transport.'

Halper nodded, setting his travelling case down and heading for the kennel door. If Brunning was willing to forgo a regular greeting, that suited him fine.

Major was already awake and alert, sitting in his own part of the kennel. He gave a slight whine of recognition as Halper approached. The lieutenant called him and the dog followed, back into the office.

As Halper unbolted the access door that led to the parking area, Brunning came forward, extending a leash. 'Here — I want you to use this until you board the plane.'

Halper looked at him strangely. 'I don't think that's really necessary, sir.'

'Probably not, but there's no sense in being careless.' The

29

colonel watched as Halper reluctantly attached the leash to Major's collar, then asked, 'Do you have all your training materials?'

'Yes sir,' Halper replied, picking up his travelling case. 'Right here. Packed them away last night, before I left the facility. Joyce picked up her records, too.'

Halper opened the access door and started for the van used to transport animals and equipment around the facility. Brunning's hand stayed him for another moment.

'One other thing —' the colonel began slowly, carefully, his voice lower. 'About Miss Kandell . . .'

Halper turned to face him. 'Yes?'

'I don't like to have to worry about unknown factors on something this vital — whether those factors are conditions, equipment, or people. To be perfectly frank, I can't say that I have complete confidence in Miss Kandell. To me, she's something of an unknown factor.'

Halper was surprised. 'I don't understand, sir — so far as I know, her work has been excellent . . . above and beyond what's expected.'

'It's not her skill that I question, Lieutenant. It's a matter of her loyalty to the programme. I don't think I have to remind you that she has disagreed, rather vocally at times, with some of our established procedures.'

Halper chose his words carefully. 'I'm sure that she's only tried to suggest changes that would benefit the programme.'

'Perhaps. But such matters are not for her to decide. And in the mission we're about to undertake, there's no room for personal philosophies. If it wasn't for Dr. Braydon's illness, I'd be tempted to risk using him on this assignment rather than Miss Kandell.'

Halper could not help looking sceptical. 'Dr. Braydon may be the resident genius behind the CAM project, but he hasn't worked with Major the way Joyce has.'

'I realise that. I wasn't suggesting we had a choice in who would be involved. The point is, Lieutenant, I am concerned about Miss Kandell's . . . weakness, in a sense, towards the animals, and especially towards this one in particular. I wouldn't want that to jeopardise this mission in any way. We can't *allow* the mission to be jeaopardised in any way.' He hesitated briefly. 'I'm aware of your friendship with her. Don't allow that to cloud your judgment. This matter is too critical. I want you to keep a close eye on her – report to me any indications you have that she might become un-cooperative, or a threat to the mission, just in case.'

'Are you asking me to spy on her?'

'No, Lieutenant – I'm telling you to watch her objectively.'

Halper stared in disbelief. 'Colonel, I happen to think Joyce can be trusted with this responsibility, regardless of her personal views. And I don't think it's fair to –'

Brunning opened the door of the van with an irritated swiftness. 'I caution you to remember your military training, Halper. I didn't get these eagles on my uniform by winning a popularity contest. I prefer to keep on a friendly basis with my associates, military or civilian. But I will not tolerate insubordination from anyone. Especially not now . . .'

An unexpectedly chill breeze whipped low over the airfield, prompting Joyce Kandell to pull the collar of her raincoat more tightly about her neck. On the eastern horizon, grey-purple light was beginning to augment the tiny spots of electric white that dotted the edge of the field.

There seemed to be almost no gap in Joyce's mind between the 'staff' meeting of the night before and the present time. For it was still night, virtually. And she had not slept . . . *could* not. There were too many questions, too many vague and ominous elements concerning this strange mission for her mind to relax enough for sleep.

She had been at the airfield since four, waiting with a kind of controlled agitation. The plane had landed at four-thirty and began refuelling almost immediately. Sleek, with swept-back wings, the VC-140B light jet transport stood nearly ready now, its last remaining fuel tank feeding from the truck's long hose.

Joyce watched the Army ground crew completing their preparations under the supervision of one member of the plane's flight crew. They had all been quietly efficient, keeping conversation down to the absolute minimum necessary for their work. Even in those details for which Joyce was responsible, they had followed her instructions almost wordlessly. She realised suddenly that they all must be under orders to avoid conversation as much as possible, and again questions about this — *mission?* — flooded her mind. What could possibly be so imperative to the national interests to involve the ARDCOM staff in this kind of intrigue? Whatever was behind it, these cloak and dagger games were both ludicrous and frightening.

Three years before, when she had first come to work at ARDCOM as Dr. Braydon's assistant, it had seemed an ordinary enough job, working under laboratory conditions with the test animals. Of course there was the realisation that in any work done in the area of military research, security would be a factor. But it had all seemed routine before . . . a part of the background. Now it was no longer background. She was caught up in the middle of it, and she did not even know why.

She heard a motor, and then the transport van rounded the corner of a building and pulled to a stop. She smiled faintly as she saw Halper appear out of the driver's side and walk around the vehicle. A moment later, he reappeared with Colonel Brunning and the dog.

Two of the ground crew personnel came trotting up, halted at attention, saluted, and spoke briefly, then quickly returned to their work. Brunning and Halper walked towards her.

Brunning spoke first. 'Is everything ready?'

'Yes, Colonel,' Joyce replied. 'If anything, we're ahead of schedule. The food supplies and my medical kit are already on board.'

'And the travelling cage?'

'The first thing loaded. They had to rearrange things a little to get it in.'

Halper noticed for the first time that Brunning had no travelling gear of his own. 'Won't you be flying with us, sir?'

'No. I still have a final briefing with General Raskin, and a few other details to attend to. But I'll be arriving there not long after you.'

Joyce sensed that despite Brunning's clipped speech and look of urgency, he was somehow enjoying all this. But there were other matters on her mind as well.

'Colonel, will there be some sort of accommodation for us there at one of the bases?' she asked.

'Certainly. Don't worry about any of the practical problems . . . they've all been taken care of.'

'And we will be completely briefed when we arrive?'

'Yes.' Brunning glanced at his watch. 'Quarter after. You'd better be moving, and so had I. Have a good flight, Lieutenant. . . .' His eyes shifted to Joyce — 'Miss Kandell . . .'

He turned about and headed back to the van, taking the driver's seat himself. Pulling away, he accelerated smoothly, and the vehicle was soon out of sight in the darkness.

Halper watched Brunning's departure with a tightness in his face. Then he turned to Joyce.

'We'd better head for the plane. Do you have a bag?'

'It's already loaded.' She walked on his right, the dog between them. 'Did you know I had an MP escort over here this morning?'

'No, but it doesn't surprise me.'

'I guess you've seen these kind of security measures before.'

'Not since Vietnam.' They reached the steps and started up to the plane. 'Did you get any sleep?'

'No. Did you?'

Halper shook his head. 'Too keyed up, I guess.' He glanced back briefly at the lights of the installation behind him. He had left it many times before since being reassigned there, all on occasions much different from the present. There was a certain melancholy about having to leave the place, especially with the unknown before him.

Inside the small jet, there was the slight, muffled whine of the plane's various systems operating, and the occasionally fluctuating internal lights. The remaining member of the flight crew followed them into the ship, waited as the men on the ground rolled the steps away, then sealed the hatch. Saying nothing, he entered the cabin and shut the door behind him.

Halper headed towards the rear of the plane. 'Let's get Major secured.'

Joyce nodded reluctantly. 'I almost wish we didn't have to use the cage.'

'I know. But the way it's padded, he'll be better off in there if we hit turbulence.'

The interior of the aircraft had originally been desiged to accommodate eight passengers. As it was arranged now, two of the seats in the rear had been removed to allow sufficient room for the travelling cage and the supplies. To provide access to the door of the cage, located on the right, it had been necessary to move the six remaining seats together on the left side of the plane.

Halper opened the cage door and motioned for Major to enter. When the dog had arranged himself on the padded floor, Halper fastened the door and checked it. Then he stowed his own suitcase next to Joyce's, between the rear seats and the cage, and checked once more to be certain everything looked secure.

Turning, he looked into Joyce's worried gaze. The expression had seemed a part of her for the past several days.

'You look tired,' he said, steering her back towards the front of the ship. 'Come on, let's take our seats.'

'Too many long hours lately, I guess,' she said disconsolately. 'You know we were supposed to have some time off at the end of our last training cycle. Of course I didn't mind the extra work with Major so much, but with Dr. Braydon's breakdown, and now . . . this!'

They took their seats. Looking at the tension in her face Halper could not help but remember Brunning's words. It seemed foolish to doubt her . . . to mistrust her. And yet he could not deny that Joyce had given Brunning reasonable cause for doubt on more than a few occasions. Call it a personality confict or a mere difference of opinion. Whatever, it had never been critical before. Now it might be.

'You're being a civilian, they can't really order you to go along with this . . . not like in my case,' he said.

She leaned her head back, looking straight ahead. 'Maybe

not officially, although I'd be willing to bet that my contract with the government has some interesting loopholes.' She sighed. 'Besides, with what I know now, however little it may seem, if I did refuse to go they would probably have to lock me up until it's all over. So I may as well go.'

Halper nodded in agreement, but wondered if her answer told him anything. Finally he tried to put it out of his mind. He did not like playacting, especially with Joyce.

He slipped the end of his seat belt through the buckle and pulled it snug. 'Something else we missed out on –' he remarked dryly, '– *breakfast*.'

She winced. 'Don't remind me!'

The two pairs of turbojet engines located to the left and right of the rear fuselage suddenly increased their whine, building up to a steady roar that could be felt as much as heard, even though most of the sound was shielded out.

The plane's interior lights dimmed almost to nothing. The ship rolled and swayed smoothly down to the end of the runway, then turned. Locking for a moment while it built up thrust, it released suddenly and headed down the strip, increasing to takeoff velocity.

In seconds they were airborne. Halper looked at his watch. Five twenty-nine.

'Not bad,' he said softly. 'Not bad at all. With any luck, we should be in Texas in just a little over two hours. I wonder if they show a movie on this flight?'

There was no reply, and he turned to see why his joke had been wasted. Joyce was sound asleep, fatigue finally catching up with her. She twisted slightly in her seat and her head rolled over to one side, coming to rest on Halper's shoulder.

The lieutenant looked back momentarily towards the padded cage to make sure Major had gotten through the takeoff without any ill effects. He then returned his gaze to Joyce, gently brushed a few loose strands of raven hair away from her face, and settled back for the remainder of the flight . . .

In the nation's capital, at ten minutes before seven in the

morning, a grey government limousine arrived at the 21st Street entrance of the State Department. Second largest building belonging to the United States Government, the structure dominated a two-city-block area between 21st and 23rd Streets. Its influence and power in matters of world affairs were second only to that of the White House. Some political insiders gave it a slightly better edge.

Emerging from the car, Secretary of State Charles Wellmont did not pause to observe the Washington dawn. He ignored it as he did the chill in the air, heading for the doorway with a controlled and purposeful stride. The night security guard was still on duty at the door, and the man admitted him quickly, with a quiet greeting.

Wellmont looked a good deal older than his fifty-five years. His snow-white hair rose in a crest that added to his already impressive height, and lent his appearance a dignity that would have been fitting on the Supreme Court bench, or even in the Oval Office itself. But his ambitions had always been in the field of international diplomacy, and in his meteoric rise to power he had not hesitated to use his appearance, his steady voice and cool demeanour, as effective tools in dealing with representatives of other nations. His direct and unwavering gaze had often been as effective as the threat of economic sanctions or military intervention.

But now his eyes held a worried concern as he reached the door to his office and opened it.

Hanging up his topcoat, he moved directly to his desk and the phone, and began dialling a number. He sat down but did not lean back. There were several clicks on the line as matching security equipment came into play at the Pentagon, then the phone at the other end rang. It was picked up before the second ring.

'This is Wellmont. Give me General Baker, please.' There was a brief pause, then he said, 'General? How is it going?'

There was a longer pause as he listened carefully, nodding. While he listened, his office door opened and Jonathan Bennet, one of his two undersecretaries, entered the room.

'Yes, I see,' Wellmont replied over the phone, acknowledging Bennet's presence with a quick glance. 'All right, General. Do what you can, and keep me informed . . .'

Wellmont replaced the receiver quietly, then unlocked his lower left desk drawer and extracted a heavy courier's folder with classified markings and the remains of a seal. He slid out the contents – an eighty-four page report in photocopy form, fastened at the top with a metal binder.

'Jonathan –' he began, looking not at Bennet but at the first pages of the report, 'have you attended to everything that I asked?'

The undersecretary stepped closer to the desk. 'Yes, sir. It's all been taken care of. But are you certain that we don't need to inform the Secret Service?'

Wellmont continued to flip through the report. 'The Treasury Department knows nothing of this yet. Let's keep it that way. The crews on Air Force One and the back-up plane will receive what orders they need from the Pentagon.'

'Yes, sir.' Bennet's expression was grave. 'Have you had any further reports on the buildup in Egypt and Syria?'

'Yes. I'm afraid they only confirm our fears. Automatic weapons shipments have tripled this month, and camouflaged anti-aircraft missiles are being transported to border installations for use against Israeli air defence. It's not good at all.'

Bennet shook his head. 'I can't understand why the Russians would risk this kind of confrontation with us, just before the summit.'

Wellmont glanced up from the report with carefully controlled features. 'Yes, that is hard to answer.'

'What about the possibility of just calling off the conference, in protest of their actions?'

'No,' he replied quickly. 'No . . . we can't afford that just yet.'

The Secretary of State took another minute in looking through the document in his hands, then closed it and placed it back within the courier folder. He held it firmly in both hands for a moment, as if making certain he had read it well enough that he would not need to refer to it again. Then he rose from his seat and walked to the other side of the room, to the document shredder.

Wellmont turned the device on and inserted the folder with its report. When the machine had shut off, he removed the receptacle from the bottom, glanced briefly at the confetti-like material within, then turned and brought it over to Bennet.

'I want the contents put in the incinerator,' he told him.

Bennet nodded and started out.

'I want *you* to do it, Jonathan.'

'Of course, sir.'

Wellmont began placing his briefing reports and other information he would need for the conference into a leather briefcase. His actions were methodical and detached, as if his thoughts were on matters far removed.

Bennet paused at the open door. He clutched the receptacle close to him as if fearful it might be stolen. Vague doubts seemed to cloud his features, and with a certain hesitancy he spoke again.

'Sir —'

Wellmont looked up. 'Yes?'

'I was wondering . . . that is . . .' He looked questioningly at his superior. 'Has the President been fully briefed?'

Wellmont studied him a moment, a haunted look within his own eyes. He looked back to his work.

'He's . . . aware of the military situation. . . .'

There was a sudden, sharp squall of sound, accompanied by a faint but disconcerting thump. Halper jerked re-flexively, then as his mind cleared, realised he had been dozing and that the plane was landing. The noise of the tyres quickly faded after their initial touchdown on the pavement below.

The light jet transport was slowing now, losing momentum with the aid of reversed engines. Rolling almost to the end of the runway, the plane swung smoothly around and on to a lengthy exit strip that led to a large complex of hangars and other buildings. As the plane finished its turn, sunlight poured in through the cabin's windows on the side where the two passengers were seated, spilling a rectangular patch of brightness across their faces.

Joyce Kandell blinked and rubbed her eyes, frowning in puzzlement as she looked out the window, then around the interior of the plane. The expression changed as her eyes met those of Halper.

'*Oh* . . .' she said, and smiled. 'You know, for a moment I couldn't remember where I was or why. It was nice while it lasted.' She paused a moment. 'What time is it?'

Halper checked. 'Quarter to eight.'

'Then I take it this is Texas?'

He leaned across and peered through the window port at a large, plainly lettered signboard.

'Ellington Air Force Base, to be exact,' he said. 'On what you might call the outskirts of Houston.'

'Hmmm.' Joyce fumbled in her purse and extracted a mirrored compact, checked her appearance, and sighed.

Halper thought of making some appropriately encouraging remark, then decided against it. For the moment at least, the girl was in no mood to be easily cheered.

Instead, he unfastened his safety belt and went to the rear of the cabin. Their luggage and the supplies were still in a secure position. Alert and ready, Major sat in the centre of the cage, swaying slightly as the plane moved along. Halper made his way back to the seat.

Joyce undid her own belt as he sat down. 'How is he?'

'I wish I felt as good as he looks,' Halper sighed. 'I don't know what they have planned for him, but I'm pretty sure he can handle it. Maybe we'll find out soon.'

Joyce nodded, and they waited for the plane to stop rolling. But it did not stop when it reached the loading area in front of the third hangar. Moving ahead smoothly, it rolled on into the hangar through the open, wide door, leaving behind the clear morning brilliance for the cooler light of the hangar's interior.

As the jet finally came to a stop, the door was already beginning to close behind it, electrically moving along its tracks as if sealing them off from the outside world. It shut with a dull clang. Engines stilled, the jet sat in a vacuum of sound.

The third member of the flight crew appeared at the door

39

to the flight deck and began to open the hatch, while below, two men in Air Force coveralls quickly positioned the ramp for the disembarking passengers.

Halper unlatched the cage door and let Major out, reluctantly attaching the dog's collar and leash. He handed Joyce's suitcase to her, then picked up his own, led Major to the hatch, and started down the ramp. The girl was close behind him, glancing about the interior of the hangar as she walked down the steps.

Waiting for them at the base of the ramp was a lieutenant in dress blues, young, about Halper's age. 'Good morning, Lieutenant,' he said briskly. 'I'll need a copy of your orders . . . you too, miss.'

Each of them tore a single sheet from the stapled group in their folders and handed it over. The Air Force lieutenant took the papers, glanced at them briefly and fastened them to his clipboard.

Halper realised the information contained on those sheets bore little or no resemblance to the real truth of their mission, whatever it might be. He wondered if the reason for the subterfuge was truly security, or if perhaps it was also a self-protective measure for the various agencies involved. By the care that was being taken, he knew there would be no trace of the coordinated activities required for the mission. No trace at all for anyone who might study the written records that had been kept. No trace . . . in case anything went wrong.

'Where do we go from here?'

'Nowhere. For the moment.' The Air Force man tucked his clipboard under his arm. 'Before you leave here, I'll have to brief you on those areas of the complex to which you'll have access. You'll need to know your way around, for today and tomorrow at least. And there are a few other . . . minor matters that need checking.'

Halper had a rough idea what he meant, and it annoyed him. 'If you really need an ID verification, surely you can get it from ARDCOM Headquarters. Their files are quite extensive —'

'Oh, I'm sure that the Army has done a good job,

Lieutenant. We intend to do a good job, too. The D.O.D. likes it that way.'

The man's tone was patronising, and that irritated Halper more. But there was nothing to be gained from arguing with the procedures. For the moment, it was the Air Force's ball game. It would have to be played by their rules.

The men wearing coveralls had entered the aircraft and now reappeared with the supplies and medical kit. Returning to the floor of the hangar, they stacked the boxes on a hand cart, then set about assisting the flight crew. The lieutenant, momentarily through with Halper and Joyce, headed off in the direction of the pilot.

Joyce set her bag down on the floor. 'Well . . . now what?'

'Brunning probably won't be here for a while yet,' Halper replied. 'So we won't be getting a further explanation of all this just yet, I don't imagine. For the moment, we'll have to take care of Major's immediate needs.'

'Speaking of immediate needs,' she said, 'there are a few of our own to take care of, one of which is food . . . if that's not against regulations!'

Halper nodded and looked towards the group of Air Force officers who were conversing just out of hearing range. After waiting a few seconds, he managed to catch the eye of the man who had greeted them at the ramp, and motioned him over.

'Lieutenant, since we'll have to rely on you to acquaint us with the facilities around here, do you think there's any chance of us getting breakfast?' With raised eyebrow, he added, 'Without endangering anything?'

Consulting his watch, the man replied, 'I think something can be arranged. We're not far from one of the mess facilities – we can bring something in for you. Although there's no great problem . . . all areas through which you'll be travelling have been temporarily closed off to ordinary traffic.'

'Really?' Halper said. 'What about the men who flew us here . . . and the landing crew?'

'When they have completed their work here, both the flight and ground personnel will be enjoying the accommodation of our security centre for the duration of your mission.'

'And you?' Joyce inquired. 'I suppose you're with Air Force Intelligence?'

The man smiled faintly, for the first time.

Of course.'

CHAPTER TWO

'It is now zero nine-thirty,' Colonel Brunning announced briskly. 'So far, we are on schedule.' He started off down the hallway, forcing Joyce and Halper to follow at an uncomfortably fast pace.

Halper studied the man, wondering if his haste was due to fear of being late or whether it was merely the enthusiasm of a career officer suddenly swept up in a highly important project. Whatever the answer, it was not to be found on the colonel's impassive face.

Brunning had only arrived a fraction under five minutes ago, and he was already halfway into the next building complex with his subordinates in tow. There had been plenty of time for Joyce Kandell and Ryan Halper to finish breakfast in relative leisure, but the tension had once again caught up with them.

Major was the only one who seemed unaffected. He trotted along evenly at the end of his leash, easily keeping pace with Colonel Brunning. His features also were impassive, patient; he awaited the next test that would be demanded of him . . . the next game.

Two guards, surprisingly burly for Air Force men, waited outside the door at the end of the hall. After formalities and a brief check of identity papers, the door was opened to Colonel Brunning and his party. It closed again as soon as they were inside.

The spacious office in which they now stood appeared to be some manner of briefing room for visiting VIP's, since its interior was decorated more for civilian tastes than the other areas they had seen thus far. No windows, skylights, or vents of any kind were visible, but recessed fluorescent lights gave out an even, slightly more than adequate illumination, and from some unseen duct cool air circulated, bearing a faint odour that almost had to be filtered stale cigar smoke.

Looking over Brunning's shoulder, Halper saw two men

waiting for them in the centre of the room. One was dressed in civilian clothes, the other in Air Force blues. There was a solitary silver mark of rank on the officer's uniform, and as Brunning's hand snapped up in a smart salute, the details of that insignia sharpened in Halper's vision. It was a star.

'Good morning, sir,' Brunning said. He motioned the people behind him forward. 'This is Lieutenant Halper, and this . . . this is Miss Kandell. I believe you've been briefed on both of them.'

'Yes, good morning,' the general responded, nodding. His face was full, with soft, padded features broken by an occasional furrow suggestive of middle age and too many worries. He stepped forward and shook their hands, but his eyes were riveted on Major. 'This is the dog, is it? This is the heart of the mission — what we're hanging everything on?' He studied Major for a moment, and the dog returned his gaze. 'Beautiful animal. Are you sure, though . . . sure that he will perform in the field as well as under controlled laboratory conditions?'

'Yes, sir. Quite sure,' Brunning replied, and quickly added, 'At least, barring unforeseen events for which we have not conditioned him.'

The general smiled and nodded, then looked towards Halper and Joyce. 'I'm Brigadier General Matthews, First Strategic Aerospace Division. This particular briefing is solely for your benefit, Lieutenant — Miss Kandell. We've decided that it would be better if you know what's involved — more than just the necessary data required by the various technicians.'

Halper cleared his throat. 'Yes, sir?'

General Matthews continued. 'Before the need for this mission — the absolute necessity of it — will be clear, you will have to be made aware of certain information. You will consider this information classified, even though the extent to which you will be briefed is by no means complete . . . nor, as it turns out, is the information itself completely secret.'

Joyce spoke for the first time. 'General . . . I'm not sure I understand. . . .'

'I will have to explain as I go along. First things first.' He

44

turned to his associate in civilian clothes. 'Are you ready to begin, Doctor?'

The man nodded, then walked to a large display stand and pulled the cover from it. He folded the cloth methodically and placed it on a nearby chair.

'All right then. Lieutenant, Miss Kandell, if you'll come over here . . .' General Matthews led them to the area of the display stand, a yard-high wooden cabinet surmounted by a four-foot cube of Plexiglas. 'First of all, this is Dr. Wendell Byers, civilian scientist in charge of the Cerberus Defence System.'

Byers nodded and extended his hand to them.

'Sir,' Halper turned to the general, 'Cerberus . . . is that strictly an Air Force system?'

'Yes, in the sense that it is under our immediate command. It began four years ago as a research and development project headed by Dr. Byers and a number of Air Force electronics specialists. Once the feasibility of the system became apparent, the entire project was placed under the jurisdiction of the Strategic Air Command. Our mission thus far has been to deter an aggressor from launching an attack against the United States or other free-world nations by maintaining a superior retaliatory capability, including long-range bombers and a variety of missile systems.'

General Matthews paused momentarily, stroking his eyebrow thoughtfully. 'But lately, especially in the area of our missile systems, we have encountered a number of difficulties, some of which are technical and some of which are political. The Cerberus project came along at an excellent time, since it lacks many of the problems of our current systems structure, and especially since it affords us a more direct form of defence than the mere threat of retaliation.'

'You mean Cerberus is something other than the usual antimissile system . . . something totally different?'

'Yes. But Dr. Byers here is the one best able to explain it.' He turned towards the scientist, motioning for him to begin his part of the briefing.

'Well, to put it simply, Cerberus is a total defence system,

45

complete within itself – a whole . . .' Byers began, his voice a monotone that suggested he had explained the system many times before. He was roughly the same height as General Matthews, with dark hair turning grey at the temples and combed neatly back. 'We had to devise a system better suited to cope with the Soviet Union's newer weaponry. Their multiple warhead missiles constitute quite a threat to our present system. The controversy over our *Spartan* and *Sprint* systems has not helped matters, and it's doubtful we can rival their *Galosh* antiballistic missile defences which have been in a state of readiness for more than a few years now. I don't have to tell you what that kind of imbalance can lead to, if allowed to progress.'

Byers hesitated, clearing his throat. 'Now another factor we had to consider was their development of the Fractional Orbital Bombardment Satellite. Although it carries a smaller warhead and has a lesser degree of accuracy than a ballistic missile, it can be used against targets in the U.S. with less warning time. And for our ground-based defences, every second counts. All of these things were primary considerations in our decision to adopt a different strategy, and to go ahead with Cerberus.'

The scientist reached out to the first of a series of switches located along the side of the cabinet and pressed it. At once, the interior of the large Plexiglas cube became illuminated. Curving up from the lower surface was what resembled a third of a world globe, filling up most of the cube's lower half. Thick black lines delineated the outlines of continents and nations, and the United States was positioned uppermost on the exposed portion of the sphere.

'This, of course, represents our country and much of the surrounding land and sea space,' Byers continued. He pressed the second switch, causing a considerable scattering of tiny green dots to appear on the globe – around the U.S. coastline, in the interior, in Alaska, Hawaii, and a number of the island territories. 'What you see now is, with certain limitations, the placement of our present radar and compatible systems-alert network. Information from all of these installations and others is sent directly to the NORAD facility at Ent Air Force Base in Colorado, where it is all coordinated. And in another second, you will see the scope of the system.'

A new series of lights sprang into view. Little fan-shaped tints of green stretched out from the points of brighter emerald, overlapping in a chain that surrounded the nation.

'Now this system has served us well so far,' Byers continued. 'But despite the praise it is often given, it is a long way from being perfect. For example, you have undoubtedly heard of instances where low-flying aircraft have entered our airspace without detection. So far these incidents have been innocent enough, but it is conceivable that bombers and even missiles launched from ships at sea could accomplish the same thing. And even our most effective antimissile missiles are totally dependent on radar, both for knowledge of when enemy rockets have been launched and for initial tracking of targets. Heat-seeking missiles have to be within a certain reasonable range before they are effective. And . . .'

The scientist pressed the third switch. Several of the dots of light and their resultant fans winked out.

'And if anything happens to the radar facilities themselves, whether due to equipment failure, power failure, or actual sabotage, we are left with a hole in our defensive system. There is a great deal of overlapping, of course, and certain back-up measures . . . but not so much that we can feel completely secure. You see, the basic weakness with the present radar system is simply that it is not a whole, but rather a combination of many, many individual units.'

'I always thought that was one of its strengths,' Halper said.

Byers nodded somewhat impatiently. 'Yes, yes . . . in the sense that it is virtually impossible to put the entire system out of operation all at once. In that sense you are quite correct. But you see there are ways to insure that same measure of security for other systems as well — systems with a greater advantage.'

'Dr. Byers,' Joyce said, 'you said before that we were totally dependent upon radar for the detection of enemy missile launchings. Yet I seem to recall a project of some kind, I think having to do with satellites equipped with infrared sensors.'

'Yes, that was MIDAS,' Byers replied. 'Missile Defense Alarm System.'

General Matthews interrupted. 'You're quite right, Miss Kandell — MIDAS is a satellite system utilising infrared sensors to detect launchings throughout the world. And it's not without value, even though in the beginning phases we did have some trouble with the system picking up heat sources other than missile exhausts. That's pretty much solved now. But again we're stuck with the problem of its specialisation. Detecting the extremely hot exhaust of an ICBM is one thing — detecting various forms of aircraft is something else. And of course missile-carrying ships and submarines present special problems all their own.'

'So what you're saying,' Halper replied, 'is that this new system, this . . . Cerberus, takes care of everything; it has all of the advantages of the others, and few of their defects?'

'Yes,' Matthews answered. 'Exactly.'

'How does it work?'

Dr. Byers held a finger up for a moment's patience, then again activated the display unit. Instantly the lights designating the radar installations and their range of coverage disappeared from the globe. In the back corner of the cube, glowing letters appeared, spelling out the words *CERBERUS SYSTEM*. After a second's delay, ten new lights appeared within the outline of the continental United States, roughly forming a circle. They pulsed steadily in bright red.

'Unlike the radar network,' Dr. Byers began, 'there are not hundreds of individual installations in Cerberus. Instead, there are ten primary transmission commands, which you see now.' He paused. 'And, I might add, the positions of the lights on this map do not necessarily indicate their true location.'

Halper nodded, fascinated by the pulsing circle of light.

'Next, these primary transmission commands are backed up by a chain of secondaries.' As he spoke, a smaller circle of lights sprang up within the first, brilliant yellow in colour. 'So if anything should happen to one of the first chain, its function will be assumed by one of the second. In fact, only five functioning units are essential for the minimum operational security of the system. This makes the possibility of sabotage highly unlikely.'

After a few more seconds, three triangles of cool blue colour appeared within the concentric circles. Dr. Byers pointed towards the area.

'And that is the triad of final command centres into whose computer complexes all information is fed. There are, between them, fifteen new Cyber 70 computers with cross-linked processing units to handle the enormous amount of data necessary to coordinate the system. And from these centres issue all coded instructions to the rest of the system.'

Still gazing at the globe, Halper asked, 'Those three command centres — is one of them in charge of the others, or are they all equal somehow, with separate jurisdictions?'

'Technically, one is designated as high command, to fulfill certain requirements of the military structure,' Byers replied. 'However, the installations are completely duplicative in their function, from equipment to personnel, and any one of them can operate the entire defence system alone ... should the need arise.'

'Dr. Byers,' Joyce inquired, 'there's one thing that I don't understand about the placement of the transmission points which you described.'

'Yes?'

'In the conventional radar network, the installations are located as close to the coastline as possible, since their range is limited by the Earth's curvature. But these new Cerberus installations seem rather far inland ... some even in mountainous areas. Won't that affect them?'

Byers smiled. 'It would affect them very greatly — in fact, make them almost useless — if they operated in the same manner as conventional radar. But they do not, Miss Kandell. They are the transmission points for signals beamed not out to our horizon, as radar, but rather straight up ... into space. I can anticipate your next question — but I am coming to that, if you will watch the display.'

Silenced momentarily, they watched as Byers pressed

49

another of the display controls. Now, suspended in space above the Earth model, were ten tiny objects. Halper blinked in surprise. There had been no objects there before, and he wondered what intricate mirror or optical system was built into the transparent cube.

Halper studied the circle of objects. 'They seem to be in roughly the same position as the transmission command points,' he said.

'They are in exactly the same position, Lieutenant. Twenty-two thousand, three hundred miles above the surface, which places them in a synchronous orbit. They move precisely with the Earth's rotation, so that they are always over the same spot. Of course here in this display both their size and altitude are distorted for the sake of convenience in viewing them. Here,' he said, again pointing as another object appeared, larger, near the top of the cube. 'Here is a greatly enlarged view of one of the individual satellites.'

Joyce looked carefully at the three-dimensional image floating near the top of the cube. 'And this satellite is different from those of the MIDAS series?'

'Completely!' Byers said with the first trace of enthusiasm he had shown thus far. 'First of all, the Cerberus satellites do not rely on infrared sensors, nor for that matter on any other conventional detection system. And, secondly, their function is more complicated than the MIDAS satellites, since the latter were only used to detect the launchings and perform initial tracking.'

'But these do more?' Halper asked.

'Quite. But let me show you.' Again Byers turned his attention to the controls.

From each of the ten primary transmission points, two faint beams of light rose up like elongated V's to the two nearest satellites. The effect was like a tall zigzag form wrapped around in a circle.

'As you can see,' Byers explained, 'each of the stationary satellites receives beams from two of the ground transmission points, which in turn send commands *to* and receive information *from* two of the satellites. And, as I said before, only five of the ground transmission points are necessary to control all ten satellites.' Byers proceeded to demonstrate different patterns of beam transmission, simulating emergency measures used in case of failure of any of the primary or secondary ground installations. He faced his audience. 'Since there are a maximum of twenty installations, counting both the first line and their back-up units, an enemy would have to knock out more than three-quarters of them to seriously damage the effectiveness of the system. And that would require an organised act of sabotage almost beyond anyone's capabilities. Needless to say, all installations are under maximum security conditions.'

Colonel Brunning had been silent through the demonstration thus far, but now he spoke. 'Those security conditions include, by the way, a number of the dogs trained at ARDCOM facilities. In fact, five of the last training cycle were slated for one of the bases involved.'

Dr. Byers seemed impatient with the interruption. 'Yes, well – to get back to the function of Cerberus,' he said, touching another switch. A circle of light appeared within the cube, spreading out from the satellites at a forty-five-degree angle towards Earth. Its edges met the surface of the globe many thousands of miles beyond the coastline, forming a great inverted dish over most of the Western Hemisphere.

'What you see represented here,' Byers continued, 'is not actually a screen or scanning pattern in the usual sense. Rather, it is an area of sensitivity made possible by a fairly recent discovery in field electronics, and by taking advantage of the Earth's natural flow of magnetic forces. The essential thing about it is that it is a total field – not just a conglomerate of individual scanners as with the present radar system. And it is highly accurate.'

After a moment's silence, Joyce said, 'I have the impression from what you've said, Doctor, that this ... area of sensitivity will pick up more than just missiles and aircraft.'

Byers nodded. 'Cerberus will detect ships and submarines as well – in fact, virtually anything produced by man which utilises energy and is large enough to constitute a threat. Of course commercial air and sea transportation, as well as our own military craft, will be picked up as well, but these will be

51

recognised and ignored in the same manner as is presently done by our radar network.' Byers paused a moment, then reached for the display controls again.

'But,' he said, 'detection is only half of the job. The other half, quite naturally, is preventing the missiles or whatever from achieving their purpose. And to that end, the Cerberus satellites are fully equipped. If you will please look at the enlarged image . . .'

They saw that the suspended image was undergoing changes. On four sides, protective blisters moved away, revealing underlying equipment. And on the bottom, panels opened as a stacked array of tiny rockets swung down and into view.

'Each of the satellites is equipped in exactly the same way as the image you see,' Byers stated. 'But don't be misled by the rockets – they are only a back-up measure, to be used in certain instances should the primary system fail.'

'And the primary system is – ?'

'Watch.'

As the automatic cycle of display now operating within the Plexiglas cube continued, a tiny, elongated spot of light appeared from the direction of the Eurasian icelands.

'That represents an ICBM,' the scientist explained.

With slow precision, the spot advanced along its predetermined course, crossing above the Arctic regions and inexorably heading towards the United States. Steadily it drew nearer to the edge of the great dish of energy superimposed above the United States, then intersected the edge of the transparent field.

Instantly, the defence system seemed to respond to the intruder's presence. The glow of the ground-station lights increased in intensity; the transmission beams seemed to fluctuate in odd patterns, and the satellite nearest the missile's path became brighter.

Byers said quickly, softly, 'In actual use, the system will only need fifteen to twenty seconds to identify, countercheck, and respond.'

Halper glanced at the larger image at the top of the cube, and saw that it represented the satellite being activated. On the forward face, just behind the opening made by the removal of the protective blister, a device was moving ... repositioning ... aiming. ...

Halper looked back to the circle of lights above the sphere of Earth just in time to see an intense beam of light flash out from the satellite and reach the oncoming missile. In a simulated explosion, the ICBM vanished.

'Basically, what the primary system involves is an improved form of laser beam,' Byers said coolly.

'Something like Project Spade?' Halper asked.

'Yes, but considerably more advanced.' Byers put his hands in his pockets, seemingly more relaxed now that the simulated attack was over. 'The Pentagon had to discontinue Project Spade in 1971. At the time, the available laser systems simply were inadequate. But research has continued since then, principally at Kirtland Air Force Base in New Mexico, and we now have systems nearly a thousand times more powerful than before.'

The remark prodded Halper's memory, and he recalled having read somewhere that the Pentagon had spent well over a hundred million dollars on laser experimentation in 1973 alone. He wondered how much had been spent altogether.

'Do you see the real advantage of this system?' Byers asked. 'The satellites are in a better position to deal with missiles, and they do away with the dangerous time lag involved in launching our own antimissile missiles from ground level, since the laser system is instantaneous. It is even much better equipped to handle the multiple warhead rockets that have posed such a problem for the Safeguard system.'

Joyce frowned slightly. 'But hasn't there been some opposition from civilian space researchers to an in-space defence system?'

'Well, yes,' Byers said evasively, 'but it is the only truly workable system, so the advantages far outweigh the objections. Any other questions?'

Halper nodded. 'Couldn't an enemy circumvent the system by simply attacking the satellites first?'

'What could that accomplish?' Byers countered. 'The satellites are quite capable of defending themselves against missiles in the same manner you just witnessed. And if an enemy should use some version of the laser beam weapon employed by the satellites to destroy one of them, the others would take over its function. Even if they could destroy them all before our own system could eliminate the source of the beams, then that enemy would be inviting complete and instantaneous retaliation from our remaining nuclear arsenal – part of which will always be maintained.'

'I see,' Halper said. 'It seems you've developed a foolproof defence system.'

A cloud settled over Dr. Byers' features. 'Not quite, unfortunately. Of course the satellites will need periodic replacement, but that's no insurmountable problem, especially once the space shuttle project is fully operational. But there is a greater, more urgent problem at the moment . . . one which is the reason for your being here.' He switched off the display.

At Byers' cue, General Matthews began to move away from the Plexiglas cube. The others followed, finally congregating in the centre of the room.

Matthews spoke. 'Now that Dr. Byers had filled you in on the background of Cerberus, I can explain further. As he told you, there are still a few relatively minor details to iron out – but nothing that would prevent the system's use. At least . . . so we hope!'

'Sir,' Halper asked as the general paused, 'when will Cerberus begin operation?'

'It's scheduled to go into effect next week,' Matthews answered. 'However, there has been a problem. You see, about a year ago we had reason to suspect that information about the project had leaked out somehow to the Russian spy network. A report, later confirmed, from our own intelligence sources proved that Russian military scientists were not only aware of the system and its principles, but also that they were actively engaged in seeking some technological loophole in the field of sensitivity that they could exploit for their own purposes – to negate the effectivness of our defence system.

54

Several of our own government operatives were assigned the job of keeping track of the Russians' research project, and to alert us if it seemed their scientists might have found a way to bypass Cerberus. Two months ago, we received a partial transmission from one of the operatives in Russia indicating that their scientists had apparently found a way of defeating the Cerberus satellite system. We don't know exactly how, since as I said the transmission was only a partial one. We have heard nothing from that operative since, and can only assume him dead or captured.'

They all stood in silence for long moments. Finally Joyce broke the spell. 'Are you sure that report is reliable?' she asked.

Matthews sighed. 'We just don't know. To our best estimates, Cerberus is better than ninety-nine per cent effective against all known weapons systems, and almost everything that we've been able to postulate that could develop anytime in the near future. But of course trying to anticipate new discoveries is haphazard at best.' He paused. 'The point is, we simply can't afford to risk switching over to Cerberus, knowing that the Russians may have a way to defeat it. Yet we've already made commitments of personnel and equipment to the new Cerberus installations. If we don't make the changeover next week, we'll be caught between systems and there'll be serious gaps in our defences. Therefore, we have to find out what their research has yielded — we *must!*'

Ryan Halper seemed puzzled. 'Sir, exactly what is it that *we* have to do?' he asked. 'And if the information you've given us about the Cerberus project is already known to the Russians, then why the need for all this secrecy?'

'It boils down to this, Lieutenant,' Matthews said quietly. 'Due to our operative's capture, Russian intelligence has been alerted to the presence of the rest of our people in the area of the research laboratory. Things are closed down even tighter than normal in Communist Russia, and I don't have to tell you the advantages their security forces have over those in our open society. I doubt if we could get another man near enough to the source of the research

55

documents to do any good. In fact, after we heard no more from the first operative, all direct intelligence efforts on our part in Russia were halted for fear that further pressure would only succeed in driving their research efforts completely underground, under a security blanket we'd have no chance of penetrating. So . . .'

General Matthews paused, stroking his eyebrow again.

'So,' he repeated, 'a special emergency council of the Department of Defense and other related agencies agreed that some other way had to be devised to secure the information we needed. A number of possible methods were suggested – and discarded as being unworkable. As much out of desperation as logic, we finally decided to try a totally unorthodox approach, to be planned by our best and freshest strategists.

'All projects carried out under the D.O.D. are of course known to their planners – all facilities, equipment, and personnel are constantly kept in mind to be utilised in special missions, whenever the need arises, depending upon the particular situation.' He paused a second, looking down at Major. 'And so it was with your work at ARDCOM, Lieutenant . . . Miss Kandell. Especially your new "second memory" project. That is why the order went down to have one of your specially trained dogs adapted for the mission, along guidelines furnished to your facility's commanding officer, General Raskin, and passed on to Colonel Brunning here.'

'You mean,' Joyce said faintly, 'all this time you've known that we would be expected to participate actively in this mission – more than just in the final training of the dog?'

Matthews nodded. 'Of course we could not tell you of this ahead of time. It would have served no useful purpose and only would have been an unnecessary risk. You see, what we plan to do – what we've got everything riding on – is to utilise this animal, with its special training and brain implant, to get the information we must have. If we can pull it off – and it's going to take more than just a little effort – this dog may succeed where our human operatives have failed.'

56

Joyce Kandell looked stunned. Her mouth opened as if to say something, then slowly closed.

Halper said, 'You mean you intend to use this dog for espionage purposes?'

'Counterespionage is a better term,' Matthews stated. 'We're running out of time and options. This has a chance of working, and it may be our only chance. So I hope you can see now exactly why there's a need for absolute secrecy with this mission. The only chance it can possibly have of succeeding depends entirely on the element of surprise. It's a one-shot effort. Once the plan is known, it's worthless. But if it succeeds just this once, it will have paid off . . . completely.'

'And if it doesn't?' The girl's voice was hollow and dry as she thought of Major's fate.

General Matthews grimaced slightly. 'If not . . . then we will likely be stuck with the most ridiculous intelligence effort ever undertaken. To say nothing of the loss of an important defence system in which a considerable amount of time, effort, and funds have already been invested.' Again a look of resolve settled upon the officer's features. 'But we can't fail . . . we can't afford to. And I have confidence in our ability to pull this whole thing off, as wild as it may seem.'

'But isn't it quite a risk, sir?' Halper began. 'Attempting something like that just before the summit conference?'

'There's a greater risk if we don't. In fact, those arms talks are the most pressing reason for the mission. The Russians have the edge on us and they know it. They won't bargain when they're ahead. That's why we need the information as quickly as possible.'

'But even assuming the dog can be used for that purpose, how on earth do you intend to get him into Russia, not to mention the specific area you want?'

Matthews smiled faintly, as if amused by Halper's particular choice of words. He crouched down next to Major and scratched the dog's ears gently.

'Lieutenant,' he said finally, 'have you ever heard of the Trojan Horse?'

It was quarter after seven that evening, civilian time, when the door to the restricted section of the Officer's Mess swung smartly open. Holding the door, and standing out of the way, was the same sergeant major who had escorted Carter out of the ARDCOM centre the previous night. Still wearing what appeared to be the same dress-green uniform, he looked no less trim than before.

Carter was a remarkable contrast to the Special Forces soldier as he eased past and into the room. Haggard looking, his clothes rumpled, he accepted the soldier's courtesy with a grudging reluctance. Once inside, he glanced nervously around. His eyes finally settled on Lieutenant Halper and Joyce Kandell, and he headed towards their table.

Halper smiled as Carter reached them. 'It looks like our resident computer technician has been logging overtime.'

Carter pulled out a chair and sagged wearily into it, uttering a faint groan that was more of the spirit than of the flesh. 'You don't have to be so cheerful, Lieutenant. As a civilian, at least I can get overtime.'

Halper's smile faded. 'True, alas,' he said.

Carter looked up as a young airman came up to their table and placed a mimeographed sheet with the evening menu next to his hand. He looked it over briefly, pointed to a few items and handed it back silently. After the airman had gone, he said, 'You wouldn't believe what I've been through since I saw you last.'

'Try us.' Joyce's tone was sympathetic. 'Right now I'd believe almost anything.'

'Well, first of all they rushed me over to the airfield without a chance to stop at my place or anything. And when I got there, the jet was warmed up and ready to go — and I don't mean a passenger plane! It was some kind of a fighter jet, and I practically had to fly piggyback with . . . with Godzilla over there.' He motioned towards the door where the Special Forces man still stood.

If the soldier caught any of Carter's words, he made no show of it. Standing at parade rest, with his dress trousers tucked neatly into his boots and the green beret tilted at a businesslike slant over his weatherbeaten features, he looked like a recruitment poster. The .45 at his side seemed a part of him, not an accessory.

'Keep one thing in mind,' Halper said soberly. 'If anything had happened . . . if there had been any threat involved . . . that man would probably have laid down his life, if necessary, to see that you got here.'

Carter's irritation faded. 'Yeah, I guess so. Anyway, after we landed I was shuttled over to a large building with a computer system almost identical to the one we have back at ARDCOM. And keep in mind that I got there around midnight — not the best time to start work. There, I spent the next . . .' he checked his watch, 'the next sixteen hours completely reprogramming their system to match the function of our own — the one we've been using for the canine project. And that was no small task in itself, considering I had to start almost from scratch. If it hadn't been for the encoding cards and tapes I brought with me, I might have been at it for weeks.'

He halted quickly as the airman returned with a tray of steaming dishes. The man set them before him and left.

Carter looked at the food, sighing. 'I wish I were hungrier. This is the first decent meal I've seen since sometime yesterday.'

Joyce frowned and asked, 'Didn't they bring you anything while you worked?'

'Just some kind of vending-machine sandwiches. The Green Beret had the same, but I think he would have been happier with K Rations.' Carter glanced again towards the Special Forces soldier, this time with a curious respect. 'That man is something else, you know? He's been everywhere I have — and I do mean everywh.e — gotten no more sleep than me, and he still looks like he could take on an armoured division.'

Halper was still curious. 'What happened when you finished reprogramming the computer? Did they give you any kind of a briefing?'

'You mean Dr. Byers and the SAC general?'

Halper nodded.

'Oh, yeah. Soon as they could get me over to that

demonstration room I got the whole fifty-cent light show.' Carter smiled. 'And I hope you took notes, because I have the strange feeling we're going to be quizzed on it later!'

Almost as a reflex action, Halper glanced again to the table where his commanding officer sat. Colonel Brunning was still engaged in low-key conversation with General Matthews and a man in civilian dress whom Halper had not seen before. And over in the corner, by himself, sat the Air Force lieutenant who had met Halper and Joyce Kandell when their plane landed. The young intelligence officer had already completed his own meal and was sitting, quietly surveying the room with the alertness of a hawk.

'Well,' Carter said, swallowing quickly, 'what have you been up to since you got here?'

'Not all that much,' Halper replied. 'We had our briefing first thing this morning – I imagine the details are the same. Then you can sandwich in Major's exercise period, an electronic check of the implant, and a complete medical exam with the assistance of some kind of Air Force veterinary specialist. That pretty much rounds it out.'

Carter finished another bite. 'They did at least give me about an hour and a half off before I came in here. I tried to get a little sleep, but I think it left me more dragged out than before. Oh, well . . .' He concentrated on his food again, then looked up suddenly at Halper and the girl. 'Did you . . . well, were you . . . filled in on this mission any more than I have been? I mean, specifically in the area of just how they intend to utilise the dog . . . transportation and everything?'

Halper shook his head. 'Not completely. Except for the basic reason behind this whole operation, they're still feeding us what we need to know on almost a minute-by-minute basis.'

'I see.' Carter seemed relieved. 'I was wondering if maybe they considered me some kind of security risk.'

'If they did, you wouldn't be here.'

Carter nodded to himself. 'I guess they're just keeping a tight rein on everything . . . which is understandable.'

Joyce folded her arms and leaned against the edge of the table. 'Their computer centre – is it far from this building?'

Carter looked surprised. 'Oh, didn't I tell you? It's not even on the base. It's over at the Johnson Space Center.'

'The NASA installation?' Halper asked.

'Yes. I imagine it will be our base of operations once this whole thing gets going.'

'Why there? Surely that isn't the only computer system in the area. There must be a half-dozen or more military bases within a few hundred miles of here.'

'Yes, but not with a system suitable for the kind of programme structuring required by our project.' Carter took a sip of water, then pushed his plate away, the food half eaten. 'Besides, there aren't that many places with a communications link-up as extensive as that complex has available. Most of the ones that do are either too tied up with high priority duty, like the national defence, or else they're needed in some other capacity in this mission. At least that's what I've been able to figure out from what little information I've received.'

'Then I gather you think our part will take place here in Houston,' Joyce said. 'We won't have to be directly involved in any other part of the world.'

'No, not likely. Certainly not in Russia – that much is obvious. Probably not in Europe, either. I have a feeling that things will be happening fast . . . no time to transport us, bag and baggage, to some point across the ocean. Besides, there's no need to. If this thing can be run by remote control, so much the better.'

'Better for a number of reasons,' Halper said. 'I have a feeling myself – that the Defence Department is as concerned with what happens *after* they pull this off as they are with the matter of *if* they can pull it off.'

Joyce frowned. 'How do you mean?'

'Simple. The United States can't just stage an espionage mission this complex against the Soviet Union without making waves in the rest of the world. If any of our personnel were captured by foreign governments unfriendly to the U.S., or were even witnessed doing *anything* that could lend credence to Russian claims of espionage, it would hurt our national image.'

Carter snorted. 'As if espionage between both countries didn't go on all the time!'

'Doing it is one thing,' Halper said dryly. 'Getting caught at it is another. No, you can bet that the D.O.D. wanted a way to get the information they need — a way that would be almost impossible to prove was espionage.'

'Should be quite a trick to pull off.'

'A dangerous trick,' Joyce added. 'With Major right in the middle of it.'

A note of apprehension in her words caught Halper's attention. Brunning's warning came to mind again, and he found himself wondering at what point Joyce's natural concern might become a problem. He tried to sound resolute. 'We're just going to have to do the best we can at our end of it and hope that everything goes as planned.'

'I know,' she said, hesitating, 'but what if the plans have only been figured for a one-way trip?'

Halper shook his head. 'I don't think so. They'll have every reason to want to bring him back. If he stays in the communists' hands, there's too great a chance he may be exploited for propaganda purposes. Even if he weren't ... even if he weren't alive. No, you can bet they've figured a way to get him out of there once the job's done.'

Carter sighed and shook his head. 'Spy business! Working at ARDCOM, I expected that we might be the subject of espionage. I didn't expect to participate in it.'

Joyce suddenly held her hand up in an unobtrusive signal for silence. 'Company . . .'

Halper looked over and saw that Colonel Brunning and the civilian that had been at his table were walking towards them. General Matthews was leaving.

Carter and Halper rose to their feet almost simultaneously. As usual, the colonel wasted no time in petty conversation.

'Gentlemen, Miss Kandell,' he began, 'this is Arnold Smith, a representative of one of the civilian agencies. You'll be working with him.'

The three shook hands with Arnold Smith and introduced themselves. Smith had a quiet friendliness about him, eyes that twinkled with alert interest, and a balding head that made him look fatherly and kind. And he was shorter than he had seemed while seated.

'Welcome to the club, sir,' Halper told him. 'It looks like this will be quite a project for us.'

'Yes. Yes, it will,' the man said quickly. 'Colonel Brunning has told me a lot about you — all of you. If you're as good at your work as he says, we shouldn't have any problems here in Houston.'

'And if we do, you'll be helping out?' Carter asked.

'With technical and advisory problems, yes,' Smith said. 'My work is research, Mr. Carter. What you might call supplying raw material.'

Joyce was about to ask a question, but Colonel Brunning broke in. 'There'll be more time tomorrow for you to exchange the necessary information. And if your temporary quarters are satisfactory, I suggest you turn in early and get as much rest as possible. Needless to say, for the time being you will be restricted to authorised areas only. I'll see you all in the morning.'

Smith nodded politely to the three, then turned and walked with Colonel Brunning towards the door.

After a moment, Halper said, 'So much for that.'

Carter shrugged. 'We may as well go to our rooms and try to catch up on our sleep.'

The others nodded in agreement and left the table. The Special Forces man was waiting to join them as they left the mess facility, and he walked with them in silence back to the area in the building complex where their temporary quarters were located: four rooms at the end of the hall, two on either side, Vistors' Section *B*. He continued directly to his room and closed the door behind him, leaving the others in the hall.

Halper looked down the corridor for signs of other rooms being occupied. He saw none. 'Do you think Arnold Smith is billeted in this section?'

Carter shook his head negatively. 'Probably in the *A* section, where Colonel Brunning is. I passed by there a while ago before dinner. Looks about like this, but the furnishings are a bit higher class.'

'Rank Has Its Privileges,' Halper said resignedly. 'Did you

notice that Brunning was rather vague on which civilian agency Smith is representing?'

'Yes, and Smith didn't clear it up any, either,' Carter agreed. 'Research, he says . . . which is a pretty good way of describing the gathering of intelligence information. And civilian. And you can add to that the fact that groups like the FBI don't generally work out of the country.'

'So you think he's CIA?'

'I'd be willing to bet on it.'

'Makes sense, I guess.' Halper rubbed the back of his neck, where muscles were beginning to ache from tension. 'To run this show from back here, we're going to have to know the layout of the area where the Russian research is being done. And if anybody has that information, the CIA does.'

Carter stifled a yawn. 'Well, whatever they've got planned for us, we'll find out tomorrow. I'm turning in. See you . . .'

He went into his room and closed the door. In a moment Joyce and Halper followed suit, too weary to talk further.

It was eight-thirty p.m. in New York City. In the offices of *News-Scene* magazine, standing near the desk of science editor Josh Stuart, D. Thomas Lawrence struck a weary pose. Coat slung over one shoulder, he watched as Stuart shuffled through the jumble of paperwork that covered the desk.

'What's the problem, Josh? I'm about to leave – can it wait?'

'Just had it a second ago,' Stuart muttered to himself. Then, finding a slip of paper, he repositioned his glasses and glanced over it. 'This is it. I'm afraid we can't have that feature article on the new NASA Administrator. At least not for the issue we'd planned.'

'Why not?'

'Got a call a few minutes ago. I was out but one of the girls took the message. Dr. Laswell's cancelled out the interview session . . . said it would have to be set up sometime later. I called back as soon as I got the message, but I was told he had already left Washington.'

Lawrence was still not sure whether he should be

interested ... whether the information was worth delaying his dinner date. 'Did Laswell give any reason?'

'No. None at all.' Stuart frowned, tossing the note back into the clutter on his desk. 'I guess that means we'll also have to hold the related articles on the joint Soviet-American space projects, since we wanted to tie it all together.'

Lawrence grunted unhappily. 'That would foul us up but good. We'd have to find new material for a quarter of the magazine if we hold up the other articles.'

'Wouldn't be the first time we put out a thin issue.'

'True. But precedent is not much of an excuse to hand old Harry J. when he wants to know why we're short copy.' Lawrence hesitated a moment. 'Funny — Laswell was only appointed to the post a few months back. He hasn't been in long enough to get uppity with the press.'

'Maybe you haven't been following his career like I have. He's been pretty uppity, as you put it, with a lot of people over the years. He can afford to be, with his background. He's one of the few original pioneers in space science who's still pioneering.'

Lawrence nodded in vague recollection.

'Also,' Stuart continued, 'his views on international politics haven't made him too popular in some circles — especially the military.'

'He must have friends somewhere.'

'You mean the appointment? There was no one better qualified for the job. Besides, his views fit in nicely with the President's policies on improved relations with the East ... joint research and all that.'

'An interview with him should make good copy. Just try to set it up again as soon as you can.'

'Sure. But what puzzles me is why he should cancel on such short notice.'

A voice came from behind them. One of the reporters still in the building was motioning for Lawrence.

'Sir, there's a call for you in your office.'

'All right, thanks.' Lawrence started to turn around and head back there, but abruptly changed his mind. He picked up the phone on Stuart's desk and pressed the button for the switchboard. 'Hello? This is Lawrence – transfer that call for me to this phone, please.'

He waited a moment for the shift to be made, then gave a surprised frown when he recognised the caller. 'Jeremy – where are you calling from?'

'Here,' Jeremy Meeker's voice replied. 'In Washington, that is. Haven't you heard?'

'Heard what? I haven't been near a TV or radio all day.'

'The flight to Brussels has been delayed. I thought I'd better check in with you.'

'Delayed? What for?'

'Bad weather conditions over the Atlantic. At least that's what the Air Force says.'

'Is it true? I mean, could there have been trouble with the President's plane? Kook threats, or anything?'

Meeker's voice hesitated. 'Not that I've heard of, but I'm not sure they would say so even if there were. You know how they are.'

Lawrence considered it. 'Is there . . . any hint that maybe the conference isn't going to come off after all?'

'No. We're still scheduled to leave in about five hours. But obviously it's going to throw us almost a day behind schedule. The NATO meeting will have to be moved back a little, and I can't even guess about Moscow.'

'All right, Jeremy, Keep me posted.'

Lawrence hung up the phone. He was silent a long moment, still thinking about Meeker's call. Josh Stuart was busily sorting through another stack of papers, looking for something and seemingly unaware of Lawrence's phone conversation.

Stuart looked up finally as Lawrence was about to walk away. 'What shall I do about the other articles – the ones related to the Laswell interview?'

'Plan to run them anyway,' Lawrence tossed over his shoulder. 'There's nothing to fill in, so we'll just have to play it by ear.'

By nine in the evening, Halper was still debating whether or not to turn in early himself. He had spent the last several hours in his temporary quarters poring over all the accumulated notes and training records he had compiled during the months spent working with Major. He had worked with other dogs as well during the last training cycle, and had kept scrupulously complete records on them all.

It was a different kind of training from the usual Military Police guard dog progamme in which Halper had participated, both stateside and in Vietnam. He had been a dog handler originally, prior to OCS. So when his orders came down assigning him to ARDCOM he was not greatly surprised, even though he thought he might be assigned to the security section rather than the experimental projects staff. That had been over a year and a half ago, and it seemed unlikely there would be any new assignments as long as the project continued and his work was satisfactory.

As he forced his mind back to the records before him, he heard a knock at his door. Joyce's voice followed, softly.

'Ryan —'

Halper left the small desk and opened the door. Joyce stepped inside, a troubled look on her face.

'Ryan . . . can I talk with you?'

'Sure.' Halper gestured towards the desk. 'I've been going over my notes. I could stand a break.'

Joyce closed the door behind her. 'I've been looking through my own records on Major, but I can't seem to concentrate on them.' She walked over towards the desk, eyes downcast. 'I wish Dr. Braydon were here. If something should go wrong —'

'You can't worry about that.'

She shook her head, not in answer to Halper but in response to her own confused feelings. 'I know. It's pointless to worry. And I guess it's selfish of me to wish any more work on Dr. Braydon. The poor man's been in charge of virtually every project at ARDCOM since the beginning. They've been overworking him for years.'

Halper nodded. 'We're lucky he was able to perform the implant operation before his breakdown.'

'Lucky?' Joyce looked at him oddly. 'I suppose. But I think this unexpected project was exactly what brought it on.

The last straw ... the last strain on his system' He just couldn't take it anymore.'

Halper studied her a moment. 'How about you?'

'What?'

'I said, how about you? Are you going to be able to take it?'

She remained silent, surprised by his remark. He had said it calmly, despite the concern on his face. But she could not tell whether the concern was for her ... or for something else.

'You know, you haven't exactly been a pillar of confidence since this started,' Halper continued. 'I'm going to need your help on this thing. It will take both of us — doing our best — to pull it off. You know that.'

'And ... you're not sure whether I can handle it?'

'I think you can.'

She studied him a long moment, then smiled sadly. 'Sometimes ... sometimes it's almost frightening, Ryan. There are times when I can almost see you transforming ... becoming another Brunning.'

The remark caught him off guard. 'I ... I'm not like the colonel ... not that much. I'm not that hard-core. You know better.'

'Do I? I thought I did, but lately ...' She trailed off. 'Don't you realise what you're doing right now? A pep talk, like one of Brunning's, to get me into line.'

'It's not like that.'

'Isn't it? I mean, maybe I do need it, but I didn't think that sort of snow job was your style.'

'Quit it!' Halper was on the verge of losing his temper with her, and he could not allow that. How simple it might be to tell her of Brunning's distrust ... to be perfectly frank and open with her. That was what he wanted, even though a voice akin to conscience spoke to him of military duty and the responsibility of an officer. There had never been a clash before — minor skirmishes, perhaps, but never a real clash. There was one now, growing minute by minute. And the horrible thing about it was that Brunning and Joyce were both right.

'Just quit it,' Halper repeated, bringing his emotions into

more complete control. 'I don't want to argue with you ... not on this or anything else, for that matter. Please don't force it, or start finding motives for things I say. I think we both have good reason to be concerned with this ... this mission. It's obviously important.'

Joyce took a step closer to him, her look more pleading. 'Maybe it is important. But the thing is, what are we doing in it? Whatever the reason, it's still plain out-and-out espionage, Ryan. That's not our job. There's no war on.'

'You heard General Matthews explain the need for it – the danger of a defence system that we can't be sure about. Maybe the Russians haven't cracked it. But we have to know, one way or another.'

'I can understand that. But I can't help but feel that if it wasn't this, it would be something else....' She sighed, shaking her head slowly, turning away from him. 'I don't know. Maybe it's just been a long time coming, but I'm beginning to wonder about our work. Are we doing the right thing? I mean – where is it all leading to?'

Halper looked at her strangely. 'What are you getting at?'

'The experimentation with the animals – is it just to improve their value in guard applications and in sniffing out drugs and explosives, or is it leading up to something else? If this mission succeeds, what will they want to try next?'

'You heard them say this is a one-shot affair – once the plan is known, it would never work again.'

'Maybe. But how many variations must there be ... how many plans that wouldn't depend on the element of surprise?'

'I don't know. I honestly don't know.'

Joyce was silent for several moments. Her hands on the chair, she leaned forward slightly, not really seeing the desk and the papers arranged upon it. 'Am I being so unreasonable? For wanting to know?'

Halper had no answer ... not for her and not for himself. His own thoughts were too uncertain to voice. He tried to sort them out, but there were only a few that seemed clear and important. He did not want to sacrifice Joyce's friendship for the sake of the mission. And he would not sacrifice the mission for anything, if indeed it was as important as it seemed. He hoped the two goals would not be irreconcilable.

He moved to her side and placed a hand on her shoulder.

'Try to see this thing through. Please. We can't afford any rash decisions right now. I'm going to be depending on you, and Major will, too. . . .'

She turned at his words, her eyes searching his face. Some new emotion welled up within her.

'And I'm depending on you, Ryan. But I don't think you understand that. I don't think you understand that at all.'

In a moment she had reached the door and opened it. She disappeared from view, closing the door with slightly more force than necessary.

Halper stared at the plain wooden panel for nearly a minute, trying to sort out his own conflicting feelings. Then he realised that he had a decision to make. An unpleasant and difficult one.

Brunning had said to report any potential problems concerning Joyce. The colonel would almost certainly be interested in their conversation, but to tell him of it might jeopardise Joyce's continued work at ARDCOM . . . at the least. And to ignore the matter would be to take the responsibility into his own hands.

Halper put away his papers and turned out the light. The decision could wait until morning, anyway.

CHAPTER THREE

Lieutenant Ryan Halper sat bolt upright in bed.

He had been dreaming about a number of things, some vague, some clear. But something had intruded, something which had begun as a part of the overall background and quickly forced its way through the fabric of his dreams.

It came again – a moderately quiet but incessant knocking on his door. He listened for another second, clearing his mind and remembering finally where he was.

Swiftly on his feet, he reached the door and opened it. The young Air Force Intelligence officer was outside.

'What is it?'

'Lieutenant, Colonel Brunning wants to see you. At once. In the Medical Lab.'

'What about the other ARDCOM personnel?'

'Just Miss Kandell – she's already been awakened.'

Halper's pulse was increasing. 'What's up? Is something wrong?'

'I couldn't say,' he replied, looking like he himself had been roused from sleep only a short time earlier. 'You'll have to speak to the colonel.'

'All right . . . I'll be there.'

'Colonel Brunning asked that I wait for you and Miss Kandell, and take you there personally.'

'We know the way, Lieutenant,' Halper said with irritation. 'We were there earlier today . . . I mean yesterday.'

The Intelligence officer shrugged, his tone becoming apologetic. 'I'm sorry, but the colonel's orders specified that I escort you there. They're in a different section of the Med-Lab, and it will be faster if I show you the way.'

Halper sighed and gave in. 'Okay . . . no argument.'

He closed the door and headed for the closet. Halfway there, he stopped, rubbed the sleep from his eyes and looked at his watch. In the windowless room, with the lights out, it was hard to see. Only a faint amount of light came into the room from the hall outside. At last his eyes were able to

71

perceive the dimly glowing points of radium on the face of the watch.

'Three in the morning!' he groaned. He grabbed his uniform from the closet and began dressing. Two minutes later he was out in the hall.

The Air Force lieutenant was waiting there several yards away from their rooms. A few seconds after Halper had closed his own door, Joyce Kandell appeared in the hall, rushing towards him. Her hair had been hastily combed, and she was still buttoning the brown jacket that matched her skirt.

'Ryan — what do you think is wrong? Is it Major?' Her voice was low and she seemed out of breath.

Halper tried to calm her. 'Take it easy. I don't know yet. We'll have to find out from Brunning. It could just be something routine.'

'But the colonel said nothing about starting this early.'

'Relax,' Halper told her. 'For that matter, he's said nothing at all about this mission until he had to — you know that.'

A sound behind them brought their attention around to the last door on the other side of the hall. The Green Beret had just emerged, straightening a few pleats in his uniform caused by the web belt and holster. Satisfied with his appearance, he took up a position against the wall and remained stationary.

Halper looked quickly to the Air Force lieutenant. 'Did you get him up?'

The young officer nodded. 'Since it was necessary for you and Miss Kandell to keep your paper work and classified materials here, I thought it would be advisable to have someone keep an eye on the rooms. It makes things a lot easier on security if we use someone already cleared and involved in this project.'

As they hurried along the hallways, their footsteps echoed in the stillness. Activities in the complex were at a minimum now. Only the occasional whine of a jet engine could be heard, and even that sounded alien and remote in the night-time surroundings. They left the main building and

72

crossed a short, open area that separated it from the Medical Lab wing. In the blackness of the early morning Texas sky, the pole-mounted lights stood out like brighter stars, spilling pools of brightness in odd patterns. A small, completely enclosed cargo truck was backed up to a loading ramp on one side of the Medical Lab wing, but it was impossible to tell if there was any connection between that and the matter that had called them to the building with such apparent urgency.

An Air Force guard snapped to attention as the three approached, recognised the Intelligence officer and waved them on through the entrance. The outer office was deserted, as it had been earlier. Ordinarily there would have been a number of military and civilian personnel present during the normal working hours. But the circumstances of the last few days were far from ordinary.

Halper reached the swinging door of the inner lab section first and pushed through, pausing to hold it open for the others. He looked around, breathing a sigh of relief as his eyes settled on the cream and black form of the dog, sitting alert and ready next to Colonel Brunning.

Joyce went directly to the dog, crouching beside him. She looked up at Brunning. 'Is Major all right, sir?'

Brunning was his usual self — formal without seeming so. 'Yes, of course. He's fine. I'm sorry to have gotten you up at this hour, but the entire schedule has been updated; we have to begin at once.'

'Updated?' Halper responded. 'Sir, has anything happened?'

Brunning shook his head impatiently. 'No, nothing's wrong. The mission is not jeopardised. But a number of factors have forced us to move up the launch window, and that means we've got to get Major ready as soon as possible.'

Halper had entertained a vague suspicion that transporting Major to some as yet undesignated area in Russia would involve more than just ordinary ships or aircraft, considering the time factor alone. But he was still surprised by the colonel's words.

'Then ...' he hesitated. 'Then Major's going to be launched into space?'

'Quite right, Lieutenant,' Brunning chided. 'If we don't take too long and miss our opportunity!'

At that precise moment, the door to lab facility D swung part way open and General Matthews leaned around it. He spotted Halper and Joyce.

'They're here — good! Get them started processing immediately.'

'Yes, sir.' Brunning headed towards the door to the lab. 'Come along, and bring the dog.'

The door led into a short hallway, one side of which was glass, offering a view into the laboratory area which glistened with the highly scrubbed gleam of a hospital operating room. Inside the lab, the veterinary specialist who had earlier assisted in Major's medical examination waited.

Brunning motioned to the door at the end of the hall. 'You'll have to go through there first. Special coveralls will be required in the lab, and there'll be someone in the ready room to assist you.'

Leaving Brunning and the general behind in the hall, the lieutenant and the girl moved into the ready room with Major. Inside, several booths were located at the far end. Standing near the door was a woman wearing white slacks and tunic, with a close-fitting cap that enclosed her hair.

'Here, Lieutenant. If you take off your coat, you'll be able to slip this on over your uniform,' the woman said, handing the folded garment to him. To Joyce Kandell she extended an outfit like her own. 'And you, miss. I'm afraid you'll have to change that suit to get into this.' She motioned towards the booth on the right.

When both were ready, they cleaned their hands thoroughly with disinfectant soap and stepped into white slip-on shoes. The lab assistant busied herself with a checklist of prelaunch procedures.

Joyce watched silently for a moment, then volunteered, 'The last solid food he had was a little over seventeen hours ago. ...'

74

Without looking up, the assistant answered, 'Yes, I know. That information is in the log. Since that time, the dog's system has been voided, and he's received a special nutritive injection which should last him for the duration of the flight.'

The woman set down her clipboard and picked up a spray can of disinfectant. She used it discriminately on Major, concentrating on the pads of his feet, lifting each paw. 'We've already given him a complete antibacterial bath,' she explained. 'This is just a minor touch-up.'

Halper asked, 'Is he ready now?'

The woman nodded. 'We can take him into the lab.'

Another door connected with the spotless room beyond. As they approached the veterinary specialist, the man began to pull layers of sealed plastic sheeting from a large object near one wall of the facility. Once the last bit of plastic was removed, they could see that the object was a six-foot-long, cylindrical satellite, tapering at the ends and some three and a half feet in width. The plastic had protected the open hatch, the cover for which rested, similarly wrapped, on the lower shelf of the special dolly supporting the satellite. The specialist was as sober-faced as his assistant as he greeted them. 'Good morning, Lieutenant . . . miss.'

'Good morning,' Halper replied. 'How can we help?'

'For the moment, just your presence here is a help. It's important that the dog be at ease . . . that he associates this project with the previous experiments in which he's been involved.'

Halper nodded. 'I don't think there'll be any problem. He's pretty adaptive.'

'Good. But I want you both to behave normally around him. It will make things simpler.' He handed Joyce his own copy of the medical checklist. 'We ran another examination about twenty minutes ago. The results are the same as the one twelve hours ago, but if you would check it over you may find something I've missed.'

Joyce quickly checked through the data. But it was soon apparent that the man had missed nothing in his examination of the dog. Every test that had been necessary, or even merely advisable, had been performed. The information was thorough and positive.

She handed the checklist back to him. 'It looks like Major's ready.'

The man nodded, slipping on a pair of disposable plastic gloves. 'Is there any particular procedure you've used in your training programme to get him started into a new experiment?'

Halper answered. 'No, not really. Aside from generalised commands that are necessary under certain circumstances, nothing in that manner is needed.'

'I see. Then we can go ahead.' He turned slightly as his assistant brought forward a hypodermic with a carefully measured amount of colourless liquid. He double-checked it, voided the air in the needle, and administered the shot to the dog's hindquarters. 'This is just a mild sedative to make sure he doesn't become too excited, and to keep his respiration and heartbeat at a lower, smoother rate. He won't use up the stored oxygen supply quite so fast that way.'

Joyce studied the metallic object resting on its dolly. 'There doesn't seem to be much room in there for life support systems. How ... how long will the oxygen last?'

'Seventy-two hours,' the specialist responded. 'That should be an extra day more than necessary. A larger margin than that would be better, of course, but the limitations of the satellite are rigid.'

Joyce pressed the matter further. 'Does that seventy-two hours begin once the capsule is sealed?'

'No. Fortunately, an external oxygen supply can be hooked into the internal system until about twenty minutes before launch. The launch technicians will disconnect it and seal the inlet valve then.'

The specialist leaned forward and examined the dog's pupils, then checked the heartbeat with his stethoscope. After a moment, he straightened.

'All right,' he said. 'Let's get him in the capsule. I can use your help, Lieutenant.'

Halper reached down, and together with the veterinary

76

specialist lifted Major up to waist level. They carried him over to the open hatch of the satellite and gently lowered him inside, where the specially padded interior had been fitted out for a dog Major's size.

Cushioned restraining straps were put into place and their Velcro fasteners secured. This accomplished, the specialist began to fasten the tiny electrodes, connected to the life-function monitors, upon Major's body with circular adhesive patches.

Halper noticed that besides the radio transmitter attached to the life-function monitors, another device sent its cables into the system. Two rollers were visible beneath the transparent plastic cover of the device, with a thick coil of paper accumulated mostly on the first roller. Several tiny marking arms traced a series of almost microscopically small lines across the roll of paper. At least they had at one time; for now the device was not functioning.

He also noticed a number of other devices built into the satellite. 'How much of this paraphernalia is really essential for the mission?' he asked.

The specialist looked at him strangely. 'All of it. Maybe not in the sense you're thinking, but it's still absolutely necessary for the outcome of the overall mission.' He hesitated a moment, concentrating on a particular bio-connection. 'You see, both the United States and Russia are working along similar lines in outer space research, out of simple, practical necessity. There are a certain number of goals common to both programmes, and there aren't that many possible ways to achieve them. We've got a pretty good idea of what they're experimenting with, and vice versa. But there's a lot of grey area on the actual details.'

Completing the final connection, he continued, gesturing towards the satellite's devices. 'About 65 per cent of what you see in there is for appearances only. Bait. We know the Russian scientists are interested in our experiments towards developing a workable means of extending the effectiveness of the basic life-support system for long space flights over great distances. It's a common problem for both sides. You just can't carry enough supplies for a

77

manned mission to the other planets with our current systems.

'The water supply can be recycled through filtration processes for a considerable amount of time before too much is lost, or the filters' effectiveness is diminished. The oxygen supply is another matter. And the amount of food carried is strictly limited by space within the craft. Reaching the moon was one thing ... making it to Mars and beyond is quite another. Unless we can slow down the body processes to use less supplies, we may have to abandon long-range missions until such time as we have developed faster, better means of propulsion.'

Joyce had joined them. 'You mean you've actually been working with reduced metabolism research for the space programme?' she asked.

'Oh yes. I suppose there wasn't that much news coverage at the time, generally for good reason. But both NASA and the Air Force have spent millions on hibernation research, as it can be applied to manned space missions. And a good number of civilian scientists received grants for the work. One of the principle researchers has been Dr. Henry Swan. He's in Denver, with the Research Institute for Biological Studies.'

He paused to check Major's continuing reaction to the drug. 'In fact, it was Swan's work that pointed the way for much of our later research. He and his associates, Dr. Dalton Jenkins and Dr. Kerwin Knox, were working under a NASA contract studying lungfish from Uganda. Lungfish aestivate in summer — a kind of hibernation without temperature loss. Anyway, the experiment helped prove the existence of antabolone, an antithyroid hormone which suppresses metabolic functions. There are other anti-metabolites, we've since discovered, and we're on our way to developing an integrated system of chemical enzyme inhibitors that should give us a reasonable and safe means of control over metabolism.'

'But ...' Halper queried, 'you haven't got it yet?'

The specialist's mouth twisted in a grudging smile. 'No, not yet. But the Russians don't know that. Not for sure.

Their own research is about as far along as ours at the moment. The work in both countries has suffered mainly from budget problems. What with the money that went into Southeast Asia and a few other places, the NASA budget was cut considerably. That meant that everything but top priority projects went by the boards ... including the ones involving reduced metabolism.'

'Won't that fact create a problem?'

'No, not really. The Russians know we're still doing some research, mostly through government grants to scholarly research institutes. Besides, by a peculiar twist of Soviet thinking, they tend to be suspicious of any announcements we make about discontinuing an area of research. They are somewhat devious with their own scientific announcements, and I guess they expect the same from us. You can bet they're still interested in reduced metabolism.'

Halper nodded understandingly. 'So if they see what looks like an experiment along those lines, they'll grab the opportunity to examine it.'

'Definitely,' the specialist replied. 'Of course, it won't fool them forever. Despite the fact that we've had our best chemists and engineers working on this, even to the point of designing it around some of our actual experiments, it still won't take the Russians more than a few days to determine that this is phony. But hopefully that will be long enough to allow your dog to do his job.'

Joyce shook her head. 'I'm afraid I still don't understand how you intend to pull it off. You can't just drop Major, satellite and all, in on them without arousing suspicions.'

'No, of course not,' the man agreed. 'That would be too obvious. Far too obvious. For this to work as planned, we have to not only deliver the entire package to the right area, we also have to make it look accidental ... and convincing. But that's General Matthews' job, and I'm just as glad I don't have to worry about that end of it.'

Halper noticed Joyce's sober expression, and knew that she would be worried about all aspects of the project. For that matter, he would be also.

Approaching quietly, the lab assistant handed another hypodermic to the veterinary specialist. Again he checked the level of the liquid, this time a pale blue in colour.

'What's that?' Halper asked.

'Just a little frosting on the cake. It won't hurt the dog's performance any ... but I think it might just confuse the Russian scientists for a while.'

He gave Major the injection, disinfected the area again, and reached into the satellite. His hand located the end of a long flexible tube connected to one piece of equipment. At the end of that tube was a tiny plastic housing, terminating in an injector needle. He brought it near Major's hind-quarters, near the spot where he had just injected the blue liquid. Then, surprisingly, he wedged the point into the padding of the satellite's interior.

With that completed, he began a slow and methodical check of the satellite's systems. For long moments, there was no sound except the ticking of the wall clock. Minutes ticked by ... became hours. When at last everything had been checked and double-checked, the clock showed quarter of six. Outside, it would be dawn soon.

With Halper's aid, the large hatch cover was lifted up and fitted into place. Special bolts were tightened, making the seal airtight. Looking through a small window in the hatch cover, the specialist checked once more the reclining form inside, then closed a metal cover over the unbreakable glass.

The man moved out of the way as his lab assistant came up to them pushing a low cart upon which rested four cylinders of oxygen. One by one, they were transferred to the lower shelf of the satellite dolly, and their outlets interconnected through an automatic valve system. That valve system ended in a lenghty air-hose connection, which in turn was plugged into a recessed panel of the satellite.

Outside somewhere, at a distance of a hundred yards or more, the engines of a propeller-driven plane started up. The specialist and his assistant seemed to notice it and glanced at the wall clock.

'Let's get it covered,' the man said suddenly. He pointed to a grey tarpaulin lying folded on a nearby counter top.

Halper picked it up and brought it over to the satellite, beginning to unfold it as he walked. With the four of them working on it, they had the cover completely over the satellite and tied down in a matter of a few minutes.

In the hall behind the glass, General Matthews was signalling. He nodded and quickly motioned towards the thick metal sliding door at one side of the laboratory.

The lab assistant threw back the locking devices, and Halper began to push open the door. Abruptly, he received help as two airmen on the other side also pushed. As the door stopped at the end of its tracks in the open position, Halper saw that the airmen were standing in the open back of the truck he had seen earlier. One of the men stepped through the door and headed for the covered satellite. The other paused long enough to place a wide steel ramp across the gap between the truck and the building, then followed the first man.

In a moment, they had rolled the satellite on its dolly over to the ramp and carefully manoeuvred it into the truck. Floor-mounted chocks held the dolly rigidly in position, and tie-down cables secured it more firmly. When they were satisfied that the dolly was properly secured, they removed the ramp, waited a moment as the truck moved forward a few yards, then closed the rear door from the inside.

Halper slid shut the laboratory door and turned in time to see General Matthews walking towards the end of the hall, out of view as he passed the edge of the glassed-in section. Brunning was motioning for them to join him.

The veterinary specialist was next to Halper suddenly, thrusting his hand towards Halper's. 'Good luck, Lieutenant. Maybe we can exchange ideas sometime ... when matters are less urgent.'

Halper nodded, smiled back. Joyce Kandell seemed not to hear the remark. She was already hurrying to the ready room. Halper reached it a few moments later, and slipped out of the coveralls he had worn over his uniform. By the time he had put his coat on, buttoned it, and picked up his cap, Joyce was emerging from the changing booth, again in her civilian clothes.

Swiftly, they made their way out of the room and down the hall, in the direction General Matthews had headed. Brunning was waiting at the end door.

'You'd better hurry if you want to see him leave,' he said crisply.

They made the door and all three left the building. It was still relatively dark outside, but the glow in the eastern sky, combined with the electric floodlights of the facility, made details fairly discernible.

General Matthews stood over by the truck, leaning in towards the cab. He spoke briefly into a microphone connected to the truck's mobile radio equipment, then listened as a quick reply came. He turned, exchanged salutes with Colonel Brunning, and moved around the front of the truck, climbing in the passenger side and slamming the door.

Almost at once the truck moved out, following the roadway part of the distance, then cutting across the field in the direction of the airstrip.

Halper could see the source of the engine sound now. A C-130 cargo plane was poised at the end of the airstrip, its bulbous nose, high-lifted tail, and rear opening ramp making it easily identifiable. In another minute, the truck had reached the plane and carefully lined itself up with the ramp. Shifting into low gear, it began to move up into the plane until it was completely out of sight.

They would be tying it down now, Halper thought. Making the truck fast within the hold. An instant later, he saw the ramp pulled up into flight position and an upper section swing down from the top to meet it and lock into place.

Brunning checked his watch. 'They should be at the launch site in less than an hour.'

Halper replied, 'I take it, sir, that our presence won't be needed at the launch.'

'That is correct,' the colonel answered, noting the tone of curiosity in Halper's voice. 'So the location of that particular military installation shall remain one classified secret on which you won't be briefed.'

'Colonel,' Joyce's voice was strained. 'What do we have to do next, and how long do we have —'

'Next,' he began before she had finished, 'you will both return to your quarters and collect your bags and paper work. Carter will have been awakened by the time you get there.'

Halper suddenly realised that the young Intelligence officer who had brought them there had somehow left their presence without him noticing. The man was presumably rapping on Carter's door at that moment.

'After that,' Brunning continued, 'there will be transportation waiting for you all at zero seven-twenty.'

'Yes, sir.'

At that moment, the whine of the cargo plane's engines increased, louder still, and the ship began to move down the airstrip. It continued to pick up speed until at last, two-thirds of the way down the strip, it lifted off and soared into the morning sky. As the plane became a dot, fading into the distance, Joyce Kandell gazed after it.

'Good luck,' she said, her words almost inaudible. 'Good luck, boy. . . .'

At seven-fifteen the sun was beginning its upward trek over Houston. The humid an air was gradually beginning to warm and there was a clearness, an awakening quality to the morning light, that helped to evaporate the unreality of the night before. The difference was only a matter of a few degrees on a clock face, or a thermometer, or a light-intensity scale. But that difference was felt . . . tangible . . . real.

Lieutenant Halper and Joyce Kandell stood on the side-walk near the entrance to the building in which their temporary quarters had been located. Halper surveyed the area of the base that stretched out before him, then his eyes came to rest on Joyce.

She had been silent most of the time since the dog's departure with General Matthews. And if that silence was encouraging after her emotionalism of the night before, it was also puzzling. Halper could not be sure whether it signified a grudging acceptance of the present state of affairs, or whether it was only a temporary quiet ... a calm before some greater storm. It would do no good to surmise. He could only wait and watch, and try to head off any future disputes. For he had already made up his mind about what to tell Brunning. He would tell him nothing. Yet.

At that moment, footsteps came from behind them and they turned to see Carter approaching. The Air Force had managed to supply him with a change of clothes, apparently from the Base Exchange, and Carter looked as if he did not entirely approve of their choice. Still, from his expression, he seemed to be facing the morning with a kind of tired, grim humour.

'Morning,' Carter said without enthusiasm. 'What's up, besides us?'

Halper filled him in quickly on the events of the night before. Carter's interest picked up as Halper described the intended transport system for the dog.

'A satellite? But how are they going to –'

'We weren't told,' Halper replied. 'We'll just have to wait and see.'

They fell silent as the Special Forces soldier came up behind them and halted. Out in the morning light, his rugged features seemed even more weather-beaten, but he appeared rested and alert. There was the faint scent of gun oil with him, suggesting that he had just recently cleaned his automatic.

Halper checked his watch. Exactly seven-twenty. He looked up suddenly at the sound of a truck's engine, and saw a white van, marked with the insignia of the NASA facility, turning the corner. It angled in towards the sidewalk and stopped in front of them. The tinted windows were rolled up tightly.

Colonel Brunning was already in the vehicle. He opened the right front door part way and looked out.

'Have you got everything, Lieutenant?'

'Yes, sir. We're ready to go.' Halper reached out and opened the rear door of the van, then picked up his suitcase and placed it inside. Turning, he took the girl's bag, put it in next to his, then helped her step up into the van.

Carter shifted the OD overcoat that had been across his left arm to his right as he climbed in. 'One thing about travelling light,' he said, dropping on to the rear seat. 'It doesn't take long to pack.'

Joyce and the lieutenant had already taken the centre seat of the van, leaving the Green Beret to join Carter in the rear. As soon as they settled themselves, the driver pulled away from the sidewalk. In a few moments, the air-conditioner managed to remove some of the moisture present in the Houston atmosphere.

'All right,' Colonel Brunning said, turning to look back at the other passengers. 'One thing we can take care of right now —' He gestured towards the man driving the van. 'This is James Neston from NASA headquarters. Mr. Neston is Assistant Administrator, Office of D.O.D. and Interagency Affairs. He is the official liaison between the Defense Department and the NASA personnel we'll be working with on this mission.'

Neston turned as he stopped the van briefly at another corner. 'Good morning. Welcome to Houston.'

He looked to be in his early forties, with a pleasant, tanned face and sandy hair. Neston wore no coat, but a short-sleeved shirt and tie. His manner was congenial, but he had the appearance of a man under a certain amount of pressure.

Brunning continued, speaking to Neston. 'Lieutenant Halper and Joyce Kandell, immediately behind us, are my chief training personnel at ARDCOM, and the ones who have prepared the dog for this mission.' He pointed to the rear. 'The other civilian back there is our computer technician, Carter. He has already spent a little time at the Johnson Space Center, yesterday.'

Carter nodded, smiling grimly at the memory of his sixteen-hour stint at reprogamming their computer system.

'Mr. Neston has a top security clearance, and is aware of all operational aspects of the mission.' Brunning continued, obviously with no intention of introducing the Special

Forces soldier riding with them. 'Understandably, there are only a very few members of the NASA team who are in on this.' He turned his attention again to the driver. 'Is everything running smoothly at the centre?'

Neston seemed to hesitate a fraction of a second. 'Yes, Colonel. I can promise you that our technical facilities are all operable and ready.'

If Brunning noticed anything unusual about the man's response, he did not press the matter. He was about to settle back in his seat when Joyce Kandell spoke up suddenly.

'Colonel, that man you brought to our table last night – Arnold Smith –' she asked. 'You said he would be working with us. Won't he be going to the Space Center?'

'Mr. Smith will be joining you there a little later,' Brunning answered dryly. He glanced at his watch. 'At the moment, he has a schedule of his own to follow. . . .'

The van neared the gate and slowed down. Then, as the military policeman on their side of the guard station waved them through, they picked up speed and headed off along the access road, leaving Ellington Air Force Base behind.

In another minute and a half, they were turning south on to Galveston Road, the major highway running south-east from Houston almost to the bay coastline. The van eased into a steady, safe rate of speed and maintained it. Conversation ceased, and the passengers seemed occupied instead with their own thoughts.

After covering five miles of Galveston Road, at a point near the centre of the town of Webster, the van turned east on NASA Road 1. Exactly twenty-eight minutes after they had left the air base, they reached the Second Street Gate entrance to the NASA installation.

The 1,640-acre Lyndon B. Johnson Space Center facility was almost a city in itself, with its dozens of multilevel buildings and parking areas. But its layout was more organised than all but a very few cities. The arrangement was more neatly planned, the open spaces more numerous, and the buildings themselves all modern and almost identical in style.

Yet it was a city in a very real sense. A city with nearly ten thousand workers directly involved there or nearby. And a city, unlike most, with a single, driving purpose.

The van turned off Second Street and headed for a building on the east end of the main complex. It seemed somewhat newer than the rest — a squat concrete two-storey structure about three hundred feet long — and it bore no signs to label its function.

It had a main entrance facing the roadway, but also bore a set of doors on the northern side, opening onto an alleyway created by a concrete fence separating the building from the adjacent parking area. It was the latter entrance to which the van now drove. Stopping a few yards from the doors, the driver stilled the vehicle's engine and got out.

'This way, please.' James Neston opened the door to the building as the ARDCOM personnel filed out of the van. 'It's not one of our more decorative spots,' he said apologetically. 'But it's functional.'

They followed him down the hall, which was more than adequately lit, considering there was little worth seeing, then turned to the right and headed down a connecting corridor. A short distance farther and they were in front of a series of multiple doors that apparently could all be swung aside to permit bulky equipment to enter the room.

Immediately in front of the right-hand door, a member of the centre's security police stood on guard. Moving aside, he opened the door for them.

'Good morning, sir.'

'Morning, Mike,' Neston replied. 'How's it going?'

'Quiet so far.'

'Good.' Neston disappeared into the room, and the others followed.

As the door closed behind them, a cooler wave of air-conditioned air enveloped them. The steady, faint hum of the building's cooling equipment seemed more noticeable in this area than it had been in the hall.

Carter winced slightly as he looked around the spacious room. 'Home sweet home ...' he remarked, with an unmistakable tone of distaste.

The room was more than just large. It had the look of an almost empty warehouse, with plain grey walls that were bare except for electrical conduits and fixtures. What equipment there was sat in an improvised arrangement at the centre of the great area of floor space. A massive computer system with its console dominated the grouping. Near it stood a bank of communications equipment, its great array of indicator lights glowing in soft iridescent tones. A short distance behind the computer system, a dark panel had been suspended from the ceiling at a point a little higher than eye level. Its four-by-six-foot form had baffles leading back from the edges to a point behind it. Several wooden folding tables had been set up, with sufficient chairs for at least a dozen people. And everywhere, leading from each piece of equipment, cables were strung out. Some interconnected with other pieces of equipment, and some only ran across the bare concrete floor to disappear into wall outlets or open sections of conduit. The electronics gear sat like a spider in some huge, free-form web.

Neston cleared his throat, and the sound echoed in the vast room. 'We've been using this area so far for running a few experiments in various electronics systems,' he explained. 'There are other plans for the building later on, but for the moment this was the most logical choice of locations for running the mission. We not only had the room and the excuse for bringing in whatever gear we needed, we also avoided some potential problems. Since this particular facility is little-used, there was no need to displace regular personnel, creating an observable break in normal activities.'

Colonel Brunning nodded impatiently. 'Yes, this building fits our needs perfectly.' He turned to his computer technician. 'Carter – check out the system again, just to make sure it's set up correctly.'

Carter seemed about to protest, to explain that he had already double-checked the system the day before. In the same instant, he realised it would be pointless. 'Yes, sir,' he said instead, and headed for the equipment.

Lieutenant Halper and Joyce Kandell opened their bags

and extracted their research data, then put the suitcases out of the way in a spot near the wall. They placed their folios of notes and charts on the table nearest the computer console.

James Neston looked at a group of clocks arranged above the communications equipment. Of the top two, the left one was set for Houston time, the right for Omsk, Russia. In Houston it was eight in the morning. In Omsk, it was seven in the evening. Between those two cities stretched a distance of over six thousand miles.

'We've got a little over an hour before launch,' Neston remarked. 'I may as well explain some of our setup now.'

Halper and Joyce gave him their undivided attention. Brunning began to pace slowly, while Carter was starting his equipment check.

'All right, to begin with,' Neston continued, 'as far as communications go, we've taken advantage of the existing NASA and military facilities around the world. If something goes wrong with any one of them, there are quite a number of alternate channels we can still use. The various networks for communications and tracking are all handled by the Goddard Space Flight Center in Greenbelt, Maryland. They're tied directly to the Mission Control Center here, and we've patched in a remote system to this building. I can't tell you too much about it since it's a little out of my field, but one of our men who'll be in here will be able to fill you in on the details if you're interested.'

Neston turned to the computer unit. 'That, as you probably know much better than I, is the computer required for your canine project. It, and all other equipment in here, are on a power line separate from other working systems, and with standby generators waiting in case of power failure. It's the same procedure we use on manned missions.' He shot a finger at the suspended four-by-six-foot panel. 'And that, hopefully, will give us a ringside seat on the action.'

'What is it?' Halper asked.

'Actually, Lieutenant, it's just a rear-projection television screen, similar to the ones we use in our Mission Control

Center.' He stopped momentarily as a coiled section of cable dropped from an open conduit and hung a few inches above the floor. A moment later a man appeared at the door, walked over to the cable, and began untying the twisted wires that had held it coiled.

Neston continued. 'It's part of a discontinued experiment ... something that we thought about using in future manned missions. NASA had been interested in a secondary visual system apart from the cameras. Some way that the scientists and engineers here at the Center could see what the astronauts see – directly.'

Joyce was first this time. 'How could they manage that?'

'Simple,' Neston said, then smiled. 'At least, it should be, theoretically. The basic idea is to tap the minute electric currents that travel along the optic nerve, amplify them, transmit those coded signals back to Earth, then process them through a computer system where they're interpreted and used to form an image on a television scanner like the one you see here. We had done some work with computer-generated televison images before – General Electric's Visual Simulation Laboratory developed a special system for us to use in training astronauts for docking manoeuvres in space. So we combined our computer graphic technology with the results of some vision research projects being carried out at M.I.T. and Stanford University.'

'Did it work?'

'It would have. But unfortunately, try as we did, we could find no other way of tapping those impulses without a direct implant in the brain itself. Understandably, we were a bit reluctant to wire up our astronauts in that manner. They put up with enough as it is. Of course, in this case, since your project already involves the use of a brain implant in the dog, it was relatively simple to add to the existing sytem. In fact, it dovetailed quite nicely.'

Halper nodded. He had not been present in the operating room a little over three weeks ago when Dr. Braydon and the others had worked on Major, putting the tiny implant in place. And even if he had been there, he probably would not have noticed any modification in the device. More and more, he realised just how much work had been going on without his knowledge.

'Anyway,' Neston concluded, 'as I said before, such topics are a little out of my field. I'd feel a little more at home behind a desk right now.' He turned then, looked back over his shoulder, and called to the man who had just entered a moment before. 'Bill — when you get through, c'mon over.'

The man finished attaching a connector to the end of the cable. He brought it to the rear of the communications console and plugged it into a labelled socket, then joined the group.

'Bill,' Neston addressed him, 'this is Lieutenant Halper and ... Joyce Kandell — did I pronounce that right?'

The girl nodded, smiling faintly.

'Good.' He continued, 'They're both with the ARDCOM group.' He put his hand on the man's shoulder. 'And this is Bill Stanton, from our Tracking and Data Acquisition Office. Bill's our chief technician. In fact, he usually doesn't have to pull his own cable like that.'

Stanton was already shaking hands with them. 'No — not recently, anyway.' He smiled keenly. 'Actually, I asked for a full crew to help out with the wiring ... but these people have some kind of strange idea about security!'

'So we've noticed.' Halper's smile was ironic. 'Will you be in on the operating end of this mission?'

Stanton nodded. 'Running communications. Should be interesting. From what I've been told so far, this should be a real, one-of-a-kind effort.' He turned his attention to James Neston. 'I've hooked up a spare line into the commo network.'

Neston looked at him strangely. 'Don't we already have a back-up line on that?'

'Sure — but if the first line overheats or shorts out, all we'd have to fall back on is the second line. If something happened to that while we're getting another connected, we'd be out of contact for a while.'

'Not much chance both lines would go out in that short a period.'

'Maybe not, but why risk it?'

Neston considered it and shrugged. 'You're right. No sense in risking anything we don't have to on this.'

A sudden intermittent buzzing interrupted further conversation at that point. Neston looked to the two phones on top of the communications console, one red, the other black. It was the black one whose buzzer sounded, its small light flashing simultaneously.

Neston walked over to it and picked up the handset. 'Yes, sir? No, Norm, the general isn't here yet ... sometime after launch, probably thirty minutes. Is Dr. Laswell still planning on coming over?' He listened for several seconds, frowning. 'I was afraid of that. Can't be helped, I guess. Look – see what you can do, will you? All right ... thanks, Norm.'

He returned the handset to its cradle and walked back to the others. The uneasy expression on his face was more noticeable now than earlier.

'Well, is there anything else I can go into – anything I haven't explained?' he asked.

'I was wondering,' Halper said after a second's pause, 'if it would be possible to test out that television system before we actually have to use it under working conditions.'

'Yes ... briefly.' Neston pulled a small pocket notebook out and consulted it. 'We're due for an operations check of the system. They should have the capsule in place on the rocket by now.' He put the book away. 'But we can't use radio transmissions from the capsule yet. They'll have to patch in through the external connections and send the signals here by ground line.' He turned to Stanton. 'Bill – get hold of the launch-site crew, find out if they're ready for the test, and get the video-display circuits operating.'

'Right.' The technician swivelled into the seat before the communications console and pulled a lightweight headset and microphone combination over his black hair and greying sideburns. He pressed several switches in rapid succession, and began speaking softly into the microphone suspended an inch from his lips.

Neston again faced Halper and the young woman. 'The video signal from your implant is separate from the main core of signals and is processed through a section of our real-time computer complex over at Mission Control. From there the reconstructed images are patched into our circuits here, for the big screen and also for facsimile printout, if we need it.'

'In black and white?' Halper inquired.

'Yes. Actually, our facilities here could produce colour images, if they could be transmitted from the implant. But we're not that far along with the system — we've only broken down the optic nerve impulses into light and dark codings, for the purpose of transmission.' He smiled faintly, as if reading Halper's thoughts. 'And yes, it's rather a moot point anyway, since a dog can't perceive colour.' He paused a moment, looking towards Stanton.

'One thing that I haven't found out yet,' Joyce Kandell said. 'I know the approximate range of the implant's radio transmission. It's no more than five or ten miles, depending upon conditions. So even using a relay point somewhere near the Russian border, how will the signals be sent back and forth between Major and us over the remaining distance?'

'Major ... is that the dog's name?' Neston seemed vaguely amused as the girl nodded silently, but he continued. 'Well, as you suggested, there is quite a relay system involved. But as for the actual details, you might do better to ask General Matthews when he arrives.'

'Jim —' Stanton called back to Neston. 'I've got it set up from the launch site to here.'

Neston glanced at Brunning. 'Colonel, is your man through with the computer checks?'

Carter nodded his head in affirmation, and Brunning replied, 'Yes, sir.'

'Good,' he said, then directed to Stanton, 'Check the big screen out first — run some test patterns.'

'Right, Jim.'

Halper and Joyce Kandell watched with interest as the NASA technician manipulated a series of switches on a

93

free-standing unit adjacent to the communications console. At once, the four-by-six-foot screen blazed brightly as the video projector behind it was activated, flooding the area with a surprising amount of light. A second later, the light diminished almost by half as the panel formed a checkerboard pattern on its surface, with alternating squares of light and dark.

Stanton located a special videotape cassette in a recessed box in the top of the unit and inserted it into the slot. He depressed the button for automatic test and waited. A split second later the checkerboard changed, dark squares becoming light and light becoming dark. Next, the entire pattern began shifting to one side, flowing from right to left in a steady progression. Then, the movement stopping, the squares began to expand, moving off the panel as the centre square filled the screen up more and more.

When the screen had gone entirely black, a white dot formed in the centre, gradually becoming a circle. As it reached the edges of the panel, another circle was forming in the centre, moving out as the first had done. Soon there was a series of circles constantly expanding, creating the effect of moving forward through a tubular tunnel. It was almost hypnotic, watching that shifting image, and the sensation of movement was hard to shake off.

Finally Stanton seemed satisfied with the system's operation, and he pulled the cassette from the machine. Pressing the main input button, he patched the unit and screen into the computer circuits. A simple grid pattern at once formed ... remained steady ... waiting for a signal which would give it an image to depict.

Stanton turned. 'Jim, the system's working and ready.'

'Fine. Patch in to the launch site.'

Stanton punched the button opening the circuits between the large computer system and the signals coming in through his console from the distant launch site. On the display screen, the grid pattern faded, swirled, and disappeared completely into a disconnected barrage of light bursts and patterns. Finally the image cleared.

The right half of the picture was a middle grey tone,

marked by a slightly irregular border running from top to bottom. The left side was darker grey, punctuated here and there with partial views of bits of equipment, bolts and fastenings, and tie-down points for a number of the straps which held Major securely in place.

It took Halper several seconds to realise that the grey area on the right was the padded section of the capsule, and that Major was lying on his side even though the image they were now seeing was of course upright from the dog's point of view. At the bottom left of the image, the front edge of the dog's paws could be seen. There was the slight suggestion of glare from a bulb off the left side of the screen. The light was apparently near the top of the capsule, and had been turned on by the launch crew for the test. That notion was amended as the angle of shadow shifted suddenly, and Halper realised that the source of light must be from outside the capsule, aimed in by hand through the small window area in the hatch. Obviously a built-in light would be out of place in the kind of capsule that it must appear to be to fool the Russian scientists.

Noticing a slight movement of the image, Neston remarked, 'Looks like your dog is a bit restless.'

Halper nodded, a look of concern setting his features. Joyce studied the image for a moment.

'I guess a stronger tranquiliser would have been too dangerous,' she replied at last. 'I hope he won't try to move around too much.'

Neston sighed. 'Yes ... if he gets too active in there, it could conceivably jeopardise the mission.'

'Is medical telemetry data also being patched through to the Mission Control Center?'

'Yes. Do you want a readout?'

Joyce nodded. 'Please.'

Neston pointed to a small televisor in the communications console as Stanton selected the channel for the medical data. 'Of course we won't have access to that telemetry once the dog is out of the capsule.'

Joyce studied the glowing figures that suddenly appeared in electric green across the face of the small screen. It was almost hard to relate the abstract letters and numbers to the living, breathing dog that had been in her charge.

Major's breathing was slow and somewhat shallow, but steady, as was his heartbeat. Blood pressure was only a degree below normal, and his temperature was what it should be — 101.2 degrees.

Neston asked, 'Any problems?'

Joyce shook her head. 'No . . . for a sedated condition, all the readings are normal.' She studied the figures a moment longer, then shifted her gaze to the large image screen where the tilt-angled view of the satellite's interior could still be seen. That she was seeing it through Major's own eyes was a fact both difficult to comprehend and faintly disturbing.

'Seen enough?' Neston asked. They nodded. 'All right — shut down!'

Stanton switched off the linkup to the launch site and the display screen went blank. An instant later the computer reestablished the grid pattern, but even that faded as Stanton deactivated the unit.

Halper looked to Neston with appreciation in his eyes. 'That's quite a system. Of course it's not exactly as good as watching TV . . . a little grainy, maybe.'

'You're right there,' he replied. 'We can't really get the clarity we'd like with it. But I think for our purposes it will do fine . . . certainly a lot better than nothing.'

'Mr. Neston,' Joyce began, 'maybe we could keep Major calm by using the equipment during launch . . . feed the right patterns to him, reassure him, as we've done before.'

Neston shook his head. 'No chance. From here on out, until we get the word, there'll be no transmissions to or from the capsule through any of the systems. Those signals could be picked up by the Russians and blow the whole game.' He looked down at the floor and sighed as if tired. 'No, we'll just have to trust to the dog's own composure . . . and to your training techniques. . . .'

A little less than three hundred miles away, in a desolate area of sandy soil and limited foliage, in the centre of a large tract of land protected by armed guards and high fences topped with barbed wire, the rocket stood on its launch pad. Seemingly unused roadways crept purposefully amid carefully laid out areas of concrete and steel, and it was near the centre of these that the rocket waited alongside its gantry.

Tall and rigid, powerfully sleek in its design, it gave the impression of being more permanent than it was in reality. For in what now amounted to a matter of minutes, it would no longer be a part of the complex. A little over a hundred feet tall with its modified nose cowling, the Atlas-Centaur rocket had been the best choice for size, payload capacity, and economy. A workhorse of the American space programme, the Atlas-Centaur had played an important role in unmanned launches for nearly a dozen years. The *Mariner* series had been sent into space by it, as well as the *Surveyor* series and other space probes. And now it had a different mission. Limited, unorthodox, and perhaps less idealistic than pure scientific advancement, it was still a mission of the utmost importance.

Within that modified nose cowling capping the top of the launch vehicle, a bulky satellite was mounted. Its thickset form and lack of markings suggested an ominous purpose, and it was like no satellite normally known to the general public.

There were a number of satellite series which were destined never to be featured in newspaper or magazine articles ... which in fact did not officially 'exist'. *Sky Hunter* was only one of several such classified series of space hardware. It had been developed by SAC's Vandenberg facilities in response to continued Russian experimentation with a satellite system too dangerous to ignore.

The first published reports had come late in 1970, carried in such magazines as *Aviation Week*. Always watchful of Soviet launchings, the North American Air Defense Command (NORAD) had followed with special interest the testing of a new class of satellites. NORAD had observed for three years the continued use of a Russian launch vehicle classified by the U.S. as the F-1-m, which not only served to place a payload in orbit, but also functioned as a platform for continued orbital change. The purpose of such manoeuvrability in space had been suspect from the start.

The satellites had been launched from the Soviet Union's largest site, Tyuratam, in the open steppe country of the Kazakhskaya region, and announced as part of the *Kosmos* series. Kosmos was a loose and ill-defined designation which had been applied to launches of a military nature as well as some that were more or less purely scientific. Both observation satellites and the newer, offensive, Fractional Orbital Bombardment satellites had flown under the cover name of Kosmos, and shared the launch site of Tyuratam. But while the FOBS series was designed for earthly targets, the new manoeuvrable Kosmos hardware had a different aim.

In the tests from 1967 through 1970, a familiar pattern evolved. Two or more Kosmos satellites would be launched separately over a period of days or weeks. Frequently both achieved adjusted orbits after initial entry. One always assumed a passive role, while the other became an active intercepter, seeking a matching orbit which would allow a near pass. Always, one or more of the satellites were destroyed after rendezvous by an unknown explosive force.

On January 2, 1972, *The New York Times* carried an Associated Press release stating that Kosmos 462 had been launched from Tyuratam, intercepting the earlier launched Kosmos 459 within hours, and destroying both the target craft and itself 150 miles above the earth. The distance was significant, since most American reconnaissance satellites operate at that orbital range. A follow-up article on January 28 disclosed that a special staff report issued a month earlier by the Congressional Research Service for the U.S. Senate Committee on Aeronautical and Space Sciences had detailed the scope of Soviet experimentation along these lines. The report pointed out the potential threat such a capability posed to American satellite systems ... a threat which could not be ignored.

A comparable American system was needed. *Project Saint*, an earlier programme by the U.S. using inspector satellites, had been abandoned, but it served as invaluable groundwork for the new research. And there was no lack of incentive. For to allow Russian forces the sole use of military inspector/destructor satellites would be to grant them a weapons superiority in space too devastating to even consider. Literally hundreds of communication, navigation, and reconnaissance satellites were in use by the American armed forces. In the event of limited, non-nuclear war, those satellites would be early targets.

On an official basis, *Sky Hunter* did not exist. On a practical basis, it had to exist.

And now, poised atop the waiting Atlas-Centaur was a satellite identical to those of the *Sky Hunter* series. Identical, with one major exception . . . and one minor one. Its purpose, in the first place, was entirely different. And in the second place, the satellite was little more than a shell, since more than half of its interior had been vacated of certain pieces of equipment and a number of storage tanks for propellant fuel which would have given it an extended range of manoeuvrability in space.

In the hollow provided by the alterations, held rigidly in place by a nylon harness equipped with explosive fastenings, was cradled the satellite containing the dog. Major was more restful now, his ordinary alertness dimmed somewhat by the mild tranquiliser administered to him almost five hours earlier. Its effects would last for at least another fifteen hours, and would fit in well with the rest of the mission.

The primary satellite was little more than a carrier for the second, then. And yet there was one other purpose for it to perform, and towards this end, part of its equipment still remained intact. Near the nose of the primary satellite were located a dozen miniature rockets, equipped with warheads of remarkable explosive power. In a ring beneath a cover that would be jettisoned once in space, the mini-missiles surrounded a core consisting of television cameras, heat sensors, a specialised version of a radar unit, and a transmitter-linked on-board computer. All this could be — would be — controlled from the ground. As could the tiny detonating device that was imbedded at the beginning of a lengthy line of plastic explosive that meandered around the inside surface of the primary satellite's lower section.

Everything had been checked and double-checked. All was in readiness. The end of the countdown was approaching.

Drawn away now from the rocket, the gantry was in launch position. At its top level, in the area designated as the white room, General Matthews stood with the last of the Air Force technicians. The extendible flooring which had before surrounded the upper end of the launch vehicle was pulled back and in the open position, like the jaws of some great vice.

Matthews gazed across the span of open air that stretched between him and the launch vehicle. His eyes were hard and cold, his features firm-set and almost without expression, giving his padded face the look of sculpted sandstone.

'Nothing must go wrong,' he said to the man next to him. 'Absolutely nothing.'

The technician studied him gravely. 'We've taken every precaution, sir. *Every* precaution. But of course, as you know, with any launch there's always a certain latitude for mechanical failure, or human error —'

'There had better be none with this mission,' the general said sharply. 'Because there's just no second chance. If we fail the first time, even if it happened in a way that would not tip off the Russians to another attempt, the big boys in Washington would never authorise a second try. The whole thing is just too unorthodox, too costly, to try again.'

The technician hesitated, then asked, 'Do you think another method would work?'

Matthews sighed and shook his head. 'No, not really. If there were anything else left besides this lunatic idea, we would have tried it. If we fail ... if *I* fail ...' His voice trailed off. He checked his watch, then compared it with the clock on the wall of the white room. 'We'd better move it. There's not much time left.'

'Yes, sir.'

The man opened the door to the white room and ushered the general out, then followed him to the elevator. The descent was slow, steady, and controlled, a reminder that aspects of every mission could never be rushed, especially those involving rocket launches. Everything had to follow in step-by-step succession. There was no room for haste.

At the bottom, a closed vehicle waited for them. A few minutes later they had arrived at the blockhouse and were safely sealed inside its steel-reinforced concrete walls.

General Matthews walked past the second row of technicians and approached the centre of the first row. Stopping behind the launch commander, his eyes locked onto the television viewing screen before them. Displayed there was a full-length view of the rocket, gleaming in the morning sunlight, vapour pouring off its fuselage as vented liquid oxygen from the vehicle's fuel tanks spilled out into the moist air of Texas.

Matthews stood rigid and erect, almost mimicking the immobile posture of the rocket. He glanced at the clock that was synchronised with all others on the base. The second hand was sweeping around to the top of the dial. On the control board, the digital readout clicked off the final seconds. Matthews watched, and knew that people in Houston and other scattered locations around the country were waiting for the outcome as well. In the next moment, the mission could be safely underway, the dog beginning a journey that would test its training and capabilities to the limit. Or, in the next moment, it could all be finished. . . .

The general barely heard as the launch commander repeated verbally the numbers turning up on the digital readout.

'. . . Eight . . . seven . . . six . . . five . . . four . . . three . . . two . . . one . . . ignition –'

Flame and vapour roared out from the Atlas-Centaur as the vehicle's three engines fired. An instant after the television image showed the ignition, the beginning of the shock wave started to thunder through the launch complex. No amount of soundproofing could filter it all out, not at that range. For much of it was a deep-throated vibration that spread out through the ground itself, enveloping everything in its droning note.

Smoothly, with deceptive ease, the rocket lifted off and slowly pressed upward into the sky. The angle of the television image changed gradually as the tracking cameras followed it higher and higher into the atmosphere. Fading into the blue haze of the stratosphere, the rocket became no more than a faint speck of light.

Listening to information relayed to him through his headset, the launch commander also studied several glowing screens before him as tracking data rapidly flashed on in letters of iridescent green. 'Sir,' the man said after a moment, 'it's *go* for orbital entry.'

Matthews heard him and nodded slowly. The launch had gone perfectly — that much at least was done and over. Already the first stage of the rocket was beginning its plummet down to the waters of the Gulf of Mexico. A few minutes later, the second stage would start to drop into the Atlantic off the eastern coast of Florida. And the primary satellite, with its odd, secret cargo, would begin to circle the Earth . . . for a while.

'Okay . . . wrap it up.' The general reached for his briefcase and signalled silently to the guard at the door of the blockhouse to have the car ready. 'Good job, boys. Excellent launch. Maybe . . . just maybe, we won't all have to pack up and go to Australia after all. . . .'

It was ten-fifteen a.m. in New York at that moment, and *News-Scene*'s D. Thomas Lawrence was at his desk. Before him was a copy of the *Times*, with an article on the summit conference and the trip's delayed start.

He read it through again briefly, then picked up the phone. Dialling an outside line, he checked the number for Kennedy International Airport and continued dialling. Reservations and information lines were usually busy, and he was not surprised to have to wait a few minutes. Finally he heard a click, and a cheerful female voice answered.

'I wonder if you could help me,' Lawrence began casually. 'I'm trying to find out who many flights left yesterday for Europe.'

He waited again, while the woman checked.

'Sixteen? Throughout the day? And these left at their regularly scheduled times?' Lawrence listened, then replied, 'Okay, thanks very much.'

He hung up the phone. Leaning back in his chair, his eyes again fell on the article's first paragraph and the official statement blaming the delay of the President's flight on bad weather conditions.

Lawrence stroked his chin, frowning to himself. A puzzled, curious frown. Then he pressed the button on his intercom.

'Sarah, I want to send a cablegram at once – to Brussels – for delivery to Jeremy Meeker, as soon as he arrives. . . .'

CHAPTER FOUR

In Moscow, thirty minutes after launch, it was six forty-five in the evening. A light afternoon snowfall was in the process of being cleared from the streets even as more of the crystalline flakes tumbled gently down from a rapidly darkening grey sky. The Russian capital city was preparing for night, and many of the street lamps were already on with a glow that seemed abnormally white against the grey of the sky.

An Intourist guide, warm coat covering her severely trim uniform, methodically checked the members of a tour group back aboard their bus. The boxy vehicle was one of several parked along the edge of Red Square.

And not far from Red Square and the Kremlin, within view of the Lenin-Stalin Mausoleum and the Cathedral of St. Basil, an unimpressive government building stood tall against the bleak skyline. Its architecture was mid-1930s Western Hemisphere, executed in tones of grey and brown, and it made a kind of ungraceful half step between the ornate style of the czarist period and the cold, plain design of the newer buildings.

It was a building not open to tourists, nor even to the average Russian citizen. State Police maintained what appeared to be a casual guard around the entrances and immediate grounds, and an occasional Russian military officer could be seen among the plainly dressed civilians entering or leaving the building.

On the tenth floor, at the end of a cramped hall dotted with office doors behind whose frosted glass panels light still showed, a larger door was located. Heavy looking, of dark reddish wood, the door seemed to possess a brooding countenance of its own, cool and imposing. Near the top of the door, slightly above eye level and painted in a silver tone, were the Russian letters spelling out the words *Director, Internal Security*. The official state seal was painted above that, and the whole of the words and design glowered down at the hall that stretched away, and at all who might find themselves there.

Behind that door was an office that matched the darker red wood of the portal. It was decorated in a style that was simple without being plain, luxurious yet restrained. Dark grey carpeting ran flush with the wall panelling, and in the centre of that carpet sat a wide mahogany desk, behind which a man was looking through a file folder of typewritten papers.

The man, Miklos Nikovitch, was of medium height, thickset yet not truly fat. His jet-black hair was combed straight back, neatly, in contrast to eyebrows that were ragged and wild. Ice-blue eyes rested within a full face that was lined with soft-edged crevasses and an occasional faint scar. It was a face that was expressionless, that appeared to have already held a lifetime of emotions within its craggy features, and could hold no more.

Nikovitch closed the file of papers, gripped it for a moment in both hands, fingers tapping noiselessly on the manilla surface. Then he walked to a safelike cabinet built into one wall, opened the drawer, placed the folder inside, and closed the drawer. He pressed the centre button of the cabinet's combination lock, then returned to the desk.

He was about to reach for his overcoat and hat when a knock came from the door that connected with the office to the left of his own. He turned.

'Yes?'

The door opened quickly and smoothly, and a man, thin and balding, entered. 'Director Nikovitch ... I know you are about to leave, but I thought I should tell you ...'

'Yes?'

'I have just received a call from one of our people in the space-tracking network....' The man seemed more concerned about having disturbed his superior than about the information he had been given. He looked down at a sheet of paper he held. 'It seems the Americans have launched a new satellite.'

Nikovitch picked up his hat, brushed the edge with his fingers and examined it. 'That is not so unusual, Alexi.'

'No,' the man agreed reluctantly. 'But from the size and configuration, it is possible that the satellite is one of their destroyer series. Of course it is hard to be positive from the limited information we can obtain through tracking.'

'Odd, that they should launch such a craft just now . . .' He frowned briefly, then shrugged it away. 'Assuming you are right, we will study this new one as we have the others. But I doubt if it is anything new or unexpected. We have heard nothing from our operatives indicating any change in the American programme.' Nikovitch placed his hat on his head, straightened it carefully, and reached for his coat. 'So far, they have only tested destroyer satellites on some of their own derelict space equipment. The time to worry is when they begin testing them on our satellites!'

'Yes, Director. I . . . I am sorry to have troubled you with this.'

Nikovitch shook his head. 'No — you are doing your job. You were right to tell me. Go ahead and start a report on it, find out what you can. In the morning we can pursue it further.'

'Yes, Director.'

In the meantime, we certainly have enough to keep us busy. There are still several important matters concerning the summit conference. I want you to personally supervise the security measures for the meeting here. And at the airport, arrange for extra agents to be present. Our citizens must be briefed — our leaders feel that crowd reaction should be somewhat subdued this time.'

'I will attend to it. I have already drawn up a new schedule, since the American President will be arriving later than we expected.'

'Yes,' Nikovitch replied, frowning sceptically. 'That is a disturbing matter.' He started to leave. 'See what you can find out about it.'

'As you wish.'

'Oh, and Alexi,' he paused at the door, slipping into his overcoat. 'See if any of our observation satellites are in an orbit near enough that of this new one to give us a good look at it. The photos we got of the last one were poor . . .

very poor. You know who to contact. And if anything comes up, of course –'

The thin man nodded. 'Of course.'

Nikovitch opened the door and stepped into the hall. 'Good night, Alexi.'

Fifteen minutes later, ten a.m. at the Johnson Space Center, General Matthews was just arriving at the warehouselike building being used for the mission. A small jet plane had brought him from the secret launch site back to Ellington Air Force Base in a little over twenty minutes. A sedan made the trip to the centre in exactly nineteen minutes, cutting nine minutes off the trip the van had made earlier.

Matthews breezed through the door held open by the guard and entered the room where the mass of interconnected electronic equipment sat huddled in the centre. He removed his cap and placed it on one of the wooden folding tables.

Colonel Brunning approached him. 'Congratulations, sir. We heard through the communications relay that the launch was perfect.' He extended his hand to the general.

Matthews shook it briefly, without warmth. 'The hardest work still lies ahead of us, Colonel. Is everything in order here?'

Brunning's smile faded. 'Yes, sir. Everything is operational. We've already tested the circuits for the computer control and the visual-display screen.'

'Good,' Matthews replied, then glanced towards Halper and the others. 'Do your people know that they may have to spend the next forty-eight or more hours in this building?'

Brunning hesitated. 'I haven't told them in so many words, sir, but they know the general nature of the mission and its requirements.'

'Never take anything for granted, Colonel. Never.' His tone was becoming irritable, and Matthews seemed to notice it. He paused. 'Never mind. You and your people have done an excellent job so far and I have no reason to criticise you. Without your dog, this project couldn't work.'

Brunning became silent. If Matthews' apology offered

praise for his group, it also implied a responsibility for the success of the mission.

'And speaking of the dog,' Matthews added, 'I want to find out more about your control system.'

'Yes, sir.'

Over at the communications console, James Neston had been talking with Bill Stanton. Neston now came over to the two military officers, wearing a hesitant smile.

'Good news, sir,' he said, addressing the general. 'We've heard from both the NASA tracking network and the space tracking centre at NORAD. The primary satellite has assumed proper orbit and is maintaining it.'

Matthews nodded. 'What's the distance between it and the Bio 12 satellite?'

'About four thousand miles. But launch control has already fired the primary's thrusters to slow it down, so Bio 12 will be catching up to it in three hours.'

Matthews checked his watch. 'That will make it around thirteen-fifteen, Houston time. That should be compatible with our schedule. Anything else?'

'Well ...' Neston seemed reluctant. 'I had a call a while ago from Norm Ripley. It seems that Dr. Laswell is here in Houston and he's coming over to see you.'

'Oh?'

'That's all I was told, really, so I don't know exactly what he's got in mind.'

Matthews frowned. 'You're a lot closer to the Administrator than I am, Jim. You must have some idea.'

'I ... I do know that he's unhappy about some of the aspects of this mission. But I'm afraid you'll have to get the details from him, sir.'

'All right ... when will he be here?'

'Any time, I guess. He knew when you were due back.'

Matthews' features set in an unpleasant look of resolve and he nodded unhappily. Turning his attention to his briefcase, he opened it and withdrew a clipboard with a dozen or more sheets of coded information attached. He glanced through them quickly, then placed the clipboard on the table.

He turned to Brunning. 'In the meantime, you may as well brief me on the details of your system. I don't want any surprises once we really get under way.'

Halper was already on his way over, summoned by Brunning's glance, and Joyce was close behind. The general sat in one of the chairs by the table, but Brunning remained standing.

'First,' Brunning began, 'I feel I should emphasise the fact that the system does not exercise forceful control over the dog. But it does enable us to feed information directly to the animal in a new way.'

Halper was searching through his project folder for a particular diagram. He found it and placed the open folder before Matthews.

'We're using a nine-channel micro-implant,' Halper told him, 'although I believe there's also a separate circuit now for the visual-display screen being used for the mission.'

Matthews looked at the diagram and nodded in understanding.

'Of course, this is enlarged here . . . the actual implant is about the size of a nickel. Perhaps a little thicker. There's a length of platinum wire looped beneath the scalp that serves as the receiving antenna, and also for transmitting some of the feedback signals.'

Neston broke in: 'There's a second transmitter loop for the video system, General. It was added to the original design.'

'I see.' Matthews looked to Halper. 'What about commands?'

'I can give the dog voice commands, if necessary, through an audio circuit which sends impulses direct to the dog's right ear. He responds to twenty-four separate commands, but he also has been trained to initiate his own actions once he's been given a particular objective.'

'And the Computer Augmented Memory system?'

Joyce spoke up, somewhat reluctantly. 'That was developed by our chief scientist at ARDCOM, Dr. Marcus Braydon, based on certain civilian research projects.'

That was an oversimplification and she knew it. But

Matthews' interest was not historical or scientific. He did not need to know that Braydon had based his work on a number of separate research efforts whose results had been published in scientific journals throughout the country and the world. Memory researchers such as Karl H. Pribram and Nico Spinelli, and even R. W. Rodieck of the University of Sydney, had laid much of the groundwork for the exploration of the mind's function of recall. Computers had been used in some studies to help decipher the myriad of complex impulses involved in memory. What had been learned was only a faint scratch on the surface of a still vast unknown, yet some progress had been made, and there was evidence to indicate that the mechanisms of visual recollection, at least, could be plotted mathematically. The similarity of the convolution integrals used in that plotting to Fourier transformations, used in holography, suggested that visual images might be stored in the mind much as they are stored in laser-created holograms ... by interference patterns. It had already been demonstrated that specially programmed computers could create hologram simulations, producing three-dimensional images of objects which never existed. The possibility that such computer techniques could be applied to memory experimentation as well was too irresistible to ignore. Dr. Braydon had already made extensive use of 'stimoceivers' — small implantable transceivers used to stimulate certain portions of a test animal's brain, and to allow feedback between an animal and a computer system. Tests conducted from 1968 on by many researchers — Delgado, Bradley, Wallace, and Johnson among them — had inevitably attracted the attention of military scientists, always alert to potential military applications of new discoveries. But it was when Braydon decided to combine both areas of research that ARDCOM's Computer Augmented Memory project began.

'Actually,' Joyce continued, 'the system is limited to one mode of information. Memory traces are very complex. Almost hopelessly so. At present, the best we can do is influence the area of the brain concerned with visual recognition. Dr. Braydon ...' she said, pausing uncomfortably, '... hopes to expand his research to other areas of sensory input. But that's still in the future.'

She hesitated, glancing towards Carter. 'Most of the electronics and programming systems we use were engineered by computer, from Dr. Braydon's initial calculations. The computer sorts out the images we wish to transmit – of people, buildings, whatever – and breaks them down into the proper impulse signals for the implant. Then the implant's probes regenerate those impulses in the lateral geniculate nucleus, which is a kind of collection point between the optic nerve and the occipital cortex, where the function of visual recollection is housed.'

Matthews frowned. 'I'm not sure I understand. At the moment you're transmitting, is the dog then "seeing" these images?'

'No, sir. That would confuse him ... make him uncontrollable. I should have explained – the impulses are sent in a very rapid sequence, so that the dog is not conscious of them. It's done subliminally. But the information enters his mind nonetheless, and is available for comparison with real-life surroundings.'

Halper pointed to the diagram once again. 'There are also circuits for other impulses – a quelling signal to help override fear, and an arousal signal to wake him, if necessary.'

Halper flipped to another diagram showing the interior of a building on the ARDCOM site. 'In our test maze, we photgraphed the arrangement of the panels, sequencing the views the way the dog would see them if he were actually running the maze correctly. We ran those through the optical scanner portion of the CAM equipment for the computer to translate. Then when we transmitted the signals to the implant, the dog was able to "recall" the pattern of a maze it had never encountered before.'

'That's one thing I wanted to check,' Matthews told them. 'In your laboratory situation, you could use any number of photos you might need. Here we may not have that luxury. Arnold Smith will be able to supply us with a certain number of photos and diagrams, but I'm concerned that it may not be enough.'

Halper considered it. 'As long as we at least have maps or floor plans, and photos of each general area, I believe the computer can generate enough simulations to fill in the gaps. Besides, Major's not totally dependent on the system. He's been trained to respond to visual cues more than an ordinary dog would.'

'Good. We'll find out just how well soon enough. . . .'

In the next instant, the door to the cavernous room swung open and two men entered. Dressed similarly and of about the same height, the men differed in most other respects. The one slightly in the lead had thinning blond hair, was somewhat heavier in build, wore silver-framed glasses and looked to be in his sixties. The other man was nearer thirty, had an abundant amount of red hair combed left to right, lean athletic features, and a lanky gait. As they approached Matthews, Brunning, and the others, James Neston headed to intercept them.

'Sir, you know the general, of course,' Neston said quickly, 'but I don't believe you've met the colonel, here, from ARDCOM Headquarters, or his staff. . . .'

Neston began to introduce them. The red-haired man was cordial in his reception. The other was far less than cordial.

Neston moved next to him. 'This is Dr. Stephen F. Laswell, the Administrator of NASA.' He motioned to the man who had entered with Laswell. 'And this is Norman Ripley, our Associate Deputy Administrator.'

Laswell ignored the others and turned to Matthews. 'General, I have to speak with you — immediately!' His tone bordered on open hostility.

Norman Ripley glanced anxiously at Neston, who returned a look of apprehension. Brunning seemed faintly surprised.

'All right, Dr. Laswell,' Matthews said softly. 'We can talk now.' He placed a hand on the man's arm, steering him away from the others towards the side of the great room.

Neston avoided the questioning looks of the ARDCOM personnel and walked over to the communications console.

Stanton took his eyes off the equipment for a moment and swivelled around to face him.

'Bill,' Neston ordered, 'get hold of launch command and the trackers by ground line — ask them to double-check their computer coordinates on the reentry path and landing site, and to make sure the point chosen for detonation is within the range of the Russians' tracking facilities. We wouldn't want them to miss the show.' He watched as Stanton turned and switched on the phone circuits. 'And remind them to avoid radio communications except for generalised reporting of the primary satellite's position.'

'Yes, sir.'

As Stanton set about his task, Brunning and the others approached Neston. The colonel reached him first.

'Is anything wrong?' Brunning asked.

'No, sir. The mission is going smoothly so far.'

'But Dr. Laswell seems upset about something.'

Neston looked briefly to Norm Ripley, then replied. 'It's in the nature of a personal disagreement, Colonel.'

Brunning frowned. 'I wasn't aware that there were any problems, personal or otherwise, involved.'

'Well, sir, due to the secrecy of the mission we weren't able to smooth out all of the details ahead of time. And not quite as tactfully as we would have liked.'

'But the administrator has been in on everything, hasn't he?'

All Neston would say was, 'He is now, sir.'

Norm Ripley spoke up suddenly, asking, 'How long before we get this show on the road, Jim?'

'Roughly three hours.' Neston was beginning to look tired again. 'And I've got a feeling,' he said, almost under his breath, 'that it's going to be an exceptionally long three hours.'

Laswell and Matthews, meanwhile, had reached the wall. Despite the general's precautionary move, they were not quite out of earshot of the others.

Matthews kept his voice low. 'All right. What is it?'

Laswell made an impatient gesture and shook his head.

'You know what it is! You *must* have known how I would react to this mission when you began —'

'Settle down,' Matthews said firmly, the sound of command coming into his voice. 'There's no need getting worked up over this. You know what's at stake.'

'Of course I know what's at stake ... your *job*, more than anything else. You're afraid your project to turn space into the next zone of combat will be undermined, and you're exploiting our facilities to save it!'

Matthews' eyes were grave. 'I didn't invent warfare, Dr. Laswell, nor did I invent the ballistic missiles the Russians have available to destroy us. The purpose of the Cerberus project is defence ... *defence*, not aggressive warfare.'

'But how far does it go? Will the next "defence" installation be on the moon? Perhaps we should have armed our Skylab — fit it with nuclear warheads,' he added mockingly. 'I'd sooner keep these international conflicts out of space.'

'So would I,' Matthews said coldly.

'What do you expect of me?' Laswell continued. 'Why wasn't I even given the consideration of being trusted with the information concerning this mission?'

'There were only a limited number of people who could know the full details of it at any given time,' Matthews replied. 'Security demanded that.'

'Security? Others knew. I should have been informed immediately about the true nature of this effort! Instead, all I received were vague statements from the Defense Department and an urgent request for certain equipment and facilities to be placed at their disposal. How do you expect me to feel when my assistant administrator has been privy to almost the entire mission from the start, while information was denied me. Only yesterday was I made aware of the fact that this is all for the sake of espionage.'

'All right!' Matthews thundered. 'Call it espionage if you want — I really can't deny that's what it is. But the simple fact remains that the Russians have obtained information about the Cerberus defence system, information that has apparently helped them find a way to circumvent it. That could place this country in jeopardy, Doctor, and don't fool yourself into thinking that international problems have been ironed out between our two nations to the point where we no longer have to worry about the possibility of attack. Even discounting that possibility, by having the means to penetrate our defences, the Soviet leaders would have an incredible bargaining position in international affairs. We could be forced into the position of having to sit by and watch them do whatever they please in the world. You wouldn't want that, would you?'

'I think you're exaggerating the danger. That kind of argument would ring truer, General, if you hadn't bludgeoned the President and Congress with it every time you wanted an increased defence budget.' Laswell shook his head, pausing. For a moment, there was a flash of something other than anger in his eyes. 'Don't you realise what something like this could do to the space programme? We have just finally reached a stage where joint Soviet-American efforts are possible. The information exchange programmes alone are invaluable. But all that could be destroyed forever by a . . . a stupid blunder like this.'

Matthews' gaze hardened. 'I have my orders.'

'And I have my responsibility to NASA. I have spent too many years of my life working in the programme to stand by and see it endangered by some militaristic venture. The President saw fit to appoint me to this post, and I will not have my authority subverted.' He paused, studying Matthews' implacable features. 'But I see there is no point in discussing it further. At least not with you, General . . .'

Laswell turned and headed for the door. Norm Ripley hesitated for a second, then followed him.

Halper watched their departure with a sense of foreboding. He had been able to hear most of the conversation . . . at least enough of it to understand what was happening. And he knew that Joyce had heard it as well, which would not help matters any. No — it would not help matters at all.

. . .

A short while later in Brussels, capital city of Belgium, it was five-thirty in the afternoon. The official airport ceremony honouring the President's arrival and presided over by Belgium's king had concluded at five. The entourage had made its way through town with a minimum of difficulty, despite the crowds, and had arrived at the residence of the U.S. Ambassador. Because of the late arrival, a limited and informal press conference was immediately arranged at the steps of the building, primarily for the benefit of foreign correspondents. But the American journalists were also present.

Secretary of State Charles Wellmont emerged and surveyed the gathered reporters, looking as if he did not relish what lay ahead. But that look was quickly submerged beneath the calm, certain composure of the master diplomat.

After several casual opening remarks, questions were accepted. The first came from a reporter near the front of the crowd:

'Mr. Secretary, the NATO meeting scheduled for today has been postponed until tomorrow?'

'That is correct.' Wellmont paused to clear his throat. 'There was not adequate time left this afternoon. Rather than attempt any meetings this evening, it was decided to wait and begin fresh in the morning.'

Another asked, 'Do you expect the United States and other NATO members to be in agreement, as they were last time, especially on the matter of defence funding?'

'Yes, I believe so. We have everything to gain from cooperation and mutual accord. I foresee no major difficulties in our meetings here. I would say that the details of our present agreements have been worked out for the most part and are at least 90 per cent complete. There is really little left but the formal ceremonies.'

'Isn't that rather optimistic,' the man pressed, 'considering the current internal problems among several of the NATO member countries?'

Wellmont did not bat an eye. 'If it is optimistic, it is an optimism based on a working knowledge of the present political situation. I would hardly call it mere wishful thinking.'

116

He acknowledged another man near the rear of the crowd.

'Mr. Secretary, about the upcoming summit conference in Moscow, which is certainly the most important part of this trip — the final stages of the SALT talks are supposed to be drawing to a close. But in light of the reports that the Soviets have now deployed their new SSX-19 multiple-warhead missiles to replace their single-warhead SS-11's, isn't it true that they stand to lose more than they could gain from agreements that would limit such missile systems?'

'Not necessarily. You should realise first of all that the United States has also kept pace technologically with the Soviet Union. Even without multiple-warhead systems, we still have a greater number of retaliatory missiles available. No, *both* nations would benefit from such limitations. The financial benefits alone should be incentive enough.'

'But isn't it true,' a different voice interjected, 'that there's continued speculation concerning a disparity of systems? That the Soviet Union now has a technological advantage of some kind?'

Sober-faced, Wellmont replied, 'I do not indulge in speculation.' He paused. 'Are there any other questions?'

Jeremy Meeker was near the front of the crowd. He had his notepad before him, and Lawrence's telegram was clipped to the top edge.

'Secretary Wellmont,' Meeker began, 'I was wondering about yesterday's delayed flight, which was blamed on weather conditions. There were sixteen commercial flights which made the trip to Europe yesterday under the same weather conditions. Do you have any comment on that?'

Wellmont hesitated briefly, his features tightening. 'All I can suggest is that considering the passengers on Air Force One, and the importance of this trip, additional caution seemed warranted.'

'But sir —' Meeker pressed, to be immediately interrupted.

'That will be all for now,' Wellmont stated quickly and firmly. 'There will be a full press conference tomorrow, at the conclusion of the NATO meetings. . . .'

'Is Dr. Laswell going to be a problem?' Brunning asked, keeping his voice low in the Houston Mission centre.

General Matthews reflected a moment. 'I don't know yet. At the moment, of course, he's still angry. I have to admit I did expect his reaction.'

'Is that why you wanted him kept in the dark?'

'It's part of it.'

Neston was with them, and he added, 'I guess if I have to put my job on the line . . . this mission is worth it.'

'There's a lot more on the line than that,' Matthews said soberly. 'A lot more.'

Joyce Kandell had approached them, drawn by their whispered remarks. Her look was urgent and questioning. Brunning noticed her first, but she directed her words to Matthews.

'I don't understand, General – I thought this mission had been fully approved by everyone involved.'

'That authority rests with the Defense Department. We thought it best to delay full disclosure of the plan to Dr. Laswell until a few days ago. He's only just assumed the position of NASA Administrator, and during a mission such as this, changes of leadership in any agency can create problems.'

Joyce was sceptical. 'He may be newly appointed, but he's been connected with the space programme for decades! I've heard quite a bit of Dr. Laswell. He's a highly respected man.'

Matthews nodded grudgingly. 'I agree, although I feel some of his personal views are unrealistic. But you need not concern yourself with that. Everything is under control.'

Joyce seemed about to press the matter further when the door to the great room suddenly swung open. Arnold Smith entered, wearing a light grey business suit and carrying a bulky black case. The other hand held a folded newspaper. He picked an empty table near the computer console and set the case down carefully. He began to thumb through his fresh copy of the Houston *Post*.

Looking up, he greeted the others with the unconcerned good humour of a man waiting for the bus. Returning his attention to the paper, he finally found the item he wanted and smiled faintly. He showed it to the others.

Halper read it first. 'It's an item about a new Navy navigation satellite being launched this morning. What is it ... some kind of cover story for the rocket that launched Major?'

'Basically,' Smith replied.

'But the Russians will know it's not a navigation satellite, won't they?'

'Certainly. However, what they most likely will think is that it's one of our manoeuvrable inspector satellites ... a misconception which we will encourage, hopefully, by appearing to hide the fact.'

Halper considered it and shook his head. 'I'm afraid I'm not very good at chess, either.'

'No matter, Lieutenant. It's only a minor element of the overall plan. There are more important at the moment.' He opened the case. Inside were maps, diagrams, and information sheets. Occupying the rest of the case's interior were two computer tapes and a massive stack of programming cards.

Carter looked at the materials and sighed, knowing what was to come. 'Looks like I'll be busy for a while. . . .'

He gathered up the tapes and cards, and with Smith's help took them over to the computer console. He began organising them into programming sequences.

A brief silence fell over the others. Rather than let the conversation return to the matter of Laswell, Halper changed the subject.

'General, I've been wondering how the Bio 12 satellite you mentioned fits into all of this. Is it something new?'

Matthews seemed relieved to speak of something else. 'No. Actually, the satellite originally had nothing whatsoever to do with this mission. It was launched into orbit a year and two months ago, and is the same general type as the one in which you placed your dog.'

Joyce showed a spark of interest. 'Did it have a dog aboard?'

'No. It had forty-five sealed containers of various kinds

of microorganisms, as part of an experiment to test out certain effects of spaceflight and medications to counter those effects. The experiment was a failure. Five days after it was launched we lost control over its equipment, and even from the beginning we were unable to receive signals from the satellite. It remained in orbit, and because of its type, its time of launch, and the fact that it has no further use to us, it was selected by the Defense Department experts who planned this mission.'

'But,' Halper replied, 'if it can't be controlled, then how can you use it?'

'In a very important way. The satellite itself is worthless. What we want is its history ... its recorded presence over the past year and two months. It will all begin to make more sense when we start the next phase, as soon as the Bio 12 satellite catches up with the one we've just launched.'

Joyce nodded pensively. 'I hope Major is still all right. I wish there was some way to know. . . .'

'So do I,' Matthews replied. 'But unfortunately, we can not afford to find out just yet. Any telemetry data sent back from that satellite now would destroy the plan.'

'And yet,' Joyce said softly, 'if anything's wrong with the dog, there is no plan.'

'True enough. One way or another, we'll find out a little after one o'clock. Until then ... we shall just have to wait. . . .'

'I wish you would reconsider, sir.'

'Reconsider?' Dr. Laswell sat behind the desk in an auxiliary office of the Project Management Building, the phone in his hand. He studied Norman Ripley with grim animosity. 'Under the circumstances, you're hardly in a position to offer recommendations. Can you give me one good reason why I shouldn't dismiss you and Neston both?'

'We were acting under orders.'

'Whose orders? As long as you are a part of NASA, you are subject to *my* directives. I can understand Matthews' desire for secrecy, but not your complicity in this. I'm very

120

disappointed in you, Norman. How can I trust either of you after this?'

He looked away from his associate deputy and continued to dial the number for a security line to Washington, D.C. He waited impatiently for the call to go through.

When the phone rang at the State Department, it was answered by undersecretary Jonathan Bennet. His voice sounded more remote than it should have for the distance involved.

'This is Stephen Laswell of NASA. I'm calling from Houston.'

'Yes, Dr. Laswell?' Bennet's tone seemed immediately cautious.

'I've got to get in touch with the President.'

There was a pause. 'The President has already left the country some hours ago —'

'Yes, of course,' Laswell said irritably. 'I'd be calling the White House, otherwise. But if he's arrived in Brussels you can arrange a call for me. I must speak to him. It's quite urgent.'

'Perhaps I could be of some help . . . if you could tell me the nature of the problem?'

'I'm sure you know what the problem is. Why do you think I'm here in Houston? I know what's being done, and I strongly disapprove of the needless involvement of NASA facilities and personnel in this kind of questionable activity.'

There was an odd silence at the other end. When Bennet spoke again, he said calmly, 'If it concerns an agency policy matter, than I suspect you will have to wait until after the President's return from Moscow.'

'This can't wait until then. If I'm going to remain administrator, then there simply must be an understanding as to my authority, and what will be allowed. I must speak with the President about this at once.'

'I'm sorry, sir, but I'm afraid that's impossible to arrange.'

'If the President is in a meeting at the moment, at least you can give him a message. . . .'

'I'm afraid that's impossible too, sir,' Bennet's voice was beginning to sound strained.

Laswell shook his head in exasperation. 'But why isn't it possible?'

'I'm sorry, sir. Secretary Wellmont's instructions were quite explicit. I'm sorry. . . .'

Laswell replaced the phone receiver quietly, staring across the office at Norman Ripley. Ripley's stance was tense, and he had followed the phone conversation with a troubled look.

Laswell's voice became cold and hard. 'Norman, I know you have a phone line set up to the test building. I want you to use it. I want you to call General Matthews . . . *now*!'

In utter silence, the primary satellite hung in space as the Earth rotated slowly beneath it. Brilliant white sunlight illuminated half its surface, and reflected Earth-glow tinted the other half with a faint blue. Nothing in its outward appearance suggested the strange cargo it held as it waited for Bio 12 to draw nearer.

Inside the primary satellite, within the secondary satellite suspended in its harness, Major also waited. At least in manned space flights there would be the sound of the radio bearing familiar voices from Earth, or the sound of another human voice within the capsule. But for Major there was only the sound of his heart beating, pulsing blood through his veins; and of his breathing — steady, in and out, through nostrils that at times seemed not to be a part of him.

The mild sedative was doing its job, helping to keep him calm. His training made up for the rest of it, and Major waited for whatever lay before him. Any normal dog, brought up in the usual manner and with the freedom to develop at least partially on his own, would be hard-pressed to cope with the isolation, with the darkness that enveloped all, with the oppressive silence, and perhaps worst of all, the odd feeling of weightlessness that tugged at the insides of his body.

No, that was not the worst.

There was one thing worse than all these. And it was the

knowledge of being alone — a feeling that would reach to the core of any normal domestic dog. Those stresses, over a period of time, could work to destroy the mind of such an animal.

But Major was no ordinary dog. As soon as possible after birth, he had been isolated. He and hundreds more like him. He had been fed a carefully controlled diet, exercised regularly, and even while still a pup had begun the long series of training programmes that would make him much more than just a military guard dog. He had been subjected to intense cold and heat, spun at dizzying speeds in a small centrifuge, and confronted by bizarre situations that would prod his mind to the utmost level. But if his intelligence had been polished to an extraordinary level, it had also been formed and shaped. Shaped to a particular end.

The research had really begun so long ago. Breeding and training dogs for a specific purpose was an old art, and an art brought to practical perfection in the Kaiser's Germany. During World War I American soldiers had seen, with a certain amount of surprise and admiration, the effectiveness of the Germans' trained dogs used in warfare. American training programmes began, some coming into effect well before the onset of the next world war to follow. After that, the interest had waned somewhat. Newer types of warfare relegated the dogs to use by military police for a variety of less heroic, if not less hazardous jobs. Then someone began wondering how to improve the effectiveness of the animals. New research programmes had begun. The Army's 'super dog' operation to develop smarter, hardier guard dogs was part of it. The Navy's use of dolphins was proven to have surprising worth, especially in areas or conditions dangerous for divers. And with the age of computers and microelectronics, new ideas sprang forth. . . .

Major waited, hour after hour, at times in a dreamlike state. Although he could not know or appreciate the fact, the compartment within the larger primary satellite in which his own satellite was suspended had been emptied of air. Pressure within the area where reserve fuel tanks should have been located was now equal with the almost perfect vacuum of space. That was an important factor, since the plastic explosive placed around the interior of the primary would otherwise transmit its concussive force through the air, directly to the capsule Major occupied. But without that air, there would be no blasting force to tear at the capsule, no sound or vibration.

Another hour passed.

Major waited patiently, unaware of the gleaming object in space that was now only five hundred yards away, and steadily drawing nearer. . . .

'Status report?' Matthews demanded. He had come up behind Neston, who was standing alongside of Bill Stanton at the communications console.

Neston took away the extra headset which he had been holding to one ear. 'Everything's on schedule, sir. Bio 12 has caught up with the primary satellite, which has now completed acceleration so that they're both moving at the same speed.'

'What's the distance between them?'

'About two hundred feet.'

'That won't be too close — the explosion won't affect the primary satellite?'

'No, sir. The missiles will be directed at the leading edge of the Bio 12 satellite, so the force of the explosion will be away from the primary. Besides, we can't risk having the two satellites any farther apart. The discrepancy might show up on the Russian's tracking system when the secondary satellite is released. At two hundred feet, with the confusion of the explosion, we should get away with it.'

'Good enough. The engineers who planned this gambit must know what they're doing. What about the timing sequence?'

'I asked launch command to check on that earlier, sir. The final sequencing is all under computer control now.'

'How long?'

Neston brought the headset up to his ear again and listened for a moment. 'Four minutes and thirty-one seconds.'

Matthews frowned anxiously. 'Here's where we find out if we're still in the game or not. . . .'

Bio 12 and the primary satellite moved in tandem orbit as the Pacific Ocean passed beneath them. The primary was a degree or two below the position of the other, angled slightly down towards Earth. Thousands of miles below, a machine controlled their destinies.

Minutes ticked off, then seconds. At the exact predetermined instant, the signal flashed up from the Canberra relay point in Australia. Picked up by the primary's antenna and receiver, the coded electronic instructions were immediately acted upon by the satellite's on-board computer. The radar unit had already locked onto the Bio 12 satellite, and at the minor distance involved there could be no such thing as a miss.

Relays clicked, tiny rocket engines fired. Eleven of the twelve mini-missiles left the primary satellite and rapidly crossed the distance between the two objects. At the same instant, other relays were closing to send power back to the firing core of the plastic explosive.

Bio 12 erupted in a blinding flash of light, the violence of the explosion all the more bizarre since there was no attendant sound of the blast. Simultaneously, the thin line of plastic explosive that ran around the interior of the primary satellite's rear compartment also detonated.

Fragments of the shattered rear compartment careened away from the primary satellite in all directions. Their mooring points destroyed, the straps holding the secondary capsule in place separated and drifted away. And a specially designed jet nozzle, made to look like a simple hose fitting, fired a three-second burst of pressure at Major's capsule, forcing it out of the primary's damaged shell and into a slow downward drift towards Earth.

Twenty seconds out from the primary, circuits within Major's capsule were activated by a signal from the ground, a signal that was an encoded 'rider', a signal that was part of a larger transmission apparently aimed at the primary satellite. A slight variance from the proper trajectory was studied by the ground-based computer at launch command, relayed back, and adjusted by a two-second burst of the capsule's own thrust jets, all in less than half a minute. And the encoded signal did one other thing as well.

The capsule's own equipment had been activated, and data on Major's heartbeat, breathing, and other vital signs began to be transmitted for the first time. It was a continual, automatic transmission that would not cease now as long as the capsule's batteries held out. Also, automatically, the device Halper had observed earlier began to function. The roll of paper began to advance extremely slowly, and the tiny marking arms started recording Major's vital signs in great zigzag lines on the surface of the paper roll. What had before been minute tracings were now wide arcs of ink, almost superimposed one upon the other. As the servo-clock mechanism continued to turn, marking the date and time automatically, it became impossible to tell that the device had not been working all along.

Leaving the scattered debris of Bio 12 and the damaged hulk of the primary satellite behind, Major's capsule headed earthward in a gradually descending arc.

In the NASA control room, nine people breathed a sigh of relief as the first signals were received from the capsule, carrying news of Major's health. The steady rhythm of the dog's heartbeat and breathing were comforting sounds after the long silence.

Joyce Kandell sat down at one of the wooden tables and leaned forward against two elbows, chin propped on folded hands. She remained silent for several minutes.

Halper sat down opposite her. 'At least we know he's all right so far.'

'Yes ... so far.' Her eyes remained focused on the tabletop for a moment, then raised to his. 'But the landing is just as dangerous as the launch ... maybe more so.'

'Everyone's done an extraordinary job so far. He'll make it.'

'That's not the only thing that's bothering me,' she added, lowering her voice. 'Ryan, there's something wrong with this whole mission. Why else would Dr. Laswell be so upset about it? He's not the type of man whose advice is taken lightly.'

'I know. But don't you think it could just be due to what General Matthews said — the fact that Dr. Laswell was informed quite late about the mission, and an unrealistic attitude —'

'No ... no, I don't think that's true at all. Ryan, I heard what he had to say, and he's right! If news leaked out about this mission, the space programme would *have* to suffer. We're not just talking about a government agency, we're talking about an important area of scientific research. I've read some of Dr. Laswell's papers and articles on the potentials of the space programme. We can't just be satisfied with a few hops to the moon. There's so much more to be gained from further exploration and research. So much. And if something like this mission could jeopardise all that, then I have to agree with him — it's wrong to involve NASA.'

Halper drew in a deep breath and let it out slowly. 'But if it's all necessary —'

'Is it? That's what I just don't know.' Joyce shook her head. 'How can we be sure this isn't all some pointless exercise in power politics. You were in Vietnam — you know how often things were done that turned out to be unnecessary.'

'Sometimes ...' Halper said softly. 'And many times they *were* necessary. But how can anyone be sure ahead of time what's necessary and what isn't? World affairs aren't that simple.'

'But by that argument, *anything* can be justified.'

Halper held up a hand to silence her. 'Looks like we have some work ahead of us. ...'

Arnold Smith came up to their table and began laying out maps and information sheets in a neat and precise order. There were generalised maps of Russia, one concentrating on the southern part of the West Siberian Lowland, and several detail maps of the city of Omsk and its surroundings.

127

While Smith continued with his maps and papers, General Matthews had more work for James Neston and Bill Stanton. The general stood behind the communications console and checked his watch automatically, despite the wall clocks in front of him. 'All right, gentlemen ... it's time to send out the alert to the Pentagon for relay to units in Europe. We'd better look like we're *trying* to intercept that capsule!'

'Starting transmission now, sir.' Neston replied.

'And when that's done,' Matthews continued, 'remind launch command to complete their calculations on the exact touchdown time for the capsule, and give us a countdown so we can switch on the ARDCOM equipment. I don't want those transmissions starting one second before or one second after the instant of landing.'

'Yes, sir.' Neston was about to attend to that last order when the black phone buzzed suddenly, its light flashing. Neston answered it, then turned back to Matthews.

'It's Laswell again — the second time he's called in the last hour.'

Matthews shook his head. 'I can't speak with him now. We're going into a critical phase of the mission.'

Neston hesitated. 'From the way he sounds, sir, I think maybe you'd better try to see him as soon as you get a chance.'

Matthews considered it, chewing his lip. 'All right. But tell him the soonest I can get away from here is an hour from now.'

'I'll tell him, sir.'

While Neston set about his work, Colonel Brunning walked slowly up to the communications console. His steps were cautious, but in his eyes there was still a trace of excitement.

'What next, General?' he asked.

'Next?' Matthews paused briefly, his eyes seeming to focus on some inner thought. 'Next ... we wait a little while longer. And hope that Arnold Smith's people have done their homework well enough. ...'

CHAPTER FIVE

Most of the lights were out in the building as Miklos Nikovitch made his way down the cramped hall. It was ten-forty in Moscow now, and only a few of the offices in this section of the building were occupied. Nikovitch did not go all the way to his own door, but instead stopped in front of the second door down from his own. The office on which it opened was one of the few with its lights still burning.

Nikovitch paused, taking a second to brush away the remaining flakes of snow from the shoulders of his coat with a few gruff sweeps of his hand. Then he reached out to the doorknob, opened the wooden panel with its upper section of frosted glass, and strode inside.

He squinted momentarily in the harsh electric glare, then his eyes settled on the approaching form of his subordinate. 'What is it, Alexi?' Nikovitch asked, even before the man reached him. 'What have you called me back for at this hour?'

'I am sorry to disturb you, Director, but I thought it necessary.' Alexi's manner was still deferential, but in his tone there was a trace of vindication. 'It seems there are new developments concerning the satellite launched by the Americans earlier this evening. Important developments that required your presence.'

'And I am here now. What is the problem?'

'A few hours ago, our tracking ships, Chazma and Sakhalin, discovered the destroyer satellite's target. It was as you said, one of their own derelict satellites.'

'Yes?'

'It had been launched a little over a year ago, one of their bio-satellites. We had always presumed that it failed to function. There had never been any return transmissions from it, and it was never brought down.'

'And they have already destroyed it?'

'No, Director. That is, they tried to destroy it, but

apparently something went wrong. Our tracking equipment registered an explosion in that area, but the bio-satellite is still there. Their destroyer satellite, however, was damaged and is now functionless. Our equipment has picked up the presence of debris in that area, and the satellite no longer responds to signals from the American transmitters.'

'That is strange, in a way. They have had very few equipment failures in that series.' Nikovitch had his hands folded, rubbing his thumbs together slowly. 'But this much you could have waited to tell me tomorrow.'

'There is more.' Alexi was becoming agitated now. 'Some of the force of the explosion must somehow have deflected the bio-satellite from its normal orbit. It is falling to Earth, and if its present trajectory holds, it will land in one of our central provinces.'

'Here . . . in the Soviet Union?'

'Yes, Director.'

Nikovitch smiled faintly. 'Good. Perhaps if we can recover it intact, we will be able to learn something from it.'

'We've also received word that the American Naval forces in the Mediterranean are on alert status, as are their ground and air forces in Germany and other European bases.'

'But if they are aware of the falling satellite's trajectory, why —'

'Perhaps they think they will be able to deflect it somehow by radio signals to another area.'

'Can they?'

Alexi shrugged. 'It has not responded yet to any transmissions. But . . . but there is another possibility. They have aircraft outfitted for capturing equipment as it drops by parachute from the sky. Perhaps . . .'

'No.' Nikovitch's features clouded. 'No. They will not attempt to violate our airspace. There could be nothing in that derelict satellite so important for that, to risk a direct confrontation. Not anymore.'

'But there is something I have not yet told you . . . something which would seem to be impossible. . . .'

'Well?'

'Director — that satellite is now transmitting life signs. Medical telemetry. There's some kind of living creature in it!'

Nikovitch shook his head automatically. 'Nothing could have survived for that length of time.'

'Something has,' Alexi insisted. 'And not a lower organism. Whatever it is has a heartbeat and respiration. We're sure it can't be a man. It might be a small ape of some kind, or a large dog.'

Nikovitch considered it a moment. His ice-blue eyes raged with energy under the ragged overhang of his eyebrows. 'If what you say is true,' he said, pausing, 'then why have the signals from the satellite only now begun?'

'I ... I don't know.' Alexi shook his head defeatedly. 'Perhaps a circuit which was open, closed when the satellite was deflected off course. A relay might have become unjammed. Or perhaps ... no, I really cannot say.'

Nikovitch had started to take off his overcoat, but stopped. 'Did you do as I asked regarding our observation satellite?'

'Yes, Director, I already contacted the control centre. There is a satellite relatively close to the orbit of the American's destroyer satellite. Operations for manoeuvring it into photographic range have already begun, but it will be a while before it is close enough for the first pictures.' The thin man with the sparsity of hair paused. 'But is it still necessary, Director? Now that the object of those photos is no longer functional?'

'Yes, of course it is still necessary. Maybe it is more necessary now than before. You say you have the location where the other capsule will land?'

Alexi nodded. 'In the province of Omsk.'

'When?'

'Within the hour, if nothing changes.'

'This is a bad time to have to be concerned with unknown factors ... a very bad time.' Nikovitch methodically rebuttoned his overcoat. 'Alexi — listen carefully: there are a number of things you must do. First arrange for a jet aircraft to transport me to Omsk. Next contact the military command there and tell them they are on immediate security alert until further notice — no civilians must interfere with recovery operations. And finally you must inform the Premier, the Presidium Chairman, and the General Secretary of the situation. Can you do that, Alexi?'

The subordinate's face looked drained of both blood and emotion. 'Yes, Director.'

'Very well, then. I will be at the airport by the time the plane is ready.' He opened the door and started out. 'I am sure I can trust you to take care of things while I am gone, Alexi.'

Alexi nodded a bit reluctantly, and watched Miklos Nikovitch leave the office, his footsteps fading away down the hall. . . .

General Matthews made it to Dr. Laswell's office by two o'clock that afternoon, almost exactly on time. He was ushered in by Norman Ripley, who remained standing near the door even after it had been closed.

Matthews faced Laswell with a look of firmness reserved for special adversaries. But Laswell's countenance was equally firm.

'I don't have much time,' Matthews said immediately.

'This shouldn't take long, General,' Laswell came around in front of the desk and stood before him. 'I really hadn't intended to pursue this further with you, but it seems I am left with few alternatives.'

There was an angry edge to his words. Matthews assessed them in silence, waiting.

'I called the President a while ago,' Laswell continued. 'Or rather I should say I tried calling him. He seems to be unavailable at the moment. But I don't suppose that surprises you?'

'As I understand it, the President is quite busy with his current trip to Brussels and Moscow.'

'Busy, yes. But there is no earthly reason for him to be totally unavailable . . . unless someone wants to be sure I do not speak to him.'

Matthews remained silent again.

132

'Who authorised this mission?' Laswell asked suddenly.

'It was planned and approved of by the Department of Defense.'

'And that's all the authorisation needed?'

'Military intelligence missions do not have to go knocking on every agency's door for approval.'

Laswell seized on his words. 'And military intelligence operations should not be using civilian help!'

Matthews hesiated. Then he said calmly, 'When it comes to the defence of this country, all publicly funded organisations, especially those operated under federal jurisdiction, may be called upon for support.'

'In time of war, yes.'

'If we ever get involved in a direct war with the Soviet Union, Dr. Laswell, it could very well be too late to do anything. I frankly don't understand you, or how you can be more concerned with some esoteric philosophy of science than you are with the safety and well-being of this country.'

Laswell sighed. 'I may not share your nationalistic views, but I most certainly do care for this country. But you must understand –' he stopped, as if considering his words. 'General, one of the primary goals of our space programme has been to insure that the exploration and use of space will be conducted for peaceful purposes. And with relations improving for more joint operations between the Russian space teams and our own, something like this, now, is especially bad. Any connection between NASA and an espionage operation could forever blacken the image of the programme. And with the funding problems we're already experiencing, we don't need any more blows to our image.'

'Have you considered the possibility,' Matthews began carefully, 'that something like this, as you put it, could be the justification for an increase in funds?'

'If it succeeds! But I don't like the idea of becoming dependent upon military grants to continue our work. And what if it fails? A debacle of that order, if news of it was given out by the Russians, would be exploited by the world press for all it was worth.'

'You might keep in mind the fact that the Russians do

not hesitate to use their space programme for other than the most idealistic purposes. And they openly suggest the same of us. They will know, afterwards, that we've used NASA's services for this matter. Their own intelligence organisation being what it is, we can count on that. But the trick is to handle the whole thing in such a way that they *can't* make use of it for propaganda purposes.'

Laswell looked at him disdainfully. 'Do you really believe that's possible?'

'Yes, I do.'

'I doubt it very much, myself. But I suspect that's not the worst of it, is it, General? I have the definite impression that despite the alleged importance of this mission, the President of the United States does not even know it is taking place.'

Matthews hesitated a long while. 'It was not necessary to concern him with the details of this yet. There are enough pressures on him already.'

'Is that the reason? Or is it just that you knew he'd never approve of your plan?' Laswell paused, shaking his head. 'Have you done it all behind his back? *Lord* – what kind of madness could have inspired this!'

'Did you have anything else to say, Dr. Laswell?'

He seemed to draw himself up. 'Yes, I have something else. I didn't ask you here for a debate. I wanted to tell you that I have friends in the Senate and the House of Representatives ... friends who would be interested in knowing what you've done, and what you're continuing to do, without presidential approval.'

The general studied him. 'Is that a threat?'

'It's an ultimatum. Since I seem not to be able to express my views directly to the President himself on this, I find it necessary to resort to other means to put a stop to it.'

'That's blackmail at best ... I can think of worse names.'

'Call it what you will. But it is a promise I intend to keep, if you force me to.'

Matthews said nothing at first, though anger raged within him. 'I ... would need time to consider it. It would not be easy to cease operations.'

'You have until eight o'clock tomorrow morning,' Laswell said flatly. 'If I haven't heard from you by then, and if the equipment you've had assembled is not dismantled, I will make Congress aware of the situation in a matter of minutes.'

Matthews left the office, feeling the added weight of a new problem. He had not the slightest intention of complying with Laswell's demand, despite the warning. At least he still had a little time ... time to resolve it somehow. ...

Captain Dimitri Storkas concentrated grimly on securing the fastenings of his parka, trying to avoid the other thoughts that were in his mind. The last place he wanted to be right now was here in the same military base outside of Omsk where he had spent the last ten months. He should have been off duty an hour ago, and already on his way to the small Ukrainian village so many miles away ... the village that was his true home, and home of his beloved Rina. That was where he should be going — home — and not out into the barren, snow-covered forest lands beyond Omsk.

He fumbled with the last fastening, his movements becoming more aggravated. Suddenly aware of another person's presence, he looked up in time to see his superior officer stop before him.

'Angry about something, Dimitri?' The man's stern gaze studied him knowingly.

'No, sir,' Storkas lied. 'I am only anxious to begin the search.'

'Oh, yes.' Smiling wryly, the officer automatically interlocked his hands behind his back as he stood. 'And anxious to conclude it, as well. Do not worry, Dimitri — you will still have your leave time. But you will have it after this is done. I do not have to explain to you the matter of priorities, I am sure.'

'No, sir.'

'Good. And you should be glad at least about your recent promotion. A captain's pay will keep a new wife and family better than that of a lieutenant. I have been able to help you that much. Am I right?'

'Yes, of course.' Storkas' tone was controlled. 'I am grateful for your assistance, sir.'

'When is the wedding to be?'

'It . . . was to be tomorrow, sir.'

The officer shrugged, but his expression was not unsympathetic. 'Well, such a thing as a wedding may be postponed a day or so much more easily' than an event of this nature. I would rather disappoint you and your bride-to-be than the whole of the Soviet Government. But you understand this.'

Storkas nodded disconsolately. He tucked his heavy gloves under the belt of the parka, and snapped down the trigger guard on his automatic rifle. He extended the carry-strap and slung the weapon from his shoulder.

'This wedding,' his superior pressed the point further, 'is it to be a traditional village ceremony?'

'Yes, they've been making preparations – I had to send a message to let them know my arrival would be delayed. They . . .' He paused, becoming somewhat self-conscious. 'They prepare special foods, make decorations. . . .'

The officer breathed out a pleasant sigh, looking away from Storkas. 'Ah yes, I have seen a few such weddings . . . years ago. I remember the music, the happiness and warmth of those occasions. They have so much more feeling than those cold civil procedures in the big cities. You are lucky.'

Storkas smiled faintly, thinking of Rina, 'Yes, sir . . .'

The officer's smile abruptly faded. 'All right, I see you are ready to go. Do you understand your instructions, Dimitri?'

'I understand, sir.'

'Then go . . . and try to please all concerned, with a quick success.'

Outside, as snow drifted down in the darkness, Storkas pulled the hood of the parka over his chestnut-brown hair, then walked towards the two snow-tracked vehicles twenty feet away. Beside the vehicles waited two teams of five soldiers each, dressed and armed similarly to Storkas.

As Dimitri neared the snow-tracks, another man approached from another section of the building. A younger man than Storkas, he seemed closer in appearance to a teenage student than to a junior officer in the Soviet military, though in fact he occupied the position vacated in the course of Storkas' promotion. Stopping briefly as he reached Dimitri's side, he held out one of two radio units, each of which was equipped with a directional loop.

'Here, Captain,' he said, exhaling a cloud of vapour in the cold. 'They have both been set on the same frequency as the capsule's homing signal.'

'Fine. Have you attended to everything else?'

'Yes, sir. The vehicles are fully fuelled, and there are extra cans of petrol loaded on the back.'

'And the regular radios – ?'

'One man with each vehicle has a back-pack transceiver.'

Storkas pulled the heavy gloves from his belt and put them on. 'Battery lights?'

'Already loaded, Captain.'

'Then let us begin at once. It will only get colder between now and dawn. . . .'

Storkas climbed into the lead vehicle, his junior officer commanding the other. When the last of the men were aboard and the engines started with an ether choke, the two snow-tracks rumbled off across the compound. The gate in the tall, all-encompassing fence was held open for them as they reached it, and in another few moments the two vehicles left the military base behind and headed off, away from Omsk, into the vast expanse of open country beyond.

The stationary tracking facilities had already estimated the general area of the landing site from knowledge of the capsule's trajectory. But how far the wind-borne, para-chuting capsule might have drifted within that general area, or perhaps even out of it, remained to be discovered.

Soon lost from sight in the darkness and drifting snow, the military base and the city of Omsk ceased to be a part of their reality as the recovery team pressed on. Throwing long ovals of yellowish white ahead of them, and trailing long and winding tracks behind them, the two vehicles seemed overwhelmed by the scale of the countryside around them. Tiny and fragile, they crept across the great blanket of frost-white made glistening grey in the night.

The cold also added to the feeling of isolation, and there was no escaping it, not even within the enclosed vehicles. Despite the heaters, which poured out tepid air through their vents, there was simply not enough warmth to overcome the gnawing chill. It was a cold that rose from the depths of earth and rock and pressed down from the heavens. But it was a part of their existence usually accepted, if not enjoyed.

Miles passed, and more miles.

Storkas watched the twin ovals of light trace out their jerky path across the snow, and watched also to the right and left of their course, in case some evidence of the capsule's whereabouts might be revealed in the residual glow. For the moment there was nothing to see except the endless, undulating cover of snow and the black skeletons of trees, which were appearing all the more regularly.

He listened to the steady tone being received by his radio unit. That tone was growing louder and more clear even as he rechecked the direction by means of the radio's loop.

As they rolled relentlessly on, the elements of their surroundings — the cold, the unyielding snow, the changeless sounds — all began to form into a whole, a solid, tangible and enclosing. It enveloped them and held them tight within its grip.

The droning sound of the engine began to assault Dimitri's ears, and as had happened before on occasions, he started finding melodies within the motor's rhythmic hum. One was dominant among them, and it played through his mind for a while before he devoted conscious thought to it and remembered what it was: Prokofiev's *Peter and the Wolf.*

Perhaps it had not been well-favoured by the critics, but the symphonic fairy tale had always been well-loved by the common people, including Dimitri. The music was perfectly suited to this panorama of snow and forest through which he now moved. The melody continued in his mind as his eyes searched for some sign of the capsule, even though he knew they could not yet be close enough to the source of the signal. For a moment he thought he caught a brief glimpse of a wolf among the snow-skirted trees. Whether it was real or illusion, Storkas was not sure. It might have been prompted by the music which still coursed through his head, or it might actually have been a wolf. Whatever, it served as a reminder of the possible dangers of the forest, dangers that had not really changed over the centuries. And it also brought to mind other recollections of Storkas' youth. Recollections of —

Something interrupted those thoughts, something that had really begun a moment earlier, and had just now tugged at his mind. Almost in the same instant, the radioman seated behind him thrust forward the unit's handset.

'Captain —'

Storkas took the instrument, held it to his ear. 'Yes?'

His junior officer's voice came over the receiver. 'Sir, we are no longer picking up the signal from the capsule!'

'What?' His own attention was jolted back to the tracking unit he held, and Storkas found that it was true — the signal from the capsule was gone. There was not the slightest trace of it. He automatically checked the power-indicator light of the unit, even though he realised it was not likely due to a power failure since both radio direction units stopped receiving the signal at the same moment. 'A high point in the terrain must be blocking the signal — keep going along the same course.'

'Yes, Captain,' the reply came back.

The two snow-tracked vehicles crept on through the white timberland, heading in the last direction indicated by their radio units. The ground was becoming more irregular in this area, and a gentle slope of some fifty feet elevation still lay ahead of them at a distance of perhaps a quarter mile.

Storkas withdrew a map from his parka and unfolded it. He checked the circle that had been marked on one section indicating the general location of the capsule. Even with this as a guide, the area covered by the circle was still many square miles. He knew he would have to rely completely on the tracking units. It was even possible the capsule was not visible to the eye. By now it would likely have a fine covering of snow upon it, and it could be indistinguishable from the rocks and fallen tree trunks on the forest floor. He reached into the compartment below the windshield and pulled out a pair of binoculars with yellow filters, then used them to scan the area ahead.

Still nothing in sight. And still no homing signal from the downed capsule.

Slowly the vehicles started up the incline, heading for the top of the ridge. They had to shift down into a lower gear, and even then there was some difficulty with the treads slipping in the soft snow on the slope. Steadily they made their way up until, a few minutes later, they were almost at the very peak. And then . . .

'Stop!' Storkas bellowed. He grabbed the radio direction finder suddenly as an abrupt burst of sound came out of it. the capsule's homing signal had begun again, much louder now than it had been before. Storkas manipulated the directional loop until he reached a null spot. He looked forward, but the vehicle's headlights were much too high in the air, the snow-track still partially on the upward incline, and only the tops of the trees were illuminated.

'Ease forward,' Storkas commanded of his driver, 'a little to the right.'

As the vehicle inched over the peak of the ridge, the spots of light thrown out by its lamps moved downward, creeping along the trees towards the ground. Halfway down, a spot of bright colour showed with sudden intensity.

'There!' Storkas cried out. 'The parachute!'

Starkly illuminated in the headlight's glow, the tangled orange and white form of the capsule's descent parachute hung snagged from several branches of a tree. As the lights angled down more, the shroud lines were revealed, taut and silver-white. At the end of those shroud lines hung the capsule, swaying slightly in the faint breeze.

Dimitri drew in his breath suddenly. For he saw now

that the tree on which the parachute had become entangled was at the edge of a precipice. The capsule was dangling over open space, precariously suspended above what must be at least a hundred-foot drop to the forest floor below.

'Forward — quickly!' he commanded. 'If those branches should break before we can secure a line to the capsule, it could be destroyed!'

The vehicle lurched forward and headed down the other side of the ridge, the second vehicle following at a safe distance. Two-thirds of the way down, the first snow-track gained too much momentum for its unsure footing, and started to sideslip across the snow. There was the momentary danger that the second would crash into it, but the driver of that snow-track braked expertly, and the driver of Storkas' vehicle finally managed to steer back into a straight course. Using slightly more caution, they both moved as quickly as possible in the direction of the dangling capsule.

'Stop here,' Storkas ordered as his vehicle came within twenty feet of the tree. He opened the door and slid out of his seat, then grabbed a heavy, coiled cable from the door of the vehicle, and tossed it to the first soldier out after the radioman. 'Here — secure one end of this to the winch-mounting on the front. Hurry!' He turned to the radioman with more quick instructions. 'Report back to headquarters — tell them we have located the capsule — explain the situation.'

While the man sent his message over the back-pack radio, Storkas headed for the edge of the precipice. His junior officer caught up with him at the base of the tree. Dimitri placed a gloved hand against the trunk and leaned forward, looking down into the darkness below.

'Here, sir,' the younger officer offered. 'I brought one of the battery lights.'

Storkas switched on the light, like a small auto head-lamp with handle and battery case, and directed the beam down past the edge of the precipice. He saw that his previous estimate had been close. There was a drop of close to 150 feet. Soft snow was on the ground below, but not enough to cushion the fall of such a heavy capsule from that height.

Storkas switched off the light and handed it back. He turned and faced the vehicle. 'Soldier – have you secured that cable?'

'Yes, Captain.'

'Bring the rest of it here!'

In what seemed a few quick steps, the soldier had covered the distance between them. He extended the cable to Storkas, who took it without further comment.

Dimitri coiled the loose half of the cable. He looked at his junior officer. 'How are you at climbing trees?'

The young man looked up at the tree and its branches, assessing its footholds. 'Reasonably good, sir.'

Dimitri hesitated a moment, studying him. Never mind . . . I'll do it. I need the other cable from your vehicle. See to it.'

'Yes, sir.' The man's tone might have been of disappointment or of relief. Dimitri was not sure which.

Aiming carefully for a moment, Storkas tossed the coiled cable over a sturdy branch well above the position of the suspended capsule. He waited as the end of the cable swung down within reach and grabbed it, then tested it briefly with his weight. Satisfied with this, he knotted the end of the cable through his belt to free his hands for climbing, and began his ascent.

Cautiously, Storkas climbed up along the great tree's trunk, finding what hand and footholds he could among the branches and limbs. His target was a heavy, near-horizontal limb that passed a few feet above the shroud-line rings of the parachute. Reaching this limb, he started out slowly across it, his bulky parka making his movements more difficult.

Out from the tree a distance of twice his own body length, the limb began to sag slightly under his weight. This had the beneficial effect of bringing him a few inches closer to the shroud-line rings, but it also made him unpleasantly aware of his tenuous position.

Carefully, lying along the top of the limb and holding on

with the pressure of his legs, he loosened the cable end from his belt and reached down towards the rings. They were almost out of reach, but he managed to slip the cable through the first and then the second ring. He closed the loop between the two rings as tightly as the tension of the lines would permit, then tied the cable securely.

Calling down to his vehicle's driver, he ordered, 'Start the winch — take up some of the slack.'

As the solder complied, the long curve of cable from the snow-track to the upper tree limb slowly straightened. At last it was almost taut.

'Enough!' Storkas again checked the knot he had made, then looked down towards the base of the tree. His junior officer was there, waiting with the other cable. 'All right,' he called out to the man below him, 'hang on to one end, and toss the rest up to me.'

'Yes, sir.' The officer uncoiled part of the cable, held it firmly, then aimed and threw the remainder directly at Storkas.

The cable began to spiral out as it flew, lost momentum, and passed a few inches out of reach of Storkas' outstretched hand. Dimitri made a futile grab for it and missed, almost losing his hold on the tree limb in the same instant.

He grabbed hard with both hands to the limb, and the sudden breath of air he drew in hurt his lungs with its sharp, cutting chill. For a brief instant the image of his beloved Rina's face was before his eyes. Then he looked down at his junior officer again, and saw that the young man was gazing up in near terror. He huffed the cold air out of his lungs and shouted down at him.

'What are you waiting for — coil up the cable and try again!'

'Yes ... yes, Captain!'

'And aim higher this time!'

Again the cable flew out, and this time it was high enough to be caught in Dimitri's gloved hand. He reached down and looped it also through the shroud-line rings, tying it as solidly as the first knot.

'Now' he called down, 'take eight men over there on the

far side of the vehicle and have them pull on the cable. If there is not tension on it, when I cut the lines from the parachute the capsule may swing over against the tree.'

'Yes, sir.'

In less than a minute, eight of the soldiers were assembled at the extreme left of the vehicles, ready for a tug-of-war against the force of gravity, for the point over which the first cable passed on the overhead limb was not directly above the capsule. As they pulled against the second cable, less of the capsule's weight was on the parachute.

Storkas looked down at the men, then at the capsule dangling below him. He pulled out his bayonet from its sheath. 'Are you ready?'

'Yes, Captain.'

'Then brace yourselves!' Storkas yelled, and began to cut away at the shroud lines.

As each line severed, it snapped upwards with a distinct twanging sound. Above, smaller branches lashed back as the weight on them was suddenly released.

With the cutting of the last line, the capsule jerked suddenly to one side as its full weight came onto the cable, almost pulling the soldiers off-balance. Struggling against that pull, they managed to keep the metal cylinder from smashing into the tree, and its position finally stabilised.

Storkas crept backwards along the limb until he reached the trunk again, then climbed carefully back down.

'Keep a tight hold on that cable,' he ordered the soldiers, 'and move back over towards the vehicles. We've got to swing the capsule in away from the ledge.'

When the soldiers had moved en masse to the area indicated by Storkas, he turned towards the soldier manning the winch.

'Start playing out the cable — slowly!'

Whining, the winch began to unreel the cable that had been taken up earlier. As the capsule lowered, the eight soldiers backtracked, pulling mightily on the second cable. The capsule swung steadily in towards them, and by careful jockeying of the two cables, they moved it, still in a suspended position, to a point roughly eleven feet away from the edge of the precipice. Storkas and his junior officer steadied it from swinging as the men lowered the cylinder.

It was almost on the ground when an odd shudder ran through the great tree behind them. Then, with a sound like a rifle shot, the limb over which the first cable ran parted from the tree abruptly and fell, releasing the main support of the capsule.

Instantly the cylinder pivoted about and dropped the remaining few feet to the snow-covered ground. Storkas was knocked to one side, clear of the capsule, but his junior officer was pinned partially beneath it.

Storkas was on his feet again in a flash, and struggled with the end of the capsule. 'Quickly — help me with this!'

The driver of the first vehicle reached him before the other soldiers, who were farther away. When five of them had gathered at the capsule's end, they were able to lift it up long enough for the others to pull the young officer out from under it.

'My leg!' He grimaced in pain, felt all the more keenly in the cold. 'It is broken!'

Storkas, at his side, was not surprised. 'You are lucky the snow cushioned you a little. It might have been worse.' Concern showed in his features, though, as he checked the man over for other possible injuries. Finding none, he turned his attention totally to the broken leg.

'It is not a bad break,' he said in a relieved tone. 'Just a simple fracture. It will mend.'

The young officer groaned at the prospect of spending long weeks with his leg in a cast. Especially since his duties would still await him back at their headquarters.

Now that the need for his initial concern was past, Storkas smiled faintly. 'You can believe that I am sorry it was you to which this happened,' he said softly. 'But I am also glad it was not me!'

The man managed a strained smile of his own, and Storkas gave him a comradely slap on the shoulder.

'All right, now clench your teeth,' Storkas told him. He

set the broken bone, using the man's rifle for a splint and strapping it firmly in place, then helped carry the injured man to the second vehicle.

Returning to the capsule, he motioned for his radioman to follow. Storkas knelt beside the cylinder, darkened from its re-entry into the atmosphere, and examined it. Finding the protective metal cover over the hatch window, he released the catch, raised the small panel and peered into the capsule's dark interior.

'Where is the battery light?'

There was a moment's pause, then one of the soldiers brought it to him. 'Here, sir.'

Storkas switched it on and aimed the glaring beam through the window. The recumbent form inside was motionless at first, then, after a few seconds, Major stirred and raised his head to gaze out at the sudden new source of light, blinking at its intensity.

Staring into the light, Major could see little of Storkas' features. And although he could not know it, that same blurred image was being viewed by the people in Houston.

'Let me have the radio handset,' Storkas directed.

The radioman next to him detached the unit from the back-pack transceiver and gave it to him.

Storkas thumbed the switch and blew once into the microphone, out of habit. 'This is Patrol One ... we have secured the capsule. ...'

After a second's pause, a reply came through the earpiece. 'What is its condition?'

Storkas looked it over once again. 'It seems to be undamaged, sir.'

'And the contents?'

'A large shepherd dog,' Dimitri replied. 'Alive ... and so far, apparently well. But it is hard to be certain without examining the animal.'

'That will be done by our own doctors,' came the reply. 'You have done your job, Captain. Return as soon as possible.'

'Yes, sir. One thing, though – should I open the hatch of the capsule partially?'

'No — leave everything as it is. A special team will study the capsule when you bring it back. Nothing must be disturbed — we are under orders to that effect.'

Storkas frowned. 'But what if the enclosed air supply becomes exhausted . . . the dog will die.'

There was a pause at the other end of the transmission. 'Then it will not be our problem, but that of the diplomats. We are under orders, and you will comply with them.'

'Yes, sir. Shall I . . . shall I bring the capsule back to the base?'

'No. You are to take it directly to the Omsk Technical Institute, at the edge of the city. They have complete laboratory facilities, and I am told that due to their present research work, they already have special security forces.'

'All right, sir. And I have a man with a broken leg. Shall I take him to the city hospital or send him back to the base in the other vehicle?'

'You will take both vehicles to the institute,' his superior ordered. 'If one of them should break down, you can use the other to transport the capsule. After you have delivered it, then you may attend to your injured man.'

'Understood, sir.' Storkas handed the phone unit back to the radioman. There were other questions in his mind, but he knew better than to ask them. It was not wise to ask too many questions, especially in matters like this. Best to follow orders — and hope that it would not be long before he saw his bride-to-be.

He stood up. 'Quickly — let us get this loaded on the back of the vehicle.' He shouted his orders. 'Do you want to stay out here all night?'

At the same instant that Captain Dimitri Storkas was boarding his snow-track in the province of Omsk at four in the morning, it was five o'clock in the afternoon in Houston. In the near-empty building on the NASA grounds all was momentarily quiet — after the brief moment of elation.

With the cover again in place on the capsule's hatch window, no light entered the cylinder that was halfway

147

around the world. And with no light, there was no visual feedback from Major's implant. The great display screen was dark for now, but the circuits were still ready and waiting for whatever might come.

Carter had completed programming the additional material brought for the computer's memory bank, and Arnold Smith had checked it over with him to insure that all the information had been entered correctly. Carter was now leaning back in his chair, feet stretched out in front of him in a relaxed position. Arnold Smith, on the other hand, was pacing nervously around the circumference of the electronic equipment consoles.

Colonel Brunning was seated at one of the tables with Lieutenant Halper and Joyce Kandell. Behind them stood the general, looking down over their shoulders at the map which covered the tabletop.

'Well, at least we know he's down and safe,' General Matthews said suddenly. He checked his watch. 'And by now, on his way to Omsk. So far, so good.'

'Sir —' Bill Stanton called out from the communications console, 'we've received a report from our tracking stations in Europe. As accurately as they can tell from the capsule's final trajectory, it must have landed no more than a mile from the target site, right in the wooded area we'd chosen.'

Matthews smiled grimly. 'Chalk one up for the boys in logistics. I just hope the Russians don't notice the coincidence of the location too soon.'

Joyce studied the map before her. It was all just so many ink markings on paper, but she realised that those markings were symbols of a real and distant place, where Major would be a microscopically small speck of ink.

She looked up at Matthews. 'General, you're sure that they will take Major to the institute?'

Matthews nodded. 'They have to ... no place else around there with what they need. Omsk has quite a large veterinary research centre, but they're not equipped to handle anything like a downed American experimental capsule ... not from the point of view of security, and not from the point of view of equipment. Before they even

148

acknowledge the fact that they've recovered the capsule, they'll have their best scientists going over it to find out what they can about it.'

Brunning added, 'And they'll have their best scientists going over the dog, too.'

There was a brief silence after Brunning's remark, then Halper looked up from the map which he had been studying. He leaned back in his chair.

'General, you told us that the counter-Cerberus research was being conducted at the Omsk Technical Institute,' the lieutenant began. 'But if that was over a month ago, isn't there a strong possibility that the research has been moved to another location ... especially since one of our agents was captured in the area? If that's the case, then all this preparation could be wasted effort.'

The general frowned slightly. 'We've considered that, Lieutenant. But the circumstances are not as simple as they might appear. In the first place, for them to shift the location of the research, they would have to relocate all the personnel who are involved in the work, as well as the paperwork and research data ... they can be just as bureaucratic as we are. Another factor is the simple truth that their present location is almost perfect. Besides the personnel and facilities already there, its position in the interior makes it well isolated and inaccessible to outsiders without being so far from Moscow that occasional supervisory visits can't be made.

'Travel to and from Omsk can be watched most carefully ... regulated, screened. Outsiders would be easy to detect. The fact that we even had *one* agent in that area was a stroke of pure luck. The truth of the matter, from the information I've received, is that the man was already there in the city working under a cover identity, and had been there for the past five years.'

'Five years!' Halper sounded incredulous. 'How?'

'He was recruited in one of the Scandinavian countries by the communists, where a background identity of a civilian scientist had been built up for him. He was a legitimate, competent physicist, and ended up being

149

assigned to the Omsk Institute, where he worked on projects of relatively minor importance. He passed along what information he could through our intelligence system, but was always cautious enough to avoid detection. . . .'

Matthews paused. 'That is ... until this last bit of information. He must have decided that the results of their counter-Cerberus research were important enough – urgent enough – to jeopardise his position. And a man as careful as that – to work undetected in their midst for five years – must have found out something really big to risk everything, including his continued usefulness as an intelligence agent, and even his life. We've got to find out whatever it is their research has yielded ... we can't afford not to find out!'

Joyce Kandell absorbed this additional information with scepticism, then asked, 'And there was no effort made after that to find out more by direct means?'

Matthews shook his head. 'It was too impractical, too impossible, to have any chance of success, especially on such short notice. It could take months ... years ... to infiltrate their research group again. We can learn some information, of course, observing the moves they make – new missile installations, large shipments of heavy materials, many things like that from satellite observation and our regular intelligence network. But interpreting that information, separating one project from another and guess-timating, all takes time ... too much time. And it requires us to wait until work has already begun before we can know what they're up to. That wouldn't give us much time for countermeasures of our own.

'Now, as I said before,' Matthews continued, 'since we've made no further push in the area to find our more about their research, there's no pressing reason for them to move the site of that research. In fact, since we've done absolutely nothing in the way of intelligence probes, they may even assume that we never received any information from our agent. They may think he independently stumbled across their plans but was unable to relay it before his capture. That would be to our advantage.'

Halper was wondering what advantage the unnamed U.S. agent had been given ... and what difference the results of their mission would make for him, if any. Was he dead now, buried in some unmarked plot reserved for captured spies? Or was he still alive, being pumped for information in some ghastly prison? And which fate would truly be the worse? Halper was glad of one thing, at least – if he himself had to be a part of some espionage operation, then better by remote control, safe and secure in his own part of the world. A second after that thought, he also realised the irony of it, and the callousness. ...

He looked across at Joyce, and knew her own thoughts would be with Major. Perhaps her affection for the dog was misplaced, but it was there nonetheless, and for the girl, at least, the success of the mission would depend on more than just the acquisition of the desired information.

Arnold Smith, who had completed another few laps of the room in the course of his nervous pacing, stopped suddenly and consulted his watch. Looking up again, he directed his intense gaze at the general, who caught his look.

Matthews himself checked the time, looking at the large clock in the room instead of his watch for the first time. 'All right,' he said abruptly. 'So much for the silent part of the operation. It's time a few appropriate remarks were made to the right ears.'

He turned to face James Neston and Bill Stanton. 'You've got the official statements ready for release?'

'Yes, sir,' Neston replied. 'We're ready to transmit them at once.'

'And you're patched in to the international wire services?'

Stanton patted a device next to the communications console. 'Yes, General. Through this facsimile unit we can put out anything we need to have known.'

'Then begin as we planned,' Matthews instructed them. He turned back and reached into the briefcase he had brought in with him. From a folder within, he extracted several eight-by-ten black and white photos, then carried

151

one of them to the communications console and handed it to Stanton.

Halper and Joyce Kandell could not help but see the remaining prints left behind on the table. One form in the photos stood out immediately to them — for it was the dog, Major. The human standing next to him in the picture was also recognisable after a moment's look.

'General,' Halper said as Matthews returned to their table, 'This man ... it's the veterinary specialist at Ellington Air Force Base, isn't it? The one who prepared Major for his space flight?'

'You're right, Lieutenant. His name is Dr. Corby, and his work has gone a bit beyond simple veterinary medicine. The photo was taken yesterday, outside the medical building, in an area that will be difficult to recognise.'

'Then you're going to transmit the photo to the Russians,' Joyce replied, 'as part of the plan?'

'It will be made available through the right channels.' Matthews paused. 'Yes, they'll see the photo, all right, including the slight alteration we made in it ... an alteration which I sincerely hope they discover. ...'

In Brussels at that moment it was a little after midnight. In the residence of the U.S. Ambassador a light still burned in the room occupied by Secretary of State Charles Wellmont. Seated behind an antique desk in the well-furnished room, Wellmont studied his notes and State Department intelligence reports.

There was a soft knocking at the door. Dan Hillman White House Press Secretary, looked in.

'Sorry to interrupt —'

'That's all right — come in,' Wellmont said tiredly. 'I haven't really been able to concentrate on NATO matters anyway. What's up — have you heard anything?'

'Yes, sir. Word was just relayed from Washington.' Hillman paused as he took a chair near the desk. 'The capsule is down and safe. A Soviet recovery team has already reached it, so the operation seems to be on schedule ... so far.'

'Yes ... so far,' Wellmont said worriedly. 'But we don't know how long it will take before we can get the information we need.'

'Perhaps we'll have a better idea by morning.'

'Perhaps. I just wish we had more time to work with it. There's just no latitude in the plan ... no margin for error.'

Hillman nodded in agreement. Dark-haired and in his early thirties, he had served as press secretary for the past year. His appointment to that post had been influenced as much by Wellmont's recommendation as by any other factor, and yet he did not like the present situation thrust upon him by the Secretary of State. But he did not have to like it to go along with it.

A sound from outside the building caught their attention at that moment. Hillman rose, crossed the room, and looked out through the window at the ground below.

A dark vehicle with military markings stood at the gate, headlights spilling out twin scoops of brightness on the dark ground ahead of it. Two men emerged, both in uniform, paused to show identity cards to the secret service guards on duty at the gate, and headed towards the building.

Wellmont remained seated, but stared intently at Hillman. 'What is it?'

'Not sure ... two soldiers, I think. They're coming in.'

Hillman left the window as the men below disappeared from view. He went to the door and held it open a crack, looking down the hall.

'Could just be embassy business, I suppose ...'

Wellmont left his chair, an anxious frown on his features. 'I doubt it.' When he reached Hillman's side, he asked, 'Has the President retired for the night?'

'Yes. About an hour ago.'

The hall was silent. Several long moments passed, and they began to wonder if the men were coming upstairs or not. The grand staircase of the residence was too well-carpeted for footsteps to be heard.

Suddenly, the men appeared on the landing, escorted by three secret service men. It was clearly apparent now that they were Air Force officers, and in fact were wearing flight uniforms beneath their top-coats. They moved soundlessly down the hall, halting at the now open door of Wellmont's room.

The taller of the two officers, a Captain, unzipped a slim leather case and extracted a sealed folder. Extending it to Wellmont, he explained, 'We've just flown over from Wiesbaden, sir — these are from the Aerial Intelligence Division. Copies are being sent to Washington through regular channels, but the base State Department representative wanted these forwarded to you immediately.'

'Yes, thank you.' Wellmont accepted the folder. 'Is there any reply necessary?'

'No sir.'

'Very well . . . thank you again.' Wellmont watched them depart, then stepped back into the room and closed the door. At his desk he used a letter opener to break the seal. His hands moved quickly to open the folder and remove its contents.

Hillman looked over his shoulder as the Secretary of State looked through the photos and report. After a minute of silence he said, 'Problems . . . ?'

'Yes — it seems there's no end to them. These are new reconnaissance photos taken over the Mid-East. They show the anti-aircraft missile placements along the borders of Egypt and Syria. At least three-fourths of the sites are ready for use — more than we thought they could have operational so soon.'

'Enough to afford to start things up again?'

'More than enough, I'm afraid, with the tremendous increase in weapons they've received.' Wellmont shook his head. 'Yes, *more* than enough. I think we can safely assume that they are only waiting for some word from Moscow — an assurance that the United States is in no position to intercede in any new conflict.'

'And that word could come at any time, couldn't it?'

'Yes, at any time.' Wellmont laid the report on the desk. 'We still don't know if the Soviet counter-system, whatever it may be, is operational or not. Or what they intend to do with it.'

Hillman sat down in the chair near the desk. 'At least they don't know that we're on to it.'

'So we presume. But that's hardly enough at this stage of the game.'

Hillman nodded, frowning.'Are there any other options for handling it? Can we alert the United Nations — furnish them with evidence of the build-up?'

'I'm afraid that might only trigger an early attack. Besides,' Wellmont said sceptically, 'I doubt that the U.N. could rise to the occasion this time, any more than it has in the past. Certainly, the Communist block nations in the General Assembly will rally against any action.'

'So ... it still boils down to one thing — the success or failure of the mission.'

'I'm afraid so. And the rest of the conference will be riding on it as well. If we can't obtain the agreements we seek from the Soviets this time, we may never get them. We *can't* afford to return to the cold war status of the fifties.'

Wellmont sighed. 'And we have these other matters to attend to as well. We have to try to put an end to the divisions in NATO. The skirmishes in the past few years ...' he shook his head slowly. 'These petty wars threaten to tear down everything we've worked so hard to build.'

'I know. And what's frightening is the possibility that one of these days some stupid, minor territorial squabble is going to lock the superpowers into a conflict they can't avoid.'

'Which is all the more reason we can't afford to lose ground in our dealings with the Russians.'

Hillman was silent for a time. Then he said, almost to himself, 'I wish there had been some other way. ...'

'So do I,' Wellmont replied. 'I don't like these covert operations any more than you, Dan. But there simply was no other way. We can only hope and pray it will work.'

Hillman rose from the chair, 'We'll find out tomorrow, one way or another.' He glanced at his watch. 'I guess I'd better turn in — things are going to be starting early, and we've got a full day ahead of us.'

'All right. Good night, then.'

Hillman paused at the door. 'You should try to get some rest, sir.'

Wellmont's attention was already back on his notes for the conference. 'What? Oh, yes ... later, perhaps. I still have a few things to go over. See you in the morning, Dan.'

'Good night, sir.'

CHAPTER SIX

The sun was not yet up in Omsk when Miklos Nikovitch arrived at the military air base. After a brief phone call to the main military compound where Storkas' superior still waited, Nikovitch was in a government car heading for the Omsk Technical Institute.

Snow covered the road and progress was slow into the section of town where the institute was located. There were relatively few cars in Omsk anyway, but even had there been a greater need for clear roads, it would still have been impossible to keep them clear for very long from the continually settling flakes.

Nikovitch stirred impatiently in his seat as the car plodded forward. For all his country's might, he was being held in check for the moment by a simple whim of nature. Perhaps, he thought, the greatest obstacle they had to overcome was their own nation's intractable scale and natural phenomena.

Omsk was a relatively large city. Not as large as Moscow, of course, but comfortable enough in its close clutter of buildings. Nikovitch preferred it that way, having a quiet distaste for the great open expanses of land that so characterised the Soviet Union. It was perhaps a strange outlook for a man whose own humble beginnings had been in a small village on the edge of just such forest lands as those beyond Omsk. But it was not a strange outlook for one who preferred not to be reminded of his beginnings, of those times and conditions which preceded his slow and perilous rise to the top of his field. Nikovitch had no desire to think of those times, and even if he had, there could be no thought devoted to such recollections now. Not when there were important matters at hand.

The flight from Moscow had taken almost three hours, and although he could have used the time for sleep, he did not — in fact, could not. Instead, Nikovitch, the solitary passenger on the military jet, had spent the flight considering what he must do in the next several hours. And there would be much work for him. Depending on what he found when the capsule was brought in, he would have to alert sections of the network. Operatives in the United States would have to be contacted quickly, faceless people in obscure jobs who could get information about almost anything when necessary. Nikovitch did not like making even seemingly minor decisions without all the background information he could possibly accumulate. Perhaps none of this would be needed. Perhaps not, but Nikovitch thought it would . . . even hoped it would.

There had been occasions before, twice in fact, when charred fragments of American satellites and space hardware had dropped into regions governed by the Soviet Union. They had yielded little useful information in comparison to that easily gained through other means. But those had been only fragments, and in poor condition at that. Never before had an intact satellite been recovered for study, let alone one that posed the kind of bizarre problem this one posed.

Official statements would have to be made about the recovery of the American capsule and its canine occupant. These statements would be made by men higher in authority than Miklos Nikovitch, but the timing and the content of the official announcements would depend greatly on the status report received from Nikovitch. He would have the assistance of others in Omsk, but it would be his recommendation that would carry the most weight. For this reason, his decisions would have to be most carefully made. He could not afford to be wrong.

In the last remaining minutes of his ride, Nikovitch watched the factories move by his window in the immediate distance. Omsk was a true industrial centre and manufactured everything from farm machinery and electrical equipment to lumber products and foodstuffs. And there was a different kind of industry as well, an industry of research institutes and laboratories that produced quite another class of products, not all of which were for the direct benefit of mankind. Largest of these was the Omsk Technical Institute, and it was that research facility which lay immediately ahead.

The official car turned into the wide, curving driveway of the institute and stopped in front of the gate. Momentarily leaving the warmth of the tiny gate house, the guard emerged to check credentials before admitting the car. Appearing more decorative than defensive, the tall ironwork fence and gate that surrounded the institute grounds was more than adequate protection in this land of rigid enforcement of laws, especially with the squads of guards that could be called forth at a moment's notice.

Letting Nikovitch out at the entrance, the driver took the vehicle around the back to a sheltered parking area. More than just a driver, the man was one of Nikovitch's agents in Omsk, as were most of the institute guards, and would be assigned to him during the director's stay.

The thickset Director of Internal Security moved up the steps of the institute's librarylike façade with surprising lightness, and was quickly ushered in by another guard. As the door was closed, shutting out the cold and bleakness behind him, a man appeared from the opposite end of the large foyer, coming towards him with a deliberate swiftness.

'Miklos . . .' the man said simply, stopping in front of the director and extending his hand. 'When you called from the air base I was still asleep . . . the night guard gave me your message, but I am afraid it was not very clear.'

'I know, Otto,' Nikovitch said flatly, his words accompanied by a short, sweeping gesture of his hand. 'I will explain further. We can use your office.'

'Yes, of course.' As they walked, the man checked his watch. 'None of our regular personnel will be arriving for almost another hour yet. Do you wish that I close the institute? Shall I order any emergency precautions taken —'

Nikovitch shook his head. 'No. Unnecessary. You will conduct your daily routine as usual, Otto. And there is no need for above-average precautions. Once the capsule is delivered here, we will take it directly to the security section. There will be more than adequate safety there.'

'Good. I am glad that we do not have to disrupt activities. We have too many projects which must not fall behind schedule.' The one addressed as Otto fell silent as they entered a hall at the end of the foyer. He was as tall as Nikovitch, but more slender in build. His light brown, almost blond, hair was combed to the side from a high peak above his forehead. And although his words were in almost flawless Russian, the colour of his accent was decidedly German.

At the point where the hall turned to the right, a door was located in the left wall, just before the corner. The metal plaque on the door bore the name *Otto Hurdein*, and below that in smaller Russian letters, the title, *Administrator, Omsk Technical Institute*. Otto admitted Nikovitch, then entered and closed the door behind him.

It was forty minutes later, six-thirty a.m. Omsk time, when Captain Dimitri Storkas and his recovery team arrived at the institute. Their tracked vehicles rolling smoothly forward on the snow-carpeted road, they were checked through the gate and were soon at the side loading entrance of the building. Engines stilled, Storkas climbed out of his vehicle to supervise the unloading of the capsule.

Storkas was tired, cold and tired, and he knew his men could be no less so than he. He was glad that his work was over now, but still his relief at completing his mission was diminished by the presence of the institute guards who now swarmed out of the building to assist them. Dimitri had always felt uncomfortable around these coldly efficient men who masqueraded as simple guards, but who were in truth much more. He seldom had official contact with these men, but he encountered them often enough in unofficial activities. They, like he and most other officers from the army base, spent what free hours they had in the public places of Omsk. In that respect at least, they were the same. But in all others, they were worlds apart. The institute guards, agents of what government group Storkas could only guess, were tight-lipped men who avoided direct fraternisation with the army personnel. And their enmity seemed to Storkas not so much due to suspicion or duty as to plain elite arrogance. Whatever the case, Storkas was a soldier and had no appreciation for intrigue or the questionable methods of secret police.

The leader of the institute guards was directing his own men as the capsule was lifted down from the rear of the snow-track, and he made no attempt to address Storkas. Under ordinary circumstances, such disrespect would have irritated Dimitri, even though he would have done nothing to incur the wrath of the guards' higher-ups. But on this occasion Storkas wanted nothing more than to leave quickly and to be on his way to the tiny Ukrainian village where guests were preparing for a wedding.

Moving carefully, the guards carried the capsule through the loading entrance and down a ramp within the building. The leader of the men paused momentarily at the door, looking to Storkas.

Dimitri ignored him and returned to the lead vehicle, reached for the radio transceiver handset and pressed the switch. 'The capsule has been delivered, sir,' he said into the mouthpiece.

There was silence for a moment, then the voice of his superior officer came through the earpiece. 'Good — there were no further difficulties?'

'No, sir. About my injured man — it seems needless now to transport him further without a proper cast on his leg. Shall I take him to the city clinic?'

'Yes, you may as well,' his superior directed. 'His vehicle and crew shall remain there to bring him back as soon as he is attended to ... and you are to report back here now. Once everything is taken care of, we can all use a little rest.'

'Yes, sir.' Dimitri paused briefly, and when he spoke again, his tone was slightly different. 'And sir — about my leave ... ?'

There was a hesitation at the other end of the transmission. 'All right, Dimitri. As soon as you've returned and checked in your equipment we'll get the information for the necessary reports. And you will have to change uniforms before you begin your leave. I will arrange for transportation back to the railroad station if you wish.'

Storkas managed a smile. 'Thank you, sir.'

There was no further reply from the radio unit and Dimitri placed the handset back in its latched position. He was about to re-enter the vehicle when a firm hand tapped his shoulder.

'Captain,' a voice said, and Dimitri turned to see that it belonged to the leader of the institute guards. 'One moment.'

'Yes?' Storkas stood rigidly still, eyeing the man, fearful that he might be detained.

'A few questions first ... before you leave.' The man had a detached confidence in his manner that struck Dimitri the wrong way.

'I am under orders to report back as soon as possible.' Storkas replied stiffly.

'Yes, of course. But this will not take long, Captain. First of all, I must know if anything on the capsule has been disturbed.'

'It is exactly as we found it – my orders stated that we do nothing to the capsule, and those orders have been followed.'

The man seemed sceptical. 'You are sure the cover was not opened at all ... perhaps to let air in or to check the animal inside?'

'No,' Storkas said. He sensed the man's arrogance becoming more pronounced, and it irritated him. Still, he tried to avoid showing it. 'As I told you, we did nothing to disturb the capsule or its contents. Our orders were explicit.'

'Very good. I am sure our leaders will be pleased by your efforts.' The man smiled annoyingly, then looked back towards the rear of the first vehicle, then the second. 'And one other thing – I notice that you seem not to have brought the parachute which was attached to the capsule. ...'

'It was ensnared in the branches of a tall tree. I had to cut the lines on it to retrieve the capsule. It was impossible to retrieve the parachute as well.'

162

'Impossible?'

'Yes,' Dimitri replied, a bit of his irritation creeping into his tone. 'But you should know this ... since you seem to be aware of our radio transmissions during the mission.'

The man's features lost some of their sureness. He avoided a direct answer. 'I do not know if our scientists will need the parachute or not, Captain, or how soon they might require it if they do ... but I am sure if it should be needed, your superior will send someone to retrieve it.'

'No doubt he will,' Storkas said flatly. Had he been a fool, he might have added that unless the order came within the next few hours, he would be well on his way out of Omsk — that someone else would have to head the retrieval mission. Had he been a fool, he might have said many things ... things he would have regretted later. But Storkas was no fool. And he also doubted that such a mission would be necessary anyway. What purpose would be served in retrieving the parachute? No, he was sure the man was only toying with him, flexing his power.

Dimitri managed a cold and casual look of his own. 'Is that all you wished to ask?'

The man studied him a moment, eyes narrowed. Then he nodded affirmatively and turned on his heels, entered the building and bolted the loading doors from the inside.

Storkas quickly entered his own vehicle, waited while the engines of the two snow-tracks were started, then directed his driver to leave the institute grounds. Once clear of the gate, the lead vehicle turned in the direction of the city clinic, with the second vehicle following. And once he had left his junior officer in capable hands, Storkas would waste no time in returning to the base. ...

Miklos Nikovitch and Otto Hurdein were walking quickly from the administrator's office in the institute at that moment. They were continuing along the other hall this time, heading deeper into the building.

'I want a complete photographic series,' Nikovitch was saying, 'from the moment the capsule is opened. We must have a complete record of all details of the capsule's interior. If we should overlook something in the process of removing the dog, then at least we will have everything on film.'

'Yes, you are right. We have the necessary equipment here, and several security section personnel are standing by — I sent for them as soon as I received your message.'

'What about an expert to examine the dog?'

Otto nodded. 'Someone is on the way by now, or should be. I contacted the Veterinary Institute and au nor their best and most trusted doctor.'

'We will have to work quickly,' Nikovitch said, his features impassive. 'It is a certainty that we will be hearing from the Americans soon.'

The men turned a corner and walked a short distance further, past several administrative offices, until they reached the polished metal door of an elevator. Nikovitch entered first, then Hurdein, who pressed the close-door button. But instead of pressing the button for an upper floor, he inserted a key from his vest pocket into a small opening at the bottom of the panel.

Instantly the elevator began moving down to a basement level not frequented by the regular institute personnel. As it whined to a halt, its door opened on a narrow corridor, white and clinical.

'The capsule will be in laboratory four,' Hurdein was saying as they emerged. 'I ordered it completely disinfected and sealed off. We will have to have routine bacterial testing of the interior of the capsule, and that was the easiest laboratory to isolate.'

'Will we be able to view the procedures?'

'Yes, there is a window between the outer section of the laboratory and the disinfected area.'

'Good. I will be interested in seeing what is found.'

Otto Hurdein paused a moment, then asked, 'One thing, Miklos ... are you sure you have explained everything to me — everything that you can, I mean — because you said before that the capsule containing the dog has been in orbit about the earth for over a year. I simply cannot understand how that could be possible, and the dog still be alive. . . .'

'At the moment,' Nikovitch replied, 'I am in no better position than you, Otto, to suggest an explanation.' He hesitated. 'I . . . I have a possibility in mind, only a theory. But I want to find out much more than I know now before I suggest it.'

At that moment, they reached the door to the outer section of the laboratory numbered *four*. Inside, their attention was drawn to the scene on the other side of the double glass panel.

The capsule was resting on an improvised stand near the window. Two men and a woman, dressed in white and all wearing surgical masks, were involved in the task of cleaning the outer surfaces of the capsule with disinfectant solution. The job was made more difficult by the roughened and scorched areas caused by re-entry into the Earth's atmosphere.

Nikovitch and Hurdein took up their places in front of the window. As the three on the other side of the glass completed their work with the disinfectant, the man in the centre looked up briefly at Hurdein, nodded, then returned his attention to the capsule.

'You have met Vladimir Dubuokov before, of course,' Hurdein stated, pointing towards the man. 'With his background in satellite systems, I thought it advisable to bring him in on this.'

Nikovitch nodded. 'How is he progressing on the counterdefence system?'

'He has almost completed the final calculations for us to adjust the equipment. How is the construction progressing?'

'Done, except for minor electrical connections. The communications system has just been tested out this week.' Nikovitch looked back to the man in the sealed-off laboratory. 'But Otto, I do not want Dubuokov distracted from his work too long by this satellite matter. When the Americans' Cerberus system goes into operation next week, we *must* have our own countermeasures in operation as well. I do not have to tell you the threat their system poses to us — the danger if they can destroy our offensive and defensive missiles, while their own can still be launched

165

against us. That kind of untouchable power would tempt even the most benign of nations.'

Hurdein nodded, but with something less than conviction. 'Would it not be enough, Miklos, to merely operate our own Cerberus-like defence measures?'

The Director of Internal Security shook his head slowly. 'It will be more than a year before we can activate a system comparable to that of the Americans. Much could happen in that time. Besides, our leaders do not feel it is enough to just equal the Americans' system. For safety's sake, we must be in a position that is superior to theirs.'

'I suppose,' Hurdein replied. He watched as the scientist in the sealed-off laboratory worked on removing the bolts which held the capsule's hatch in place. 'But what if the Americans develop a countermeasure of their own — we will again be where we are now . . . a standoff.'

'That is not our worry, for now.' Nikovitch thrust his hands into his trouser pockets and gazed through the window into the lab. 'Anyway, they apparently could not think of an adequate countermeasure, or else they would not have decided on the type of defence system they chose. No — they think it is foolproof. It will take them some time to find out it is not.'

At that moment, the scientist removed the final bolt securing the capsule's hatch. He leaned towards an intercom unit on the wall.

'We are ready to begin, sir,' said the metallic voice from an overhead speaker.

'You have checked to be sure the satellite is pressurised?' Hurdein inquired.

'Yes. We could have assumed it, anyway, since from all indications this is the same as the other American bio-satellites. But we have tested the pressure at this valve —' he pointed to the oxygen inlet, '— so we do not have to worry about a sudden pressure equalisation.'

Hurdein nodded. 'Good. Go ahead and remove the hatch.'

The scientist reached over and flipped a switch that activated the large cameras located in an overhead rack.

Colour photos would be taken from this point on, one every quarter-second by each camera.

Next, he reached into the recessed area near the left side of the hatch and pried up the lever that would cause the seals to be broken about the inside edge of the large metal cover. He waited a moment, listening for a hiss of air that would indicate unequal pressure, but confident he would not hear it.

No sound came forth.

Quickly, he and his assistants grasped the lifting bars at the ends of the hatch. Raising the cover, they carried it to a laboratory table alongside the capsule stand and gently placed it there.

Through the window, Nikovitch and Hurdein stared hard at the reclining form within the capsule. The dog was lying motionless.

Nikovitch leaned closer to the glass. 'Is the animal still alive?'

Dubuokov, the scientist, reached into the capsule and placed a hand on the dog. One of his assistants, the woman, picked up a stethoscope.

Suddenly, Major started. His eyes opened, blinked several times, then focused on the strangely garbed people leaning over him.

In the dog's mind, there was a recollection of a similar scene. Less than a month ago, there had been other people dressed the same, bright lights, a strong scent in the air that assailed his nostrils and seemed to wipe out all other scents. Then another odour that brought drowsiness and finally sleep.

Major looked at these people. They were strangers, but there was nothing to indicate that they meant him harm, and there were as yet no voices from that new part of his mind that sometimes warned him of danger, or suggested answers to problems. For the moment, he felt safe.

For several long moments the assistant listened through the stethoscope, occasionally changing the position of the bell to another spot on the dog's chest. After the last check, she removed the instrument and replaced it on the stand to her left.

'Heartbeat and respiration appear normal,' the woman said. 'Shall I take the dog's blood pressure?'

'No,' Miklos said. 'We may as well wait for the veterinary doctor to arrive. He will make a complete medical examination.'

Dubuokov touched the padded harness that held Major in place. 'Shall I loosen the straps, Director?'

'Yes, go ahead,' Nikovitch began, raising a finger as his tone became more urgent. 'But as you do, be careful that you disturb nothing else. Observe how everything is connected.'

'Yes, Director . . . but the film —'

'Film is only a two-dimensional reality,' Nikovitch stated. 'Assuming it comes out properly, it is still only a helpful record. Do not trust completely to the automatic cameras to observe things for you.'

'Yes, Director.' Dubuokov fell silent and began to examine the straps and the rest of the capsule's interior. He checked to be sure there were no electrical connections of any kind within the strap sections, then began unfastening them.

Major lay still during this process, and did not attempt to move even after the last remaining strap had been undone. Dubuokov patted the dog, then examined the bio-sensor connections adhered to the animal's body. Tracing the wires back to their source, he noted with no great surprise the radio telemetry unit to which they were attached. Then he noticed the other device that received input information from the life-function monitor. Staring through the transparent Plexiglas plate of the device, he studied the two reels of paper within, and the tiny marking arms that were still tracing muddled, overlapping lines across the faint chart markings.

After several minutes' examination of the strange mechanism, Dubuokov turned his attention to other things within the capsule. A few of the devices were not familiar to him as being part of a standard bio-satellite — either

168

American or Russian. One thing in particular attracted his attention – the device whose connecting cable and needle probe was now apparently out of place. He reached in and pulled the needle probe from the side padding of the capsule, then examined it, calling for a magnifying lens from one of his assistants. Enlarged with the aid of the lens, the needle bore traces of a crusty brown residue that was dried out, but still relatively fresh.

'What have you found?' Nikovitch called out.

Dubuokov looked through the lens another two seconds, then looked up to the director. 'I am not sure yet. This device here seems to have been connected to the dog at one time – until just recently, in fact. But I do not know what it is, not without further examination. And there is a paper graph roll which is connected to the medical telemetry equipment. We will probably have to have a computer analysis of the information before we can be sure of anything.'

'See that it is done, then.' Nikovitch seemed to be losing patience as his interest in the nature of the satellite increased. 'I want everything in there examined completely – everything! And see that you are careful not to leave too many traces of your work. Everything must be replaced before we return the satellite to the Americans.'

'Yes, Director.'

'Miklos,' Otto Hurdein said softly. 'The Americans will know anyway that the capsule has been thoroughly examined. They will expect it.'

'Of course,' Nikovitch answered, a slight smile curling his lips. 'They will know it . . . but why leave the evidence there in plain sight to tell them? Let us not make our counterparts' work too easy for them, Otto. These things must be done properly.'

Hurdein sighed. 'I am afraid the rules of the game are too complex for me, my friend. But we each have our jobs to do, and I am glad you can do yours with such skill.'

At that moment, one of the institute security personnel came down the hall and into the room. He carried with him several wide sheets of facsimile printout paper.

'This information as just been transmitted to us from Moscow,' the guard said, addressing them both but handing the printout sheets to Nikovitch. 'They are copies of news releases which have come out in various American and European newspapers and television sources, only a while ago. Translations are alongside each article. And —' he pointed to the bottom sheet, 'and the last is an official message received by Moscow from the Americans, regarding the satellite.'

Nikovitch dismissed the guard and quickly scanned the information contained in the articles. 'The same. All the same — a general news release and accompanying photo.' He handed one of the copies to Otto Hurdein.

Hurdein read briefly through the text, looking also at the photo alongside it. He looked up suddenly, a look of vague surprise upon his features. 'But — this states that the satellite was launched less than a month ago ... that the dog was merely part of a project to test a new medical telemetry system.'

'Yes, but we know better! We have tracked that satellite for over a year, since the time of its launch. And there were no launches of any kind on the date mentioned in that article.'

'Yet this photo,' Hurdein continued, looking back to the printout sheet, 'it clearly shows the dog at some facility in America ... and there is a car in the picture, with a licence plate showing this year's date — I need no translation to recognise that!'

Miklos shrugged. 'Then either it is another dog in the picture or it has been retouched. You do have someone on your staff who can detect such things?'

'Yes, of course.'

'Then see it is done.'

Hurdein nodded, still frowning at the photo and article. 'This statement explaining the satellite is puzzling, though.'

Nikovitch folded his hands and began to rub his thumbs together. 'Probably that is not designed to mislead *us* so much as their own people. Unless they think us so foolish as to not recognise the experiment for what it is!'

'But why should they try to keep their experiments in the space programme secret from their own people?'

'Who knows? Perhaps they are afraid of failure. Besides, the Americans are a strangely sentimental people. They might permit thousands of stray dogs to die of starvation in alleys, and thousands more to be put to death in dog pounds; but just launch *one* into space and the cries of protest will be heard from every quarter.'

'What is the content of the official message from the Americans?'

Nikovitch glanced down at the sheet. 'It is what we could expect — a carefully worded explanation of how their satellite has "accidentally" lost orbital velocity and descended here, coupled with an appeal for all possible assistance in recovering it. All the right diplomatic manoeuvres.'

'Then we are going to be pressed for time.'

'Yes, we will have to work fast. Obviously, the Americans would like to pressure us through public opinion, so that the satellite does not become an extra bargaining piece in the conference tomorrow. But we can buy some time yet. We will send word back to Moscow for an official statement to be made ... the content of which is that our technicians are aware of the satellite's descent; recovery teams have been sent out to find it, but are hampered by difficult weather conditions in the search area; all possible aid will be given, and we will inform the Americans as soon as the capsule is retrieved and its condition determined.'

'I understand,' Hurdein replied. 'And I will have someone working on this photo immediately.'

'Excellent. Oh, and one other thing, Otto —' Miklos added. 'Send word to my subordinate, Alexi, to keep me informed of all new intelligence information. And regarding my earlier orders to him about one of our observation satellites — as soon as possible, I want the photos it takes of the American's destroyer satellite. He can transmit them to me here through the facsimile printout equipment.'

'Yes, Miklos, I will attend to that as well.'

'There are still several questions we must answer,' Nikovitch stated coldly. 'We must learn why the Americans decided to destroy their experiment in suspended animation ... and we must learn also why they failed.'

CHAPTER SEVEN

A round of brief but joyous cheers went up in the mission control centre as the first real images appeared on the surface of the giant visual-display screen. The momentary flash of light earlier when Captain Dimitri Storkas examined the capsule had told them that the dog was on the ground and alive, but little else. The continuing medical telemetry data had already told them that much, anyway. What they needed was to 'see' exactly where he was, and the circumstances in which the dog now found himself.

And now they *could* see. Everything Major was seeing.

'Have we done it?' General Matthews was asking. 'Can we be sure of the exact location?'

All eyes were on the display screen. The image was at a slight angle, and only showed the upper part of the laboratory, the people from the waist up, and occasionally the overhead cameras and lights – Major's view as he lay in the capsule.

'Sir, I've checked through the communications network,' Bill Stanton addressed the general, turning from his console. 'We've tried triangulating the signal from our stations in Europe and from the military satellite system, but the best we can do is determine that the capsule is somewhere near the centre of Omsk. At this distance, we just can't pin down the exact area.'

'But we must know.' Matthews continued. 'We cannot simply assume that the dog has been taken to the Omsk Technical Institute. The course of the mission from this point on will depend entirely on the dog's present location. We have a very limited amount of flexibility in the plan.'

Arnold Smith was staring at the display screen with an odd concentration. He seemed to be doing mental comparisons, trying to match the image with something already stored in his mind.

'General,' Joyce Kandell said quietly. 'What if ... what

does the plan call for in the case that Major can't complete the mission?'

Matthews turned abruptly and stared at her, as if the mere mention of such a possibility was a bad omen. After a moment, his look of reproach faded. 'In that case, Miss Kandell, our orders are simply to play out the charade to the end. We will recover the dog, extend the gracious thanks of the American people for the generous assistance of the Russian people ... make all the appropriate arrangements, let rumours slip out through the right channels that new projects are underway to adapt our suspended animation techniques to future manned missions ... the works. If necessary, the "experiment" can be termed a partial failure later on, and it will be forgotten by their scientists. Hopefully. They may guess what this was all about eventually, but I would rather have them wondering than knowing.'

Joyce nodded in understanding. 'And if they should discover the trick before the dog has been returned ... then what?'

Matthews looked down, his patience dwindling. 'Miss Kandell ... I understand and appreciate your concern about this mission, and the dog. But have *some* trust in us. There are certain bargaining pieces we can use, if necessary, to insure the return of the dog. But I should add that the primary need for recovering the dog is to deny the Russians what propaganda value they might derive from the incident.'

'Yes, sir ... I understand.'

There was silence again in the huge room, a silence which was broken a minute later by Arnold Smith.

'I don't think we have to worry just yet, General,' Smith said softly. 'It is fairly certain that the room which we are seeing is a laboratory somewhere within the Technical Institute.'

The General looked back to the display screen, then over to Smith. 'How can you be sure?'

'For one thing, the only places they would have been likely to take the dog and capsule were either to one of their veterinary research centres or the institute itself. For studying the capsule, the institute is far more likely. Besides, the equipment I see in the room is more typical of a multipurpose laboratory than a medical one.'

'I can see your point so far,' Matthews replied. 'Go on —'

'The real clincher is the man you see leaning towards the capsule, examining the internal devices.' Smith paused, while they all stared at the image. 'That man is Vladimir Dubuokov. I have seen a photo of him before, and I know from an earlier report from our lost agent that Dubuokov is at the Technical Institute, and *working on the counter-Cerberus project.*'

Matthews stared at the figure on the display screen image, and his eyes narrowed as a smile formed. He sucked in a breath of air and exclaimed softly, 'Well, hallelujah and praise be to the General Staff!'

Ryan Halper had been watching the unorthodox scene before him intently. The image on the display screen had an almost hypnotic effect on the viewer. The high-contrast picture with its shades of black, white, and one intermediate grey was somehow eerie and unreal, an effect heightened by the total silence that accompanied the scene.

'I just wish we could hear what they're saying,' he said suddenly.

Matthews turned slightly. 'You're not the only one, Lieutenant!'

Over at the communications console, James Neston frowned self-consciously. He walked over to the table where Halper and Joyce were standing beside their pushed-back chairs.

'The choice wasn't entirely a free one, Lieutenant,' Neston explained. 'We found that the broadcast unit of the implant could handle only one coded signal. Actually, it would have been considerably easier to tap the dog's auditory input and relay that back. But when it boiled down to a choice of either hearing what was going on, or seeing it, the decision was relatively simple.'

Halper nodded. 'Makes sense.'

'We're not completely shackled by our lack of sound, however,' Neston continued. 'Fortunately, I understand that

Mr. Smith has a rather thorough knowledge of Russian. . . .'

Matthews nodded grimly. 'And unfortunately, there are a great many languages easier to lip-read than Russian.'

'Worse yet,' Smith himself added, facing away from the image-display screen for the first time, 'as long as they're wearing those surgical masks, they may as well not be speaking at all!'

'That shouldn't last too long,' the general said. 'Once they've completed their bacteriological analysis of the capsule I'm sure they'll dispense with the masks.' Matthews studied the image a few moments more, then turned to look at the clock over the communications console. The hour was quarter after eight in the evening. 'Now that contact has been established, is it possible someone could attend to the matter of dinner?'

James Neston reached for the black phone. 'I'll have something sent over from the commissary.'

'But see that the regular security precautions are maintained,' Matthews cautioned. 'We don't want to blow it at this stage of the game!'

'Of course, General.' Neston busied himself with the phone call for the next several minutes, slighly irked by Matthews' unnecessary warning regarding security. In his job as Assistant Administrator, Office of D.O.D. and Interagency Affairs, he had dealt with a considerable number of Pentagon bigwigs and other high-ranking military personnel. All of them had the same things in common – a rigid adherence to rules and procedures, job pressures that often led to a kind of mild paranoia, and a general distrust of civilian security operations. That last tendency was ironic, he thought, since military security personnel had endured more than their fair share of leaks and monumental errors. So Neston had heard on his own and from associates, at any rate. Or was that, he wondered, just a *civilian*'s general distrust of *military* security?

The system for ferrying food over to the mission control would be the same as it had been for the noon meal – an appropriate number of covered trays, destined supposedly for the VIP Guest Centre on the NASA facility, would be taken by an unmarked van to the alley behind the squat grey two-storey building which housed the mission team. The plain metal box containing the trays would attract no great amount of attention as it was carried into the unfinished building in which work still presumably continued. Left with the security guard inside, it would be brought to the door of the big room, and the Green Beret, who had little to do now but stand and watch the activities, would transport it the final short distance.

It was a relatively simple procedure, compared with some that had been necessary on occasion. But the simple plans worked best. That had been Neston's experience in the past and there was no reason to believe it would not hold true now. There always had to be a careful balance between the minimum amount of security necessary and the maximum amount that would be possible. In fact, even the minor precautions involved in this particular food transfer might seem unnecessary to the average person. It seemed unlikely that Russian agents would be on the facility's grounds ... or on the NASA payroll. Neston knew better than to accept that premise on blind faith ... knew better than to risk it. He completed the call and hung the receiver on the telephone's cradle.

Colonel Brunning left the table at Matthew's silent beckoning, leaving Halper and Joyce Kandell by themselves. Both had again taken their seats, and they glanced at each other with tired expressions.

'Dinner! I'd forgotten all about it,' Joyce said. Her finger drew aimless circles on the tabletop. 'In here, it's hard enough to keep track of time under ordinary circumstances. And these few last few hours have been a long way from ordinary. ...'

Halper nodded slowly. 'We still have a ways ahead of us, too.' He sighed. 'That's the real killer — having your real work ahead of you and having to wait, unable to do anything ... trying to stay alert for it.'

'How long do you think the Russians will be examining Major?'

He shrugged. 'Four or five hours, at least. More likely

177

half a day or more. But they'll have to take a break sometime, if only to wait for lab reports or something. My guess is that's when we'll have to make our move.'

Joyce sighed. 'I guess that will give us a chance to sleep tonight . . . if I can.'

'You'd better – we've been up and going for the last seventeen hours.' Halper gestured towards a stack of Army cots near the far wall. 'It may have to be in shifts, but we should be able to get at least a few hours sleep.'

On the other side of the room, Brunning was in conference with Matthews. The subject of their discussion was the NASA Administrator, Dr. Laswell.

'If you ask me, General,' Brunning said evenly, 'the man's actions border on treason.'

'Perhaps.' Fatigue was showing in Matthews' features and stance. 'But we must remember that from his point of view as administrator, he's entirely justified. Although I don't agree with him, I can at least understand his position. We've put him in a bind and he's fighting back the only way he can.'

'But he's endangering the mission,' Brunning replied. He glanced towards Joyce Kandell. 'In more ways than one.'

'Perhaps he is. But that does not make our options any pleasanter. We can't comply with him, of course. But his deadline will be firm, I'm sure, and I don't see how we can conclude the mission before tomorrow morning. In fact, there's almost no chance of it. And if we continue after that hour, Laswell will go ahead with his threat to notify congressional leaders. He has to – he feels it is the only way he can save the image of the space agency. What else would he have left, short of a public protest and resignation?'

'Maybe his resignation would be for the best.'

'But it would not help us here and now, and probably not in the long run, either. What it boils down to is this – somehow we must prevent him from contacting anyone tomorrow.'

Matthews paused, rubbing his fingers across the creases in his forehead. Talking more to himself, he said, 'I'm

178

supposed to retire this month. If I have to end my career with a failure ...' He let out a tired, trembling breath, then turned back to the colonel. 'Have you any suggestions?'

Brunning considered. 'It would be pointless to merely prevent any communications from leaving the space centre. Laswell would simply leave, as long as he had his freedom.'

Matthews nodded.

'We could place him under house arrest.'

'Yes ... we could.' Matthews was silent a moment, looking off into space. He turned to Brunning with a grim, hard look. 'And we may have to. But Colonel, I want you to realise how dangerous ... just how *very* dangerous, such an action would be.'

In New York City at that moment, it was twenty minutes after nine in the evening. Most office buildings were empty of people, except maintenance workers, for the night. But the offices of *News-Scene* magazine never closed completely.

D. Thomas Lawrence wrapped the remains of a corned beef on rye in its wax paper shroud, shoved it unceremoniously off the edge of his desk and into the wastebasket below. After a final sip of tepid coffee, the paper cup followed the same path.

Tie hanging at half-mast below his open shirt collar, Lawrence leaned forward against his desk, studying the evening newspaper. He seemed not to notice when Jack Myerson ambled up before him and stood waiting for several moments.

'If you're going to goof off, Larry,' Myerson said finally, 'you may as well do it at home.'

'So who's goofing off?'

'That's right – don't tell me, I've heard it before. The Lawrence credo: "the professional reporter works twenty-four hours a day ... mind always alert and gathering information." Is that how it goes?'

'Roughly,' Lawrence said. 'But as usual, you have a tendency to misquote your sources, Jack. What are you doing out of the sports department?'

Myerson sat on the edge of the desk. 'It's a dead night. A dead week, for that matter. We go to press tomorrow afternoon, and there isn't one significant sports story for this week's issue — would you believe it?'

Lawrence began to tear the front page article he was reading from the paper. 'So run a filler on the evils of government intervention in the field of professional athletics.'

'We did that two weeks ago — or don't you read my section any more? Anyway, we'll probably have to run another personality profile ... unless the Green Bay Packers announce their simultaneous retirement before two p.m. tomorrow ... or Muhammad Ali challenges Arnold Palmer to fifteen rounds. ...'

Myerson watched as Lawrence folded the newspaper clipping and placed it in a file folder in the top right-hand drawer of his desk. The rest of the paper was tossed overboard, perching rooflike on the brimful wastebasket.

'All right, Larry.' Myerson sighed. 'So what's up?'

'I'm not sure yet.'

'You must have a rough idea — any time you get that predatory look in your eye —'

'You read about that dog — that U.S. space project that fizzled somehow and landed in Russia?'

'Sure, who hasn't by now? But that's the dailies' big item for the moment. We'll probably have a follow-up on it next week, but that'll be handled by our regular correspondents.' He tapped the nameplate on Lawrence's desk. 'It's certainly nothing to worry an associate editorial writer with ... not unless you want to tackle it from the point of view of government waste.'

'That's not quite what I had in mind.'

'What, then?'

Lawrence hesitated. 'Something's up — what, I'm not sure. But it strikes me as odd that something like that would happen right now. Especially with that delay in the President's trip.'

'But that delay was announced yesterday.'

'Yes, I know. But certainly it must have been known

180

before then that the satellite's orbit was decaying, and where and when it would land.'

'So?'

'So it's possible there could be some connection between the two. I've been wondering anyway about that thin excuse they gave for delaying the trip.'

Myerson shrugged. 'There could be any number of political reasons. And maybe there really were technical problems.'

'Maybe. But there are other "coincidences". Yesterday, out of a clear blue sky, the new NASA Administrator suddenly cancelled out of a special interview session for a feature we had scheduled to run soon. He's reportedly left Washington, but I've been unable to find out where he's gone. So I can't help thinking that lost satellite has created quite a stir.'

'Wouldn't it ordinarily?'

'To some extent. But it could create even more problems if it wasn't just a simple medical telemetry experiment. The fact that a dog of that type was used started me thinking.'

Myerson seemed more interested. 'How do you mean?'

'Do you remember a short news item about six or seven months ago about the military's experimentation with animals? Not long after the "super dog" programme ... and the Navy's dolphin programme?'

'Yeah, I think so — but there wasn't much said about it at the time.'

'No, I know — just a few sparsely worded statements. Then nothing. A complete clamp-down on information from military sources.'

Myerson digested the statement for a moment. He frowned. 'You're suggesting the satellite might have had a military purpose of some kind, and that our side is just falsely claiming it was connected with civilian research?'

'Why not?'

'That could get pretty tacky. Both for them to attempt it and for us to try to expose it.'

Lawrence snorted. 'As far as our side attempting it, I'm sure it would be no more restrictive from a political

181

viewpoint than any of the other projects the military-science boys have been involved with lately. And as far as I'm concerned, if there has been any irresponsible experimentation in outer space funded by public money, then people have a right to know about it.'

'If it is some kind of military project, though, then how do you figure the NASA Administrator is involved?'

'I don't know ... I haven't put it all together yet. But I will.'

'I thought your main assignment right now was the summit conference.'

'Every newspaper and magazine in the country will be covering that in one way or another. Some might even mention the satellite incident as a political factor. But if I can get a different angle on it — if I can uncover a real story ...'

Myerson looked uncomfortable. 'You know, this isn't exactly the best time for another super exposé of military matters, Larry. You know what a touchy state of affairs the media is in right now.'

'Which is a good reason not to back down. You never win anything by surrendering. I'm convinced that the only way to insure that no political restrictions are placed on the press in this country is to have the support of the people — and the best way to do that is to keep them informed of what's really going on behind the scenes. Especially the corruption and deception, when we find it.'

Myerson slowly shook his head. 'It's not that easy to figure out the American public.' But Lawrence's slight look of disgust demanded a further response. 'All right — so maybe I'm not as avid a crusader as I should be! You do well enough for both of us, anyway. But the thing is, I'm beginning to think the situation isn't so simple, isn't so ... black and white as it may look. How do you balance the public's right to know with the genuine need for secrecy in certain instances? What if — just supposing you're right about this item — what if an article on it causes real harm either to our country's security or the national image? What then?'

Lawrence forced his chair back suddenly from his desk

with a brief grunt of a laugh. 'Sure! The fate of the entire free world depends on one dog!' His mocking expression quickly faded. 'No, I'll give you the benefit of the doubt and assume you're merely stating a hypothetical situation. Okay. Look at it this way — if I investigate, the most I can find out is the truth. If there's nothing to my pet theory, fine. All I'll be out is some time and effort, and maybe a plane fare if ol' Harry J. is in a bad mood.'

Myerson nodded. 'The boss has made it pretty clear that the days of unlimited travel expenses are gone for good.'

Lawrence shrugged off the interruption. 'Even in that case, I should still get enough to work up an editorial on the whole issue of animal research for military purposes. I'll have that at the least. If the incident is somehow connected with some top-secret programme, I'd be willing to bet that it's only a secret to the American public! The old war-secrets angle doesn't apply anymore. We're not at war with the Russians. The Cold War itself has faded, and all we're stuck with now is a *Hardware War* which is draining the country's finances. No, Jack — I just can't agree with your theories. The only way to put an end to that kind of wasteful nonsense is to expose it.'

'Yeah. The only trouble is, the Russians don't have a free press to expose their military shenanigans. So how do we stop them?'

Lawrence sighed in exasperation. 'Look — go write your World War II memoirs or something, will you. I've got to get ready if I'm going to catch a plane out tonight.'

Jack Myerson shook his head sadly and ambled away.

With no further distraction, Lawrence concentrated on his own thoughts. Jerking open the top file drawer on his desk, he quickly flipped through the crowded manila folders of accumulated clippings until he came to the one clipping he sought. Skimming through the lines of type, his finger abruptly halted on the word *ARDCOM*, and he jotted down the midwestern location of the base, grateful that information on the installation had been made known at a time before the security clamp-down. Slipping the small notebook back in his shirt pocket, Lawrence reached for the phone.

3   He punched out the sequence of digits on the buttons, this time unappreciative of the number's melody on the touch-tone unit. He waited. Three rings and the beginning of a fourth, then he heard the receiver at the other end lift up and a silky voice answer.

Lawrence smiled. 'Angie, this is Larry. Look, I want to stop by for a minute. ... No, just a minute – I've got to leave something off before I go to the airport. ... No, I shouldn't be gone more than a few days at the most – look, I'll explain when I get there, okay? ... Okay, see you in about forty-five minutes.'

Hanging up, he shoved the file drawer closed with his knee and grabbed a scratch pad. He scribbled out a quick message, slipped the sheet of paper into an envelope, sealed it and scrawled the executive editor's name on it, and tossed it into the *Out* box on his desk.

Pulling open the top left-hand drawer, Lawrence extracted a small cassette recorder and a handful of extra cassettes. These he dropped into a flight case which was already packed with underwear and toilet articles. The case was always kept ready and waiting beneath his desk for just such spontaneous travel plans.

Lawrence took a brief moment to scoop the personal items from the top of his desk into the knee-well drawer, then locked everything. Pulling his tie up snugly against his collar, he left his chair, grabbing his coat on the way out of the office.

The garage where his car was parked was seven blocks away. It cost him a small fortune for the luxury of keeping a car in the city, but he valued the increased mobility it gave him. He walked swiftly, avoiding others on the side-walk with an instinctive caution in the late evening's chill.

Traffic was still fairly congested when he pulled his car on to the avenue. As he drove, he used one hand to bring out his cassette recorder and set it on *record*. Speaking into the microphone, he stated his name and position with *News-Scene*, the date, and an introductory 'to-whom-it-may-concern' explanation of his plan to investigate a possible connection between the satellite incident and an earlier report concerning military experimental research with dogs. He stated his plan to travel by commercial transportation to the ARDCOM facility, then began to record some initial ideas for the article. He was done long before he reached the apartment building, the cassette in his pocket.

It took him twenty minutes to find a parking space, and he considered himself lucky at that. His own apartment building had a basement parking level, and he decided he would leave his car there later and catch a cab to the airport.

Once in the foyer of the building, he singled out the buzzer button labelled *A. Simons* and pressed it for two short bursts. He waited for a long moment in silence, then a voice issued forth from the wall-mounted speaker. The tone was slightly raspy, the speaker-cone perforated where some-one had poked a pencil through the grille, but the voice was still immediately recognisable.

'Who is it?'

'It's Larry, Angie.'

'Come on up.'

There was a buzzing snap as the lock at the end of the foyer released momentarily. Lawrence was through it in a second, closing the door behind him. The automatic elevator carried him to the twelfth floor and the door to 12-C was opening before he could knock. Lawrence frowned disapprovingly at the girl who stood within.

'What have I told you about that?'

'I checked through the peephole first!' She smiled. 'So no lectures. Besides, you said you don't have time. . . .'

Lawrence scowled unconvincingly and entered the apartment, watching as the girl bolted the door. Her long hair was in layers of blonde and light brown, falling casually about her shoulders, over the dark-coloured African print caftan she wore. She fit well with the room, he often thought. It was offbeat, its style a kind of pop-contemporary-antique mish-mash of furnishings that some-how worked well together despite their seeming incongruity. Angie was not the kinky type, just blessed — or cursed —

with a decorative bent, one whose variety and extremes seemed to balance in direct proportion the plainness of her secretarial job.

She turned from the door and faced him, a wistful smile on her lips. 'So — what perilous news mission is taking you away this time?'

'Please don't humour me, Angie — I'm in no mood for it tonight.'

'That's easy to see.' Then with more concern, she added, 'Okay, I'm *sorry*.'

'Let's call it even. Peace?' They kissed for a long, lingering moment, then Lawrence broke free, sooner than he really wished to.

'Look,' he began, fishing in his coat pocket for the cassette tape. 'I want to leave this with you, the usual arrangement.' He handed it to her, then removed his office desk key from the ring of keys in his pocket and handed that to her. 'You'd better hang onto that, too. It might be safer with you than with Myerson at the office.'

The girl looked at the tape and key, a growing expression of doubt and apprehension setting her features. Her eyes found his again.

'Larry, you're ... you're not going to investigate something that can get you into trouble, are you?'

He smiled faintly. 'These days, trouble is an occupational hazard for a reporter.'

'You know what I mean — be serious.'

'I am serious.' He studied the look in her eyes for a moment, then gently placed a hand against her cheek. 'All right, Angie — don't get so uptight. I'm certainly not going out looking for trouble ... not trouble for myself, at any rate. Just the facts. And it's probably no big deal.' He tapped the cassette. 'This is just for insurance. A preventive measure in case I should need it — nothing more. You know that. This isn't the first time I've left something with you for safekeeping.'

'No ... it isn't the first time. I just hope it isn't the last —'

'Now don't start that —'

'I mean it! I'm all for the crusading writer bit, Larry. I

186

understand what you're doing.' Her voice became less steady. 'But I keep having this crazy fear that one morning I'll read in the paper that you've been tossed in prison for exposing something top-secret, or ... or found in the river after you've done an article on organised crime. ...'

'I haven't done anything so terribly reckless yet.'

'No ... not yet.'

'And I don't intend to start now. But when I sense an important story in the works, I have to do something about it. I didn't get this far by just sitting in my office writing stories about the city beautification programme.'

'Is the job all you care about?'

Lawrence sighed wearily. 'You know it isn't.'

The girl turned and walked over in front of the glass and bamboo coffee table, placing the cassette and key in a square ceramic box on the table's surface. After a moment of silence, she again faced Lawrence.

'All right, you don't have to worry ... I'll take care of things at this end.' The silky quality of her voice was now somewhat strained.

'Fine ... I knew I could count on you. And like I said, there's nothing to worry about.' He hesitated a moment, checking his watch. 'Look, can I use your phone – I need to make sure there's a seat available on the midnight flight.'

'Why not.' The corner of her mouth curled down. 'Maybe I'll get lucky and all flights will be delayed.'

Lawrence checked his pocket directory and dialled the number of the airline's office at Kennedy Airport. The clerk on duty had the information he needed.

He hung up the phone. 'Flight's still on schedule. I'll have to go now, Angie – it will take me a while to get to the airport.'

'Well ... keep in touch, if you can. Drop me a postcard or something. ...'

'Of course.' He went to her, kissed her somewhat less enthusiastically than he would have liked, and headed towards the door.

Her voice called softly after him. 'Be careful. ...'

CHAPTER EIGHT

At eleven p.m. Houston time, most of the ARDCOM staff were sleeping, or trying to, despite the occasional hum of communications equipment and the steady glow of both the visual-display screen and the command building's interior lights.

In New York City, Larry Lawrence was boarding his midnight flight, ready for the usual droning, soporific journey through darkness. A journey of a few hours that would be punctuated by air pockets, stale cigarette smoke, and an occasional cheery visit from the stewardess.

In Brussels, Belgium, it was six a.m. The presidential party was already up and beginning preparations for the day's activities. The NATO meetings would not start for a few more hours, but in those few hours most of the diplomatic manoeuvring between parties would be settled, one way or another.

And in Omsk, U.S.S.R., it was ten in the morning. The city's daily activities were well under way by then, people working in the various industrial or manufacturing plants, buying what weekly needs they could afford, or working simply to maintain the city. Crates of cotton and woollen textiles, leather goods, and foodstuffs were being loaded into train cars of the Trans-Siberian railroad, bound for cities in both the eastern and western parts of Russia. New farming machinery bound for communes in the south also would be transported at least part of the way along the tracks of the Trans-Siberian and its branches . . . fragile threads of metal that spanned great sections of the Eurasian land mass.

And there were other activities as well, activities not known to the populace of Omsk.

In a small, simply furnished office on the far side of the security section beneath the Omsk Technical Institute, Miklos Nikovitch sat studying the Wirephoto of Major and the man with him. A celluloid cover sheet had been attached, with a red circle around the area of the car's licence plate. A number of other papers and messages nearly covered the top of the table behind which he sat.

Otto Hurdein abruptly entered the room, carrying another sheaf of papers in his hands. His brows were knitted in a look of concentration.

Miklos looked up. 'More information?'

'Yes, quite a bit.' Hurdein carefully laid the papers on the least occupied portion of the table. 'I had facsimile copies of the tracking logs sent from our satellite-watcher stations. They cover the period that the American capsule was in orbit — just over a year. I do not know if it will help us or not, but I thought —'

'Yes, yes ... a wise decision, Otto,' Nikovitch replied impatiently. 'What of the photos showing the American destroyer satellite?'

Hurdein sifted through the pile of papers he had just deposited. 'I have them here — they were just transmitted a little while ago. Our photo-analysis personnel have looked them over briefly and formed some conclusions.'

'Good.' The Director of Internal Security pointed to the photo he held. 'And about this one — are they sure about the manner in which it was retouched?'

Hurdein nodded. 'Only the licence plate on the automobile was retouched ... that is really the only part that needed modification. It would have been too difficult to superimpose the dog on to the background, and there was nothing significant in the background anyway to suggest when the photo was made — except for the licence plate. And the edges of such an object are fairly sharp, making the retouching more simple. It is a good job, of course, but not quite perfect enough to avoid detection by an expert.'

'What about the man in the picture?'

Hurdein's eyes became more intense. 'That is the interesting part — for in checking through our file on American scientists, we have found one whose photo seems to match perfectly the man with the dog. His name is Corby, and he is a scientist with a background in veterinary medicine. He has worked on a number of government space projects utilising animals.'

'Well then, do you think his presence in the picture could be part of the American's charade — making it seem the project was ordinary?'

'Perhaps, but I do not believe that to be the case. You see, from what we have learned in recent months, this man Corby is also involved in their research efforts towards finding a workable reduced metabolism technique.'

Nikovitch leaned forward. 'That would seem to fit. But if that is the case, then why would they take such a photo?'

Hurdein shrugged. 'That I do not know. Perhaps at the time it was taken they had some other purpose for it. Perhaps they did not plan that it would be put to such a use as this.'

'Perhaps . . .' Nikovitch studied it a moment more, then placed the photo to one side and gestured towards the new stack of papers. 'Now, what of the pictures from our observation satellite?'

'Here —' Otto handed several of the facsimile printout sheets to him. The black-and-white images were remarkably sharp and clear, and superimposed upon the pictures was a faint sector grid for the sake of measurement approximations.

The first photo showed the disabled American destroyer satellite from an almost perfect side view, the odd tilt of the orbiting device obvious against the horizon line beneath it. Detail at this angle was relatively flat, the surfaces showing little in the way of shadow. But little detail was needed to display effectively the raw, gaping maw that remained where once the aft portion of the satellite had been.

In the second shot from the Russian observation satellite, taken with a long lens at a distance of less than a mile, the view was nearly three-quarters front. Orbit modification had swung the Russian device partway around the broken shell, offering greater shadow depth and proportionately better detail. It had also made visible the 'business' end of the unit — the area where the tiny missiles were launched.

'Here —' Otto pointed, 'you can see the vacant tubes, and some signs of the missiles' exhaust heat marring the front surface.'

'Yes ...'

Hurdein extended a third facsimile sheet. 'And here in this enlargement of that area, look at this spot, right ... *here.*'

Nikovitch strained to make it out. 'It ... it looks like the nose of one of the missiles.'

'It is.'

'Then one of them was not fired?'

'I think probably they all were activated, but apparently that one malfunctioned.'

'Why?'

Hurdein again shrugged. 'There is only so much we can tell from these photos. But I would guess that the release mechanism for the missile failed somehow, and the tube became jammed.'

'Could that explain the explosion?'

'Certainly it is possible.' Hurdein traced a line with his finger from the launching end of the satellite back to the rear. 'If the missile jammed, held in place within its tube, but the engine was still activated, there would have been an enormous heat buildup, perhaps more than the insulation had been designed to tolerate. And there are likely connecting pipes running back to the propellant tanks, or what were the propellant tanks, somewhere in this area, because several of the attitude-correction jets are located near the front of the device. If the heat burned through one of those pipes, or even if it was transferred back to the propellant tanks ... well' He made an expanding gesture with his hands, signifying an explosion.

'All right,' Nikovitch replied finally. 'We now know what might have caused the satellite's failure. But what we still have to answer is why the missiles that *did* fire did not totally destroy the bio-satellite and the dog, and for that matter, why the Americans should want to destroy it at all!'

Hurdein pondered the statement for a moment. 'The only thing we can assume, since the bio-satellite was unscathed, is that the missiles detonated before reaching their target. How or why I am not sure, unless it was tied in with the partial launching failure. That would explain why the dog's capsule was deflected from its established orbit. And as far as why they wished to destroy their experiment ... well, perhaps they did not. It might have been a simple miscalculation. Their target might have been some other bit of space debris.'

A chilling frown set Miklos' features. 'I cannot really believe that they made so large a mistake as to try destroying the wrong satellite!'

'Perhaps not, but the possibility must not be ruled out. It would be a colossal blunder, assuredly. But such mistakes have been made before. Even we, on occasion ...' he trailed off, shrugging his narrow shoulders.

'I think it more likely that they made the attempt out of some need to deny us the knowledge of their research, or to hide their work from the rest of the world.' Nikovitch leaned back in his chair. 'Hopefully, the answers will become clearer when we have learned more about the dog and the capsule.'

Hurdein checked his watch. 'If you wish, we can return to the laboratory. They should have some indication of the satellite's function by now.'

'Has the veterinary specialist arrived yet?'

'Yes, Miklos. The examination of the dog has been under way for an hour and a half so far.'

Nikovitch rose from his chair. 'Let us go see then what they have found out. ...'

Vladimir Dubuokov looked up from his work as Nikovitch and Hurdein entered the laboratory. He straightened from his bent position over a work table.

'Director,' Dubuokov addressed him, 'we are almost through with our initial studies. We have learned much already.'

'But obviously not everything.' Nikovitch studied the man and the carefully disassembled equipment laid out on the table before him. Then his eyes settled on a new face. On the other side of the laboratory, a woman garbed in white was in the process of taking a small blood sample from Major. 'Who is that?'

Dubuokov glanced over his shoulder automatically. 'That

192

is Dr. Ludmila Petrokova, from the Korsky Institute. She has been working on the medical examination of the dog.'

'I will want to talk to her later,' Nikovitch replied, looking back to the disassembled equipment. He folded his hands. 'But first I want to know what you have found out about the technical aspects of the satellite.'

'Yes, Director.' The scientist stepped over to the satellite, which was still resting on its improvised stand. 'Once we had completed out bacteriological tests on the capsule's interior, we were able to begin further examination of the equipment and systems. The bacterial analysis of course was completely negative ... we assumed that from the beginning.'

'Go on –'

Dubuokov took a breath and looked back at the capsule, rather than into the penetrating gaze of the director. 'As far as the majority of the equipment is concerned, it is the usual life-support and medical telemetry system used in previous bio-satellites – at least, from what we know of their satellites. The most obvious difference is simply that the available life-support resources are not enough for the amount of time the dog spent in space ... they are in no way near enough. Not if the dog's metabolism were operating normally.'

Nikovitch began to rub his thumbs together. 'But, if the dog's metabolism were abnormal?'

'Exactly. And there is a complete record of that metabolism ... here –' He returned to the table, pointing to the partially unreeled chart roll which had been removed from the automatic graph device. 'This was the easiest piece of equipment to disassemble, and the most important to study first. Obviously, the Americans employed this device to record the readings from the bio-medical sensors. Direct telemetry would have been difficult and risky since the rate of heartbeat and breathing – everything – was slowed to an incredible degree.'

'And also, undoubtedly, because such direct telemetry would have been picked up by us as well!'

'Yes ... but as I say, it would be exceedingly difficult, if not impossible, to monitor such a slow metabolic rate from Earth. This automatic mechanism makes more sense.' Dubuokov picked up a slender tool and used it as a pointer, indicating the flow of information lines on the elongated graph. 'As you can see here, the very beginning of the graph must represent the period just prior to the launching of the satellite. The dog's metabolic readings are already somewhat slower than normal, most likely due to the action of some drug administered shortly before launch.'

He traced the flow of graph lines further. 'The readings continue to slow, as their system gradually begins to take effect. See here – this minor variation on the graph – this must have occurred during the launch itself, but the dog's metabolic reaction to the stress is minimal. The heartbeat has slowed to less than one beat per hour at this point. Breathing also has decreased to an incredibly slow rhythm.'

Dubuokov had covered only the first few inches of the slow-motion graph. Dozens of yards more remained, of the unreeled portion alone.

'After a few days' time had elapsed,' he continued, 'the dog's life functions slowed even more, then finally settled into a regular pattern which continued until shortly after the moment the satellite began to fall back to Earth. At that point, with the graph device continuing at the same rate of speed, the dog's normal metabolism caused the readings to be compressed into a completely indecipherable mass of lines. But in the interval between the launch and re-entry, the graph shows that the dog's heartbeat rate was one per *day*. We have programmed the information on to tapes and are subjecting it to computer analysis now.'

'Very good,' Nikovitch said, without much enthusiasm. 'And while you have been working with that graph roll, have you had photos made of its entire length?'

Dubuokov hesitated. 'No, Director. Not as yet.'

'Well, see that it is done. The computer records of the information will assist in our research, but should any questions arise after we have returned the dog and capsule to the Americans, we may need to see how the original graph looked.'

'Yes, Director.'

'And it would be wise to photograph the monitoring device in its disassembled state. It may turn out to be useful. Now, what of the other equipment?'

The scientist moved to another table along the side wall of the laboratory. 'The medical telemetry transceiver could not be examined, unfortunately. Both the primary and back-up circuits are in the same sealed module, and the entire unit is encased in a solid plastic material – there is no way to open it without forcibly breaking it or cutting into it. And since you instructed us to leave no obvious signs of tampering . . .'

'Yes, of course. Do not worry about the transceiver, Dubuokov. I am sure its design is familiar to us.' Nikovitch headed towards the table where the scientist waited. 'One thing, though – have you any idea why the transmitter, which had been silent for so long, suddenly began to function once the capsule was deflected from its orbit?'

'Without checking the circuits, I can only guess, but I feel certain it was an automatic reaction once the dog's metabolism became normal again. Obviously while the project was going as planned, and the readings were being recorded on the graph roll, there was no need to waste the batteries' energy. The solar cells on the satellite's outer surface assisted in maintaining enough electricity for the device used to keep the dog dormant, but not enough to waste on needless transmissions. However, once the status of the animal changed, some signal would be necessary to alert their ground stations.'

'And what could have caused the dog's . . . return to normal?'

'It must have been quite a jolt,' Dubuokov said appreciatively, 'when the satellite was deflected. The intravenous connection that we found stuck in the interior padding of the capsule was apparently dislodged from the dog at that moment. The device to which it was connected controlled the dog's state of suspension – once it became disconnected, its control ceased.'

'But would it begin to revive so quickly?'

195

The man shrugged apologetically. 'You would do better to ask Dr. Petrokova about that, Director.'

Nikovitch frowned. 'I will ... in a moment. This device here,' he indicated the equipment on the table. 'It is *this* that accomplished the Americans' miraculous feat?'

Dubuokov looked down at the device, nodding. 'I admit, it does not look to be an excessively complicated machine. But in its simplicity it hides a great many mysteries.' He lifted the cover, having already removed the bolts during the course of his examination. 'In here is a reservoir of some type of liquid – Dr. Petrokova is attending to its analysis – which is part of the system. There is also a small pump which seems designed to give periodic injections of the liquid, depending upon feedback from the dog's life-function readings. This small device here is a miniature generator which produces a negative static electric charge, which presumably is transmitted through the bloodstream. And the entire process is controlled by a complex transistorised circuit, located here – and all of this I have photographed.'

Nikovitch ignored the last remark. 'So you are saying that you understand what this device is ... ?'

'No – what I am saying,' Dubuokov corrected, 'is that I recognise the *components* of the device. Exactly how it works is still unclear.'

Miklos' eyes were narrowed beneath the ragged crests of his brows. 'And when do you think you *will* know?'

'Soon, I think. We will know more as soon as the chemical analysis of the liquid is complete.'

'Was there anything else unusual about the satellite?'

'Nothing significant.'

Nikovitch paused. 'Do you have any idea, from what you've seen of their experiment and from your own knowledge in this area, why they would want to destroy it?'

Dubuokov gave an inaudible sigh. 'It is hard to understand, especially after seeing how successfully their project operated. It would seem to make no sense ... unless ...'

'Go on –'

'Well, we know that the Americans tried to divert its trajectory after the destroyer satellite misfired. They wished

196

to bring the capsule down in some area other than our country or those of our allies. But their efforts to activate the capsule's guidance system failed. Now unless there was damage done to the receiver circuits during the orbit deflection, then we could assume that the radio was faulty prior to that time. In which case they may have tried previously to bring about re-entry, and failed.' Dubuokov made it clear with his tone and facial expression that he was only theorising. 'If they thought that the satellite was no longer controllable, it might have seemed preferable to destroy it rather than let it drift on in orbit towards an eventual re-entry in some part of the world out of their reach.'

Theory or not, the answer pleased Nikovitch. It was a plausible and workable explanation for an otherwise bothersome inconsistency. And it fit with Miklos' knowledge of American security tactics.

'It would appear then,' he replied, 'that through a few mechanical failures, and perhaps an error in judgment, they brought about the exact thing they feared the most. By accident, they have delivered their precious experiment into our hands.' He smiled faintly. 'It would be an unpardonable crime if we did not take advantage of this opportunity to study their work. Do you agree, Dubuokov?'

'Of course, Director.' Dubuokov's smile was strained. Nikovitch had much authority and power; there were rumours that he might some day ascend to an even higher position of responsibility within the government. One must tread carefully around such individuals.

Nikovitch turned slightly. 'If that is all you can tell me about the satellite, then I will talk with Dr. Petrokova next.'

Dubuokov nodded and led the way. Hurdein followed behind Nikovitch, still silent.

Dr. Ludmila Petrokova was a woman in her early forties, of medium height, and somewhat heavy in build by Western standards. Yet her overall appearance was pleasant enough, despite the rather severe effects of the white laboratory garments she wore, and her plainly tied-back hairstyle. Her firm, steady gaze met that of Nikovitch as he approached

... met it and matched it with the same imperturbable strength found in Miklos' ice-blue eyes.

Dubuokov spoke first. 'Director, this is Dr. Petrokova,' and then, to the woman. 'Director Nikovitch is the head of our country's internal security force.'

'Doctor ...' Nikovitch acknowledged the introduction. Petrokova replied only with a courteous nod.

'You are considered the best in your field here?' Miklos asked bluntly.

'Director, I have worked at the Korsky Institute for the last five years, the last two of which I have served as senior veterinary researcher. Prior to my assignment here, I worked towards my doctorate at the University of Moscow. Before that, I served as a laboratory assistant for ten years.' All of Ludmila's educational and professional background was being related in a totally matter-of-fact manner, without embellishment. Such a tendency was not uncommon among scientists anywhere. It was considerably more common within the regimented society of Soviet Russia. She continued. 'And because of my recent work in certain experimental areas, I have a top-secret security clearance. There was simply no one else suitable.'

'Very well.' Nikovitch looked down at Major, who now sat patiently next to Dr. Petrokova. A heavy band of leather circled the dog's neck, and was attached by means of a strap to the table behind them. 'He seems to be in good health.'

'He is,' Petrokova replied. 'Remarkably good, considering the amount of time he has spent in space without exercise or normal food.'

'What can account for it? Has any of your work produced results nearly as impressive as this?'

Petrokova took the second of his questions first. 'No, none of our efforts in this area have succeeded for that length of time. Few test animals have survived more than a month under such restrictive metabolic controls. But from this animal's state of health, I could almost doubt that he had been in space for a week, let alone a year and two months.'

Nikovitch dismissed the statement with a quick gesture

of his hand. 'That much we have proof of. Our facilities have tracked that satellite from the instant of its launching until it landed here in the Soviet Union.'

'So I understand.' Petrokova reached down and stroked the top of Major's head. The dog looked up, eyes alert and friendly. 'Yet there is absolutely no sign of physical or mental deterioration such as is normally associated with a prolonged spaceflight.'

'Is that not the ultimate goal of such research?'

'Naturally. But it is still surprising to find that the Americans have perfected this technique so soon.'

Nikovitch shrugged. 'I am sure that our own scientists are not far behind in this research. It may be that the Americans have only stumbled onto some new principle accidentally. If that is the case, then we shall soon be as capable as they.'

'Of course,' Petrokova added quickly, 'since they are using a dog, it would seem they have not yet advanced to the level of primates in their experimentation.'

Otto Hurdein, who had until now remained silent, spoke up. 'Have you been able to analyse the liquid found in the control device yet?'

Dr. Petrokova turned to the table behind her and picked up a sheet of handwritten notes. 'Using the equipment available here, I have been able to isolate a number of the liquid's components ... but a complete analysis is not possible in this laboratory.'

Both Nikovitch and Hurdein frowned at this revelation. Dubuokov, however, obviously expected it.

'Well then,' Hurdein pressed on, 'of the components you have been able to isolate — what can you tell us?'

Petrokova glanced at the notes briefly, then handed the sheet to Hurdein. 'The components are suspended in a liquid which is essentially the same as blood plasma in that it is composed of serum albumin, but lacking the usual clotting agents found in blood. Its salinity also makes the liquid a conductor of mild electrical impulses, although I am not sure yet just what part the small static electric generator in the control device plays in the system.'

'Could they have patterned it after our electro-sleep devices?'

'Possibly, although its manner of operation is no doubt different since it is not connected to the brain. It seems to work throughout the entire body system. But as I said, just how it works is still unclear.'

She paused while Hurdein and Nikovitch looked over the notes she had made. 'As you can see, the fluid also contains a wide range of amino acids, necessary for maintenance of cellular tissue, and traces of several chemicals. Some of those chemicals are identifiable as controllers of body functions — breathing, heartbeat, and the rest. The others I have not been able to break down sufficiently for analysis, but I expect to be able to within a few days to a week.'

'We may not have that long,' Nikovitch said suddenly. 'Unless you can continue your experiments with a small sample of the fluid, you may have less than a day and a half. The Americans will be expecting us to return the capsule and the dog as soon as possible. Our political leaders may find an adequate excuse to delay the return, but we cannot count on much time.'

Hurdein inquired, 'Have you taken a blood sample from the dog?'

Petrokova nodded affirmatively. 'Once already, about an hour ago. And I am due to take another in a few minutes, to determine if any change has taken place.'

'You have found the same chemical from the device to be present in the dog's bloodstream?'

'Yes, but to a lesser degree than I first expected. I think what has happened is that since the dog's return to normal metabolism, much of the fluid's content has been cleansed from its system by the kidneys. There are ways of checking this, but again, not with the equipment present here.'

'But,' Nikovitch stated firmly, 'you have checked all other medical aspects that you can —'

'Yes, all that I *can*,' she replied, reaffirming the qualification. 'From all outward signs, the dog is perfectly healthy. Their technique resulted in a perfect state of homeostasis during the dog's time in orbit — a kind of super balancing of

200

its metabolic functions, so that only a minimal amount of air and nutritive supply was needed to maintain a healthy state. The enormously slow rate of its life functions apparently accounts for the lack of muscular deterioration. In effect, the dog has clinically aged only a few days during the last year and two months.'

'Incredible!' The exclamation was voiced by Nikovitch, but it was equally in the minds of Otto Hurdein and Vladimir Dubuokov.

'I must make a report to Moscow as soon as possible,' Miklos continued. 'The importance such a technique could have to our space programme – perhaps even in other fields –'

'To be sure about it,' Dr. Petrokova interrupted firmly, 'we will have to continue our examinations. The only way we can be really certain, of course, would be with a partial dissection.'

'That is out of the question,' Miklos said flatly.

'We could always claim that the dog was injured during the landing impact and required an exploratory operation.'

'No. That would not be accepted. And remember that we would rather have world opinion on our side, whenever possible. No, we shall have to be content with the photos and samples, and attempt to duplicate their technique in our own laboratories.' Nikovitch's cool gaze was fully on Petrokova as he said, 'You are our only veterinary authority present at the moment, Doctor. Accordingly, I am making you responsible for the dog's continued good health until such time as the Americans' representatives have claimed it. I am sure that you are more than sufficiently qualified for that job. . . .'

'Yes, Director . . . and you do wish me to continue the examination?'

'Yes, insofar as the basics are concerned. And try to complete analysis of the unidentified chemicals, if you can.'

'I will do my best.'

Nikovitch turned and walked away. Otto Hurdein followed him to the door between the laboratory and the outer section.

Under his breath, Miklos said, 'The woman is a bit more of the scientist than is desirable in this instance.'

'She is just trying to do her job,' Hurdein answered.

'Her job, in this case, is to do what we want — no more and no less.'

Dubuokov joined them. 'Director, I am afraid that Dr. Petrokova is correct in one thing — further examination of the dog and the fluid will require more specialised equipment than we presently have available here at the Technical Institute. Transporting everything we might need from the Korsky building would be difficult, so it may very well be necessary to move the dog and capsule to their laboratory.'

'Perhaps — perhaps not,' Nikovitch snapped, almost angrily. 'But if that should be required, it is I who will make the decision.'

'Yes, Director — I did not mean to imply —'

'Enough. There is no need for further discussion. You are through with your examination of the capsule, Dubuokov?'

'Except for reassembly of the equipment —'

'Good. I can spare you no longer from your primary work on the Cerberus countermeasure system. Our facility is complete and we need the final adjustments necessary for its operation. Have you completed your calculations?'

'Not entirely, Director. But I am nearly done —'

'I want those calculations tomorrow ... if you have to work through the night to finish them. Do you understand?'

'Yes.' Dubuokov said resignedly. 'I will begin as soon as the satellite equipment is reassembled.'

Nikovitch watched the scientist return to the laboratory, then walked with Otto Hurdein back along the hall. Miklos' pace was brisk, impatient.

'I shall have to make my report to Moscow,' he was saying. 'They will need to know of our progress, especially with the summit so close. They will need to know what to tell the American President. He may ask when the satellite will be returned. And there is something else I must do. ...'

Hurdein looked at him quizzically. 'And that is ... ?'

'I must contact my subordinate, Alexi, and tell him to alert our operatives in the United States. There are still a few questions in my mind that are bothering me, and I need more information.'

Hurdein nodded. 'You have operatives near the military bases?'

'Not only near them ... on them. In many places of value. And also at several of their space facilities. Yes,' he said finally, more to himself than to Hurdein, 'that may prove worthwhile. ...'

CHAPTER NINE

By half past one of the following day, the President and his entourage were ready to leave Brussels. The meeting at NATO headquarters had gone more smoothly than expected, although there were still some areas in which full accord had not been reached. Gleaming in the sunlight, Air Force One stood poised on the runway's access strip, engines silent.

Within the second cabin, Secretary of State Charles Wellmont looked up in anticipation as White House Press Secretary Dan Hillman entered from the forward cabin. But Hillman's expression was as disturbed as his own.

'What is it?' Wellmont asked.

Hillman looked as if he had not slept well the night before. 'The President's getting impatient. He knows we should have left a half hour ago. I don't think we can delay any longer.'

Wellmont consulted his watch. 'I had hoped to hear from the Pentagon by now. There should be an update on the progress of things.'

'We may have to leave without it.'

Wellmont shook his head. 'I'd rather not. As long as we're on the ground, we still have options.'

Hillman seemed dubious. 'At this point, I don't know if we can come up with any further "problems" to justify moving the schedule back again.' He considered a moment, 'When is the first meeting with the Soviet leaders?'

'This evening at eight – their time, which gives us only about four and a half hours. It will be a state dinner meeting, and I'm certain it will set the tone of all subsequent talks. I tried to avoid it . . . to have the first talks begin in the morning, if possible.' Wellmont sighed. 'They preferred the dinner meeting anyway, and I didn't think I could risk being too adamant about it. We're pushing our luck as it is.'

'You don't think they suspect anything?'

'No ... not yet. We can be certain that if they did — if they knew the true nature of the satellite — we would have already received word from them cancelling the meetings.'

Hillman walked slowly to the other side of the cabin, his footsteps falling silently on the carpeted flooring. 'I wish we could have avoided telling the President about the satellite. He's concerned that it might affect negotiations.'

'There was no way we could isolate him from the news. We had to make it available to the world press. As long as he doesn't know the rest of it.'

'If we've learned nothing before the meeting, we'll have to tell him. He can't go into it unprepared.'

'I realise that.' Wellmont ran a hand through his white, crested hair. 'But it will be difficult.'

The door to the cabin opened abruptly and the second flight officer entered. Wellmont got to his feet.

'Yes?'

'A radio message from Washington, sir — unscrambled, it reads, *Status: Viable; 2, 3.*'

Wellmont's look of concern lessened. 'That means we're still in a position to learn the information we need, in two or three hours.'

Hillman frowned. 'Even at that, we'll be cutting things pretty close.'

'Yes, I know.' Wellmont chewed his lip, deep in thought. After a long moment, he looked to the flight officer. 'All right. You can announce in a few minutes that the problem with the aircraft has been remedied. We can leave as soon as you're ready.'

'Yes, Mr. Secretary.'

After the man left the cabin, Hillman turned his troubled gaze out one of the windows, looking at the Brussels airport buildings. 'Do you think we've been doing the right thing, sir?'

'I hope to heaven we have. ...'

In the central United States, day was just beginning.

By seven in the morning Larry Lawrence was driving his rented car along U.S. Highway 66, cutting southwest across

Missouri. He had been driving for the last two hours, and the increasing morning light was a welcome change from the darkness in which he had begun his drive. Another welcome change was the sky itself, which had grown more and more blue as he left St. Louis and its grey haze behind.

His flight had landed at St. Louis Municipal Airport a few minutes after two in the morning, where Lawrence got both a car and a road map from a rental agency. He then checked into the St. Louis Marriott across from the airport just long enough to shower and catch a few hours of sleep.

And now he found himself driving in the midst of rolling countryside, in an area known as the Ozark Plateau. Somewhere, a short distance ahead, lay the answer to a question that had not released its hold on his mind since it first occurred to him the day before. Getting the information he wanted would not be easy, regardless of the pressure he might be able to exert. But easy or not, he would try it. He could sense the presence of a newsworthy story, and was determined to find out what he could.

Lawrence slowed the car almost to a stop and checked the map. From what he had been able to find out, the ARDCOM facility was located on a piece of government-owned property roughly fifteen miles from a large Army installation. There was a turnoff, an access road somewhere ahead. At least there should be. . . .

Speeding up, Lawrence began to scan the left-hand side of the road. A mile rolled by without any turnoff. There was simply nothing in sight except hills and trees and open fields. And at that time of the morning, there were scarcely any cars along U.S. highway 66 either. Not even a military vehicle, which he might have welcomed as an indication he was near the place he sought.

Two more miles dragged by, and Lawrence was beginning to consider the possibility he might somehow have missed it . . . or worse yet, that his information was wrong. After a moment, he dismissed those thoughts. He was quite sure he would have seen any turnoff, had he passed it. And he was almost equally sure of his information.

Another half mile rolled beneath his wheels, then

206

suddenly Lawrence jammed on his brakes. He had chanced to look back slightly along one area he was passing, and had seen an access road that was not visible from the direction in which he was driving. The turnoff curved into the opposite lane, and was not easily noticeable except to traffic going northeast along the highway.

Turning his wheel hard left, he pulled the car around into the other lane and stopped again just within the mouth of the turnoff. There were no signs anywhere. Nothing to tell him for certain if this was the road to the ARDCOM facility or only the route to someone's farm or country home. He had not really expected to find a placard or banner proclaiming the area to be a government installation. On the contrary, he had expected almost exactly what he found — a plain, hard-packed dirt road, disappearing around a bend in the thick growth of trees and brush.

But was this the right one?

Gunning the engine, he started down the road. It twisted and turned through a wooded area too dense to yield a view of more than a few hundred feet ahead at any given time. Three miles crept by, then four, and it was beginning to seem that the road led nowhere at all ... just on and on through the Missouri countryside.

Abruptly, the curving road straightened. A section of chain-link fence came into view, and about fifteen feet beyond it was a second fence. Barbed wire on angled standards topped both fences.

A gateway, complete with guard post and military police, loomed ahead. Now there could be no doubt, no chance that this was merely some farm road.

Lawrence pulled his car up in front of the gate, instantly aware of the sharp attention focused on him by the two MP guards. Mustering a look of businesslike unconcern, Lawrence left his car, carrying the map with him, and walked up to the guard post. One of the men stationed there, wearing the stripes of a Sergeant First Class, stepped out of the small structure and waited until Lawrence reached him.

The man's tone was friendly. 'Lost, sir?'

Lawrence held the map in his hand without looking at it. 'Not that I know of ... this is the road to ARDCOM headquarters, isn't it?'

The guard avoided a direct answer. 'Do you have business with anyone from ARDCOM?'

'Yes,' Lawrence replied, stretching the truth. He extended his *News-Scene* credentials. 'I'm researching an article for my magazine, concerning the use of animals for military purposes.'

While the guard examined his credentials, Lawrence looked around the area. The other guard, still within the semiclosed hut, was watching him. Careful that he did not appear too curious, he continued to survey the fence and the terrain beyond. The road continued on the other side of the gate, but was paved from that point on, disappearing out of sight around another bend twenty yards in the distance. Nothing else could be seen yet from this position.

Movement caught his eye, and Lawrence glanced to his left. Another guard, this one on a walking post, was patrolling the area between the two chain-link barriers, accompanied by a large German Shepherd guard dog. As the pair moved past him, it was difficult to tell which of the two studied him the more intently — the man or the dog.

The MP handed back his press cards and said simply, 'I have not been informed of an appointment for anyone from your magazine.'

Lawrence pocketed his cards. 'Well, they might not have expected me at this time ... look, I'd better speak with your superior officer — no, better make that the Base Commander. You do have a phone?'

The MP stood his ground. 'I'm sorry, sir. I'm afraid that would be im —'

'It's quite important,' Lawrence interrupted. 'I'm sure your commanding officer will agree. ...'

Studying him for a long moment, the guard silently considered. Then, turning to the guard hut, he called out, 'Dial HQ.' After another second's gaze at the reporter, the sergeant stepped back into the structure and took the phone from his fellow soldier. There was a brief, low-pitched conversation with someone on the other end, then the MP took the phone away from his ear.

'I'm sorry, sir, but headquarters knows nothing about you. If you're interested in information, you'll have to apply in writing through regular channels, and —'

'I'm not interested in standard poop sheets. Look, let me talk with someone in authority . . . *please!*'

The guard considered again, consulted with headquarters, then grudgingly handed the phone over to Lawrence. Taking it, he faced a half-turn away from the guard hut.

'Hello?'

A cool, sharp voice responded. 'General Raskin's office, Command Sergeant Major Tyson speaking.'

'Sergeant Major, perhaps you can help,' Lawrence began. 'I need to talk with someone about the article I'm doing, but I seem to be running into difficulty as far as getting on the base —'

'Perhaps you don't understand,' Tyson replied, with calm but carefully accentuated words. 'This is a restricted base — the work done here is considered classified. You're familiar with the designation?'

'Yes, but —'

'No one is allowed on base except those with official business . . . and with security clearance.'

'Perhaps if I could speak to the general —'

Tyson's tone was becoming more brittle. 'General Raskin is quite busy right now.'

'I'll bet he is,' Lawrence said under his breath, quickly adding, 'I think he might find time to see me, if he understood the nature of my article —'

'As I said, the general is busy.'

'— the article concerns dogs, you see . . . dogs and satellites. And other interesting things like that. . . .'

There was the sound of a hand clapped over the phone's mouthpiece at the other end, then silence. He could imagine the top-ranking noncom hastily consulting General Raskin, who was surely within ear's reach.

Then came the sound of the phone changing hands.

Another voice spoke this time, a deeper, slightly husky voice.

'General Raskin here. Who is this?'

'D. Thomas Lawrence, General ... Associate Editorial Writer, *News-Scene* magazine.'

'What are you trying to pull, Lawrence? What's this bull about an article?'

'The plain truth, General. And I need some information, preferably an interview.'

'Well, you won't get it from me.'

'That would be a shame, sir. A real shame. It could make things difficult.'

There was a slight pause. 'What are you talking about?'

'Well, I have to write my article, one way or another. I already have a certain amount of information, and a few hypotheses, but I really need more to go on. I would hate to have to go back and write up an incomplete story ... one that only hints at the facts.'

Raskin almost exploded into the phone. *'If you think you can bully your way in here, Lawrence —!'*

'Oh no,' Lawrence interrupted calmly. 'I don't really have to see you ... as I said before, I can just go ahead and write up what I already have. I'm sure that once it's published, there'll be enough interest in the story to warrant a follow-up article on it. Perhaps then there'll be more time for an interview.'

There was a long silence, a strange vacuum of sound. When Raskin spoke again, it was quite apparent from his tone that he had much more to say, and much less pleasantly. But all he did say were two words:

'Wait there!'

There was a slamming click which made Lawrence's ear ache for several seconds, and he handed the phone back to the guard, who stared at him with a puzzled look. He waited.

Before five minutes had elapsed, the squeal of tyres could be heard coming towards the gate. An Army jeep appeared on the paved road, screeching swiftly around the bend, and halted near the guard post. Two more MP's were in the olive-drab vehicle, sporting the same white helmets and Sam Browne belts as the two at the guard hut, and armed with standard automatics. But these two were a captain and a master sergeant, and they looked considerably less friendly.

'Open the gate!' The captain stood up on the floorboards, remaining in the jeep. He waited until the double swinging gates were drawn open, then motioned for Lawrence to drive in and park. 'Leave it over there, next to the building.'

Lawrence complied, took his key out of the ignition, and got out of the car. Swinging his cassette recorder over his shoulder by its strap, he strolled towards the jeep. He was smiling faintly, but he saw no humour in the eyes of the guards.

'Get in.' The captain made no effort to help him into the back seat of the open vehicle, and remained standing until Lawrence was seated. Then he lowered himself quickly on to the canvas-covered frame and barked, 'Let's go!'

With a burst of acceleration that pressed them tighly against their seat-backs, the jeep wheeled about and headed back along the paved road. They covered a distance of several more miles before anything was visible. Then the complex of buildings came into view, and slightly in the distance, the airstrip from which Major's trip had begun.

The jeep sped past the living quarters and mess facility, on past storage buildings and a number of the labs. It slammed to a halt in front of a low, one-storey building. The signboard out front bore the stencilled legend, *ARDCOM HQ, XR DIV., 5TH U.S. ARMY*, and in smaller letters, *Commanding Officer, Brig. Gen. John J. Raskin.*

A man stood outside that building, waiting. A solitary star gleamed over his tired and angry features.

'Now we'll have that little interview you wanted, Lawrence. . . .'

At seven in the morning at Houston's Johnson Space Center, activities were just beginning. It would still be at least an hour before all the various technicians and engineers involved in current projects, including the Apollo-Soyuz mission and the Space Shuttle, would start their busy

211

schedules. But for another group, the day had begun much earlier. . . .

In the grey, expansive building being used as mission control for the ARDCOM project, lights still burned as they had throughout the night. Arnold Smith still dutifully watched the image-display screen, although he now did so from a leaning position against the back of the computer console.

Matthews and Brunning sat at one of the tables, both looking fatigued. Dr. Wendell Byers sat with them, having arrived minutes earlier. His complete knowledge of the Cerberus defence system could be essential for a quick interpretation of the Russian plans for a countersystem. They had briefed him on the progress of the mission, and also on the matter of the NASA Administrator.

'When do you expect them here?' Byers asked.

'Soon,' Matthews replied. 'I've made the arrangements.'

Byers shook his head, concern showing on his scholarly features. 'I don't like it. I wish we could avoid something like this.'

Matthews nodded in agreement. 'So do I. But I really have no choice. We can't let anything jeopardise the mission. During the night, we had several messages relayed to us by Washington. We really must get the information as quickly as possible.'

Byers sighed. 'I still wish there were some other way. . . .'

Moving among them, James Neston handed out plastic foam cups filled with fresh, hot coffee. The last cup he handed out went to Bill Stanton, who was engaged in a routine communications check of all equipment and relays.

Ryan Halper was bent over his cot, replacing his shaving articles in the bag set across the wood and canvas frame. He looked up as Joyce Kandell emerged from the lavatory at the end of the room.

She was still drying her face with a pastel towel as she returned to the area of the cots. Her hairstyle was somewhat the worse for wear, but was combed in a manner that was still functionally attractive.

'Like the accommodations?' Halper inquired.

'I suppose there are worse places.'

'I've seen a few,' Halper replied. Through his mind flashed recollections of his time in Vietnam, of wood-slat buildings with corrugated metal roofs and outdoor latrines. When there *were* buildings. He had been a corporal then, working as a dog handler. It was only later, months after his return, that he had made the decision to apply for OCS and continue his work as an officer.

Reflecting on the past, Halper was glad that Major's training had come after the U.S. involvement in Vietnam ended. Of the thousands of dogs sent there for use as sentry and scout animals, none had been returned to America. Certain well-meaning congressmen had protested the policy, without realising the necessity of it. Although each dog was valued at roughly $5,000, each had been exposed to a virulent canine disease rampant in South Vietnam. All had to remain there. Yet was Major's current work any less dangerous . . . ?

Joyce looked towards the image-display screen with reawakened concern. 'Anything happened since last night?'

'I don't know.' Halper handed her the extra cup of coffee left by Neston. 'Smith said he'll brief us as soon as we have our heads clear.'

She sipped at the steaming cup. 'Mine's about as clear as it's going to be. Smith got me up about four times last night, to double check on the medical tests they were making on Major.'

'Did he stay up all night?'

She nodded. 'Smith, and the two NASA people as well. I think General Matthews must have been up most of the time, too.'

'Why didn't they let us spell them?'

'How could we? We couldn't really replace Neston or Stanton, and Smith's the only one who has a chance of knowing what's being said by the Russians.' She hesitated a moment. 'Besides, General Matthews said something about keeping the ARDCOM team fresh until they need us.'

Pausing, Joyce gently kneaded the muscles of her arms, flexing the stiffness out of them. 'What rest I had helps, I suppose, but what I really need is to get out of here for a little while. This place is beginning to get to me. . . .'

'I know what you mean.'

Arnold Smith turned and briefly surveyed the room, then spoke a few quick words to Carter, who was just beginning to check his computer circuits.

Carter walked over to Halper and Joyce. 'Smith wants to see you,' he said casually. 'I get the impression not much has happened yet, but he still wants to brief us on current status.'

'Check.' Halper zipped up the bag and placed it beneath his cot. Then he and Joyce followed Carter back to the computer console where Arnold Smith waited.

'Good morning,' Smith said. 'Sleep well?'

'As well as could be expected,' Halper replied. 'What's up?'

Smith straightened, glancing again briefly at the visual display screen. 'So far, nothing much. They've been making all the routine medical tests on the dog, and examining the satellite — all of which we expected, of course. And apparently they're buying the explanation we want them to believe. I've been able to catch some of their conversation when they've been close enough to the dog for me to read their lips, and I don't think they're at all suspicious yet. Probably because they want to believe we've dropped something important into their laps.'

Halper found himself staring at the image on the screen, still fascinated by the notion of seeing what Major was seeing. 'How soon can we begin our operation?'

'Probably not for another hour, at least,' Smith explained. 'They're still doing more testing — the veterinary specialist they brought in isn't quite satisfied with her results so far — but there are certain limitations to how much they can experiment.' Smith thoughtfully neglected to mention Dr. Petrokova's quickly vetoed remark about dissection. 'But any time after that, once their activities have slowed somewhat, we can expect to make our move.'

Halper looked to the communications console, to the clock labelled *Omsk*. 'It's a little after six p.m. there.'

Smith nodded seriously. 'Some of their personnel have been working nonstop, and that's going to be in our favour.

If they're tired, there's a better chance they'll be careless with security ... make mistakes.'

'Let's hope *we* don't make any.'

Smith looked at Halper with a grim expression. 'You won't have any reason to. ...'

General Matthews came up behind them. His soft, padded features seemed more deeply etched than before. To Smith he asked, 'Have you brought them up to date?'

'Yes, General.'

Matthews scanned the faces of the others. 'Any questions?'

It seemed for a moment that there would be none. Then Joyce spoke up.

'General Matthews,' she began, 'would it be possible for me to go outside for a few minutes ... just to get some fresh air and walk around a little?'

Matthews shook his head. 'We haven't planned for any essential personnel to leave this building until after the mission has been completed.'

'Please, sir,' she asked quietly. 'It would help.'

The general studied the young woman carefully. In her eyes was a crying need for at least a momentary escape from the confines of the control centre. He reminded himself that he was dealing with a civilian, and one unaccustomed to such missions. Almost against his own military judgment, he relented.

'All right, Miss Kandell. All right ... but only for a few minutes.'

Brunning seemed disturbed but did not contradict the general's decision. He moved quickly to Halper's side as Joyce moved away.

'Go with her,' he said in a tense whisper. 'Watch her. If she's going to be a problem, I swear I'll pull her – throw her into NASA's security centre for the duration.'

Halper said only, 'We need her, sir.'

'We need someone, but not a troublemaker. If necessary I can bring Dr. Corby over.'

'He'd be at a severe disadvantage – he doesn't know Major's biomedical tolerances.'

'I'll take that risk if I have to.'

Halper wondered why Brunning's concern had become so intense again, but he said nothing else. As he turned to follow Joyce, Brunning motioned for the Special Forces master sergeant to go with them.

The door opened before they reached it. Norm Ripley entered, followed by Dr. Laswell. Behind them were two Air Force MP's wearing ID tags from Ellington Air Base.

Both Halper and Joyce were surprised to see them. Matthews and the others clearly were not. Joyce hesitated at the doorway, still watching in shocked silence. Then she turned and left with Halper.

Stopping before General Matthews, Laswell faced him with controlled anger. 'So you're going through with this after all.'

'I'm sorry,' Matthews said solemnly. 'I have no choice in the matter. And I'm afraid I'm going to have to ask you to stay in the mission centre for the next several hours.'

Laswell's glance took in the Air Force MP's. 'You don't really mean *ask*, do you, General?'

Matthews' voice remained firm. 'We have D.O.D. authority to temporarily detain anyone who might inadvertently or otherwise pose a threat to the mission.'

'And what about afterwards? Just how far will you go to protect yourselves – in the name of national security?'

'We'll all be leaving here once we have the information. And I hope ... I hope that by then you'll see the necessity of this.'

Laswell had no reply. But there was no doubting his thoughts.

Next to them, at the communications console, Bill Stanton suddenly turned, covering the slender headset mike with his fingers. He faced Brunning.

'Colonel, I've got a call from your headquarters – sounds important –'

Brunning's face registered surprise, followed by worry. He moved quickly to the console and reached for the black phone unit.

'Use line three, Colonel,' Stanton said.

216

'Is that line on a scrambler?'

'All lines are, sir.'

Punching the third transparent button on the phone, Brunning answered. 'Colonel Brunning.' He paused, as the ARDCOM sergeant major spoke, then, 'Yes, Ty – put the general on.'

Brunning visibly straightened as the controlled thunder of Raskin's voice came over the phone.

'Brunning, give me an update.' Raskin demanded. 'How close is the mission to completion?'

'A few hours, sir. Possibly a little more.'

'No snags so far?'

'No, General. Why, is –'

Raskin interrupted. 'We've got a problem here at the base ... one that could affect the mission. You'd better put General Matthews on the line.'

Although Brunning's features went suddenly pale, he motioned immediately for Matthews. 'Sir – General Raskin wants to speak to you. It's urgent.'

General Matthews was at the phone in a few strides. 'Matthews,' he answered, new energy coming into his tired voice.

'We've got a problem here,' Raskin replied. 'A reporter, name of D. Thomas Lawrence.'

'On *base?*' Matthews sounded incredulous.

'Yes, on base! I've got him cooling his heels in our orderly room.'

'How'd he get in?'

'I let him in ... had to. He was threatening to print his theories about a connection between our research here and the satellite unless I gave him an interview on our projects!'

Matthews fumed, a tight-lipped frown on his face as he shook his head in disgust. 'Who's he work for? Maybe if we get hold of his publisher –'

'*News-Scene,*' Raskin answered. 'It's that big weekly magazine. But it's not them I'm worried about ... their next issue won't be out on the stands for a few more days. The big danger is if he should go directly to one of the daily papers, or worse yet, television!'

'I see what you mean. You were right in holding him. The question is — what do we do with him?'

There was a hoarse, grumbling laugh on Raskin's end. 'I can think of a few suggestions.'

'So can I,' Matthews countered. 'But to be realistic, all you need to do for the moment is keep him out of circulation and try to find out what he knows.'

'To tell the truth, I don't think he knows anything conclusive. Just a vague connection, that's all. But his guessing could be extremely dangerous right now. How much time will you need?'

'Brunning's estimate is pretty close — two or three hours ... no, better make that four or five, just in case we hit any problems.'

'All right,' Raskin acknowledged. 'I'll do what I can.'

'Good. And remember,' Matthews' voice dropped slightly in volume, 'we need to be concerned not only with the immediate problem, but also the long view.'

'I understand.'

Matthews replaced the phone handset. Behind him, Dr. Laswell approached, eyes fiery behind the silver frames of his glasses.

'What is it?' Laswell questioned. 'What's wrong?'

Matthews surveyed him for a moment, hesitant to explain, knowing full well what the administrator's reaction would be. 'There's a reporter,' he said at last, reluctantly. 'At the ARDCOM base in Missouri. He's asking the wrong kind of questions at the wrong time. General Raskin is holding him there so he doesn't jeopardise the mission.'

Laswell seemed almost ready to explode. 'A *reporter!* This is exactly the kind of thing I've feared! What kind of security precautions have your people made that would allow something like this?'

Matthews tried to be patient. 'There was no way to cover such a possibility, Doctor. You know we had to make use of the news media as part of the mission. It was essential that a seemingly erroneous report of the satellite's purpose be released. There was no way to control what the press did with it after that. The possibility that a reporter should draw a connection

218

between our news releases and earlier ARDCOM experiments was a risk, a calculated risk. We'll just have to hope no others make that same connection too soon.'

'Just ... *hope*?' Laswell was outraged. 'I've warned you before, General ... if the NASA facilities are brought into this —'

Matthews' own anger was coming to the surface. 'Settle down! I know far better than you who shares the responsibility for this mission.'

The general calmed, fighting an inner battle to restore the patience that was essential. 'Just ... let us do our jobs. Let *us* worry about it. We have no intention of exposing NASA to any publicity at all concerning this mission. It would be detrimental for too many reasons, believe me. Just ... let us handle it. ...'

In the early morning sunlight outside the building, Ryan Halper and Joyce walked, the Green Beret not far behind them. For the moment at least, they were oblivious to the turmoil within the control centre. The cool morning breeze was refreshing, and at the great space centre all was calm.

'Ryan —' Joyce began, glancing back to see if the sergeant major was in hearing range. She lowered her voice. 'Ryan, do you realise what they're doing? They've brought Dr. Laswell here under guard. They're holding him prisoner because he's disagreed about the mission.'

Halper did not answer at first. Frowning, he gazed at the ground as they walked. Finally, he said, 'They must have their reasons.'

Joyce looked at him quickly. 'How can you say that?'

'Because I'm sure they wouldn't risk it otherwise. They can only hold him for a while, and once he's released, he could make a lot of trouble, if he wants to.'

'If he *wants* to ... I'd say he has every *right* to. He's been excluded from the start, and now ... this. Ryan, we were told that this was a joint operation, with civilian and military personnel involved. But it's beginning to look like the civilians don't have much say in it, except to be used by the mission coordinators.'

'You can't say that, fairly. There's still a lot about this we just don't know.'

'Intentionally, it would seem.'

Halper shook his head grimly.

Joyce studied him. 'You don't approve of my speaking out about this, do you? You think this is all right and proper.'

'I don't know! I don't think we're in any position to judge whether it is or not.'

'But you'll still go along with it?'

'I have to.'

'Because you're a soldier?'

'Partly.' He could see the discussion was returning to a familiar theme. 'And I don't have to be like Brunning to feel that way. If I didn't have a basic faith in the structure, I never would have become an officer ... never would have wanted to.'

They walked on in silence for several more minutes, isolated more by things they wanted not to say than by things already said. Then Joyce spoke again.

'I realise I couldn't do much by myself ...' she began hesitantly. 'But if both of us ... if *both* of us were to protest their action towards Dr. Laswell, then perhaps ...'

She stopped abruptly, suddenly aware of Halper's chilling look. It struck her that she had seen that look before on the colonel's grim features.

'Or am I even safe talking to *you* any more, Ryan?' she said quickly. 'Will you have them lock *me* up, next?'

Halper halted, facing her. 'That's exactly what I've been trying to avoid! Joyce, it's not that impossible. The colonel's been worried about you from the start, and it wouldn't take much to —' He bit off the words, suddenly angry with himself for letting his emotions override his reason. He had not intended to use Brunning's distrust as a tool to convince her of his own feelings. But now he had said it, and he could only hope it would not make matters worse.

'The colonel ... has been worried about me?'

Halper hesitated. 'Yes.'

She took the information with an odd calm. 'It really doesn't surprise me. We've always been on different wavelengths, even before I started having doubts about the direction the CAM project was taking. . . .' Sighing, she brushed a strand of breeze-blown raven hair away from her eyes. She gave Halper a dejected look. 'I don't know why we have to be at odds, Ryan. I don't want it to be that way. I really don't. And with Major's safety in the balance, I —'

Abruptly, the morning's stillness was shattered by the shrill wail of a siren. All three turned towards the space centre's main road as a NASA Security Force vehicle screamed its way across the base, alerting arriving motorists of its haste. An instant later, another vehicle followed it.

The Green Beret was taut, alert, his hand near his automatic. Halper followed the course of the vehicles with his eyes as far as he could.

Joyce was aghast. '*What's happening?*'

Before anyone could reply, a man came running around the corner of the building, heading towards them. The Green Beret's gun was half out of its holster when he stopped the draw, his quick eye preventing a dreadful mistake even as Halper shouted —

'It's Neston!'

The NASA Assistant Administrator slowed his pace as he neared them, finally reaching the spot where they had stopped. He was almost out of breath as he spoke.

'Trouble — big trouble —'

Halper placed a steadying hand on the man's shoulder. 'What is it . . . what's going on?'

'Everything! It started with a problem at the ARDCOM base — a reporter —'

'But those sirens —'

'They've found a spy here at the space centre. One of the maintenance workers . . . he was in a security area he wasn't cleared for . . . he tried to escape.'

'He was captured?'

'Yes, but that's not all,' Neston replied, breathing deeply. 'It's really hit the fan now. Smith is on the phone with someone — probably the CIA — and they've just learned something that may involve one of your personnel. And that's not the worst of it! The Russians have decided to move the dog —'

'Move Major?' Joyce blurted. '*Why?*'

'I'll explain inside —' Neston hastened away. 'Come on!'

CHAPTER TEN

Neston and the others burst into the command centre at a near-frantic pace, leaving the door to be closed by the security guard on duty. Matthews and Brunning greeted their arrival with anxious looks, while the remainder of the people in the room stared mutely at the image-display screen.

On that extraordinary screen, the view shifted as Major, almost halfway around the world, looked about. A group of people moved around the dog in silent unreality. To one side, as the dog faced it, there was a glimpse of a large cage being moved into position, a cage that would easily contain the German Shepherd dog.

For Joyce and Halper, re-entry into this expansive, concrete cave of a building so sparsely filled with equipment only intensified the impact of Neston's bad news. The oppressive atmosphere within again seemed almost at the point of explosion.

Halper stared at the projected image, an imperative tightness in his voice when he spoke. 'Is it over — is the mission ruined?'

'We don't know yet,' Neston replied. 'It's too early to tell.'

Joyce asked urgently, 'Are they moving Major because they found out why he's there? Will they harm him?'

'No — that's not it.' Neston tried to calm her. 'The only reason they're moving him is to take him to one of their veterinary institutes for further examination — Smith picked up that much from their conversation. They still don't suspect anything, and this has nothing to do with the spy our security people captured — he was apparently just looking for whatever information he could find about the satellite.'

'But,' Joyce insisted, 'he was right *here*, at the centre.'

'You can bet he's not the only one the Russians have alerted. There are probably a few hundred more across the nation, looking for scraps of information to send back.'

'But why, unless they suspect something?'

'Probably to find out as much as they can before they turn over the dog and satellite to us.' Neston paused. 'But it might not be long before they start figuring it all out, especially if they X-ray the dog and see the implant. The worst part of it is, for the moment, that the dog is being transported out of the immediate area of the Omsk Technical Institute, where the information we want is being kept.'

General Matthews was close enough to hear them. 'How far does the range of the implant's transmitter extend?'

Joyce forced herself to remember the statistics stored in the back of her mind. 'Five to ten miles.'

'Is that under *all* conditions, or just optimum?'

'Well ... it might be less,' the girl answered, 'if there are large enough obstructions in the way that block radio waves ... but I still don't understand how the transmissions are being relayed —'

'Through the satellite itself!' Matthews began to pace anxiously. 'There's a relay unit within the satellite's transceiver which picks up the faint signal of the implant, boosts it, and encodes it, then sends it out with the main carrier transmission of the satellite — straight out to where the signal is picked up by one of our military relay satellites over Europe. From there it's beamed down to an Army receiving station in Germany, and sent by ground line to the NASCOM Switching Center in Madrid, Spain. From there on out, it's strictly handled through NASA's facilities.

'But the point I'm trying to make,' Matthews continued urgently, 'is the fact that if the dog is moved too far away from the satellite, the implant's transmissions won't reach it. The satellite's transmitter may be powerful enough to reach the dog, but we'll have no feedback — no pictures. We'll be working blind!'

'Is there any danger,' Halper asked, 'that they might switch off the satellite's transceiver?'

'They can't,' Matthews stated quickly. 'Not without destroying it. The relay, transceiver, and its power supply are all encased in a solid block of plastic, so they couldn't

224

tamper with it — that was an operational necessity. And the equipment's reliable — best we could get — worth a quarter of a million alone. But it's all worthless if they separate the dog and satellite with too much distance!'

'We've got to stop them!' Colonel Brunning entered the conversation suddenly. 'We must prevent them from moving the dog.'

Matthews looked at him grimly. 'Any suggestions on how we might accomplish that will be greatly appreciated.'

Brunning's expression showed that for the moment he had none.

'But you're right,' Matthews continued. 'We *will* have to do something. I want everyone to return to their working positions — be ready to go if we get a break.'

Brunning and Matthews remained where they were, but James Neston moved quickly to the communications console, to wait beside Bill Stanton. Joyce and Halper went to the table immediately before the computer unit manned by Carter, the table where their notes on Major's training and command patterns were carefully spread out. Laswell and his associate deputy, Norm Ripley, waited silently.

Arnold Smith, who had been talking on the phone in a low voice, abruptly hung up. He looked quickly to Colonel Brunning.

'We have a report,' the little man began quickly. 'Our agents have been working for several months now in Europe, investigating an espionage ring that has been exploiting U.S. military personnel for what secrets they could get from them, usually by extortion or blackmail methods.'

Matthews raised an eyebrow. 'Go on.'

'Our people have turned up a list,' Smith continued, still looking at Brunning. 'A list of names. We're not sure what exact significance it has yet, but it is definitely tied in with the espionage ring. One of the names on that list belongs to someone presently assigned to the Animal Research and Development Command — your group, Colonel — ARDCOM.'

'Who?' Brunning breathed.

'A captain — last name of Stens.'

'*Stens!* We had considered him a poor security risk for this mission, but I had no idea . . .' He seemed unconvinced, inquiring, 'You're saying that he's given information to the communists?'

'We don't know that for sure,' Smith replied. 'All we know is that his name is on a captured list — that may mean that he's sold out already, or only that at one time they planned to approach him. He may be innocent of any wrongdoing, but he presents a great risk. Our people have access to military records, and we're aware of the few days discrepancy during his assignment in Germany.'

Brunning nodded, his hopes falling. 'Yes, that was why he was sent to Washington at this time, to get him away from ARDCOM briefly.'

'He knows nothing about the mission?' Smith's tone was becoming that of an interrogator.

'No — he was never informed of it.' Brunning paused briefly, then his expression grew more worried. 'But he knows about the canine Computer Augmented Memory project, and he probably is aware of the fact that he's been sent to the Joint Chiefs of Staff early — earlier than our project report should have been made. If he *is* working for the Russians, then all he has to do is pass that information to one of their contacts and the mission is destroyed!'

Halper seemed dubious. 'Can he locate one of their contacts that easily, assuming he would?'

General Matthews gave a grunting laugh. 'Are you kidding, Lieutenant? There are probably more enemy agents in Washington than there are Congressmen!'

'What if he's already done it?' Brunning continued.

'Unlikely,' Arnold Smith countered, 'unless it happened just within the last few minutes. Otherwise we'd have some indication of it in the Russians' activities. Has he had any contact with the dog?'

Brunning shook his head. 'He's never seen it. But he might eventually make the connection . . . . I'm sure he's seen the newspapers by now.'

Matthews headed for the communications console. 'I'll

have to alert the Pentagon — we'll have to work on the assumption that Stens is working for the Russians.'

'As you wish, General,' Arnold Smith replied, reaching for the phone first. 'But let me call my people in Washington, and have them pick him up. It can be handled more unobtrusively that way.'

Both Smith and Matthews proceeded with their calls. Then Joyce Kandell suddenly pointed to the image-display board.

'Look — they're starting to move the cage out of the laboratory!'

Everyone could see that the cage was indeed being removed from the lab in which the initial examination of the dog and satellite was performed. The doorway passed out of view off the edges of the display board as the cage was rolled on its casters into the hallway outside. A number of the staff at the insitute were involved in the transfer operation, that much was obvious. And also obvious was the fact that the satellite, which was Major's sole link to the American team, was staying behind.

'Halper!' Matthews called out. 'Can you keep the dog facing their key people? We need to give Smith a chance to see what they're saying.'

'Yes, sir,' Halper said. 'We'll try.'

Halper was worried as he and Joyce checked over their notes. There had been so little time to experiment with the project before this ... it had hardly been past the theory and paperwork stage when the mission had been planned. If he were by Major's side, still working as a dog handler, he could merely point to whomever he meant to indicate and give the command. Now it was more complex, requiring a more elaborate command structure to get across the idea ... requiring more time. And there was no time! Despite the slow pace of the men moving the cage, it could not be long before they left the institute.

Joyce raised her eyes to his, her voice almost a whisper. 'Ryan, how ... ?'

His mind struggled another second, then ... 'I think I have an idea ... maybe.' He turned to James Neston. 'Can you get me a photo-facsimile of the image on the screen?'

'Yes,' Neston replied. 'The equipment's been set up for that from the start. What do you want?'

'The next time Major turns towards those people in the hall behind the cage, grab a still of it.'

'Will do.' Neston kept his thumb poised over the button that would freeze one brief moment of the image. He did not have long to wait, for the dog was busily looking about him. When Major turned enough to be looking at those behind his cage, Neston instantly pressed the button. 'Got it!'

He waited as the facsimile sheet slowly extruded from the unit, then grabbed it and headed towards Halper. The lieutenant met him halfway, took the sheet, and dashed towards Carter.

'Here,' Halper told him. 'Run this through the computer's pictorial analyser, and transmit it. Quick!'

Carter dropped the facsimile into the slot of the device which would break it down into an electronic pattern capable of being transmitted, a specially encoded pattern that would fit into Major's memory as a recalled image. He typed out the three-letter code for transmitting the signal. At the same instant, Halper fitted the audio system's headset and mike to his ears. Thumbing the transmit button, he commanded, '*Major – watch!*'

It took only a fraction of a second for the combined message to pass through the NASA communications linkup. A half-second more to flash from ground station to orbital satellite, then back to the Earth's surface where the fallen capsule served as relay.

But would it work?

The answer came abruptly a second later, as Major fastened his vision on Miklos Nikovitch, Otto Hurdein, and Dr. Petrokova. His training demanded that he watch them, and watch them he would, until commanded to do otherwise.

'Perfect,' Matthews responded, but his pleasure was only momentary. To Arnold Smith he said, 'Learn what you can ... from here on, we'll just have to play it as it goes.' He turned to Neston next, almost reluctantly. 'We've got to contact Washington ... let them know what's happened. The game may be over. ...'

In Omsk, Miklos Nikovitch was unaware he was being watched, not only by the dog but by others as well. He walked in the centre of the hall, heading towards the cargo ramp and the outside world. He was flanked by Hurdein on his left and Dr. Petrokova on his right.

'Are you sure it would not have been better to give the dog a tranquilliser injection before transporting him?' he asked the woman.

'Not if we are to make further tests on him,' she replied. 'The addition of any new drugs into his system might affect the results. The dog has been very calm so far, through everything – he will present no problems.'

Nikovitch let the matter go, but there was another on his mind. 'I would rather not have to move the dog from this building, for security reasons. But if you are sure it is necessary –'

'You do agree,' Petrokova began, 'that we must learn as much about the American experiment as possible before returning the dog?'

'Of course.'

She nodded. 'As I said before, the amount of testing I can perform here is severely limited by the available equipment. At the Korsky Institute I can run a complete check.'

'All right,' Nikovitch agreed reluctantly. 'But remember – bring no one else in on this without consulting me first – no one!'

'Yes, Director.'

'Have you reached any further conclusions concerning the American's technique?'

'Not much more than before,' she replied. 'But I am convinced from what I have seen of the equipment in the satellite that the whole answer is not to be found here.'

'What do you mean?'

'I am sure that prior to the launch there must be some form of preconditioning involved which prepares the animal for a metabolic slowdown.'

229

Miklos appeared confused. 'Preconditioning? If you mean anything similar to hypnosis, I do not see how that could work on an animal. ...'

'No, not hypnosis,' Petrokova corrected. 'Although that might be of value if humans were used in the experiment. But more likely, in the dog's case the preconditioning might be chemical ... or perhaps even surgical. If so, something may show up in the X-ray series ... or certainly in the other tests.'

'As long as we can find the answers,' Miklos sighed. Fatigue was beginning to show in his eyes. 'But – nothing must prevent or unnecessarily delay our return of everything to the Americans.'

Petrokova nodded. 'One other thing I wish to check at Korsky ... I have noticed a small scar on the dog's head, which may be the remnant of minor surgery. It may have nothing to do with the experiment, but its apparent slow rate of healing may add more information to what we already know about the metabolic slowdown.'

'All right,' Nikovitch responded as they neared the ramp. 'Keep me informed of anything you learn. And do not waste any time – for there is precious little left. We are going to make an official statement within the hour, acknowledging the fact that we have finally located the downed capsule and are transporting it to a safe area. Already the American representatives are pressuring us for details of an arrangement by which we can return the dog and satellite, and with the rest of the world aware of the matter, we cannot legitimately hold them off much longer.'

'I will do my best, Director.'

'See that you do, Doctor – see that you do.'

At that moment, a member of the institute staff approached them, bearing a teletyped message. 'Director Nikovitch?'

'Yes?'

'There is a communiqué from Moscow. It seems that radio monitoring stations have picked up and isolated an unknown transmitter. The transmissions seem to be originating from here ... perhaps from the American satellite.'

'Transmissions? What kind of transmissions?'

'What appears to be telemetry data,' the man replied. 'But it is the same thing, over and over, as if some device's equipment status is being continually reported. There appears to be no urgency to the matter, but the signal is a complex one and is not entirely decoded yet.'

'Very well ... keep me informed,' Nikovitch replied, excusing the man. He then turned to Otto Hurdein. 'You think it is the satellite?'

Hurdein nodded. 'Most likely. Dubuokov said he could not get at the transceiver to examine it. Apparently it suffered no damage in the landing impact, and is still operating.'

Nikovitch thought about it. 'It must be on a different frequency than the radio beacon which enabled us to find it. We can be sure the Americans are receiving it. I am not sure I like that, but if it is only broadcasting unimportant medical information ...'

Hurdein considered. 'We could always jam it —'

'No ... that would serve nothing, really. Besides, there may be other countries monitoring that signal. If we were to jam it suddenly with a broadcast where there has been none before, our motives will be suspect.'

'Yes, that may be.' Hurdein shivered involuntarily as the wide door of the loading entrance opened, letting a draught of cold air pour down the ramp. 'Perhaps we had better wait here,' he said suddenly.

'Very well.' Nikovitch directed one last remark at Dr. Petrokova: 'I need not tell you to be careful with your cargo.'

The woman stared after him a moment, saying nothing. Then she was outside in the frigid night air of Omsk. An afternoon snowstorm had stilled momentarily, and although sunset was still an hour away in this part of the world, it was almost completely dark outside.

At the Johnson Space Center, Halper watched the men

231

disappear from his view on the screen. Without taking his eyes away, he transmitted the countermand order:

'*At ease, boy.*'

There was no longer any need to maintain Major's watch — in fact, it could not be maintained. And it was important for the dog's continued usefulness to avoid sloppiness with commands.

Without waiting for General Matthews to ask him what he had learned, Arnold Smith turned and faced the others.

'I couldn't get all of it,' he began. 'But from what I did get, it's obvious that they still are buying it completely. And I'm afraid that their veterinary specialist is planning to make X-rays as part of the further tests.'

Neston frowned. 'Once they've seen the implant, it's all over!'

'Not necessarily,' Smith said, surprising them. 'For a while, at least, they may only consider it connected with what they think is a suspended animation experiment. Of course, they would then concentrate on that, and might discover it was sending radio signals of its own — which brings up another possible problem area: they've gotten word that one of their receiving stations has picked up the satellite's transmissions.'

Matthews tensed. 'What are they going to do about it?'

'For now, nothing. They have decided the transmissions are harmless. If our luck holds out, they won't decode the relay signals until it's too late.' Smith paused, collecting his thoughts. 'Another thing of interest — I've finally gotten a good look at the man who seems to be in charge of the situation in Omsk, and for the first time I clearly saw someone say his name. The man is Miklos Nikovitch. His official title is Director of Internal Security, but his job really amounts to nothing less than supervisor of the various Russian intelligence organisations. We know very little about him other than that, and nothing about his background. But certainly he is a man to be reckoned with.'

Matthews considered the information. 'We'll keep that in mind. But for now, the only important thing is to free the dog before he reaches their veterinary facility.'

232

At the communications console, Neston was still on the phone to Washington. Covering the mouthpiece, he called to Matthews.

'General – the President's plane left Brussels a little over an hour and a half ago. They're on their way to Moscow.'

'Can't they put down at another airport ... stall for some reason?'

'Negative, sir. From what I'm told, the feeling is that any further delays will only raise suspicions and call attention to what we're doing. And then we might never get the information.'

Matthews tensed, his brow furrowing. 'How long have we got?'

'Less than three hours.'

'Three ...' Anxiety became a kind of grim resolve. 'Then the rest of it's going to be completely up to us. It's all or nothing now,' he added, thinking also of Laswell.

'They're loading the dog,' Smith suddenly said.

All in the room fell silent as they watched the image on the great projection screen. Most of it was grey-black, little being visible in the semi-darkness beyond the Omsk Technical Institute. But a small floodlight illuminated the closed van parked near the loading entrance, its rear doors open. The van's interior filled the screen as the men carrying Major's cage carefully slid it inside. The dog was studying the movements of those men as most of them returned to the building, and Dr. Petrokova could be seen climbing into the rear of the van to sit on a fold-down seat next to the cage. Once the rear doors had been closed, only the light which entered through two small skylight windows near the edge of the van's roof illuminated the interior. A partition separated the driver's compartment from the cargo area.

Dr. Wendell Byers, who was in charge of the Cerberus defence project, had been quietly viewing all about him with an intense scientific fascination. Doubtless the fact that his brainchild's future depended upon what one specially trained animal could or could not accomplish weighed heavily on his mind.

'Is it possible,' he asked abruptly, 'once the dog is free, to guide him back to the institute?'

Halper nodded. 'Yes, sir. That would be the easiest part, in fact. Almost any dog can find its way back to a place it's been, if it has the motivation. And we can give Major both the motivation and any assistance he might need.'

'But,' James Neston countered, 'first you'll have to get him out of a locked cage under the eye of their doctor, and out of a moving vehicle. . . .'

Neston's words made them aware of the fact that the van was indeed moving now. There was a slight sway to the image on the display screen, and patterns of light within the van shifted, indicating a turn.

'They're leaving the area of the institute —' Joyce began, agitation in her voice. 'Whatever we do, it will have to be soon.'

General Matthews was studying the image intensely, trying to discern as much as possible in the poorly illumined van. More out of frustration than reason, he grumbled, 'I'd be a lot happier if there were more light. . . .'

'Same here, sir,' Halper replied. 'But we can be thankful a dog's night vision is better than ours, or else we wouldn't have even that good an image to work with.'

Neston seemed suddenly angry with himself. 'What am I thinking about — we may be able to make the image better. If we feed the signal through another circuit — computer-enhance it. . .' He instantly set about adjusting the controls, while Bill Stanton assisted.

A split second later, there was a subtle change in the view afforded by the image-display screen. What dimly lit areas there were before were now intensified, yielding an even higher contrast image. The edges of objects were more clearly delineated, and their forms more discernible.

'That's a little better,' Matthews said gratefully. 'Lieutenant — can you make out the door-latch handle at the rear of the van?'

Halper looked and recognised the familiar lever lock device. 'Yes, sir.'

'Do you think your dog can open it?'

'I'm sure he can. His training has covered things like that. Even if it's locked, it will still open from the inside. But the big problem is still the cage —'

'Then *think*, man!' Matthews bellowed. 'There must be a way to do it. If not by the dog's own force, then by trickery! Is there any way we can cause their doctor to open the cage?'

Halper's mind plunged into a frustrating series of possible solutions, none of which seemed likely to work. In the back of his mind there was one idea, one recollection that he would not yet allow into his serious thought.

He continued to formulate plan after plan, bringing to bear all his experience in the programme as well as past knowledge of dog handling. But nothing that he thought of would apply, or bore the faintest hope of working. Again the faint recollection of an earlier experiment troubled his mind, and he became aware of Colonel Brunning's gaze.

The colonel's look was brooding . . . painfully perceptive. 'There *is* a way. . . .' he said softly.

Halper then knew, and knew also that Brunning had reached the same conclusion that he himself had been unconsciously hoping to avoid.

Matthews frowned, his patience strained. 'What is it — what method are you talking about?'

Halper was hesitant, but explained. 'During one of our experiments with the CAM system, we accidentally discovered a particular combination of signals that when transmitted, produces a temporary paralytic effect in the animal. As long as the signal is maintained, the animal remains in a state resembling an epileptic seizure. But — it could be dangerous, if maintained for more than a few minutes.'

Matthews followed through the train of thought. 'So, if the dog were to suddenly appear ill . . . the doctor would open the cage to examine it?'

Halper was unenthusiastic. 'It might work.'

'Then try it,' Matthews snapped.

Joyce was on her feet in an instant. 'General — that signal

could seriously harm him,' she protested. 'It's much too risky. *Please!*'

'I'm sorry,' Matthews said. 'We've got to try whatever has even the slimmest chance of –'

'Sir,' Halper interrupted, 'there's an automatic system programmed into the computer now to prevent that combination of signals from accidentally occurring again.'

Matthews looked to Carter. 'Can it be bypassed?'

Reluctantly, Carter nodded. 'It will take a minute.'

'Then work on it!'

In Omsk, the vehicle was now over a mile away from the Technical Institute, making its way to the area of town where the Korsky veterinary facility was located. A light snow was falling, and the shallow layer of smooth whiteness was marred only by the ruts left behind by the van. It was five minutes after seven in the evening, and few people were in the streets. Most workers were in their homes now, enjoying their dinner and the end of another day's work. A late-arriving lumber truck was in the process of entering a sawmill yard, and coming down a cross street was a police vehicle making its rounds.

And the van continued on towards Korsky Institute, taking Major further away from both his objective and the source of his relay signals. . . .

In Houston, Carter's work was completed. New programming had temporarily bypassed the needed portion of the complex machine's instructions. . . .

'We're ready, General,' Carter told him.

'Excellent,' Matthews replied. He noticed the strained expression on Joyce Kandell's face, but he chose to ignore the girl. 'Proceed.'

'Carter, here's what you must do,' Halper said. 'Kill the signal the instant the cage door is open, then I'll transmit the command: *Major – defend!*'

'Right.'

'And we must be ready with the countermand and escape signals,' Halper added. He had chosen the command with

236

deliberate care, since the normal *attack* signal was not to be used lightly. Despite Major's normally quiet disposition, the dog still held the power of death within its powerful jaws and sharp teeth, and the limiting command, *defend*, should be all that would be needed.

Carter nodded, hesitated a second, then with a heavy heart quickly struck the keys required to transmit the paralytic signal. Behind him, Halper kept an eye on the second hand of his watch, terribly aware of the fact that the signal could only be maintained for a few brief minutes at most.

In Omsk, the effect was immediate.

Major writhed, his tongue lolling to one side of his mouth, eyes staring out at the doctor in wild confusion. Then the dog's powerful form lay nearly motionless on the floor of the cage, except for brief involuntary twitches.

Ludmila Petrokova stared at him with horrified, unbelieving eyes. Only a moment before the dog had been normal, with no outward signs of trouble. And now, abruptly, he appeared to be violently ill. She grabbed her small bag of medical equipment, opened it, and removed a stethoscope. Perhaps, she thought, she had overlooked a weak heart condition. Or maybe the effects of the Americans' experiment were not totally successful after all.

As she quickly unlocked the cage door, she knew what Nikovitch would say: that it was her fault, that somehow she had been responsible ... that she had not been careful enough in her examination. He would believe nothing else ... would *want* to believe nothing else. ...

As she swung open the door, the concern on her face might have been for the dog or for herself. It was difficult to tell whether the steady hand that placed the stethoscope belonged to a fearful scientist or a compassionate human.

Abruptly the signal stopped, freeing Major from its mind-numbing grip. He looked squarely at the bewildered Petrokova, at the hand-held instrument near him. Suddenly there was in his mind the knowledge that this person was an enemy — an enemy to be stopped, but not killed.

Instantly, Major sprang forward from the cage. He

237

collided with the doctor, the full force of his spring carrying them both to the other side of the van.

Petrokova's head thumped the metal interior of the vehicle, and she slumped to the floor and lay motionless. Major regained his feet, then briefly sniffed at the unconscious form. The threat was gone, yet he knew there was more he must do.

Moving to the back of the van, the dog studied the broad handle that locked the doors shut. Then, turning his head almost flat against the door, he grasped the handle in his jaws and twisted. He pulled it in its downward swing until at last the latch mechanism released. Both doors swung partially open, and Major dived out the rear of the van, landing lightly on the snow-covered roadway.

As the van rolled on, the driver paused briefly to listen. He had detected a noise in the rear, and sought to clarify its source. But he heard nothing else, and returned his attention to driving. Uttering a minor curse, he reprimanded the man with him in the cab for not having secured the cage properly . . . and drove on.

Major began to run, back down the road leading to the Technical Institute. He had not seen which route the van followed from the building, but he knew the way. He was in a new maze now, a new game. And the pattern with which to solve the problem was magically in his mind . . . along with a strange sense of urgency that compelled him to hurry. All this he felt . . . all this he knew. But he could not know the elation felt by a group of anxious people, so very far away. . . .

Everyone in the mission control centre was standing, cautiously smiling tentative grins of hope and joy, their eyes riveted to the great visual-display screen and its glowing image. Grey, ghostly buildings moved jerkily by on the screen as Major ran, buildings growing out of the bleak landscape and rooted in snow. The view swung to the left suddenly as Major rounded a corner.

'He seems to be on course,' Arnold Smith said. He was standing next to Halper and Joyce Kandell, holding a map section before him. And he was quietly glad he had taken the time with Carter to program the computer's memory banks with generalised map coordinates and pictorial references, should they become necessary. For now they were necessary, and at Carter's direction the great electronic device had busily plotted a route back to the institute for Major ... making it a part of the dog's own memory. With the speed of electronics, it had taken no more than thirty seconds from the transmission of the dog's last command until completion.

Brunning added, 'Now if he can just avoid being spotted.'

'Yes,' Joyce replied, unconsciously wringing her hands. 'How long do you think it will be before they discover what's happened?'

Smith answered the question. 'Maybe only a matter of minutes ... who knows! But at least he's out of their control for the moment. Once they find out he's loose, they'll have police and military personnel combing the town for him ... but I doubt if they'll expect the dog to head straight for their headquarters!'

'The snow!' Joyce said suddenly. 'He must be leaving tracks in the snow. They'll be able to find him easily if they follow his tracks —'

'She's right!' It was General Matthews who had responded. 'Halper — Smith — you'll have to change his course. Make him wary of trackers. If he doesn't get off that soft snow for at least part of the way, he'll be leaving a trail a *boy scout* could follow.'

While Smith checked the course set out on the map, Halper looked up the code-phrase command that stood for evasive manoeuvring ... the command that would let Major know he was in hostile territory. As the lieutenant flipped to the correct page in his training notebook and saw the word, he remembered with painful clarity his capricious attempt at humour in the choice. For the code-phrase he had picked for that desired action was *dogcatcher*.

Reluctantly, Halper transmitted the command. Both Matthews and Brunning were too involved in the mission at that point to concern themselves with a lieutenant's whim.

On the image-display screen, they could see the results of the command. Major swiftly detoured from his course, heading for the edge of the road. As he neared a building with a high concrete loading platform protected by an overhanging roof, he loped towards it, building up speed. With a carefully measured leap, the dog reached the platform and landed in a shock absorbing crouch, then trotted off along the concrete surface to the extent of its length.

He turned and started down a loading ramp adjacent to the side of the building, but leaped from that ramp before reaching the snow-covered ground. Alighting on a large machinery crate, he leaped again, leaving only four muddled prints on the crate's snowy upper surface. His landing point this time was the raised base of an exterior stair, leading up along the outside of the next building and terminating at a doorway on the top floor. His target was not the door, but rather the metal ladder that began next to it and curved over the roof.

Major trotted up the stairs, only leaving tracks from the point where he landed, up to the level platform. Hesitating long enough to look around from his high perch for any signs of pursuers, the dog then tackled the task of climbing the ladder.

Ladders were nothing new for Major. He remembered well the canine corps' obstacle course, a brief part of his ARDCOM training. Halper had taught him, taking him through it the first few times, then remaining at a distance while the dog went through it alone. For Major's training had to be different from that of an ordinary guard dog. He had to also be capable of functioning independently, relying solely on the bits of information supplied to his memory by the CAM system.

Methodically raising himself up the ladder one rung at a time, he finally reached the top of the roof. Its slope was gradual enough to permit a relatively fast pace across the top of the building, and Major crossed completely to the other side of the expansive roof.

He paused at the edge, looking down and surveying the scene below. Major was breathing harder now, and the vaporous clouds of his breath drifted slowly up and dissipated.

There was a man below, moving down the street, perhaps on his way home. Had he thought to look up, he might have seen the dog ... seen it and wondered at the oddity. But there was no reason for him to look up, and he continued on his way.

Once the man had disappeared from sight, Major began looking for a way down. There were no ladders or stairs on this side of the building — no normal way to return to the ground. But there was one thing — a large, Russian-built truck parked below. A truck with a heavy canvas top, capped with a two-inch layer of snow.

Major made his decision quickly, and jumped. He plummeted fifteen feet to the top of the truck, his fall cushioned both by the snow and the give of the canvas cover. A second jump brought him to ground level once again.

Waiting momentarily in the shadow of the truck, he darted across to the opposite building. The sign on the wall was indecipherable to the dog, but it labelled the building as being a metal-working plant. After checking the doors for some way of entry, he found none that yielded to his pressure.

But in his mind was the realisation that this building was between him and his objective. To go around it would require travelling across one of the larger, more exposed streets. He knew he must avoid that if possible.

Major stood up against one of the windows, his forepaws pressing upwards against the frame. But the latch had been secured inside and it would not budge. He could break the glass, but the small spaces between the wooden framework would not admit his bulk.

The dog was about to give up that course of action and try going around, despite the possible danger, when his gaze fell on a small wooden structure at the side of the building. Four feet long by three feet deep and high, the structure had a sloping cover that was hinged against the building's wall. Padding softly to it, Major investigated first with his sense of smell.

From within the structure came the scent of more wood, but raw and unfinished. There was the peculiar tang of bark and odour of dried sap. Major raised the cover with his nose and peered into the structure.

The bin was half-filled with stacks of logs, cut to short lengths and of small diameter. On the far side, the side formed by the building's wall, there was the dim outline of a panel, around which there seemed to be faint air movement.

Major flipped the cover up, catching its weight on his shoulders, then sprang into the bin. As the cover closed behind him, he was suddenly in total darkness. But he knew where the panel was located, and in a moment had shoved it aside.

He emerged inside the building, next to a wood-burning stove and a smaller, open-topped box of logs. In here were many scents: burnt wood and ash, the sharp smell of turned metal, oil, and cloth, and the scent of man.

The dog trotted past lathes and presses and rough wooden tables where countless tools lay in the positions they had been left at quitting time. There were other wood stoves in the spacious building, whose only partitions seemed to be those forming a small office in one corner. The rest of the plant was open throughout its breadth, though cluttered with a multitude of machinery.

Reaching the other side, Major found a window. He peered out for a long moment, until sure no one was in the area. The latch was similar enough to those he had encountered in his training for him to swivel it open. This done, he stood and forced the window frame up enough with his forepaws to permit him to climb out.

Dropping to the ground, he again checked briefly for signs of people, then quickly headed away, disappearing into the shadows. . . .

The American team in Houston was more than satisfied with Major's performance so far. They were still aware that the task was not yet accomplished, but at least they were moving forward now.

General Matthews had his hand on Brunning's shoulder.

'I can see you haven't overestimated that dog's ability.' Despite his obvious pleasure, his face still showed signs of fatigue. 'As I told you before, Brunning, I'm due to retire soon. By the time this mission is through, I'm going to be ready —'

At that moment, Joyce Kandell suddenly cried out in surprise. '*The screen!*'

The girl's horror spread through the others as they saw that the image was gone. The visual-display screen had gone totally black.

'What's happened to it!' Matthews demanded, a fearful urgency to his tone.

Neston looked over the instruments of the communications console, while Bill Stanton frantically checked the circuitry. When he turned, his anxious look matched his words.

'The NASCOM circuit from Madrid has gone dead,' he told them. 'We're getting no signals to or from the dog — we'll have to try to patch in another way.'

'How long will it take?'

'Ten minutes ... maybe longer. Because of the security problems, we couldn't brief all of our facilities —'

'Work on it — do the best you can.' Matthews then faced Halper with a question. 'What about the dog? While our communications are out, will he stop?'

The Lieutenant's tone was grim. 'No, General. He's received his commands ... they're part of his memory now, and he won't forget them. Without further orders, he'll keep heading towards the institute ... *but with no idea of what to do once he gets there!*'

243

At ARDCOM Headquarters in Missouri, General Raskin was unaware of the sudden loss of communications between the NASCOM Switching Center in Madrid and the Johnson Space Center in Houston. But at the moment he faced a problem of his own. . . .

'You'd better have a pretty good explanation for this,' Larry Lawrence was grumbling. He sat on a grey metal Army-issue chair in Raskin's office, glaring up at the general who stood so imposingly before him. 'You had no right to order me frisked or to have my tape recorder confiscated —'

'Just *stow it*, Lawrence!' Raskin thundered. 'Where do you get off thinking you can extort your way onto a top-secret base, and then yell about your *rights*?'

Lawrence snorted. 'Top-secret — that classification covers a multitude of military sins very conveniently, I'll bet. And as for calling it extortion . . . well, I'm sure you'll admit that extortion only works when a person has something to hide. And the fact that I'm here in your office now pretty well proves my theories are correct.'

'Your theories are bull, Lawrence!'

'Suppose we let the readers decide?'

Raskin drew himself up to his full height and looked at the *News-Scene* reporter with chilling menace in his eyes. 'While we're playing "let's suppose", you might consider this: it will be awfully hard for you to print anything if you're not allowed to leave this base . . .'

'You can't hold me here,' Lawrence said coolly. 'You have no legitimate reason.'

'Are you going to quote me the constitution next?'

'Hardly. I'm sure I'd be wasting my breath. But it would be very unwise on your part to try anything extralegal.'

'What are you talking about?'

Lawrence smiled faintly. 'I've taken precautions, General. I never walk into anything without insurance.' He paused briefly, watching the general's increasing agitation. 'Before I came here, I left a tape with someone I could trust, explaining my theories and the fact that I was travelling here. I left the tape with instructions to turn it over to the wire services if for any reason I don't report back. I've also informed my publisher of the general nature of my article, and if anyone should check, they'll find that the airline I flew with, the agency I rented a car from, and the hotel I stayed at will all have records of my trip out here. So you see, my story will get printed one way or another.'

'I could have you declared a spy —'

'That would be pretty hard to prove, General. And the story would still be out.'

Raskin eyed him coldly. 'You think you have everything all figured out, don't you, Lawrence. If you only knew. . . .' He paused, then added angrily, 'Why try to blackmail our armed forces . . . our government? *Just whose side are you on, anyway?*'

'John Doe,' Lawrence answered. 'The American public, who always has to foot the bill for an excess of military experiments that are seldom necessary, often dangerous, and frequently immoral!'

'Oh, shut up! You're beginning to sound like your blasted editorials.'

The reporter smiled. 'So you have read some of them.'

'Only a few . . . but enough to know what kind of crap you shovel out to your readers.'

Lawrence frowned. 'I happen to think that badly planned and ridiculously expensive testing deserves to be exposed!'

'And that's what you think is involved here?'

'Don't try to deny it, General. If there had been nothing to the incident . . . nothing phoney about the capsule retrieved by the Russians, then I'd still be banging on the gate out there, and you wouldn't be talking to me now. . . .'

Raskin studied him for several moments, then turned on his heel and headed for the door. Over his shoulder, he snapped a command to Lawrence:

'Wait here!'

The general left his office, walked past the MP guard

245

posted at his door, and went directly to the orderly room. Command Sergeant Major Tyson rose quickly to his feet as Raskin entered.

'General —'

'What do we do with him, Ty?' Raskin said without looking at the lean, black-haired man whose three-up-and-three-down stripes surrounded a wreath-enclosed star. 'What *can* we do with him? He's got us over a barrel as long as we have to be concerned with publicity. And he's left word of his theories, evidently, with his associates, in case we should try to hold him.'

Tyson replied softly, 'Do you believe him, sir?'

'Yes, I'm sure he's telling the truth about that. He's clever enough to have made the necessary precautions, even if he's not smart enough to realise what he stands to ruin!'

'How much more time before the mission is out of jeopardy?'

'A few hours,' Raskin replied. 'But it's not just a case of worrying about Lawrence's news item tipping off the Russians ... in another hour or two, it will be too late to make any difference. What we have to consider is the long view ... the effect on the public if the truth gets out about this mission ... the *real* truth. And if Lawrence doesn't find the kind of story he's looking for, he may start seeking some other connection and trip smack over the fact that this is one big espionage gambit. That would look great in the papers!'

Tyson shook his head pessimistically. 'I can imagine.'

'And this comes at a time when the public's faith in us all is already pretty shaky. If word got out that our brand-new, multibillion-dollar defence system was wide open to a Russian attack ... well, that can't happen. We can't let it.'

The sergeant major considered the problem in silence. Then: 'Sir, what if we give him some kind of cover story ... something to explain the nature of the satellite ... something to throw him off the track?'

'I'm afraid we don't have time to concoct another cover for this mission.'

'Why would it have to be *another* one, sir?'

Raskin looked at the man strangely, then dawning realisation set his features. 'Of course! If the Russians bought it, why not Lawrence? And it might be the exact kind of thing he'd want to believe. We may be able to hide a greater secret with a lesser one. It's worth a try, anyway.'

The general wheeled about and started out of the orderly room. He halted abruptly at the doorway, looking back to the sergeant major. 'Thanks, Ty — I won't forget. . . .'

Raskin returned down the hall, walking quickly past Brunning's locked office and the training-records room. Lawrence was up from the chair, pacing, when the general re-entered his own office.

Lawrence halted his pacing, remaining motionless. His face was calm, but there was in his eyes an uncertainty faintly suggestive of fear.

'Well, what have you decided, General?'

Raskin did not look at him, did not even answer. He went around to the other side of his desk, pulled up the chair and sat in it. Arms resting on the green blotter pad in the centre of the desk top. Raskin stared grimly at his interlocked hands, supremely aware of the reporter's increasing restlessness. At last, after several long moments, he spoke.

'Sit down, Lawrence.'

The reporter studied the man before him. The general did not repeat his command, and Lawrence was puzzled by Raskin's new mood, unsure of how to cope with it. Then, slowly, he stepped back and lowered himself onto the grey metal chair.

He waited.

Raskin continued looking at his desk top. 'We're going to let you go in a few hours.' He paused for several seconds. 'I'll arrange for you to be driven back to the gate. Your recording equipment will be returned to you there.'

Lawrence remained silent, frowning. He sensed in Raskin's words something unsaid . . . something waiting to be dropped on him like the keen edge of Damocles' sword.

Quietly, he asked, 'What's going on, General?'

'We're letting you go,' Raskin replied. 'So be happy, go

ahead and write your little story, and let the consequences be our concern.'

'What . . . what are you talking about?'

Raskin looked up for the first time. 'You think you know so much! You're so sure you're right that you'll end up endangering our chances of getting both the dog and the satellite back.'

'So . . . it *isn't* what the press releases claim.' There was no note of triumph in his voice. Raskin's abrupt turnaround seemed to rob him of any satisfaction. 'What have your people been up to this time?'

'Not just us . . . there are other groups involved. A civilian agency needed one of our animals, trained for hardship and endurance, to be used in an important space experiment – one that could have countless beneficial applications.' Raskin shook his head sadly. 'The Russians don't know what they've got yet . . . but you'll take care of that, all right!'

Lawrence leaned slightly forward, a look of quiet concentration on his features. 'What kind of experiment?'

'One we couldn't risk a man's life on. . . .' Raskin paused, seemingly reluctant to continue. A variety of emotions played across his face, then a gradual look of resolve replaced them. 'What do you know of Project Deep Sleep?'

'I never heard of it.'

Raskin stared at him intently. 'What would you say if I told you that the satellite which has so interested you has been in orbit around the Earth for one year and sixty-four days?'

'*What?*'

The general leaned forward, his tone still quietly angry. 'I'm going to take a chance on you, Lawrence. I'm going to tell you what I can about the experiment, in the hopes that once you know what it involves, you'll be more reluctant to destroy it with adverse publicity. But I warn you –' he paused solemnly. 'I warn you, Lawrence – if you print one word of what I am about to tell you in confidence, I will deny it completely – deny that I ever spoke to you. . . .'

In Omsk, Major was truly on his own for the first time. Suddenly without the continuing signals from Houston, there was only the urgent, driving order last placed in his memory. He knew he must return to the building where he was last held, and that he must do so carefully.

He was still three-quarters of a mile from the institute, which was separated from his present position by a number of other structures, roadways, and barriers. And the snow was still falling, bringing with it a numbing chill that penetrated Major's coat more and more. The pads of his feet were already sore and icy — in another hour they might be completely frozen, if he was still outdoors by that time.

Major could endure much, but had not been adequately prepared for the cold. The prospect of his removal from the Omsk Technical Institute, and his subsequent journey back on foot, had not been considered seriously during the planning stage of the operation. It would have been impossible to anticipate every possible complication of the plan under the *best* of conditions, let alone those imposed by pressing time schedules and limited resources. But matters of logistics were meaningless to the dog. All he felt was the cold and an urge to move on ... an urge strong enough to fight his increasing desire to seek only a place of warmth and shelter.

Major hesitated in the shadow of an ash can while a small truck rumbled down the street before him. Once it had passed from sight, he trotted swiftly across the roadway, disappearing into the mouth of a narrow alley.

The dog sniffed cautiously, for there were a number of scents lingering in the alley, some easily identified, some not. There was one in particular, originating somewhere at the other end, that was vaguely familiar. But it was too faint in the bitter cold air that assailed his nostrils for the dog to be sure.

He moved on along the alleyway, past refuse barrels and stacks of empty crates. To his right was the rear of a warehouse; to his left, a food-processing plant. The rear entrance of the plant was located halfway down the alley, the door flanked by refuse barrels, some of which bore the odour of meat.

The scent only reminded Major of his hunger, for he had been fed only a tiny amount of solid food while in the institute. He had received some intravenous liquids that would not interfere with Dr. Petrokova's testing, and that at least had helped sustain his energy. But it had not filled his stomach, and the nearby scent of meat pulled him like a magnet.

But even scraps and by-products are not so carelessly thrown away in a nation which barely meets its food requirements. The barrels contained only bones, and even these were destined to be transported to yet another plant where they would be ground to dust for use in fertilisers.

Something else in the immediate area attracted the dog's attention, and Major investigated. Hanging before a wooden door marked with numerous scratches, a small section of meat dangled on a rope.

Major moved closer to it, then stopped abruptly. He had seen a faint imprint in the snow beneath the dangling meat, in a pattern familiar to him. He gently pushed a small area of snow away with the tip of his nose, and saw exposed the gleaming metal point of a bear-trap's jaw. As his counterparts had been trained for work in Vietnam and other hostile areas, so Major had been trained. The avoidance of booby traps had been schooled into him, as well as the ability to detect poisons. And now that he was closer, the tainted scent of arsenic was present in the meat that hung before him.

A twofold trap had been set for some animal, something that apparently raided or attempted to raid the processing plant. Suddenly, something about the area seemed dangerous to the dog. Major fled past the rear entrance and on along the alley.

He had reached the end of it, and was ready to dart across the next street that ran at right angles to the alley, when he saw the tracks. In the snow around the end of the alleyway were numerous sets of them, going back and forth, as if something had paced cautiously around the opening between the two buildings. They were not the tracks of a man, and they bore the scent of something like a dog, yet different . . . a scent which grew stronger.

Major heard a deep, savage growl, and looked up into the glistening gaze of a beast half again his size. Some fifteen feet distant crouched the dark and hulking form of a Siberian timber wolf.

Only dire hunger could have brought such a beast from its natural home in the wilds beyond Omsk, where the wooded plains and valleys still held deer and other game. But in winter food is scarce, and game harder to find. The fear of man fades as starvation threatens. . . .

In the next instant, the wolf lunged at Major. Despite its lack of food, it still outweighed the dog by twenty or thirty pounds. Its yellow-grey, shaggy coat glistening with flecks of snow, the wolf was virtually on top of the dog before there was a chance to run.

Forced to fight, Major needed no encouragement other than his desire to survive. He lashed back with the fury of his own teeth and nails as the two canines thrashed furiously in the snow. On Major's side was his own natural ability, augmented by ARDCOM training. But on the side of the wolf was greater weight, muscles not so numbed by the cold, and a fighting frenzy brought about by severe hunger.

For several long minutes that seemed like hours, they scrambled and fought. Major sustained numerous scratches from glancing blows of the wolf's sharp teeth, but left an equal number on his opponent.

They separated abruptly. The wolf faced Major with a madness in his eyes, teeth bared, slavering. He lunged suddenly for the dog, but his teeth snapped on empty air as Major dodged the strike at his throat, turned quickly, and nipped the wolf's ear, drawing blood.

The wolf drew back. It was tiring more quickly than the dog, who was more rested and had a greater reserve of food energy in its system.

Once more the wolf lunged, and again the quicker dog dodged, then countered with a successful strike of his own.

251

The wolf sank back, becoming momentarily caught in the snow. As he struggled to regain his feet, he still held in his eyes a look of rage and determination.

Seizing the opportunity, Major lunged in to attack. He toppled the beast, flipping it on its back. But the dog's smaller jaws could not get a good enough grip on the wolf's thickly-furred throat.

Before the beast could recover its footing, Major whirled and ran back down the alley behind him. He ran as swiftly as he could, fully aware of the sounds of his attacker gaining behind him.

Back down the alley they ran, past the stacked crates and boxes. Barely in time Major remembered the trap set in the centre of the alley, near the doorway, and leaped over it. He continued on, racing with all his speed, trying to gain as much distance as possible before reaching the street at the other end.

As the dog came within a few feet of the street, he heard a muffled clank of metal behind him, and knew without turning that the wolf had not been so fortunate in avoiding the trap. He would not be pursued further, but he could not go back through the narrow alley. He would have to go on around the warehouse and take his chances in the main street.

Major trotted briskly on, his circulation increased by the struggle. For a while, he would not feel the bitter cold so much.

At the corner, he paused to see if the area was clear. For the moment it was, and the dog started out along the edge of the roadway that headed in the general direction of the Trans-Siberian railroad station, and specifically in the direction of the Omsk Technical Institute.

He had made it nearly two-thirds of the way along the block when a police vehicle stopped at the corner in front of him. Major halted, moving into shadows at the building's edge. He looked down the road, back the way he had already travelled, seeking an escape route. But from that direction now rumbled a long, canvas-topped truck, bearing a last delivery of cargo to be taken to the railroad station.

As the distance between the truck and the police vehicle steadily decreased, Major was forced to reach a quick decision. He found no help from that odd corner of his mind that had before offered ways of doing things or issued commands from his trainer. This time, the dog had to make his own effort.

He waited in the shadows until the truck had passed him and its open back was visible to him. Then, with a sudden buildup of speed, Major ran after the truck. He leaped mightily, sailing through the open space at the rear of the vehicle, and landing atop boxes destined to be transferred to waiting trains.

Major settled down in a gap between two boxes, peering out through the space between the canvas and the truck bed. The police vehicle remained at the corner as the truck rolled past it, with no signal that the men inside had seen anything. Soon they were out of sight.

The dog knew he was still moving in the right direction. And in his mind was approximate knowledge of how far he could travel in that direction before reaching the area of the institute. So that would be his method. He would simply stay within the truck, safe from detection, until he came near enough to the building which drew him so urgently to continue on foot. . . .

The Russian transport van had almost reached the gates of Korsky Veterinary Institute when Dr. Ludmila Petrokova, buffeted by movements of the van and by draughts of cold air coming in through the still-open rear doors, began to regain consciousness. Slowly she raised herself to a sitting position, holding her head as dizziness sought to overwhelm her. Her eyes suddenly opened wide, and she stared at the empty cage. Whirling, she saw the open rear doors and a brief, bitter gasp left her lips.

Petrokova climbed awkwardly to her feet, holding onto the cage for support. With her free hand, she began to pound on the metal partition between the cargo area and the truck's cab.

In a moment, the van had stopped — the driver disembarked, running to the rear of the vehicle. With an astonished look, he surveyed the scene before him.

'The dog is gone — escaped!' Petrokova nearly shouted. 'Drive on — *quickly*. I must get to a phone and contact the Director!'.

Miklos Nikovitch was on the ground floor of the Omsk Technical Institute, in Otto Hurdein's private office, when the call came in from Petrokova. Hurdein spoke for a moment, then gave him the phone with an anxious look that forewarned of trouble.

Nikovitch took the phone and listened to the veterinary specialist's words first with astonishment, then with growing anger. 'How could you let such a thing happen!' he bellowed. He brought his anger under control then, but his carefully modulated tone was more threatening than vented fury. 'You will be held responsible for whatever happens as a result of your error, Doctor. You *must* recover the dog alive and unharmed. Send your security personnel out at once to look for it — I will send some of our men over to assist. If necessary, I will alert the Army base and have soldiers join in the search. Do you know the approximate area where the dog left the van?'

He paused, listening to the answer. 'Then begin the search at once. And this time, Dr. Petrokova — make no mistakes.'

James Neston and Bill Stanton were frantically working to restore communications at the NASA centre in Houston, and were in the final stages of patching into circuits that would connect their temporarily set-up mission control equipment with a building called Electra House, Victoria Embankment, London, England. Neston completed the final check, activated the circuits, and turned to see the results. . . .

'We're now tied in through the NASA Communications Switching Center in London,' he explained as he studied the image-display screen. 'They've established ground-line communications to the military base in Germany that is transmitting the signal to the relay satellite. The image should be coming through any time now, I hope. . . .'

For three long seconds, the great display screen remained absolutely black. Then abruptly scrambled light patterns, disturbed by interference, appeared across its surface. In another second the image had been sorted, corrected, and stabilised by the system's computer. The signal was restored — and their long-distance duplicate of Major's vision was again there to guide them and inform them.

'Thank the Lord,' General Matthews breathed softly. '*Smith!* Can you tell where the dog is? Can you fix his position?'

Arnold Smith studied the image intently. Major was now trotting along quickly and cautiously, and there were occasionally clear views of buildings and streets. Referring both to his maps of the city and to information stored within his own impressive memory, Smith compared what he saw on the image-display screen with what he knew to be in the area.

A slight frown set his features. 'I don't know how he got there so fast, with all the precautions he's taking,' Smith said. 'But the dog is apparently within a few blocks of the outer fence at the institute!'

Matthews turned first to Brunning, then to Halper and Joyce Kandell. 'How is that possible?'

Halper shook his head, a puzzled quirk setting the line of his mouth. 'I don't know, sir. Technically, he shouldn't be there. I mean, he could easily run the distance in that time if it were a straight line with no obstructions. But the route he had to take back to the institute was hardly a straight line! And I'm sure that he was being careful not to be seen, after the last command we sent him.'

Matthews sighed. 'I suppose we should just be grateful for small miracles and let it go at that. . . .' He studied the screen, not realising that the truth of the matter would never be known to any of them — that due to the communications blackout, they had completely missed Major's stolen ride on the cargo truck, as well as his bout with the scavenging wolf. Matthews turned again to Smith. 'You're sure of the location?'

'We have fairly accurate and detailed information con-

255

cerning the immediate area surrounding the institute,' Smith replied firmly. 'I don't feel there is any doubt of the dog's location.'

'All right, then,' Matthews said grudgingly. 'We'll just forget about that little mystery for the time being and concentrate on the mission. Halper — will any more commands be necessary to bring the dog to the institute proper?'

'Not unless he runs into trouble of some kind or other,' the lieutenant replied. 'But from the way he's doing so far, I don't think he'll need much help from us.'

Matthews turned to Joyce. 'What about the cold — how much longer can he keep going?'

She looked at temperature charts supplied by Smith, comparing them with her own records. 'Perhaps a half hour or more. But if he can't get inside fairly soon, the cold will begin dulling his mind. Our signals may not have any effect on him.'

Everyone's eyes were on the screen as the low-angle view of the city of Omsk continued to move across the image, occasionally ducking behind posts or under trucks. Major was following as direct a route as possible now, while still avoiding being seen.

Around a corner the image bobbed, picking up speed down a deserted alleyway. Major dodged past crates and barrels near the end of the alley, then cautiously exited from the narrow passageway and continued along the edge of the intersecting road. As he reached the halfway point along the block, a large and sprawling building surrounded by an ironwork fence came into view a short distance away.

'That's it,' Smith said quickly. 'That's the *institute*!'

The building grew steadily larger within the frame of the visual-display screen, becoming more distinct as its details were enlarged on the high-contrast and somewhat grainy picture. Soon the dog would be there.

Then suddenly Major halted. He dived into a shadowed area along the building next to him and froze in position.

'What's he stopping for?' Matthews tensed as he stared at the motionless image. 'Is something wrong?'

Before anyone could answer, two vehicles came into view at the end of the block. Each was open-topped, and in the back of each, seated on fold-down benches, were eight or nine guards from the institute. They headed on down the street, unwittingly passing the object of their search, and turned in the direction of the Korsky facility.

Major had watched them until they disappeared around the corner, giving those in Houston an extraordinary view of the men and vehicles. Now that the danger was past, the dog continued trotting towards the institute.

'Remember —' Halper said. 'All we're getting is *visual* feedback. But Major can still hear and smell things we can't detect. In that respect, he's still somewhat on his own.'

'Yes,' Matthews replied. 'And from what we just saw, we know now that the Russians have discovered the dog is loose. Probably they have only learned that fact a few moments ago, since the guards are just now being sent out to search. That means the dog has a moderately good head start on them. But their search still creates problems. . . .'

Halper looked confused. 'But sir, shouldn't it help? If part of the security force of the institute has left to assist in the search in another area, it should make entry to the grounds somewhat easier —'

'In that respect, yes,' the general admitted. 'But we don't know yet just how long it will take for the dog to enter the facility and work his way to the particular area in which we're interested. It can't take the searchers too long to follow the dog's tracks, despite his diversionary tactics. Once they see that he's heading in the general direction of the institute, they might radio back there and alert the remaining guards. If that happens, getting in will be ten times harder, if not impossible!'

Halper nodded, and his grim expression was matched by Joyce's. They turned back to the screen.

The phone-line signal flashed on the communications console and Stanton flipped on its circuit, pressing his earpiece tightly to his head. He then turned to face Brunning.

'Colonel — it's the line from ARDCOM again. General Raskin's on with an update of the situation there. . . .'

Brunning moved quickly to the phone, addressed his superior officer, and proceeded to listen to the general's report while the others in the mission control centre continued to watch the dog's progress. The colonel listened for another minute before the call was completed. Then he hung up the phone and returned to Matthews' side.

'General Raskin sounds optimistic,' he told Matthews and the others. 'He was forced to try a different tactic than he would normally have used, but it appears it might work.'

Matthews turned from the screen. 'But he will keep that reporter there until we're done?'

'Yes, sir. But as far as the long-range problem is concerned, he has decided to make use of the cover story already developed to delude the Russians.'

'The suspended-animation experiment?'

Brunning nodded. 'He's made it appear necessary to take the man into his confidence — to make the urgency of the matter more obvious by partially explaining the "project", and how long the satellite had supposedly been in orbit. He tried to make clear the logic of not ruining the project with a story.'

'I seriously doubt if that will really discourage the man.'

'So does General Raskin, sir,' Brunning replied smoothly. 'But as I understand it, that's part of the plan. The general has made sure that the logic is somewhat flawed. The reporter will in all likelihood believe he has been told a half-truth. He will suspect a different, more sinister reason for the suspended-animation experiment, and direct his article towards that idea. If other reporters should have made the same connection he has, they will probably follow his lead and tackle the matter from the point of view that it is all a wasteful military experiment.'

Matthews nodded in quiet appreciation. 'It may work. We'll find out soon enough. If it does work, at least it will give us all time enough to construct sufficient false information to cover the real purpose of the mission.' He was aware of a barely audible comment from Dr. Laswell's direction, and he turned to the NASA Administrator, undisguised hostility in his expression.

'That's what you want, isn't it, Dr. Laswell? Enough of a cover-up for this mission so that the precious sanctity of your organisation remains intact!'

Laswell glared back, but said nothing more.

'*The dog's within range —*' Smith said abruptly.

All eyes returned to the image-display screen at Smith's outcry. Major was obviously within a few dozen yards of the high ironwork fence that surrounded the institute.

'There's a guard in the gate house at the front,' Smith added. 'Even if the dog can get past him without being seen, his tracks might be spotted later. He'll have to go around to the side. . . .'

Even as Smith was saying it, Major was detouring from the road that led into the institute. Staying in shadows, he moved around the perimeter of the facility's grounds and approached from the north.

Matthews studied what he could see of the area in the dim light. 'Can your dog tackle a fence that high? It must be six feet or more.'

Halper smiled faintly. 'Just watch, sir.'

Major reached a point along the northern side of the facility which seemed to satisfy him. He began to run, swiftly and rhythmically, gaining speed at a surprising rate on the far from perfect surface.

With a strong, carefully measured leap, the dog just managed to clear the top of the fence by a few scant inches, landing almost a dozen feet on the other side. After a soft impact on the snowy ground, Major headed quickly for the shadows of the building.

'He's made it that far,' Matthews said. 'Now if he can only make it inside.'

Smith turned briefly to the general. 'The main entrance is out of the question. Once inside, the only way down to the security section below ground is through an elevator equipped with a special pass-key mechanism. Our agent there had made a duplicate of the key before his capture. But that won't help us now, of course.'

'How about the loading ramp?' Matthews asked. 'We saw the dog being taken up to ground level by that means.'

Smith nodded. 'It's the only other way down to the security section. But ... how do you propose the dog enter? Those doors will be locked, and I'm afraid that even as remarkable a dog as that one will not be able to get past them.'

'He'll have to ... somehow.' Matthews directed a penetrating look at Halper. 'How about it, lieutenant? Can it be done? Is there any way to manage it?'

The lieutenant shrugged. 'I don't know, sir. There are only so many things possible, even with the CAM system. We're still working with a dog, and a dog can't pick locks or force a door open.'

'But there must be a way ... there *must* be!' Matthews began to pace. 'Granted, it was never intended that the course of this mission would require the dog to re-enter the building. But that's the way things have turned out; it's an unalterable fact.' He stopped, directing his full attention on the ARDCOM personnel. 'And another fact which can't be altered is the simple truth that a highly expensive defence system hangs in the balance ... as well as this country's safety.'

Halper and Joyce concentrated on their training notes, and on the charts and notes supplied by Arnold Smith. Possibilities seemed nonexistent. There were no windows on the ground floor level, and those few that were on the upper floor were certainly locked and completely out of reach even for a human. There were no doors except for those massive portals which barred entrance to the loading ramp.

'Someone had better think of a way pretty soon —' Smith said urgently. 'The dog's stymied. ...'

Obvious from the picture on the image-display screen was the fact that Major had himself found no solution to the problem. The dog was trotting back and forth along the institute wall, searching in vain for some way of complying with the command that drove him steadily on.

Joyce Kandell stared at the notes and charts before her until they seemed to blur into one incomprehensible mass. If there was an answer to their present problem to be found in the accumulated material from Major's training, she could not see it. Finally, tired of looking at the papers, she began to watch the moving pattern on the image-display screen. She watched, letting her mind relax momentarily.

Major was still searching for some means of entry, and Joyce realised that the longer he continued to do so, the greater the risk that he might be seen by a guard in the area. She studied the image more intently, trying to take in all the details of the wall ... the two great loading doors ... the endless, unvarying surface of the stone.

But was that surface unvarying?

Joyce stared harder, concentrating on the moving image. She caught a brief glimpse of a surface irregularity, then had to wait until the dog passed the area again to be sure of what she had seen.

And then she *was* sure. 'There's something — there in the wall, about six feet to the right of the loading doors.' She pointed towards the image-display screen, waiting for Major to again go past the spot. '*There* — do you see it?'

'I saw *something*. . . .' General Matthews replied, still staring at the screen. 'But I couldn't tell what it was.'

Halper had missed it, and shook his head in grim silence.

'I couldn't tell, either,' James Neston added. 'But the instant you pointed it out, I hit the recall button on the photo-facsimile unit. We should be getting a printout in a few seconds. . . .'

All eyes were on the printout unit as the white slip of electrostatic paper emerged. Neston took it immediately to General Matthews, and remained next to him. Matthews called the others over; and they formed a semicircle around him.

'What do you think?' Matthews traced the outline of the wall's surface irregularity with his finger. The photo-facsimile was far from perfect, but at least it offered them time to study the image.

'Looks like a panel of some kind,' Halper offered. He pointed to a number of tiny, shaded circles near the perimeter of that panel. 'It must be bolted on to the wall.'

Neston studied the image for a moment, then added, 'No, not bolts ... bolt heads would either be octagonal or have slots. Those are round and plain. They might be rivets ... but they look more like nailheads. . . .'

Matthews frowned in thought. 'Why would anyone nail a cover panel on a wall? What's behind it? Smith — what do you know about that part of the building?'

The short, bald-headed man sighed inaudibly. 'My information only includes a rough layout of the institute. I know approximately where their project room is, and can plan out a route for the dog to follow once he's inside. But I would have to know the exact room measurements to tell what's behind any given point on the outside wall.'

'But you must have some idea.'

Smith hesitated. 'I don't like guessing. But if I have to, it's possible there's a furnace room behind there. There might be a coal chute behind that panel.'

'But would a coal chute be nailed up ... this time of year, especially?' The general looked back to the image-display screen as Major continued searching. 'And even if it is a furnace room, do you think there might be a way out of it that connects with the loading ramp?'

Smith looked at him unblinkingly. 'There's only one way to find out. ...'

Matthews considered it for a moment, weighing the alternatives. At last, he spoke. ...

'We have nothing else to go on so far ... we may as well try it.' He turned to Halper. 'Can the dog be guided to remove the cover?'

'I think so, sir.' The lieutenant picked up the photo-facsimile copy and studied it. 'There don't seem to be too many nails holding the cover in place. The cover must be wood if it's been nailed on ... and wood behind it that the nails go into ... so it's possible.'

Without another word, Halper took the photo-facsimile over to Carter, and addressed the computer technician. 'We'll have to run this through the pictorial analyser so we can focus Major's attention on the cover. Use the standard motivation programming patterns — make the cover appear to be an obstacle to him, something to be removed from his path — okay?'

'Got it.' Carter slipped the photo-sheet into the slot of the analyser and began quickly typing out the encoded signal patterns that would bring about the desired result.

After the usual momentary delay while the signal was relayed halfway around the world, Major stopped his futile pacing. A new thought was in his mind now, and the dog hurried back to the area of the wall in which the cover was located.

The cover grew large on the image-display screen as Major sniffed around it, occasionally testing its corners with his teeth. He then placed his jaws parallel with the protruding top edge of the cover, and forced his upper teeth into its wooden substance. Carefully, Major began a series of pulling, jerking motions with his head, his feet braced against the ground, his side against the wall.

At first the cover remained rigidly in place, and it seemed that it would not move at all. Then, slowly at first, then more noticeably, the wooden panel began to move away from the wall. With one final tug, Major wrenched it free.

Revealed behind the panel was a gaping open space, twelve inches square, framed by wood stripping. Major cautiously peered inside. A man would not be able to get through the opening, but Major could . . . just. He crawled through and dropped lightly to the floor . . . dropped because the floor was at a lower level than it had seemed from the outside.

On the wall beneath the opening were the marks of brackets and supports no longer present. And an unpainted section of the wall and floor showed clearly where a coal bin had previously occupied space. Near the centre of the room was a heavy-duty electric heating system, its metal surfaces still shiny and gleaming.

'Looks new —' Matthews remarked. 'That's why the old coal-chute opening was only nailed up, instead of plastered. They haven't gotten around to fixing it yet.'

Large air ducts led out from the heating unit, entering different walls to connect with various parts of the building. Some of the ducts were not yet intact, including a few leading upstairs, and several sections of the metal duct sat still wrapped in one corner of the room.

One other duct not yet connected was one leading almost at floor level to the wall on the left. The wall bracket was in place, but brown paper was taped over its opening.

Matthews was tense. 'If I've figured the distance correctly, that wall should adjoin the loading ramp.'

Halper nodded. 'Then let's make that duct opening the next target. We'll transmit an image of it, too. Major should make the connection between the first panel and that paper-covered bracket. If he doesn't get it, we'll try it another way. . . .'

Neston supplied a new photo-facsimile sheet and in a moment the transmission was sent.

Major did not need to be told twice. He zeroed in on the incomplete duct in less than three seconds, trotting over to it.

'We'd better take it easy from here on out,' Halper added. 'I'll reaffirm the danger signal . . . keep him on his toes. . . .'

Major began to paw at the brown paper covering the wall bracket. In a moment he had torn a small section of it open, and he cautiously looked through the space. On the image-display screen came a view of a wide, empty hallway, with a floor and ceiling that sloped gradually downwards, levelling off in the distance.

'That's it!' Matthews exclaimed. 'That's the loading ramp. We've found our entrance!'

Major pulled back the torn corners of the brown paper with his teeth, enlarging the opening inward instead of allowing the torn paper to protrude out into the hall. In another second, the job was done.

Neston assessed the size of the wall duct. 'It's going to be a tight squeeze –'

'He can do it.' Halper's tone was steady, encouragement in his voice. 'All we have to worry about now is getting him through the halls. . . .'

'That,' Matthews added, 'and reaching the project room before the search parties discover which way he's headed. . . .'

264

At that moment, approximately three-quarters of a mile from the institute, a team of searchers had succeeded in following Major's trail despite his diversionary tactics. They had been forced to track on foot, while their support vehicles followed the main roads and stayed within range.

Two of the searchers paused to examine two sets of prints leading off in different directions, while another continued down the length of a narrow alley. From that alley came a sudden outcry —

'*Here* — come here, quickly!'

The others ran to join their comrade, reaching the centre of the alley in a moment. They turned their flashlight beams upon the reddened snow and the grotesque, frozen form held captive in sprung steel jaws.

The leader of the searchers stared wide-eyed. 'That is no dog — it is a *wolf*! What have we been tracking?'

Then a second shout came from the roadway behind them, and they turned and headed back down the alley. The man who had addressed them stood waiting, his arm pointing to the main street around the corner.

'There are more tracks —' he told them. 'They go part way down the street, then . . . disappear in the middle of the street without a trace!'

The search leader shook his head sadly. 'I am beginning to think we are chasing a ghost instead of a dog! But that wolf back there — there may be a pack of them in the area. We will have to be more careful now. And it appears that the dog's tracks have become confused with those of the wolf, somewhere back where we picked them up the last time. We will have to backtrack . . . see if we can locate the dog's trail again.' Then, thinking of his leader's wrath, he added, 'This is going to take longer than is wanted . . . which is bad . . . very bad. . . .'

Within the below-ground level of the Omsk Technical Institute, Major prowled cautiously. Arnold Smith's knowledge of the general layout had been used to construct a route for the dog to follow, a route which was transmitted and made a part of his memory.

Miklos Nikovitch and Otto Hurdein were still in the upper level of the building. The remaining staff were gone for the time being ... all except for the scientist, Vladimir Dubuokov.

Dubuokov still worked in the project room on the far side of the security section. He was working feverishly to complete the final calculations necessary to adjust the equipment that would be employed in the counter-Cerberus system. Seated at a table strewn with papers concerning the operation, Dubuokov checked his equations. The door behind him was closed and locked from the inside ... a minor security precaution he routinely followed.

Unbeknownst to him, Major waited a short distance away. The dog hesitated at a corner, waiting while a security guard passed quietly down the hall and headed for the opposite end of the section. With the guard out of sight, and no others detectable, Major advanced on the closed door. ...

Dubuokov was suddenly aware of a sound, and was startled to hear a scratching on the door to the project room. He called out, and upon receiving no answer, laid down his slide rule and got up from the table. He peered through the small, double-glass window in the door, seeing nothing at first. Then his eyes drifted down, and a confused frown spread over his features.

Dubuokov unlatched the door, then opened it. He stared at the dog which sat for the moment so passively before him. As if expecting an answer, he said, 'But ... but what are you doing back *here*?'

Then Major underwent a drastic change of personality. Springing forward, he knocked the scientist to the floor and entered the room. Pushing the door shut, Major set his nose against the sliding latch and closed it.

As Dubuokov struggled to his feet, trying to get to the alarm button on the wall, Major advanced towards him, growling fiercely. The unmistakable threat of the dog's bared teeth, combined with his strange reappearance and behaviour were too much to fight. The scientist backed away, with Major pressing him to retreat further, until at

266

last there was no avenue of escape left open to him except for the tiny storage room off to one side.

Dubuokov entered the tiny auxiliary room and swiftly pulled the door closed behind him. Major immediately ceased growling, and insured the scientist's imprisonment by tipping over a cabinet in front of the door.

What happened after that would have seemed even more bizarre to a casual observer, for the dog proceeded to sniff about the papers on the tabletop, gazing at them with an odd fascination. Then, on further orders from Houston, Major began to open select file cabinet drawers, taking certain file folders out in his jaws and spreading the paperwork in those files across the floor.

Only those who understood the ARDCOM experiments could appreciate the performance for what it was . . . and did. . . .

Activity had increased tenfold in the mission control centre. General Matthews stared intently at the image on the display screen while he barked out orders to the others in the room.

'*Neston* – make sure it's all being recorded – and I want photo-facsimiles of those documents on the screen, every one of them! We've got to have something to work with *now*!'

He turned to Dr. Wendell Byers. 'Doctor – you'd better get over here and start examining the information. Smith will assist in translating.' The general then withdrew a folder from his attaché case. He carried it over to James Neston. 'Be ready to transmit these copies of the official photo and text announcement as soon as I give you the word. The international wire-services must have them, and so must the Russians, by their private linkup.'

'Yes, sir.'

'I don't know how long we'll have. . . .' Matthews said to everyone. 'But we'll have to learn as much as possible in the time available.'

In the administrator's office of the Omsk Technical Institute, Miklos Nikovitch and Otto Hurdein sat at opposite sides of the latter's polished desk. Nikovitch stared into space, his fingers nervously drumming on the desk's surface.

'We should have heard by now,' he was saying. 'The dog should have been found!'

Hurdein tried to calm him. 'It is night, Miklos, and it is snowing outside. Omsk is a very large place to look for one dog. He will have to seek shelter, and eventually food. . . .'

'But this is no ordinary dog, Otto, as I am sure you understand!' Nikovitch shook his head, frowning. 'What *I* do not understand is how the dog could have escaped in the first place. According to Dr. Petrokova, the animal was terribly ill one moment . . . then sufficiently well the next to knock her unconscious and leave a closed truck. It just does not make sense.'

'Perhaps it will when all the facts are known.'

'Perhaps,' Miklos sighed. 'Perhaps, but I do not think so. There is even something about the Americans' experiment that does not ring true in my mind. Something is wrong with this.'

'Everything seems normal enough, considering the circumstances. A bit strange, but still, I can see no threat. The Americans' motives in wanting to recover the dog and satellite seem genuine enough.'

'Yes. There may be no logical reason to assume otherwise. . . .'

Hurdein hesitated. 'Yet you are still suspicious?'

Nikovitch nodded, a look of grim amusement on his face. 'In all matters such as these, indeed, in everything involving contact with the West, you learn to live with suspicion always . . . and to call it a friend.'

'Yes, but like a friend, you must know when and when not to listen to its advice.'

Nikovitch ignored the remark and picked up a series of black-and-white photos from the desk. 'And these new photos from our observation satellite — they reveal another disturbing matter. The American destroyer satellite still remains in virtually the same position as before. The explosion that disabled it should have set it spinning more than it is. It would seem impossible that an accidental explosion could occur so uniformly as to leave the remaining section in a stable position.'

'So many questions . . .' Hurdein said tiredly. 'So many.'

'Yes, I know. And questions take time to answer. Time. Time for what, I wonder?'

'Perhaps you would have felt better about this matter,' Otto began, 'if it had occurred at some other time . . . when the pressing need of completing the counter-Cerberus measures was not a factor.'

The director nodded grudgingly. 'It is the worst possible timing . . . this incident could not have occurred at a poorer time if it had been planned —'

Nikovitch's mouth sagged suddenly, realisation widening his eyes. He half rose from his chair.

'Miklos — what is it!' Hurdein demanded, fear in his voice.

'The project room —' Nikovitch shouted, racing for the door. 'We must reach Dubuokov at once!'

CHAPTER TWELVE

Alarm bells were ringing in the institute as Nikovitch and Otto Hurdein left the elevator and ran down the hall of the building's security section. From intersecting corridors the few remaining security guards ran to join them.

Ahead of them, at the end of the hall, a lone security man was futilely ramming the project room door with his shoulder. Seeing Nikovitch and the others racing towards him, he paused, rubbing the battered muscles of his upper arm.

'What is it!' Nikovitch demanded of the man. 'Did you activate the alarm?'

'Yes, Director. I heard someone pounding inside the project room. Dubuokov would not answer or let me in —'

Miklos motioned to the door, addressing the other guards. 'Force it open!'

While the others stood back, two of the larger security men rammed the door simultaneously. Wood splintered on the other side as the latch mechanism began to tear apart. They hit the door again, then on the third try the latch gave way and the door shuddered open.

All was still in the project room, although a pounding sound was coming from the door to the storage room off to the side. Nikovitch, with Hurdein behind him, stood mutely staring at the scene before them.

Classified papers and documents were scattered in a wide arc across the floor. The overturned cabinet still effectively blocked the door from which the pounding originated. And over in one corner of the room, sitting docilely on the floor and panting with a blank expression of innocence, was Major.

Nikovitch breathed a silent curse.

One of the security men drew his pistol from its holster and started to take aim at the dog. Nikovitch jerked his arm down with an iron-fingered grip.

Fool!' Miklos stared him down. 'Alive, that dog is proof of espionage on the part of the Americans. If we are to be the injured party in the eyes of the world, then the dog must be unharmed. Now put your gun away and go unblock that door.'

The guard complied, freeing Dubuokov from the storage room. At the moment, a member of the institute staff came up the hall behind them, hurrying with an odd look of urgency.

'Director –'

Nikovitch ignored him momentarily. Cold fire raged within his ice-blue eyes. 'Both Dubuokov and Petrokova examined the dog – *someone* should have suspected. . . .'

Hurdein was pale. 'There was no way of knowing! That it could have been a spy mission – a trick within a trick – we did not guess!' He then directed a mildly accusing look at Nikovitch. '*None* of us guessed, Miklos –'

'All right, all right. It is too late for excuses now, anyway. We have no way of knowing for certain, but we must assume that somehow the Americans now have the details of our counter-Cerberus system. You know what that means, Otto – the communiqués we will have to send out –'

'Yes . . . yes, of course.' Hurdein looked defeated . . . tired and beaten. His face contorted in an agonised frown. 'How did they do it? How could one lone dog be used against us so effectively?'

'He was not alone – do you not understand it, Otto? The radio signals coming from the satellite? The scar Petrokova found on the animal's head?' Nikovitch's voice was full of anger directed at himself as well as the institute administrator. 'The dog has a surgically implanted transceiver – the Americans are controlling him! I knew the American military was involved with advanced experiments using animals, but I did not realise they had developed their work this far.'

Hurdein shook his head. 'All our work on developing a workable countermeasure . . . all for nothing. We are again stalemated!'

'Perhaps. At least we may have delayed the operational starting date of their Cerberus system — soon our own defence screen will be functional. Our diplomats can make new proposals to limit certain types of defensive and offensive systems. And in another year, we will not have to fear their position of power.'

'I am not sure we need fear it now,' Otto said softly. 'Fear can be very costly ... *very* costly. I have seen too many regimes ... too many nations, built upon it. ...' His voice trailed off.

Nikovitch seemed not to hear. 'And you can be certain that we will salvage what we can from this. The world shall know of this unprecedented act of espionage. There are allies of the Americans who will not hesitate to condemn their tactics!'

The waiting staff member again spoke, his tone more insistent. 'Director — please!'

Miklos turned gruffly to him. 'Yes — what is it?'

'Director, these releases have just been transmitted to us — I do not know if they are still important, considering what has happened —'

'Let me see them,' Nikovitch interrupted, taking the facsimile papers. On one was a reproduced black-and-white photo showing three men. Nikovitch looked at it, then read the accompanying text. 'How was this sent?'

'Directly to Moscow, through official channels,' the man replied. 'There was a note attached, stating that copies of the release had been supplied to all international news services.'

Nikovitch sighed deeply. 'The release states that the Americans are sending a transport plane next week, after reaching a joint agreement with our nation —'

'What!' Hurdein interrupted.

'Let me finish — the release goes on to state the Americans' appreciation for all help rendered them in the recovery of the bio-satellite and dog, and the photo with the release shows the three scientists who will travel here to examine the dog.'

Hurdein stared at him, uncomprehendingly. 'But why are

272

they sending this now? They must know we have discovered the dog's true purpose!'

Nikovitch held out the photo to him, his expression grim. 'These three men, Otto ... they are not American scientists. They are not even Americans. They are three of *our* intelligence operatives, three top men who were captured four months ago after infiltrating an American nuclear submarine base. This photo has been sent to us because they want to put us in a spot — they want a trade-off. The dog and satellite for the men. Our silence for theirs. It is obvious that if we press the matter of their espionage, they will do the same with ours. And they will have even more to bargain with shortly, if we do not send an important message —'

'But will such a trade be agreeable?'

Miklos was downcast, his ragged eyebrows close-knit in a frown. 'That will not be my decision to make ... but I know what the answer will be. ...'

In Houston, the mission team pored over dozens of facsimile printout sheets showing the papers and charts of the Russian project. Even Dr. Laswell seemed to forget his animosity as he studied the papers spread out across the four tables, which had been pulled together to form one large surface.

Dr. Wendell Byers bent over the centre of the table, reading Arnold Smith's translations pencilled over certain sections of the Russian words. The general stood next to him, waiting anxiously.

'What have you got so far?' Matthews asked. 'From all that information there must be something to go on —'

Byers did not look up yet. 'I'm not sure, General.'

'But we must find out. This mission can't have been for nothing!'

'It may take time,' Byers countered.

'We don't *have* time!'

Byers frowned in concentration, then finally looked up. 'There seem to be a number of early attempts at circumventing the system here as well, General. Some they ruled out, but kept notes covering them.'

'What sort of attempts?'

Byers picked up one of the photo-facsimiles. 'Here in this information is a plan to combat Cerberus by sending a signal of some type, possibly from a ship off our coast, to interrupt the scanning field of the system.'

'That wouldn't work,' Matthews said quickly. 'The field's too large to accomplish that, and our ground stations would instantly be aware of such an attempt.'

'Of course, and a ship-based signal could not be powerful enough, either,' Byers added. He picked up another sheet. 'This one makes more sense ... a plan to send missiles on a high apogee trajectory and through the centre of the ring of satellites, avoiding the scanning field altogether. It's almost workable, but not without problems. Evidently, too many problems, as we ourselves concluded in our initial studies of Cerberus' worth.'

'But,' Matthews stated flatly, 'our agent informed us that they had a plan that *would* work!'

'And it's in this information, somewhere –' Byers surveyed the papers with dissatisfaction. 'But I simply can see nothing complicated enough in these other papers to suggest an alternate system. Nothing to indicate the Cerberus network is vulnerable to the Russians. . . .'

'But we know it is –'

Joyce Kandell had been watching the image-display screen most of the time since the information had been relayed. She viewed with unhappiness and worry the Russians' next action. They had not yet jammed the transceiver signals relayed from the capsule, but they had placed Major in another cage, and now they surrounded it with a cloth cover that prevented the dog from seeing, and thus relaying, anything further. She turned away.

Byers was saying, 'There is a plan here for a transmitter unit which corresponds to the type used in Cerberus, but whether it's a breakdown of our unit, or part of their own system, I can't be sure.'

'What about this?' Matthews demanded. He held a facsimile sheet that included, in part, a map of the United States, 'This map of America – there is a marking almost in

274

the exact centre of the country. What does it mean? Is it a target for something?'

Byers studied it. 'Perhaps ... but it still doesn't make sense.'

Halper looked over their shoulders at the map, then inquired suddenly, 'May I see that?'

Matthews handed him the map, then watched as Halper picked up a pencil. 'What are you thinking, Lieutenant?'

'Maybe nothing, sir,' he replied. 'But the map reminded me of something else I've seen in the last few days. Another map, part of the display cube at the air base.'

Halper proceeded to draw a large circle around the dot marked on the map. He then added a slightly smaller circle within the first, finally placing three triangular marks within both circles. He held out the altered map to General Matthews and Dr. Byers.

'Isn't that the approximate position of the primary and secondary transmission points of the Cerberus system?' he asked. 'As well as the three command centres?'

Byers studied it. 'Yes ... roughly.'

'Well,' Halper continued, 'it just seems more than coincidence that the mark on the Russians' map is exactly in the centre of the Cerberus ground stations. ...'

General Matthews began to say something, abruptly halted, then stared with new interest at the map. He reached quickly for one of the facsimile sheets Byers had previously set down.

'Doctor —' he addressed the scientist, holding the sheet before him. 'This information concerning a transmitter — a transmitter similar if not identical to our own — what if that marking represents such a transmitter?'

Byers considered it only a fraction of a second, then turned to face Matthews squarely. '*A jamming station?* Are you saying the Russians wo7ld risk building a *jamming station* within the continental United States?'

'If they did,' Matthews replied, 'would it work? Would it effectively block the signals from our Cerberus ground stations to the satellite defence system?'

'It might ... if the jamming signals were powerful

enough. And that is the only position from which they could transmit such a signal uniformly to all stations, to completely block our command signals,' Byers wrestled with the idea. 'But do you realise what you're saying, General? That they would actually build such a facility here in the U.S.!'

'If you're doubting their audacity, don't.'

'But such a facility would require a large amount of land ... someplace remote, safe by virtue of its isolation. And how would such a base communicate with their superiors in Russia? Any radio-transmitted messages would be detected by our own monitoring stations.'

Matthews was silent for a moment.

Halper shrugged. 'Couldn't they just make use of our phone system? There must be a thousand or more businesses in this country that make regular calls to European countries.'

'It's possible,' Matthews agreed. 'If their messages were in code, made to sound like normal business transactions. The calls might be relayed through more than one or two other countries, just to make it less obvious. It could be an ideal system ... there's no way we could monitor every phone system in the U.S., even if we wanted to —'

Arnold Smith interrupted suddenly, an imperative tone to his voice. 'Sir, if there's the slightest chance they are using such a phone system, then there is the danger that the personnel at such a base would be alerted as soon as possible, now that the truth is known in Omsk.'

'How long would that take?'

Smith shrugged. 'Depending on how many relay points for the calls, it might only be a matter of minutes from now, assuming the Russians have already begun.'

'And we must assume that they have....' General Matthews turned to the communications console. 'Neston — get on the red phone to Washington — tell them that it's imperative to reach phone officials in —' he turned to Halper, '— what's the area?'

'North central Kansas, sir —' the lieutenant replied, checking the map.

'North central Kansas –' Matthews relayed it. 'All out-of-state phone service in that area must be stopped at once, for at least the next few hours.'

'I'll get on it, sir.' Neston picked up the red phone and began his call.

Dr. Byers was still looking at the map, his expression strained, 'How can we pin down the exact location of the base . . . if it does in fact exist?'

Matthews leaned forward on the table, looking across the array of reproduced information. 'If a piece of property large enough for such a base has been purchased recently, there will be a record of it. There should be a number of ways to track it down.' He turned to Arnold Smith. 'Do you think your people can find out . . . *quickly*?'

Smith nodded, heading for the other phone on the communications console. 'I can try.'

Smith dialled an outside line and made his call. Five minutes elapsed. Then ten minutes.

Then Smith hurried back with a handwritten list. 'We've got three possibles, General – three parcels of land purchased within the last year and a half.'

'What are they?'

'One is a farm equipment plant outside of Lincoln – but the company that bought the land there has been in business in another area for the last fifteen years.' Smith held the list in front of him, but did not have to refer to it. 'The second is about five miles from the city of Natoma – it's a large grain storage concern, fairly new and a possibility. But the most interesting one is the last. There's a large food canning and distribution company located a few miles out of Tipton. It's also new – within the last several months, in fact. And they deal almost exclusively with *European markets*.'

'That has to be it,' Matthews stated resolutely. 'You're sure there were no other large land purchases?'

'None.'

'Then that's it – we go on that basis. Tipton must be it. We'll have to alert the Pentagon . . . but we'll also have to act on our own at once. That base must be seized before its

277

personnel can escape or destroy the equipment.' Matthews took the map back from Byers. 'What's the nearest military installation?'

Colonel Brunning did not have to look it up to know. 'I believe Fort Riley, Kansas, sir.'

'Get them! Go through the Pentagon, on their lines. Get the commanding officer of Fort Riley at once – tell him it's a matter of national security! I'll explain the rest. . . .'

It was seven in the evening in Moscow. At Spasso House, residence of the U.S. Ambassador, the presidential party was stopping over and concluding preparations for the eight o'clock dinner talks between the American and Soviet leaders. Air Force One had landed at six-twenty at Vnukovo Airport, outside Moscow, to a somewhat restrained greeting by the Russian people.

In one of the rooms kept for visiting diplomats, Secretary of State Charles Wellmont conferred with White House Press Secretary Dan Hillman. Their talk involved more than just planned press releases. . . .

'Have these rooms been checked for listening devices?' Wellmont asked.

'Yes, sir. Checked and double-checked.' Hillman paused. 'The embassy staff located one last month, but it was immediately removed.'

Wellmont glanced again at his watch. 'It may not matter. Judging from the way Soviet security people are scurrying around, something must have happened.' He sighed. 'If we only knew what.'

'It could mean that the information has been gained.'

'Perhaps. But there's been no further word from Washington. It could just as easily be that the personnel in Omsk have tumbled on to our scheme. The whole effort may have been thwarted.'

Both men were silent for a moment. Wellmont paced to the window and paused there. He pulled the curtain back and looked down at the grounds surrounding the residence. Extra security personnel were posted outside, their heavy coats dotted with flakes as a light snowfall continued.

Hillman spoke. 'What are our options now?'

'Options?' Wellmont's look was as bleak as the view of Moscow outside. 'We have only two, it seems. We can go ahead and brief the President – *fully* – and be prepared for the worst. Or we can hold out till the last minute and just hope that the mission has been successful.'

'Do you think we can afford to hold out?'

'I ... I don't know. I suppose we should have told him long ago. It's only going to be more difficult now.'

'If the mission has failed,' Hillman said soberly, 'we're going to be in quite a bind. And I dislike having the President go into these meetings blind, with the kind of hostility we can expect from the Soviets.'

'So do I ... but there are graver concerns. If we don't have the upper hand, or at least a fair balance, then we can just write off any chance of a firm agreement on either the weapons limitations or the Mid-East. Once they've gained momentum, it will be worse. If we don't get the pacts signed this time, we may never get them.'

'And the President?'

Wellmont hesitated. 'Let's wait ... a while longer, at least.'

Hillman looked dissatisfied, but gave a grudging nod. 'All right. But we've only got an hour left ... only *one* hour. ...'

The staccato thunder of huge rotor blades ripped through the quiet morning air of Kansas as ten massive Chinook transport helicopters flew in open formation over the city of Tipton. Olive drab in colour with U.S. Army markings, the squadron of double-rotored aircraft flew at less than a thousand feet above the sprawling Kansas farmland, searching for a parcel of land newly circled on aerial maps.

Once the helicopters had seen duty in Vietnam, but now their rocket pods and extra weapons systems were missing. They were not an unknown sight, and people on the ground that morning would be musing as to what new training exercise the Fort Riley personnel were beginning.

The Chinooks had been flying at their maximum speed, covering the almost hundred-mile distance from the military base to Tipton in just under an hour. As they headed down towards the ground, the time was exactly ten-thirty a.m.

Below them was an extensive building complex, surrounded by several acres of land on all sides. The lead helicopter gently settled on the main road leading to the plant, while the other nine spread out, landing in positions surrounding the property.

As the roar of the turbine engines stilled and the rotors spun to a halt, the copters' rear loading ramps lowered to the ground. Each of the nine other craft disgorged twenty to thirty soldiers in fatigue uniforms, equipped with M-16 rifles, CS gas canisters, and pouches containing gas masks.

The lead helicopter unloaded an Army jeep, several officers, and a handful of troops. While one of the men raised the whip antenna for the jeep's radio unit, the lieutenant colonel in charge of the group climbed into the vehicle's right front seat. A captain slipped behind the steering wheel and started the engine, then drove off along the road to the plant, a sergeant manning the radio in the rear of the jeep.

The expressions of all three men were worried and tight-lipped. Turning to the sergeant, the lieutenant colonel snapped an order.

'Tell the platoon leaders to form up their men along the edge of the propery. All men will load magazines and chamber a round, but will not fire unless on my order.'

'Right, sir.' The sergeant quickly relayed the message over the portable unit, to be received by each platoon's radioman.

Frowning, the captain commented, 'I wish I knew what this is all about.'

'That makes two of us.' The colonel adjusted his web belt and .45 to a more comfortable position. 'All I know is what the CO told us ... some kind of potential national emergency, complete with enemy agents.' He shook his head. 'And I thought stateside duty was going to be dull. . . .'

The jeep pulled up to a stop in front of the main gate. A man in his early fifties, dressed in plain work clothes, came anxiously out of the gate house.

'What is this?'

'Open the gate,' the colonel said bluntly.

'What is this!' the man repeated. 'What authorisation have you people got coming in here like this —'

'*Open it!* Our authorisation comes from the commander in chief of the United States. Now don't waste time.'

The man was quickly losing his confidence. 'I ... I'll have to call the boss and see what he says.'

The colonel stepped quickly out of the jeep, automatic drawn. 'You'll call no one. Now open the gate at once.'

The man said no more. He unlocked the gate and swung it slowly open, then watched nervously as the foot soldiers from the lead helicopter caught up with the jeep and entered the fenced-in property.

Calling one of the soldiers over to him, the colonel ordered, 'Hold this employee here, at gun point, if necessary.' Turning to his sergeant, he directed, 'Advise the platoon leaders that no one is to leave the area. And if they're all in position now, I want one extra squad from the Second Platoon to help us search this facility.'

The colonel dropped back into the vehicle's seat and faced his captain. 'Drive on to the main building.'

With the remaining foot soldiers following quickly behind them, the jeep and its passengers continued along the short stretch of road ahead. At the termination of that road was a long building painted flat white. Two dozen cars were parked in a lot next to it.

Personnel from within the building were standing outside the door as the jeep drove up to it. Through the windows of the building looked more of the plant's office workers.

As the colonel left the jeep, one member of the plant personnel approached him. Stocky in build, the man wore a white shirt with sleeves rolled up above his elbows and a brown patterned tie. He studied the officer briefly.

'What's going on, Colonel?' the man asked angrily. 'What justifies your intrusion on our property — not even the police can force their way into a place without a search warrant!'

'This is a national matter. The police aren't involved.'

'What do you want?'

'We're going to inspect your plant facility — all of it.'

'Looking for what?'

The colonel's eyes narrowed. 'If you don't already know, then I'm afraid I can't tell you.'

The man boiled. 'I don't like your attitude, Colonel. And I don't like your implication that this plant is anything other than a legitimate business!'

'Are you the manager?'

The man fumed, silent for a moment. 'Yes, I am. And I can guarantee that the owners of this company will file charges against the Army, if necessary ... bring suit against all those involved in this ... gestapo action.'

'We'll see.' The colonel directed an order to his sergeant. 'Have three men watch the rest of these employees ... keep them all together in one area.' Turning back to the manager, he added, 'This man will be showing us around the plant. . . .'

At that moment, the sound of a single-rotor craft drew their attention to the sky. A small commercial jet helicopter, painted with civilian colours and markings, flew over the plant and landed a short distance away from the main building. Four men emerged, the pilot remaining with the craft.

The four approached the jeep and the officers. All four were in plain business suits and were vaguely similar in their manner, despite differences in their individual appearance. Two of them extended credentials.

'Lieutenant Colonel Randolph?' the first inquired.

The colonel nodded, then carefully scanned the credentials. 'Federal agents?' He then scanned the four faces with equal care.

'We flew out from Wichita,' the first agent replied. 'We received the alert from Washington an hour ago ... seems you might be needing some help with foreign saboteurs.'

Walking with the agents out of hearing range of the plant employees, Colonel Randolph told them, 'I don't know exactly what we've got here. My orders only stated that we were to isolate the plant area ... keep anyone from leaving. A search of the area was mentioned.'

The first agent nodded slowly. 'Our orders mentioned a large transmitter and antenna setup.'

'How large?'

The agent shrugged. 'I get the impression Washington isn't sure either. We'll just have to search all the buildings for any kind of unusual equipment. And we'd better find it soon.'

'Let's go then ... we'll take the plant manager and start with the office. ...'

Accompanied by the manager, the federal agents and military personnel began their check. The interior of the office was businesslike, slightly cluttered with all the desks, filing cabinets, and other office equipment, and all very ordinary. Clerks and secretaries waited at one end of the room, under the constant, watchful eyes of the three soldiers. All of the personnel appeared to belong to the area ... average Americans all.

Nothing out of order was to be found in the office or in the storerooms and extra filing offices beyond the main room. The inspection team continued out the back of the long, flat-white building, and quickly headed for the larger building behind it. Two cargo trucks were just emerging from the building's freight entrance. They were instantly halted.

'Captain —' the colonel directed. 'Take several of the men and check those trucks out ... I don't want anything left unsearched. The rest of us will inspect this building.'

'Look,' the manager protested, 'why don't you just tell me what you're looking for?'

Ignoring him, Colonel Randolph continued with the federal agents into the second building. Coming in out of the glaring sun, it took a moment for their eyes to adjust. This section of the building reached high from ground to corrugated ceiling. Loading ramps were stacked high with cardboard cartons marked with their destination. Two other trucks were still in the loading area, and loaders were moving dollies of cartons into them. Some of the workers stopped and stared at the inspection team, then continued their work. Two more soldiers went to check them.

Beyond the loading area, through wide doors over which

large down-draught fans were mounted, the canning area was in full production. Hundreds of shiny metal cans moved past them on conveyor lines, were filled, sealed, and labelled in a matter of seconds, then moved on to be stacked into cartons. There was all the canning equipment normally found in such a plant, but nowhere was there anything like a transmitter.

The men hurried out of the building, rejoining the captain and other soldiers outside. They had just finished checking the second truck.

'Nothing,' the captain stated grimly.

'The building seems clear, too,' Randolph added. 'But this is next to impossible! The equipment could be hidden behind a wall, or built into something. It might take a week of searching to turn up anything.'

'We don't have that long,' the first agent urged. 'We have to advise Washington of what we've found – if anything – as quickly as possible.'

The colonel sighed. 'Well ... we're just going to do what we can, and hope we turn up something.'

His captain nodded in agreement, a look of irony twisting the corner of his mouth even as he frowned. 'Yes, and the way we barged in, there had sure better be something here to find!'

Colonel Randolph pointed to a small concrete building less than fifteen yards away. 'Let's check it out.'

As they reached the twenty-foot-square building, the plant manager was already informing them of its purpose. 'All it houses is our emergency power generators,' the man insisted. 'In case of power blackouts, we can still continue production. There's nothing illegal about that, is there?'

The colonel did not answer as he entered the building. Inside was exactly what the man had told them ... three electric power generators, so large they filled virtually every foot of the small building. Heavy connecting conduit led down into the solid concrete floor and presumably went underground to the plant.

Randolph looked the equipment over for a long moment. 'Do you really need all that?'

'Yes, of course,' the manager stated flatly. 'There's a lot of electrical equipment involved in the processing and canning stages. If we lost power right in the middle of production, with no way to complete the processing already begun, we could lose thousands of dollars.'

Randolph turned to the agent next to him. 'Do you think a transmitter could be hidden within a mock-up generator?' He kept the manager within range of his vision, and noticed a slight change of expression on the man's face. But what that change meant was hard to determine.

The agent looked at the generators. 'It's possible. But putting a transmitter right next to two power generators could create all sorts of static problems. Besides, we still haven't seen anything like an antenna anywhere in the area.'

'No, I know.'

'Now *look* –' the manager began again. 'I still say you have no right coming into our plant this way. I'm not ignorant of government regulations! Even federal agencies need some kind of warrant before they can –'

The agent next to Randolph interrupted suddenly. 'You mean, something like this?' He pulled a folded document from his inside coat pocket and held it out to the plant manager.

The man stared at the paper, his mouth working silently for a moment. 'But – the soldiers had already forced their way in before you landed in that helicopter of yours!'

'Did they?' the agent replied.

'You know they did! You can't get away with this. I warn you, I'll see to it that –'

'Come on,' Randolph snapped to the others. 'We're wasting time here. There are other places to be checked.'

Hurrying from the generator building, they went to the last two places that remained to be checked. The first was a holding warehouse filled with sacks, cartons, and large metal cans of raw ingredients. A cold storage area at one end of the building held perishables. But nowhere was there anything even remotely resembling a transmitter or antenna.

They left the holding warehouse and approached the last building, an enormous wooden structure only one storey high, but at least two hundred feet on each side. Colonel Randolph gestured towards the building.

'What's that one?'

'Just another warehouse,' the manager replied. 'It's not in use now . . . haven't used it for some time.'

A large, partially rusted padlock was fastened securely on the door. Randolph examined it, then turned to the manager.

'Open it.'

The man hesitated a second. 'I haven't got the key. It's back in the office.'

'Go get it.' Randolph turned to his captain. 'Go with him.'

The two departed, the manager still wearing an angry scowl. In their absence, the colonel and his sergeant walked about in front of the structure, while the federal agents watched. The sergeant stopped along the wall, examining an area.

'Ever see a wall put together like this, sir?'

'What is it, Sergeant?' Randolph joined him, looking at the section the man had indicated.

'It's like some of those old-fashioned buildings in Maine — no nails to hold the planks on . . . just wooden pegs everywhere.'

One of the agents came over. 'Let's see.'

They all began to examine the wall, noting that the sergeant's observation was true. No nails had been employed in the construction of the building. No metal of any kind, for even the door hinges were made of a nylon substance.

Randolph called over to one of the federal men. 'Are the windows on your side painted over, too?'

'Yes, Colonel . . . from the inside. No, wait — I've found a spot . . . a scratched area on this one window.'

The colonel hurried to his side. 'Can you see anything through it?'

The agent put his eye close to the glass. 'Yes, I can see a little. The window frame blocks part of my vision — I can't see the floor. But the place seems to be empty, like the man said.' He continued to look, describing what he saw. 'The roof's not corrugated steel like the rest of the buildings. I can see light coming through faintly ... the stuff must be that rippled plastic sheeting, like they use on patios.' He hesitated, turning away from the window. 'That's odd. ...'

'What?'

'No vertical roof supports. The centre beam is held up by wood beams that go down diagonally to the walls.'

'Maybe it was an airplane hanger at one time. It sure doesn't look like it belongs with the rest of the buildings – they're all concrete. But whatever, if it's empty, there are going to be a lot of unhappy people in Washington.'

'Don't I know it!' The agent looked back towards the office building. 'What's keeping that manager?'

Almost as the words left his mouth, something happened back at the office building. A door on the side was thrown open suddenly and the manager ran out at breakneck speed with the captain close behind him. The captain paused to fire a warning shot into the air.

The manager raced on at a surprisingly fast pace, heading across the open field, straight towards the surrounding ring of soldiers. He had almost reached them when he stumbled and fell. He got to his feet again, staggered a few steps further, then stopped cold in his tracks, at last aware that his flight was futile.

As several of the perimeter soldiers came forward to take him into custody, the captain ran swiftly back to the warehouse where the others waited. He was out of breath when he reached it.

'Colonel –'

'What happened?'

The captain took in a quick, deep breath, and let it out. 'The manager went in for the key, or so he said. But I caught him pressing a button in his office – it might be some kind of signal – then he headed out that side door. You saw the rest –'

A faint sound came abruptly from within the warehouse. Randolph turned and listened intently. Then he pointed frantically at the door. 'Sergeant – break it down!'

'But there's nothing in there —' the federal man protested. 'It's empty!'

'*Something's* in there!'

Instantly, the sergeant took a running start, throwing his full weight at the padlocked door. After that, a number of things happened unexpectedly.

The lock snapped and the door flew abruptly open, taking less force than had appeared necessary. The sergeant's momentum carried him through the portal, past five feet of flooring, and over the top of a low guard rail of wood, anchored solidly in the flooring.

Desperately clawing at the railing, the sergeant just managed to grab hold of it, dangling from the upper rung. Dangling, because beyond that point *there was no floor*.

Where the rest of the floor should have been, there was a huge gaping chasm, fifty feet deep. It extended to all sides of the building, making the wooden structure look like some fragile cover poised delicately over an enormous pit. Grey concrete lined the walls of the excavated area and formed a smooth floor at the bottom of its depth. The area was aglow with the light of numerous pieces of electronic equipment and consoles which lined the perimeter of the floor. Power cables emerged from wall outlets and connected with the equipment.

But these features were not what dominated the pit. Dwarfing everything in its immensity, in its sheer bulk and presence, a massive dish antenna stood squarely in the centre, pointing up at the heavens. Its hundred-and-eighty-foot diameter concave surface reached out almost to the walls of the building, but was just below the ground level edge.

As the two officers quickly helped their sergeant back over the guard rail, the federal agents stared in amazement at the facility below them. One of the men stooped to pick up the crumbled fragments of the lock, and he carried them in to show the others.

'The lock isn't metal at all —' his tone was strained. 'It's some kind of ceramic. Painted. *Even the rust is phoney.*'

'It must be because of the transmitter ... and that

antenna —' The colonel drew his automatic and headed down the stairs that were positioned to the right of the guard rail. 'Nothing in the building itself is made of metal. Let's go — their technicians may still be downstairs!'

The Army personnel and federal agents hurried down to the lower level. Once below the top of the giant antenna, the stairs and handrails were metal. Desks and chairs could now be seen in some areas beneath the antenna, and one area had been partitioned off for food storage. Cots were stacked in another section.

But no people. The pit was completely devoid of any Russian personnel.

The captain looked around. 'Where are they?'

'You must have been right about the warning signal the manager sent. They've left!' Randolph searched the walls anxiously.

'But where? They couldn't have gotten past us —'

'Over here!' The colonel headed for a large metal panel in the concrete wall. He tried to open it, in vain. 'There must be an escape tunnel — the door's locked from the other side.'

'Can we break it down?'

'No — it's too strong. It's solid steel with fireproofing.'

He put his ear to the panel, listening. 'I can hear them running — they must have entered the tunnel just before we came in. Captain — send a man back to the jeep — alert the perimeter! There may be an exit to the tunnel beyond the edge of the property.'

While the others waited, the federal agents were beginning to examine the equipment and notes in the pit. One of the men had taken a small 16mm still camera from his coat pocket and began taking pictures of everything, from the glowing consoles to the massive radio transmission antenna.

Colonel Randolph and the captain waited near the metal panel.

'It's strange in a way,' the colonel was saying. 'You would think they wouldn't want to leave everything intact for us to find . . . that they would —'

Randolph fell strangely quiet. His eyes settled on a small

metal box mounted to the wall a short distance from the panel. Moving to it, he carefully opened the cover.

Within the box was a series of switches and lights, and labels printed in Russian. Near the top was a small time clock. Randolph studied it worriedly, trying to decipher the foreign words that labelled each switch and button. Only one stood out and was recognisable to him. It was on a label near a push button and the time clock.

The word was Russian for *incendiary*.

'Good Lord! We've got to get out of here – *now*!'

'But we haven't examined everythi –' the federal man taking the pictures started to say.

'Run, man! This whole place is about to self-destruct!'

Almost in panic, the men dashed for the stairs. The door above seemed hopelessly far away, but they ran for all they were worth. They ascended the first level of stairs, angled off and went up the second, heading for the door. They reached the top of the stairs and darted through the opening. One of the federal agents stumbled, but was helped up by his associates. All raced away from the building, pulses throbbing in their ears, cold sweat soaking their clothing.

The men had gone a little over twenty-five yards from the building when Randolph dived to the ground, yelling –

'*Hit it!*'

A split second after they had flattened on the ground, the building erupted behind them. A fireball of phosphorus-white flames engulfed the structure, virtually vaporised it. Pieces of the wood, popping and snapping as air cells within exploded in countless tiny detonations, fell back into the pit. Below, amidst the searing, chemically induced flames, the great antenna writhed and contorted like an enormous wilting flower. Within minutes, there would be only a molten sludge where millions of roubles worth of Russian equipment had stood.

As the flames began to fade, Randolph and the others got to their feet and headed off for the main office and the jeep. The soldier sent back to alert the perimeter troops was there, using the radio. Randolph approached him anxiously.

'Did the technicians get away?' the colonel demanded. 'Was there time to alert the men?'

The soldier was still obviously receiving a transmission on the radio unit. He held the phonelike handset to his ear for a moment, then looked squarely at the officer.

'I told them, all right, sir. And you were right about an exit near the edge of the property.' He grinned. 'But it turned out one of our big choppers was parked smack on top of their trapdoor. Those ol' boys didn't go *anywhere*!'

At two minutes after eight p.m. in Moscow, the presidential party was arriving at St. George's Hall in the Kremlin, site of the state banquet and the initial talks. In the midst of former czarist glories, two superpowers would discuss weapons undreamed of in days when sheer destructive power was limited to cannons, rifles, and bayonets. The lives of millions might someday hang in the balance, but the machineries of diplomacy demanded certain peculiar formalities.

Members of the Press Corps, arriving early from quarters at the Intourist Hotel on Gorky Street, were waiting in peripheral areas. Film and videotape teams had quickly set up equipment for later news broadcasts and were still checking their light readings. Audio men had already positioned their microphones, and could only wait for the upcoming addresses.

Charles Wellmont's features were taut, but did not display the anxiety he felt as he entered the great hall. Once the Soviets made their opening statements, they would be bound by them, and the course of all future meetings would be set. He was beginning to wish there had been some way of excluding the press from this initial meeting. But such thoughts would not help now.

Closely following the President, Wellmont and Hillman exchanged worried glances after the initial chilly Soviet reception. The sudden lack of cordiality seemed to confirm their worst fears.

Speaking in an undertone to Wellmont, Hillman said tensely, 'The axe is about to fall. . . .'

Wellmont maintained his look of controlled calm, but a fine coating of sweat glistened on his forehead. 'If it does,' he replied softly, 'it will be on our necks. If we've failed, Dan . . . *if we've failed . . .*'

Both men squinted in the sudden brightness of flash units as photographers to their right snapped pictures. Hillman nodded in the direction of the three Soviet leaders approaching from the other side of the hall. 'Looks like we've just about run out of time.'

At that moment there was a commotion at the entrance to the great room. Wellmont turned and recognised one of the security men from the embassy. His credentials were undergoing a second check at the door. Wellmont stiffened.

Finally passed clear, the man quickly approached the presidential party. Stopping before Wellmont, he extended a manila folder with the embassy's seal.

'This has been wired from Washington, sir.'

Wellmont opened the folder and looked inside. There was a ten-page initial report from the Army search team in Kansas, and a dozen or more Wirephoto prints of the jamming transmitter facility, including one of the burnt-out pit left behind.

Hillman leaned towards him. 'Is it. . . .'

Wellmont's fingers gripped the folder tightly, 'It's better than we hoped. Proof of an unprecedented plan of sabotage. It's the lever we need, Dan . . . and now's the time to use it.'

In Houston, General Matthews was conferring by phone with the commanding officer at Fort Riley, who relayed the search team's report even as extra copies of the photos made there issued from the facsimile machine. As Matthews hung up the phone, a tired, grateful smile edged across his face.

'They found it —' he said slowly, dropping the relayed photos on the table in front of Dr. Laswell and the others. 'An enormous facility, built underneath a warehouse. The equipment was destroyed, unfortunately, but the technicians and Russian agents there were all captured.'

'Incredible!' Brunning shook his head in disbelief. 'How did they manage to bring in the necessary equipment?'

'Probably flew it in from some neutral country as import material, trucked it to the site, and assembled it there. A top crew could do it in under a month. We'll have to investigate further to be sure what methods they used, just for our own peace of mind.'

Laswell still stared at the photos in awe-struck silence. He seemed unwilling, unable to speak.

Arnold Smith began packing his notes and charts back into his attaché case. Matthews and Brunning did the same.

But for Halper and Joyce Kandell, it was not truly over. They still gazed anxiously at the communications console, looking for some sign of an official message. The image-display screen had gone blank forty minutes before, indicating that the Russians had finally dismantled the sealed radio in the capsule that had transported Major to his goal. There would be no more relayed information ... no more commands to the dog. Now they could only wait. ...

Abruptly, the photo-facsimile unit began to operate again as a signal was patched through its circuits. James Neston grabbed the sheet of paper as it extruded from the machine, and handed it to the general. 'It's from Washington.'

Matthews read it, first to himself, then, 'Listen to this — an official communiqué from Moscow: "We wish to confirm that an agreement has been reached for the transportation of the American bio-satellite and dog back to the United States. We acknowledge the credentials of the three scientists who will be sent to examine the dog, and will make all necessary arrangements as you request. As an additional request on our part, we hope that certain Russian scientists presently in the United States on a scientific exchange project will be allowed to return to the U.S.S.R. on the same flight, as a reciprocal gesture of mutual assistance. ..."'

Halper asked, 'That means they want their technicians back?'

Matthews nodded. 'Part of their terms for returning the dog and for not making a world issue out of this affair. We'll comply, of course.'

293

The full impact of it all had taken a while to set in with them. But now it swept them up in its momentum. They were done — they had succeeded. The mission had worked, and Major would be coming home.

Bill Stanton slid the headset carefully off and laid it on the communications console, massaging the creases left on his ear and temple. One by one, he switched off the circuits on the console.

Neston sat wearily on the edge of a table. 'It's a NASA tradition to hand out cigars at the end of a mission . . . but I'm afraid no one thought to bring any.'

Norm Ripley came forward to congratulate everyone. The tall, lanky NASA executive gave Matthews a firm handshake. 'You pulled it off, sir. Pulled it off clean.' He smiled faintly. 'Like my granddad used to say — clean as a hound's tooth.'

But there was one there who did not share in his enthusiasm. Dr. Laswell looked about, then caught the attention of General Matthews.

'Am I free to go?' he said wearily.

Matthews nodded. 'Of course.' He hesitated. 'And I might mention that if you wish to avoid any adverse publicity, your own silence will be the primary factor.'

Laswell studied him a long moment, a quiet animosity burning deep within him. Then finally his eyes lowered and he turned to leave.

Outside, minutes later, Ryan Halper and Joyce Kandell stood on the sidewalk. The sun was nearly straight overhead, and the brilliant reality of day seemed almost strange now . . . the calm somehow unsettling. The breeze swept past them, rustling their hair.

'I don't know whether to laugh or cry,' Joyce said, her tone flat and emotionless. 'I don't know *what* to feel any more.'

Halper stood near her, looking away. 'They ended up being right, you know.'

'Yes. But I can't help wondering . . . were they right in spite of themselves? Was I really so wrong?'

'Does it matter?'

'It matters.'

Halper turned to her. 'Give it time,' he said softly. 'And have a little faith ... in them ... and in me. ...'

EPILOGUE

D. Thomas Lawrence sat on the edge of the sofa in Angela Simons' apartment, eyes fixed on the television set. He was more interested in what was to come than in the news commentator's rambling remarks about the surprising success of the just-concluded summit conference or his praise for Wellmont's diplomatic skill. For Lawrence, news of the Soviet-American agreements signed was only of secondary importance. Finally the scene shifted from the evening news broadcast to Washington, and live colour coverage of the landing at Dulles International Airport.

The Air Force jet transport had rolled to a stop, and a boarding ramp was brought out. Military and civilian personnel clustered around the base of the ramp, and a short distance away, reporters waited. Beyond them, a crowd of spectators gathered, intrigued by the odd story of the dog's landing in Russia. Although they were not clearly visible, Brunning, Halper, and Joyce Kandell were among those present at the base of the boarding ramp. After the appropriate ceremonies were indulged in, all for the sake of appearance, they would fly with the dog back to ARDCOM Headquarters in Missouri.

The crowd displayed a sudden burst of enthusiasm as the dog appeared at the top of the boarding ramp. Major's hard, lean form was relaxed, his alert eyes scanning the crowd below with interest. Behind him, Dr. Corby held the dog's leash. And behind Dr. Corby stood a number of men representing the same organisation for which Arnold Smith worked. The matter of the 'scientists' who had been sent to Russia to examine the dog would be handled quietly ... fictitious men returning to fictitious jobs, and soon forgotten.

Lawrence shifted slightly on the sofa as the girl came in from the kitchen and sat down next to him. She glanced briefly at him, failed to get his attention, then turned her own gaze to the television image.

Major started down the ramp with Dr. Corby in tow, and the animal lovers in the crowd gave another spontaneous cheer.

'Can you believe it, Angie?' he said suddenly, not looking at her. 'All those people there ... all the millions watching on their televisions ... and none of them *know*. None of them suspects the kind of experiment that was really behind that satellite. None of them has ever heard of Project Deep Sleep, just as I hadn't until that idiot general told me everything.'

The girl with the blonde and light brown hair looked at him with concern. 'Are you sure the truth *should* be told, Larry? If the Army confided in you about its experiment —'

'They confided in me only because they thought they could trick me into silence. But the dog's back safely now, and they have nothing to fear except the exposure of their secret activities.' He patted her hand. 'But the truth must be told. The millions spent on pointless military experimentation should be used for the health and welfare of the American public. ...'

He smiled faintly. 'Some people have wondered why the dog was launched into space with no publicity after the bio-satellite programme had supposedly ended. But I'm the only one to make the connection so far. And when tomorrow's issue of *News-Scene* hits the stands, everyone will know. I'll be the first to expose the project for what it really is. And I'm guaranteed a by-line on any reprint of the article.

'Tomorrow, Angie, I'll really start to make a name for myself. ...'

REFERENCES

The following research bibliography may be of interest to those who wish to delve deeper into matters presented in this book.

MATTERS OF SPACE AND DEFENCE:
1. *Soviet Space Programs, 1966–70.* U.S. Government Printing Office, publication #5271–0263, 1971.
2. *Soviet Space Programs, 1971.* U.S. Government Printing Office, publication #76–187 0, 1972.
3. *Space Agreements with the Soviet Union.* U.S. Government Printing Office, publication #79–732, 1972.
4. Ardman, Harvey 'The Laser As A Mean Mother,' *Esquire,* August 1973.
5. Davies, R. W. & R. Amann, 'Science Policy in the U.S.S.R.,' *Scientific American*, June 1969, 19–29.
6. Rathjens, George W. 'The Dynamics of the Arms Race,' *Scientific American*, April 1969, 15–25.
7. Winston, Donald C. 'SALT Pacts Face Interpretation Parleys,' *Aviation Week*, June 19, 1972, 17.
8. Wolin, Simon, and Robert M. Slusser, ed. *The Soviet Secret Police.* New York: Frederick A. Praeger, 1957.
9. York, Herbert F. 'Military Technology and National Security,' *Scientific American*, August 1969, 221, 17–29.
10. 'Soviet Satellite Intercepts Appear Planned to Deter Orbital Weapons,' *Aviation Week*, Nov. 9, 1970, 21.
11. 'Satellite Intercepter Rise Spurred by Soviet Space Moves,' *Aviation Week*, June 19, 1972, 13.
12. 'Russians Continuing Complex Military Satellite Exercise,' *Aviation Week*, Oct. 9, 1972, 20.
13. 'Secret War in Space, Where U.S. Trails Russia,' *U.S. News and World Report*, Jan. 10, 1972, 69.
14. 'Soviet Gain Seen in Satellite Test,' *The New York Times*, Jan. 2, 1972, p. 29, col. 1.
15. 'Satellite Killer Tested by Soviet,' *The New York Times*, Jan. 28, 1972, p. 27, col. 1.
16. 'Soviet Lofts Cosmos 519; Arms Observation Hinted,' *The New York Times*, Sept. 17, 1972, p. 50, col. 7.
17. 'Soviet Lofts Cosmos 520; Military Mission Suspected,' *The New York Times*, Sept. 21, 1972, p. 15, col. 4.
18. 'Panel OKs $2.3 Billion for Bases,' *The Miami Herald*, Sept. 22, 1972.

19. *NASA Fasa Fact Book*, Alvin Renetzky and Barbara J. Flynn, ed. New Jersey: Academic Media, 1971.

BIOMEDICAL ENGINEERING:

1. Delgado, José M. R. *Physical Control of the Mind: Toward A Psychocivilized Society*. New York: Harper & Row, 1969.
2. DeValois, R. L. Neural Processing of Visual Information. In *Frontiers in Physiological Psychology*. R. W. Russel (Ed.) N.Y.: Academic Press, 1966, 31–92.
3. Johnson, J. I., Hatton, G. I. and Goy, R. W. The Physiological Analysis of Animal Behavior. In E.S.E. Hafez (Ed.) *The Behavior of Domestic Animals* (2nd Edition). London: Balliere, Tindall and Cassell, 1969.
4. Michael, Charles R. 'Receptive Field of Single Optic Nerve Fibers in a Mammal With an All-Cone Retina,' *Journal of Neurophysiology*, 1968, 31, 249–282.
5. Michael, Charles R. 'Retinal Processing of Visual Images,' *Scientific American*, May 1969, 220, 104–114.
6. Prehoda, Robert W. *Suspended Animation: The Research Possibility That May Allow Man to Conquer the Limiting Chains of Time*. Philadelphia: Chilton Book Company, 1969.
7. Pribram, Karl H. 'The Neurophysiology of Remembering,' *Scientific American*, Jan. 1969, 220, 73–86.
8. Werner, B. and Mountcastle, V. B. 'The Variability of Central Neural Activity in a Sensory System, and its Implications for the Central Reflection of Sensory Events,' *Journal of Neurophysiology*, *1963, 26:-958–977*.

COMPUTER GRAPHICS:

1. Andrews, Harry C., and others. *Computer Techniques in Image Processing*. New York: Academic Press, 1970.
2. Greenberg, Donald P. 'Computer Graphics in Architecture,' *Scientific American*, May 1974, 98–107.
3. Rosenfeld, Azriel *Picture Processing by Computer*. New York: Academic Press, 1969.
4. Shulman, Arnold R. *Optical Data Processing*. New York: John Wiley & Sons, Inc., 1970.

Craig Thomas's Bestselling Paperback
FIREFOX – *Soon to be a major film*

The Soviet Mig-31 is the deadliest warplane ever
built. Codenamed FIREFOX by NATO, it can
fly at over 4,000 m.p.h., is invulnerable to radar
– AND HAS A LETHALLY
SOPHISTICATED WEAPONS SYSTEM
THAT ITS PILOT CAN CONTROL BY
THOUGHT-IMPULSES. There is only one way
that British Intelligence and the CIA can counter
the threat it poses: a scheme more desperate and
daring than any undercover operation since the
Second World War –

HIJACK THE FIREFOX!
'Simply won't allow you to put it down until you
reach the last page' JACK HIGGINS, author of
THE EAGLE HAS LANDED
'A marvellous read – a gripping, believable
thriller that flies at Mach-5 speed' IRA LEVIN,
author of THE BOYS FROM BRAZIL

'I devoured FIREFOX instantly. An excellent,
exciting book!' ARTHUR HAILEY, Bestselling
author of AIRPORT

0 7221 04456   Adventure/Thriller   95p

A MAN CALLED INTREPID:
The Secret War 1939–1945

The International bestseller by
William Stevenson

A Man Called Intrepid tells for the first time
the full story of British Security Co-Ordination,
the international Allied intelligence agency of
World War Two whose work has been a closely
guarded secret for the past thirty years. Here are
top-level inside accounts of crucial wartime
undercover operations including:

The breaking of the German Enigma code
The assassination of Heydrich
The race for the atomic bomb
Surveillance and sabotage of Nazi V1 and V2
rocket sites
The raids on the French coast that made the
Normandy landings possible
Anglo-American co-operation in the sinking of
the Bismarck
The organization of resistance movements
throughout Europe
The intelligence stratagems that delayed the Nazi
invasion of Russia

Written with full access to all the British Security
Co-Ordination papers and with the full
co-operation of BSC's director, the man
code-named INTREPID, William Stevenson's
internationally bestselling book is a uniquely
important piece of modern secret history. It is
also tremendously exciting to read.

0 7221 81582   Biography/War   £1.75

*The supersensational thriller of the man
who switched identities – to a world of
violence and murder!*

MISSING . . . AND PRESUMED DEAD
Joseph Hayes

DEATH-SWITCH!
You're Cyrus Greer, bored executive. The plane
you're piloting has crashed into the sea and
you've managed to swim ashore. Suddenly, you
realise that Cyrus Greer is dead – or at least the
world thinks he is. So you decide to start an
exciting new life under a different identity.

First the good news: you fall into bed with a
gorgeous, passionate redhead.
Now the bad: suddenly there's a whole lot of
extremely violent people after the new you, and
someone who tends to collect mutilated corpses
is threatening to kill you again. *This time, for
real . . .*

MISSING . . . PRESUMED DEAD is a violent,
breakneck adventure that shows internationally
bestselling Master of Thrills Joseph Hayes on
the devastating top of his form.

'EXCITING THRILLER WHICH COMES TO
A VIOLENT CLIMAX'
Publishers Weekly

'HERE'S THE CRAFTSMAN AT HIS
CRAFT . . . A PEACH, ESPIONAGE,
HIGH-FLOWN HORROR, BELIEVABLE
COMBAT, MYSTERY, SUSPENSE'
The Scotsman

0 7221 4420   Adventure/Thriller Fiction   95p

A selection of Bestsellers from Sphere Books

Fiction

TEMPLE DOGS	Robert L. Duncan	95p	☐
RAISE THE TITANIC!	Clive Cussler	95p	☐
KRAMER'S WAR	Derek Robinson	£1.25	☐
THE CRASH OF '79	Paul Erdman	£1.25	☐
UNTIL THE COLOURS FADE	Tim Jeal	£1.50	☐
FALSTAFF	Robert Nye	£1.50	☐
EXIT SHERLOCK HOLMES	Robert Lee Hall	95p	☐
THE MITTENWALD SYNDICATE	Frederick Nolan	95p	☐
FIREFOX	Craig Thomas	95p	☐

Film and Television tie-ins

THE PASSAGE	Bruce Nicolaysen	95p	☐
STAR WARS	George Lucas	95p	☐
CLOSE ENCOUNTERS OF THE THIRD KIND	Steven Spielberg	85p	☐
EBANO (now filmed as ASHANTI)	Alberto Vazquez-Figueroa	95p	☐
THOMAS & SARAH	Mollie Hardwick	85p	☐

Non Fiction

EMMA & I	Sheila Hocken	85p	☐
DR. JOLLY'S BOOK OF CHILDCARE	Dr. Hugh Jolly	£1.95	☐
MAJESTY	Robert Lacey	£1.50	☐
RUIN FROM THE AIR	Gordon Thomas & Max Morgan Witts	£1.50	☐
THE SEXUAL CONNECTION	John Sparks	85p	☐

All Sphere books are available at your local bookshop or newsagent, or can be ordered direct from the publisher. Just tick the titles you want and fill in the form below.

Name ....

Address ....

....

Write to Sphere Books, Cash Sales Department, P.O. Box 11, Falmouth Cornwall TR10 9EN

Please enclose cheque or postal order to the value of cover price plus:
UK: 22p for the first book plus 10p per copy for each additional book ordered to a maximum charge of 82p
OVERSEAS: 30p for the first book and 10p for each additional book
BFPO and EIRE: 22p for the first book plus 10p per copy for the next 6 books, thereafter 4p per book
Sphere Books reserve the right to show new retail prices on covers which may differ from those previously advertised in the text or elsewhere, and to increase postal rates in accordance with the GPO.